The Decameron
Selected Tales

Decameron
Novelle scelte

A Dual-Language Book

Giovanni Boccaccio

Edited and Translated by
STANLEY APPELBAUM

DOVER PUBLICATIONS, INC.
Mineola, New York

Bibliographical Note

This Dover edition, first published in 2000, includes the original Italian text of twenty stories from the *Decameron,* reprinted from a standard Italian edition, together with a new English translation of the stories selected. Stanley Appelbaum made the selection, prepared the translation, and wrote the Foreword, Introduction, and footnotes. (See the Foreword and Introduction for further bibliographical details.)

Library of Congress Cataloging-in-Publication Data

Boccaccio, Giovanni, 1313–1375.
    [Decamerone. English & Italian. Selections]
    The Decameron : selected tales = Decameron : novelle scelte : a dual-language book / Giovanni Boccaccio ; edited and translated by Stanley Appelbaum.
       p. cm.
    "Includes the original Italian text of twenty stories . . . together with a new English translation."
    ISBN-13: 978-0-486-41432-4 (pbk.)
    ISBN-10: 0-486-41432-9 (pbk.)
    I. Appelbaum, Stanley. II. Title.

PQ4272.E5 A332 2000
853'.1—dc21

00-056994

Manufactured in the United States by LSC Communications
41432904   2017
www.doverpublications.com

Foreword

Boccaccio's *Decameron* is a major, pivotal work not only in Italian letters, but in all of world literature. The earliest great literary volume of short stories, it utilized and exemplified almost all types of prose fictional narratives that had preceded it, and exerted an unparalleled influence on later storytelling everywhere. Although a product of the Middle Ages (it is only thirty years later than Dante's *Divine Comedy*, which is often taken as the most representative work of the medieval period), it also has been considered as pre-Renaissance and proto-Humanist, because of its decidedly secular attitude and its sympathetic portrayal of merchants and even members of the laboring classes.

The *Decameron* achieves literary greatness by its admirable narrative style and variety, and particularly for the prominence and excellence of its frame story, which, among its many imitators, is matched in quality only in Chaucer's *Canterbury Tales*. Boccaccio's book boasts a special place in Italian literary history, where it has been praised as a model of Italian prose ever since Pietro Bembo's *Prose della volgar lingua* (1525). Ever since the *Decameron*, moreover, the short story has been one of the most significant genres in Italian literature.

No two anthologizers of the *Decameron* would make the same selections, so rich are the pickings (of the hundred stories, surprisingly few are dull or trivial). The present editor/translator, when informed of the size the publisher desired this volume to be, had to reflect seriously on criteria for selection. It seemed to him that readers prepared to read the original 14th-century text in a dual-language edition couldn't fail to be concerned with questions of literary and cultural history, and especially with comparative literature. Therefore, while at the same time striving to fulfill the duty of any anthologist (the inclusion of representative tales of varying length, mood, and genre, not excluding the bawdry for which the book is notorious), the editor has emphasized stories with important literary affiliations in both chronological directions: stories based on eminent models and

stories that became primary models for major works by such authors
as Chaucer, Shakespeare, Lessing, and Keats (see the Introduction for
details). The commentary supplied is in the same spirit.

This commentary primarily is not contained in the footnotes, which
have been kept to a minimum so as not to disturb the reader's pleasure in the stories, and which address only special immediate prob-
lems that might hinder understanding. The basic commentary, story
by story (for the twenty selected), will be found in the section of the
Introduction titled "The Twenty Selected Stories in Their Setting." In
each case, the discussion includes (as applicable) the major characters
(when historical), the history and geography involved, the sources and
influences, and the story's particular characteristics.[1]

In preparing the translation and the commentary, the translator
consulted numerous references, including three complete Italian edi-
tions of the *Decameron* (and a fourth edition of the very first story),
and compared two 20th-century English translations. He is especially
indebted to two works: the annotated edition of the *Decameron* prepared by Vittore Branca, published by Giulio Einaudi, Turin, 1980
and 1984, as No. 169 in the series "Nuova Universale Einaudi"; and
Giovanni Boccaccio, by Carlo Muscetta, published by Laterza, Rome
and Bari, 1972 and 1974, as No. 8 in the series "Letteratura Italiana
Laterza." Muscetta's volume is the best current, handy source of information about the full range of Boccaccio's other works; its dating of
the works, including the *Decameron*, has been adopted in the
Introduction to this edition to avoid the constant use of "circa" or of
alternate dates, since these dates are the subject of much dispute (as
are some of the dates in Boccaccio's biography).

For efficient, space-saving reference to the *Decameron*'s hundred
stories (ten told on each of ten days), this volume uses Roman numbers for the days I through X, and Arabic numbers for stories 1
through 10 of each day. Thus: "(story) IV, 5" means the fifth story told
on the fourth day; or, Day Four, Story Five.

---

[1]The titles of the medieval French sources (far from standardized) are given here
in the form in which they appear in: Bossuat *et al.*, edd., *Le moyen âge*, Fayard, Paris,
1964, in the series "Dictionnaire des lettres françaises" (reprinted in the
"Pochothèque" of Le Livre de Poche, series "Encyclopédies d'aujourd'hui").

Contents

INTRODUCTION

Boccaccio: Life and Other Works

Life. Giovanni Boccaccio was born in 1313, either in Florence or in Certaldo, a town some twenty-five miles south-southwest of Florence, where his father owned houses.[1] His father, Boccaccino di Chelino, an agent of the Florentine banking house of Bardi, was not yet married at the time. The mother was most likely a servant or other lower-class woman whom Boccaccino abandoned, though he kept and acknowledged the baby boy. A few years later, Boccaccino married a woman from the Portinari clan (the family of Dante's real Beatrice) and had another son by her.

Giovanni was raised with a commercial or financial career in mind, though he soon set his heart on literature. In 1327 he accompanied his father to the Angevin court in Naples, on which the Bardi had a financial stranglehold. His father's official status opened doors to Giovanni, who could revel in the cultural, art- and book-loving atmosphere and educate his senses in the pleasure-loving court. He studied canon law as well as banking practice, but romance and writing became his primary concerns while in Naples, and he always looked back on his sojourn there as a period of bliss. He embodied the romance literarily in the figure of the charming Neapolitan girl Fiammetta ("little flame"), who appears as a character or dedicatee in most of his works through the *Decameron*; she was for him the equivalent of Dante's Beatrice and Petrarch's Laura, sharing in some of their mythical qualities, though nowhere as ethereal as they.[2] It was in

---

[1]He was *not* born in Paris! That legend (including the noble or royal rank of his mother) was deliberately fostered by Boccaccio himself in his younger years, probably as a form of psychological compensation for the shame he felt over the true facts. Nowadays the claim for Paris is made only by a few French chauvinists, and by slovenly encyclopedia editors who don't take the trouble to update their articles.
[2]For instance, Boccaccio claimed noble or royal birth for Fiammetta as well as for his mother. He also said that he first met Fiammetta at a church service, just as Petrarch had claimed in the case of Laura. While these church encounters aren't intrinsically impossible, they're suspiciously redolent of literary reminiscences: most of the lovers in the ancient Greek prose romances first meet at religious festivals.

Naples that Boccaccio created his first important literary works (see the following section, "Other Works"); he wrote original pieces in Latin and Italian, translated Latin classics into Italian, and became acquainted with the writings of Petrarch, whom he didn't meet until after his years in Naples.

Boccaccio returned to Florence in the winter of 1340–1341, unfortunately to face harder times, though he wrote uninterruptedly. The failure of the Bardi bank, due largely to a default on loans by English king Edward III, who was spending his fortune and those of others in the opening years of the Hundred Years' War, cast a pall over Florence. Between 1345 and 1348, Boccaccio tried unsuccessfully to attach himself to the courts of Ravenna and Forlì (the North Italian city states were no longer democracies of the sort still to be found in Tuscany). He was back in Florence in time to be an eyewitness of the Black Death when it struck the city in 1348, eventually carrying off his father and his father's second legitimate wife. (Boccaccio himself never married, but he had three illegitimate children by 1350.)

The *Decameron* was written between 1349 and 1351. Throughout the 1350s, Boccaccio acted in various official capacities for Florence, going on a number of missions and embassies. One more personal connection with his revered Dante occurred in 1350, when he brought a sum of money from the Florentine government to Dante's daughter Beatrice, a nun in Ravenna. The same year marked his first personal meeting with his still-living idol, Petrarch, whom he was to meet several more times and with whom he maintained an unflagging correspondence. In 1354 Boccaccio was sent as far afield as Avignon, as a Florentine envoy to the Pope. In 1355 he made an unsuccessful attempt to reinstate himself in his beloved Naples.

A political contretemps in 1360 kept Boccaccio out of official service for half a decade. It was at that time that the major shift in his literary output occurred. Practically abandoning both creative writing and the use of Italian as his medium, he turned almost exclusively to the compilation of major reference works in Latin, and the pursuit of scholarship in general (he was an early champion of Greek studies in Florence, and learned a little of that language). This shift, motivated largely by Petrarch's influence, made Boccaccio an early Humanist, and was prophetic of the situation of Italian literature until the early 16th century, when the relative neglect of Italian vis-à-vis Latin as a medium for first-class literature finally ended.

Early in the 1360s Boccaccio also took first ecclesiastic orders. At that time, he may have been primarily interested in acquiring

lucrative prebends, but as he grew older, he did become more religious, eventually disavowing the *Decameron* and beginning to collect relics, at which he had earlier scoffed (see story VI, 10). In 1361 he retired to Certaldo, but he emerged from time to time. His last bitter disappointment in an attempt at reinstatement in Naples occurred in 1363. By 1365 he was back in Florentine politics.

By 1372 Boccaccio was suffering from several debilitating conditions, including obesity and dropsy. In the fall of 1373 and in January of 1374 he delivered a lecture series on the *Divine Comedy*, but broke off after reaching only Canto XVII of the *Inferno*. He was overwhelmed by the death of Petrarch in 1374, and succumbed himself in 1375.

Other Works. Many of Boccaccio's so-called minor works are minor only in comparison to the towering achievement of the *Decameron*. Several of them would have gained him an honorable place in literary history on their own. In addition to a large number of Italian lyric poems, Latin epistles and eclogues, biographies and other treatises, and miscellaneous items, the following works stand out (the first four dating from his vital Neapolitan period):

La caccia di Diana ("Diana's Hunt"; 1335–1337; Italian verse narrative in *terza rima*, the rhyme scheme of Dante's *Divine Comedy*, in 18 short cantos). The huntress nymphs are named for ladies in the Neapolitan court; the animals they catch are metamorphosed into young men, their swains, at the moment of sacrifice. It has been suggested that this work spurred the popularity of the musical *caccia*, a polyphonic vocal form with texts based on hunting, between roughly 1340 and 1360.

Il Filocolo (1336–1339; Italian prose narrative). This is one of many retellings of the 12th-century French *Floire et Blancheflor,* a story of love and adventure. In this version the hero, Florio, adopts the pseudonym Filocolo, apparently meant to mean "love's labors" in Boccaccio's shaky Greek.

Il Teseida (1339–1340; Italian verse narrative in *ottava rima*). Largely inspired by the *Thebais* of the ancient Roman poet Statius (who figures prominently in Dante's *Divine Comedy*), this was in turn the direct source for the Knight's Tale in Chaucer's *Canterbury Tales,* though Boccaccio gives Theseus a bigger role. This work is thought to be the first major literary use of the *ottava rima* stanza, which had hitherto been employed only in the narrative ballads (*cantari*) of minstrels and in popular religious ballads. This rhyme scheme would later reach even greater heights in the hands of Ariosto, Tasso, and Byron.

Il Filostrato (1340; Italian verse narrative in *ottava rima*). Filostrato, which is intended to signify "overcome by love," is a pseudonym the author attaches to himself. The story is that of Troilus and Cressida, based mainly on the 12th-century poem *Le roman de Troie* by Benoît de Sainte-Maure. In his turn, Boccaccio was the source for Chaucer's *Troilus and Criseyde* and for Shakespeare's play. It was Boccaccio who first made Pandarus an important character in the story.

La commedia delle ninfe fiorentine ("The Comedy of the Florentine Nymphs"; 1341–1342; mixture of Italian prose and verse in *terza rima*; also known as *Ninfale d'Ameto* or just *Ameto*). This mythological-pastoral story, set in the countryside around Florence, is important in several ways. Not only did it strongly influence Italian pastoral literature, a major genre from the 15th century onward; it is constructed as a frame story with seven inserted stories, and thus directly anticipates the *Decameron*.

Amorosa visione ("Love Vision"); 1342–1343, revised 1355–1360; Italian allegorical poem in fifty *terza rima* cantos). This is an encyclopedic work containing all sorts of lore, like the second part of the *Roman de la rose* (late 13th century), and thus prefigures the scholarly works of Boccaccio's later years.

Elegia di madonna Fiammetta (1343–1344; Italian prose). The work in which Fiammetta is most prominent, this is an epistolary narrative in the first person. Fiammetta, a lady of Naples, is deserted by her Florentine lover.

Il ninfale fiesolano ("The Book of the Nymphs of Fiesole"; 1344–1346; Italian narrative poem in 473 *ottava rima* stanzas). This is the most highly regarded of Boccaccio's works earlier than the *Decameron*. A pastoral love story set in mythical times in the vicinity of Florence, it is close to the popular minstrel *cantare* tradition.

Il Corbaccio ("The Raven"; 1350s or 1360s; Italian prose). Unusual for Boccaccio, this is an outpouring of venomous misogyny. There are plenty of medieval and other precedents, but in the works of the woman-worshiping Boccaccio, the only close parallel is one *Decameron* story (VIII, 7) in which a mistreated suitor takes a cruel, ruthless revenge on the haughty woman who scorned him.

De casibus virorum illustrium ("On the Downfall of Famous Men"; 1356–1360, revised 1373; Latin prose). A group of biographies of famous people, including women, from past history and recent times, emphasizing the tragic outcome of their lives. Like the other Latin reference works by Boccaccio, this was an important source for the Humanists.

De mulieribus claris ("On Famous Women"; 1361 ff.; Latin prose). A series of brief biographies; another of Boccaccio's tributes to women.

Genealogia deorum gentilium ("The Genealogy of the Pagan Gods"; 1363–1374, a major revision of a work begun in 1350–1351; Latin prose). An encyclopedia of Greco-Roman mythology, this book also contains treatises on literature and other topics.

The *Decameron*

Italian Prose and European Story Literature Before the *Decameron*. The *Decameron* didn't spring up out of nowhere, like Athene fully armed out of Zeus's head. It has antecedents in Italy and elsewhere. For various reasons, Italian literature (not counting documentary or archival traces of the use of Italian) begins relatively late, compared with French and Provençal: around the beginning of the 13th century.[3] As is generally the case, prose appears even later than verse. But there was an explosion of Italian prose during that century, including retellings of events in ancient history, Arthurian stories, local legends, pious legends, reports of current events, wisdom literature, travel literature (especially Marco Polo, though his account first appeared in French); informational works on rhetoric, natural history, and geography; and many, many stories. In the early 14th century, there were the chronicle histories of Dino Compagni and Giovanni Villani, and that unique prose masterpiece, *I fioretti di San Francesco* ("The Little Flowers").

The most important story collection in Italian before Boccaccio, written or compiled between roughly 1280 and 1300, is *Il novellino* (also known as *Le cento novelle antiche* and the *Libro di novelle e di bel parlar gentile*). This work is hard to characterize because we have it in so many different versions, in some of which there are more than 150 stories. In general, its stories are brief and anecdotal, and many feature a witty remark. Like much of medieval storytelling, this collection has a "self-help" aspect: it professes to teach its readers to

---

[3]It has been plausibly suggested that authors in Italy retained the use of Latin longer because they felt more at home with it, and had developed an especially folksy Latin closely patterned on their everyday speech. Naturally, it must be understood that the Latin cultivated by Petrarch, Boccaccio, and the later Humanists was modeled directly on the classical Latin of antiquity that these scholars were rediscovering in their passionate quest for manuscripts of the ancient authors.

loosen their tongue and come up with a ready retort in an emergency; it inculcates eloquence (*bel parlar*). In the hundred-story version (*cento novelle*) there are traces of a ten-by-ten structure (ten thematic groups of ten stories each, but no frame story) prefiguring that of the *Decameron*. In any event, Boccaccio knew the *Novellino*, because he clearly borrowed directly from it.

Where did Italian stories come from, other than local tradition? Italian authors were quite able to read the stories already available in Latin, French, and Provençal (including the numerous tales from many other parts of the world that had been translated into those languages). This repertoire of narratives included a wealth of stories of Asian origin (indubitable, though there is much dispute over details), moral-pointing stories (*exempla*) inserted into sermons, lives of saints (definitely read for entertainment as well as edification), lives of troubadours (*vidas* or *razós*), Greek- and Byzantine-style romances, and narrative poems of all sorts: romances of antiquity like the abovementioned *Roman de Troie*, Arthurian romances, the *fabliaux* (bawdy tales of middle-class and plebeian life), and the *lais* such as those of Marie de France (courtly and magical tales of chivalry).

What was the origin of the Italian term *novella* (still used for "short story" today), which was in turn the source of *nouvelle* in French and, much later, *novel* in English? Although it is clearly based ultimately on the Latin *novus* ("new"), the intermediate stages are in dispute. Some scholars trace it to such Late Latin terms as *novellae* ("newly enacted statutes"), but a more cogent suggestion is a borrowing from the Provençal *novas*, which actually means "story," as well as "news" and "conversation." (After the destruction of Southern French society in the 13th-century Albigensian Crusade, Provençal culture was largely fostered in Northern Italy, and Italians could compose in Provençal: Dante's *Divine Comedy* mentions several troubadours and a short section is actually written in Provençal.)

General Remarks on the *Decameron*; Structure of the Work. The *Decameron* was probably written between 1349 and 1351, when Boccaccio was settled in Florence again, and while the horrors of the Black Death were fresh in his mind.

The full title, as it appears in the most highly regarded (autograph) manuscript is: "Comincia il libro chiamato Decameron cognominato prencipe Galeotto, nel quale si contengono cento novelle in diece dí dette da sette donne e da tre giovani uomini" ("Here begins the book called Decameron, nicknamed the Prince Galeotto, in which are contained a hundred stories told in ten days by seven ladies and three

young men"). The word *Decameron,* based on the Greek for "ten
days," is modeled on the title of several treatises called *Hexameron,*
especially that of Saint Ambrose (4th century A.D.), which discuss the
six days of Creation. Boccaccio's title later inspired the *Heptaméron* of
Marguerite of Navarre and the *Pentamerone* of Giambattista Basile
(both volumes were story collections). Galeotto (Galehaut) was the
friend of Sir Lancelot who eased Lancelot's way by introducing him to
Queen Guinevere (later, his name came to mean "pander" in Italian;
it was already used metaphorically, as it is here, in Francesca's famous
recounting of her love for Paolo in Dante's *Divine Comedy*).

Boccaccio's avowed purpose in writing the *Decameron* (this is expressed in the Proem and Conclusion of the work, as well as the introduction to the Fourth Day) is one of compassion: he feels sorry for
women, who, under the thumb of men, must hide their true love and
must remain idly cooped up all day; he loves and admires women and,
in these stories, is supplying them not only with entertainment but
with handy tips on asserting themselves and bettering their lot. He de-
fends himself against the blame he has incurred for his great devotion
to the sex (and for his bawdry, as well).[4] As in the *Novellino* and many
of its medieval sources, there is also a noticeable element of "self-
help" in Boccaccio's expressed intentions: the preliminary remarks to
many of the *Decameron* stories assure the listeners that they will learn
to avoid deception, improve their character, sharpen their wit, etc.

The stories in the *Decameron* include much local Italian tradition
and legend (from Florence and other cities), much observation of current life, much that was garnered from the tales of merchants and
other travelers, as well as narratives based on many of the literary
sources (Latin, French, Provençal, etc.) mentioned above in the section "Italian Prose and European Story Literature Before the
Decameron." (The following section, "The Twenty Selected Stories in
Their Setting," will discuss the individual sources for those stories.)

But the *Decameron* is much more than the sum of its hundred
stories. It is particularly famous for its elaborate and carefully crafted
frame story, the story of the tellers of the hundred stories and the occasion for their storytelling. Frame stories had frequently been used
before, especially in the story collections traceable to Asian origins

---

[4]Whenever, in the *Decameron,* Boccaccio addresses his readers directly *in propria
persona,* it is normally as "ladies." In the storytelling portions, where each of the ten
speakers has the other nine as audience, in all 90 stories in which the listeners are addressed, it is as "ladies," even though there are always either two or three men in the
audience.

(Indian, Persian, Arabic)—one has only to recall the unforgettable Scheherazade frame story of the *Arabian Nights*—but Boccaccio's takes the prize (along with Chaucer's in the *Canterbury Tales*).

The situation is this: During the Black Death of 1348, which disrupts Florentine society and demoralizes the survivors (the disease is depicted in grisly detail), seven well-to-do young women and three young gentlemen agree to escape to the countryside for the duration. Taking along the requisite servants, they live platonically in two different villas and a third garden spot, spending their days in organized pleasurable activities. The late afternoon, after a siesta, is reserved for storytelling. Each of them tells a story a day on a preannounced theme given by the master of ceremonies (whom they call "Queen" or "King") of the day. (At the end of the first day, the young man Dioneo is granted the privilege of being the last speaker on each subsequent day; moreover, he need not adhere to the announced theme of the day. He is a wag and intends to inject some humor even into days with serious or downright lugubrious themes.) The stories go on for ten days, but it is on the fifteenth day, not the eleventh (as careless article writers state), that the group returns to Florence, because they have reserved two Fridays and Saturdays for religious and hygienic purposes; when they return to Florence, all is well (the frame story ends fairly abruptly).

Each story has preliminary remarks, and there are long descriptions of the group's activities and conversations in the introductions and conclusions to each day. Moreover, each day ends with a *ballata* or dance song. The *ballata* on the ninth day, "Io mi son giovinetta," has been called Boccaccio's finest lyric poem.[5] The ten storytellers are invariably chirpy, not to say madcap. Is this gaiety unbelievable, in view of their family tragedies back in Florence, or should it be seen as a psychological escape?

Some of the names of the storytellers (which are in the nature of Greco-Roman literary pseudonyms) had been used by Boccaccio in previous writings. The seven women are Pampinea ("luxuriant"), Fiammetta, Filomena ("the beloved" or "lover of music"), Emilia (intended to mean "flatterer"), Lauretta (suggestive of the poet's laurel wreath and Petrarch's Laura), Neifile ("new to love"), and Elissa (the other name of Vergil's heroine Dido in the *Aeneid*). The three young

---

[5]The full Italian text of this poem, with a facing literal translation, is available in *Introduction to Italian Poetry: A Dual-Language Book,* edited by Luciano Rebay (Dover, 0-486-26715-6).

men are Panfilo ("universal lover" or "lover of Pan"), Filostrato, and
Dioneo ("lustful," based on the name of Aphrodite's mother Dione).
They are given varying character traits in the frame story, but only
very occasionally are the stories they tell determined by their character (with the obvious exception of Dioneo, but even *he* tells the highly
moral story of Griselda—X, 10), and even less often can traces of an
individual "voice" be detected within the stories they tell (though even
in his story of Griselda, Dioneo manages to get in one dirty joke at the
very beginning and another at the very end).

The Twenty Selected Stories in Their Setting. The "Queen" for
the FIRST DAY is Pampinea, and there is no set theme for the day. Even
so, after the long and significant opening story, the others are brief
and anecdotal, and generally conform to the theme of Day Six (witty
retorts and "bright sayings" like those in the *Novellino*).

I, 1: "Master Ciappelletto's Confession." Speaker: Panfilo.
Boccaccio took special pains with his famous opening story, in which
he depicts a thoroughly amoral man and probes into the nature of religious belief. Cepparello (or Cepperello) Dietaiuti of Prato was a real
person, not a notary but a tax collector for King Philippe IV ("le Bel")
of France and Pope Boniface VIII; his extant ledger is a linguistic
landmark of the Tuscan dialect. His sponsor in the story, Musciatto
Franzesi of Florence, was really at Philippe's court and accompanied
the king's adventurer brother Charles de Valois when Charles was invited by Boniface to meddle in Italian affairs (this was in 1301, and
that reference dates the events of the story). Franzesi also was impli-
cated later in Philippe's successful plot to capture and imprison
Boniface (1303).

I, 3: "The Three Rings." Speaker: Filomena. Outstanding among
the shorter tales of Day One for its subject, this story was borrowed
directly from the *Novellino* without significant change beyond a re-
furbishing of language. In at least one version of the *Novellino*, the
sultan is not named, whereas in others he is called Saladin, as here.
Saladin (Ṣalāḥ ed-Dīn Yūsuf; 1137–1193), ruler of Egypt (called
Babilonia by Boccaccio, but traditionally, and not through confusion
with Mesopotamia), precipitated the Third Crusade by his successes
against the Crusader states in the Holy Land, culminating in his re-
conquest of Jerusalem. A hero of Islam (not of humble origins, as in
the story), he is generally portrayed in the European tradition at least
as late as *The Talisman*, by Sir Walter Scott, as the paragon of the
noble adversary, unfailingly chivalrous and generous (he is thus portrayed in story X, 9 of the *Decameron*, included in this volume);

therefore his devious plan for extorting money in story I, 3 is out of
character; possibly the version in the *Novellino* in which the sultan is
not named is the original one. Saladin appears in a number of early
Italian tales. The story of the three rings was not new, even for the
Novellino. It has been surmised that it originated in Jewish circles in
Muslim Spain, famous home of the peaceful coexistence (*conviven-
cia*) of the three religions in question. The story, which also has echoes
in the *Gesta Romanorum* (a Latin collection of moral tales slightly earlier than the *Decameron*), is featured in the late-13th-century French
poem *Le dit du vrai aniel*, but here Christianity is adjudged the only
true religion, hands down. Boccaccio's version became the standard
one, and was adopted by Gotthold Ephraim Lessing in his classic
German verse drama *Nathan der Weise* (1779), in which the Jew
Nathan tells the story of the three rings to—Saladin!

The "Queen" for the SECOND DAY is Filomena, and the theme is an
unexpectedly felicitous ending to a period of troubles. The stories vary
in topic, mood, and length, and include legends, romances, and historical fictions. The general quality of the day is good.

II, 5: "Andreuccio's Mishaps." Speaker: Fiammetta (appropriate
for a lively tale set in Naples). One of the most highly regarded
Decameron stories for character, plot, and overall verve, this tale cannot be traced to any single source (the sources that have been suggested for individual portions of it are too remote or generic), but its
atmosphere is remarkably like those *Arabian Nights* tales in which
naïve and amorous young tradesmen's sons encounter odd adventures
in the secret byways of Baghdad or Cairo; other *Decameron* stories
have *Arabian Nights* parallels, too. The events of the story are se-
curely dated to 1301, when Archbishop Minutolo died (though in
October, not in the height of summer as in the story); his tomb can
still be visited today in the Minutolo Chapel of the Naples cathedral.
At the time, Charles II of Anjou ruled the Kingdom of Naples (all
mainland Italy south of the papal domain) and his enemy Frederick
(Fadrique) II of Aragon ruled Sicily (the Angevins had taken both ter-
ritories from the Holy Roman Empire in the 1260s, but had lost Sicily
after the uprising of 1282 known as the Sicilian Vespers). All the
streets and quarters of Naples named in the story really existed and
were well known to Boccaccio.

II, 9: "A Wager Over Virtue." Speaker: Filomena. The Lomellini
family really existed in Genoa, and included many famous merchants
and gentlemen. This story provided Shakespeare with some of the
principal plot elements for *Cymbeline* (the wager and the manner of

the deception), though the later acts diverge greatly from the story. The assassin who spares his victim in the wilderness is a frequently occurring motif in folktales (compare Snow White and Genovefa). Sources from French and Italian literature too numerous to list here have been suggested for Boccaccio's story; to mention only one, a similar wager over a wife's chastity occurs in the 13th-century French prose tale *Le roi Flore et la belle Jeanne.*

The "Queen" for the THIRD DAY is Neifile, and the theme is the gaining or the recovery of something highly desired by means of cleverness. As it turns out, the thing most highly desired in this group of stories is love or sex.

III, 9: "Gillette of Narbonne." Speaker: Neifile. This story was the source of Shakespeare's *All's Well That Ends Well,* which expands and modifies Boccaccio's plot without essentially altering it. A heterogeneous host of suggested sources or parallels for the *Decameron* version includes ancient Indian as well as ancient Roman texts, not to mention German stories that Boccaccio couldn't have known directly. The folk motif of a woman winning back her husband by accomplishing seemingly impossible tasks is also to be found in the *Roman du comte d'Artois,* written about a hundred years after the *Decameron.*

III, 10: "Putting the Devil Back in Hell." Speaker: Dioneo (who specializes in off-color humor). No specific source. The actual Thebaid, the desert home of the earliest Christian anchorites, was in Egypt, which the heroine couldn't have reached from Tunisia in "a few days," so Boccaccio must have been using the term in a generic sense. This story is an outstanding example of Boccaccio's titillating "soft porn."

The "King" for the FOURTH DAY is Filostrato, the "victim of love," and he chooses an appropriate theme: unhappy ends to love affairs. The stories are sad or subdued, except for Dioneo's obligatory humorous consolation; the characters are historical or contemporary, the latter coming from varied walks of life. The fourth day is, all around, one of the best in the *Decameron.*

IV, 5: "The Pot of Basil." Speaker: Filomena. This story is of course the sole source for John Keats's narrative poem *Isabella: or, The Pot of Basil.* Boccaccio's ultimate source seems to have been the Sicilian folk ballad he quotes at the very end, in which a girl laments the loss of her beloved basil. The ballad, which is completely preserved, mentions no murder; it is thought that the idea for the buried head in Boccaccio's story may have come from a misunderstanding of the word *testa* ("head" in Tuscan) used for "pot" instead of *testo* (or *vaso*) in the

dialect of the ballad. The ballad calls the basil *selemontano* (meaning unknown); Boccaccio changed this to *salernitano* ("from Salerno").

IV, 9: "The Heart of Guilhem de Cabestany." Speaker: Filostrato. Cabestany is a small town near Perpignan in the Catalan-speaking French province of Roussilon.[6] Guilhem was a real troubadour who wrote between 1180 and 1215; eight of his poems survive. Boccaccio's chief or only source was one of the several versions of the brief Provençal prose biography of the troubadour.[7] The story of the heart was a floating folk motif, possibly of Celtic ritual origin, that became attached to a number of historical and legendary figures from different countries. It is to be found, to cite just two instances, in Thomas's version of *Tristan* (12th century) and the late-13th-century French narrative poem *Le châtelain de Coucy* by "Jakemes." "Guilhem of Roussillon" may have been a real person, though there is some confusion of identity, and the "Count of Provence" mentioned near the end of Boccaccio's story may have been Alfonso II of Aragon (died 1196).

The "Queen" for the FIFTH DAY is Fiammetta, and the theme is happy resolutions to star-crossed love affairs. The varied stories include adventurous romances of the Greek or Byzantine type.

V, 8: "The Wild Hunt." Speaker: Filomena. The Onesti and the Traversari were real families prominent in Ravenna. The Ravenna suburb called Classe, Classi, or Chiassi is most famous today for the 6th-century Byzantine mosaics in its church of Sant'Apollinare, but in the 14th century its pine grove was renowned for its honorable mention in Dante's *Divine Comedy*. The hunt in the story, one of the very few in the *Decameron* with any sort of supernatural element,[8] reminds most readers of Woden's wild hunt in Teutonic mythology. A wide range of suggested thematic, if not specific, sources for this tale of divine retribution consists chiefly of medieval Latin-language moral and exemplary stories. In the 1480s, on the occasion of a nephew's

---

[6]Cabestany is the (Catalan) form shown on up-to-date French maps; the Provençal form Cabestanh is also found in the literature. The -ny and the -nh both represent the same sound, the one that is represented in Spanish by ñ. [7]Such biographies, called either *vida* ("life") or *razó* ("explanation"), the latter generally containing fanciful explanations of passages in the poems, were written in the 13th century (long after the poets were dead and their society had been destroyed) as prefaces to collections of their works, and include chiefly unhistorical material. One version of Guilhem's *vida* is currently available, in the original Provençal and in the French translation by Stendhal that he included in his book *De l'amour*, in: *Nouvelles courtoises occitanes et françaises*, Méjean-Thiolier and Notz-Grob, *edd.*, Le Livre de Poche, Paris, 1997, in the series "Lettres gothiques." [8]Even here Boccaccio secularizes the mystery by using it for a lover's ploy.

wedding, Lorenzo de' Medici ("il Magnifico") commissioned four large panel paintings of episodes in this story from the studio of Sandro Botticelli; three of these fine works are now in the Prado, Madrid; another is in a collection in England.

V, 9: "Federigo and His Falcon." Speaker: Fiammetta. Possibly the most widely imitated and adapted *Decameron* story: the topic has been handled by Hans Sachs, Jean de La Fontaine, Alfred Tennyson, and Henry Wadsworth Longfellow, among others. The Alberighi were a prominent Florentine family, mentioned by Dante in his *Divine Comedy*. Jacopo (Coppo) Domenichi filled numerous public offices in Florence between 1308 and 1341. Boccaccio had no need for a written source.

V, 10: "The Beloved Boy." Speaker: Dioneo. There was a real Pietro Vincioli (or Vinciolo) in Perugia in the late 13th and early 14th centuries: a very honorable and respected man (so that Boccaccio's jibes, if meant for this man, could have been a personal vendetta). Homosexuality was widespread in 14th-century Italy (Dante comments on the large number of gay men he saw being punished in the Inferno), and other wives in the *Decameron* attribute to this "perversion" their painful neglect by their husbands (other causes being old age and excessive piety). Although the story reads just like a medieval French *fabliau,* its source is unmistakably older: sections 14–28 of Book IX of Lucius Apuleius's Latin novel *Metamorphoses* (also called *The Golden Ass*; 2nd century A.D.). Boccaccio (just possibly using additional material from a 12th-century Latin poem) makes a number of substantial alterations, introducing Pietro's homosexuality, and changing the boy's fate, giving the story an especially impudent final twist. Moreover, in the Latin original, the donkey is not brought in accidentally, but is actually the metamorphosed narrator of the novel; he steps on the boy's hand intentionally to do the woman a disservice. Another *Decameron* story from Apuleius is VII, 2, which is much less heavily altered, and reads more like a free translation.

The "Queen" for the SIXTH DAY is Elissa, and the theme is escape from danger by means of a clever saying. The first nine stories are very short, so that the sun is still high in the sky in the preliminary remarks to VI, 10; these nine stories are closer to anecdotes than to short stories, but some are of high quality. They are largely based on Florentine oral history, and two of them feature Florentine cultural heroes, the painter Giotto and the 13th-century lyric poet Guido Cavalcanti, Dante's friend.

VI, 4: "The One-Legged Crane." Speaker: Neifile. This story is highly regarded, for all its brevity. Currado Gianfilazzi (late 13th and

first half of 14th century) was really as prominent in Florentine life as Boccaccio states. It's no accident that Chichibio is a Venetian; Boccaccio had a phobia for that city and made its people the butt of many of his jokes. Cranes were often eaten at Italian banquets; a cookbook roughly contemporary with the *Decameron* contains an elaborate recipe for the bird.

VI, 10: "Archangel Gabriel's Feather." Speaker: Dioneo. This story presents unconquerable challenges for translators, and an anthologist "playing it safe" might be tempted to omit it, but that would be a shame, especially in a dual-language edition, because Friar Cipolla's double talk is one of the *Decameron*'s linguistic glories. His sermon combines an endless string of puns (many of which seem to be double entendres) with a constant effort to make the commonplace seem intriguingly and bewilderingly exotic. The friars of Saint Anthony had a particular reputation for being grasping. There actually was a Tuscan surname Cipolla, and attempts have been made to identify our friar with a man who actually lived. As for his servant Guccio, his "surname," Balena, is clearly a humorous epithet, and in this volume "Imbratta" and "Porco" have been translated as epithets as well, though some scholars have thought they were actual family names.[9] The two pranksters who steal the feather bear names that are documentarily attested in Certaldo, the town in the Valdelsa (Elsa river valley) that was one of Boccaccio's homes.

The "King" for the SEVENTH DAY is Dioneo, and the theme, as might be expected from him, is women's ruses for the purpose of marital infidelity. All ten stories are on the risqué side, and this day may well have given the entire *Decameron* its reputation for lubricity. This single-minded day becomes tiresome in the aggregate, but story VII, 8 stands out for its lively and salty dialogue, Boccaccio's own addition to his source or sources.

VII, 8: "The String." Speaker: Neifile. The Berlinghieri were a real merchant family. The ruse involving the substitution of another woman for the wife is a widespread literary motif, going back to India and appearing in a variety of medieval European works, particularly the *Fabliau des tresces* (referring to the locks of hair cut off the substitute's head) of the early 13th century.[10] Boccaccio himself invented the stratagem of the string.

---

[9] If "Porco" stands for Porcellana, as believed by some, there would be an additional pun where the Porcellana hospital is named in Friar Cipolla's sermon.   [10] Original text and modern French translation available in: *Fabliaux érotiques,* Rossi, ed., Le Livre de Poche, Paris, 1992, in the series "Lettres gothiques."

The "Queen" for the EIGHTH DAY is Lauretta, and the theme is deceptions and ruses of all sorts. Although the theme is more general than on the preceding day, which was exclusively devoted to wives' ruses, the eighth day still dwells on deluded husbands to some extent. A story exceptional for the day, for the *Decameron,* and for most of Boccaccio's oeuvre is VIII, 7, the bitterly misogynistic tale already mentioned in the section "Other Works."

VIII, 3: "The Stone of Invisibility." Speaker: Elissa. This is the first of four Calandrino stories in the *Decameron*; no other figure is the hero of so many. Calandrino (meaning either "carpenter's square" or "meadow pipit") was the nickname of the early-14th-century minor Florentine painter Nozzo (Giovannozzo) di Perino, whose goofy ways are recorded in other literature as well. His cronies are historical figures, too: Bruno di Giovanni d'Olivieri and Bonamico, nicknamed Buffalmacco (meaning obscure). They reappear in several other *Decameron* stories, with and without Calandrino, as does the wag Maso del Saggio, a broker noted for his wit (he is briefly mentioned in the story "Archangel Gabriel's Feather" in this volume). The real Calandrino's wife was named Tessa (short for Contessa), as in the story; she also reappears elsewhere in the *Decameron.* The geographical terms all refer to the real Florentine countryside: the stream Mugnone and the three hills Settignano, Montisci, and Monte Morello. Although one literary source has been suggested, Boccaccio hardly needed any for this tale of recent local interest.

The "Queen" for the NINTH DAY is Emilia. Just as on the first day, the themes are left up to the speakers. The stories are thus quite varied, including both the bawdy and the macabre.

IX, 3: "Calandrino's Pregnancy." Speaker: Filostrato. We have already met Calandrino, Tessa, Bruno, and Buffalmacco. Nello is the historically attested painter Nello di Dino, or Bandino; he was related to Tessa. The doctor and apothecary Simone appears in another *Decameron* story (without Calandrino) in which Bruno and Buffalmacco play a scatological practical joke on him. There are scattered medieval references to male pregnancy, but this is essentially a Florentine gossip story.

The "King" for the TENTH DAY is Panfilo, and the theme is noble generosity in a love situation or any other. The stories are invariably uplifting and extremely well composed, and this is possibly the best day in literary quality, though story X, 8 is somewhat of a bore. The settings vary widely in both chronology and geography.

X, 2: "The Highwayman and the Abbot." Speaker: Elissa. The time

of the action must fall between 1294 and 1303, the reign of Pope Boniface VIII. Ghino di Tacco was a real robber baron, exiled from Siena; he is mentioned by Dante in the *Divine Comedy*. Like Robin Hood and many another outlaw, real or fictitious, he became renowned for magnanimity and loftiness of spirit. Radicofani and Santafiora were fortresses near Siena. Cluny was one of the most famous and wealthiest abbeys in France. There is no specific known source for the story.

X, 3: "A Contest of Generosity." Speaker: Filostrato. Oriental sources have been suggested for this story because of its Asian locales (moreover, a figure like that of the little old lady appears in some medieval Latin story collections), but Marco Polo springs immediately to mind. Very possibly Boccaccio's anti-Venetian prejudice made him attribute his information to "Genoese and others." On the other hand, by Boccaccio's time Eastern travel by merchants and missionaries was becoming more common: shortly before the *Decameron* a handbook for merchants was written by Francesco di Balduccio Pegolotti, an agent of the Bardi, like Boccaccio's father, which includes itineraries as far as the Chinese coast, with all sorts of practical advice for merchants. Since Lessing obviously knew the *Decameron,* having borrowed the story of the three rings (I, 3) in his play *Nathan der Weise,* could be have borrowed the name of his hero from this story (X, 3)?

X, 9: "Saladin as a Merchant." Speaker: Panfilo. For information on Saladin, see the remarks on story I, 3 above; in this story (X, 9) he is treated in the traditional way. Torello was also a historical figure, an Imperial magistrate in several Italian cities and Avignon between 1221 and 1237—thus long after the Third Crusade, the background of this story. Emperor Frederick I (Friedrich "Barbarossa") was drowned on this Crusade, in which kings Richard I of England and Philippe-Auguste of France also participated. San Pietro in Ciel d'Oro is a famous church in Pavia, the city that had been the capital of the Lombards before their defeat by Charlemagne. No suggested source is altogether specific, but each of the two main strands of the story has numerous counterparts in literature. The first strand, Saladin's incognito, is to be found in the *Novellino* and in the Spanish story collection *El Conde Lucanor* by Juan Manuel (circa 1335). The second strand, the absent man's journey home to forestall his sweetheart's marriage or his wife's remarriage, appears in medieval Latin stories and in an infinity of popular ballads from all over Europe; readers of English probably know it best from such Child ballads as "Hynd Horn." A special feature of the *Decameron* version, which Boccaccio

recounts without a skeptical blink, is the flying bed, clearly related to the flying carpets and horses of the *Arabian Nights*.

X, 10: "Patient Griselda." Speaker: Dioneo. No selection from the *Decameron*, however brief, can omit this famous story (the direct source for the Clerk's Tale in Chaucer's *Canterbury Tales*), despite the mixed press it has received. One feminist editor of Boccaccio is so appalled by the treatment meted out to Griselda that she denies the story any literary merit—distinctly a minority view. Other literary historians realize that it was no accident that Boccaccio placed this story last in the *Decameron*. One points to the connection between Griselda as the paragon of human virtue and Master Ciappelletto of the very first story as the wickedest man who ever lived; the entire work is thus tied together as a panorama of the human character. Another critic sees the sympathetic figure of Griselda as Boccaccio's homage to his unknown servile mother, abandoned by her lover. This was the first *Decameron* story known internationally, because, in an unusual move, Petrarch made a separate Latin translation of it that was widely circulated. As for the story's literary antecedents, they are vague, although there are famous examples of put-upon wives, such as Enide in the late-12th-century narrative poem *Erec et Enide* by Chrétien de Troyes, or the lady in the 12th-century *lai* by Marie de France called *Le Freisne*. Folklorists can read the story of Griselda as a dense tissue of well-known folktale motifs that give it a timeless quality detached from everyday reality.

Boccaccio's Language. The Italian language emerged from its Latin chrysalis at a much later date than French or Provençal, so that (as in the case of Spanish) there has been no real break, but a smooth transition, between medieval and modern Italian (very unlike the situation for French, English, and German). Since the Tuscan dialect, source of today's standard Italian, was already established as the general language of literature by Boccaccio's time (and largely thanks to him), one need only follow a few simple rules of thumb to be able to read the *Decameron* with ease. Just a handful of helpful tips is offered here.

Naturally, there have been semantic changes in the interim; thus, Boccaccio says *ebbe per costante* where a modern Italian would say *ritenne con certezza* ("considered it a sure thing"). There are slight differences in word forms—*fracidi* for *fradici* ("decayed"), or *attutare* for *attutire* ("attenuate")—and inflectional forms: *parvono* for *parvero* ("they appeared"), or *sofferrebbe* for *soffrirebbe* ("would allow"). Occasionally an obsolete word is used: *sirocchia* for *sorella* ("sister").

Here are some special features to look out for: Dependent pronouns are often suffixed to verbs that are not in the infinitive or participle form; thus: *èmmi* for *mi è* ("it is to me"), or *andronne* for *(me) ne andrò* ("I'll go away"). Unlike modern Italian, direct object pronouns precede indirect ones (or the particles *ne, ci,* and *vi*): *rimettianlovi* = *rimettiamovelo* ("let's put him back there"). Lastly, Boccaccio's style is heavily tinged with influences from Latin. Not only do verbs tend to gravitate to the end of the sentence or clause; Boccaccio regularly uses a thoroughly un-Italian construction taken over directly from classical (not medieval!) Latin, the use of the infinitive after verbs of saying, knowing, and thinking: *conoscendo lei dire il vero* ("knowing that she was speaking the truth"; in somewhat inelegant Latin, *cognoscens eam verum dicere*).

Boccaccio's excessive Latinisms disappear in his more folksy stories, and in his brilliantly vivacious dialogue, the heart of many a story and always his own personal contribution to the tale.

The Nature of This Edition

The criteria for the selection of stories have already been given in the Foreword and in the section "The Twenty Selected Stories in Their Setting."

The translation is intended to be as complete, faithful, and accurate as the differences between Boccaccio's Italian and modern American English allow. Some of the footnotes suggest other renderings of certain words or phrases in cases where even the most eminent Italian scholars disagree over nuances.

Each story is given in its entirety, including all the author's and speakers' preliminary remarks, which occasionally mention a character or incident from the preceding story.

The Italian text used as the basis for this edition was not divided into paragraphs. The paragraph divisions here were created by the translator.

The translator has felt free to break up many of Boccaccio's long sentences into two or more English ones. Many of Boccaccio's sentences strike the modern reader as rambling, if not run-on, and do not call for the same piety in a translator as, say, the architectonically structured long sentences of Thomas Mann.

The greatest liberty taken by the translator was the creation of new brief titles for the stories in modern Italian and in English. This was

done partially for convenience of reference in the Introduction, footnotes, table of contents, and running heads, but more importantly to
avoid giving away the plot, as many of the original paragraph-length
story headings do (moreover, they often give an odd emphasis to certain story elements, and sometimes don't sound as if Boccaccio himself had written them). As an example of an original story heading, in
Italian and extremely literal English, the one provided for the
Griselda story (X, 10) is given here:

"Il marchese di Saluzzo, da' prieghi de' suoi uomini costretto di
pigliar moglie, per prenderla a suo modo, piglia una figliuola d'un vil-
lano, della quale ha due figliuoli, li quali le fa veduto d'uccidergli; poi
mostrando lei essergli rincresciuta ed avere altra moglie presa, a casa
faccendosi ritornare la propria figliuola come se sua moglie fosse, lei
avendo in camicia cacciata e ad ogni cosa trovandola paziente, più cara
che mai in casa tornàtalasi, i suoi figliuoli grandi le mostra e come
marchesana l'onora e fa onorare."

("The marquess of Saluzzo, compelled to marry by the entreaties of
his vassals, in order to marry a woman of his own choice, weds a
farmer's daughter, by whom he has two children, which he makes her
believe he has killed; then, telling her he is sorry he married her and
is taking another wife, making his own daughter return home as if she
were his wife, and having driven her [his first wife] away in her shift
and finding her patient in every situation, he brings her back to his
home more dear to him than ever, he shows her her grown-up children, and honors her, and causes her to be honored, as marchioness.")

After that, why read the story?

The Decameron: Selected Tales

Decameron: Novelle scelte

LA CONFESSIONE DI SER
CIAPPELLETTO [I, 1]

Convenevole cosa è, carissime donne, che ciascuna cosa la quale l'uomo fa, dall'ammirabile e santo nome di Colui il quale di tutte fu facitore le déa principio; per che, dovendo io al nostro novellare, sì come primo, dare cominciamento, intendo da una delle sue maravigliose cose incominciare, acciò che, quella udita, la nostra speranza in lui sì come in cosa impermutabile si fermi, e sempre sia da noi il suo nome lodato.

Manifesta cosa è che, sì come le cose temporali tutte sono transitorie e mortali, così in sé e fuor di sé esser piene di noia, d'angoscia e di fatica, e ad infiniti pericoli soggiacere; alle quali senza niun fallo né potremmo noi, che viviamo mescolati in esse e che siamo parte d'esse, durare né ripararci, se spezial grazia di Dio forza ed avvedimento non ci prestasse. La quale a noi ed in noi non è da credere che per alcun nostro merito discenda, ma dalla sua propria benignità mossa e da' prieghi di coloro impetrata che, sì come noi siamo, furon mortali, e bene i suoi piaceri mentre furono in vita seguendo, ora con lui eterni son divenuti e beati; alli quali noi medesimi, sì come a procuratori informati per esperienza della nostra fragilità, forse non audaci di porgere i prieghi nostri nel cospetto di tanto giudice, delle cose le quali a noi reputiamo opportune gli porgiamo.

Ed ancor più, lui verso noi di pietosa liberalità pieno discerniamo; ché, non potendo l'acume dell'occhio mortale nel segreto della divina mente trapassare in alcun modo, avvien forse talvolta che, da falsa oppinione ingannati, tale dinanzi alla sua maestà facciamo procuratore che da quella con eterno esilio è scacciato; e nondimeno esso, al quale niuna cosa è occulta, più alla purità del pregator riguardando che alla sua ignoranza o all'esilio del pregato, così come se quegli fosse nel suo cospetto beato, esaudisce coloro che il priegano. Il che manifestamente potrà apparire nella novella

2

MASTER CIAPPELLETTO'S
CONFESSION [I, 1]

It is only proper, dearest ladies, that in everything a man does he should take his start from the admirable, holy name of the One who created all things. And so, since I, as the first, am to begin our story-telling, I intend to begin with one of His wondrous doings, so that, once it is heard, our hope in Him and His immutable nature may be affirmed, and His name ever praised by us.

It is well known that all temporal things are impermanent and finite, that both intrinsically and circumstantially they are full of troubles, distress, and labor, and are subject to infinite perils; without any doubt, we who live in the midst of them and are part of them could not resist them or protect ourselves from them unless a special grace of God lent us strength and discernment. It is not to be believed that this grace comes down to us and into us through any merit of our own; rather, it is set in motion by His own loving-kindness and obtained through the prayers of those who were once mortal as we are but, having lived in accordance with His dictates, have now become eternally blessed in His presence. We ourselves, perhaps not bold enough to address our prayers directly to so great a Judge, address them, for favors we deem helpful to ourselves, to those saints, as being intercessors acquainted by experience with our frailty.

And we observe that He is even more full of merciful generosity toward us: the power of mortal sight being totally unable to penetrate the secrets of the divine mind, it sometimes occurs that, deceived by a false reputation, we call upon someone as an intercessor before His majesty who has been driven away from His presence into eternal banishment. Nevertheless, He to whom nothing is hidden, considering the innocence of the person praying rather than his ignorance or the damnation of the person being prayed to, grants the prayers just as if the would-be saint were in His blessed presence. That will be

la quale di raccontare intendo, manifestamente dico, non il giudicio di Dio ma quel degli uomini seguitando.

Ragionasi adunque che, essendo Musciatto Franzesi di ricchissimo e gran mercatante in Francia cavalier divenuto e dovendone in Toscana venire con messer Carlo Senzaterra, fratello del re di Francia, da papa Bonifazio addomandato ed al venir promosso, sentendo egli li fatti suoi, sì come le più volte son quegli de' mercatanti, molto intralciati in qua ed in là, e non potersi di leggeri né subitamente stralciare, pensò quegli commettere a più persone, ed a tutti trovò modo; fuor solamente in dubbio gli rimase, cui lasciar potesse sufficiente a riscuoter suoi crediti fatti a più Borgognoni.

E la cagione del dubbio era il sentire li Borgognoni uomini riottosi e di mala condizione e misleali; ed a lui non andava per la memoria chi tanto malvagio uom fosse, in cui egli potesse alcuna fidanza avere, che opporre alla loro malvagità si potesse. E sopra questa esaminazione pensando lungamente stato, gli venne a memoria un ser Cepparello da Prato il quale molto alla sua casa in Parigi si riparava, il quale, per ciò che piccolo di persona era e molto assettatuzzo, non sappiendo li Franceschi che si volesse dir Cepparello, credendo che «cappello», cioè «ghirlanda», secondo il loro volgare a dir venisse, per ciò che piccolo era, come dicemmo, non Ciappello ma Ciappelletto il chiamavano; e per Ciappelletto era conosciuto per tutto, là dove pochi per ser Cepparello il conoscìeno.

Era questo Ciappelletto di questa vita. Egli, essendo notaio, avea grandissima vergogna quando un de' suoi strumenti, come che pochi ne facesse, fosse altro che falso trovato; de' quali tanti avrebbe fatti, di quanti fosse stato richesto, e quegli più volentieri in dono che alcuno altro grandemente salariato. Testimonianze false con sommo diletto diceva, richesto e non richesto; e dandosi a quei tempi in Francia a' saramenti grandissima fede, non curandosi fargli falsi, tante quistioni malvagiamente vincea, a quante a giurare di dire il vero sopra la sua fede era chiamato.

Aveva oltre modo piacere, e forte vi studiava, in commettere tra amici e parenti e qualunque altra persona mali ed inimicizie e scandali, de' quali quanto maggiori mali vedeva seguire, tanto più

clearly seen in the story I intend to tell—I mean "clearly" in accordance not with God's judgment but with man's.

Well then, it is said that Musciatto Franzesi, a very rich and great merchant operating in France, had been knighted and was due to come to Tuscany along with Sir Charles "Lackland," brother of the French king, who had been sent for and urged to come by Pope Boniface. Musciatto, finding that his business dealings, as those of merchants generally are, were quite entangled on all sides, and that he could not easily settle them, decided to entrust them to a number of people, and made a satisfactory arrangement in each case, except that he was still unsure whom he could leave behind who would be capable of collecting the loans he had made to several Burgundians.

The reason for this uncertainty was his knowledge that Burgundians are troublesome, nasty, and untrustworthy. He was unable to recall anyone wicked enough to be at all relied upon to counteract *their* wickedness. After spending a long time over this investigation, he remembered a Master Cepparello from Prato who often lodged at his house in Paris. Because this man was short of stature and very neat-looking, the French, not knowing what Cepparello means, and thinking it meant "chaplet" or "garland" as it does in their language—because he was short, as we said, called him not Ciappello but Ciappelletto.[1] As Ciappelletto he was known everywhere, whereas few knew him as Master Cepparello.

This was the nature of this Ciappelletto's life: Being a notary, he was thoroughly ashamed whenever one of his genuine documents (though he didn't draw up many) was discovered to be unfalsified. He was ready to draw up as many forgeries as he was asked for, and would have been happier to do it for nothing than anyone else would have been if handsomely paid for them. He bore false witness with the greatest of pleasure, whether asked to or not; and, great faith being placed in oaths at that time in France, and he being unconcerned about perjuring himself, he fraudulently won every case in which he was called up to speak the truth under oath.

He was especially happy, and made it his special aim, when he could sow trouble, enmity, and discord among friends, relatives, or anyone else. The greater the mischief he saw arising from this discord,

---

[1]Cepparello is really a form of Jacob, but Boccaccio may have thought it meant "little stump" (from *ceppo*). The French form of "garland" at the time would have been *chapel* (with the *ch* still pronounced like the Italian *ci*), but because the man was short, the diminutive form *chapelet* was used (with the final *t* still sounded, and the last syllable stressed).

d'allegrezza prendea. Invitato ad uno omicidio o a qualunque altra rea cosa, senza negarlo mai, volonterosamente v'andava, e più volte a fedire e ad uccidere uomini con le proprie mani si ritrovò volentieri. Bestemmiatore di Dio e de' santi era grandissimo, e per ogni piccola cosa, sì come colui che più che alcuno altro era iracondo. A chiesa non usava già mai, ed i sagramenti di quella tutti come vil cosa con abominevoli parole scherniva; e così in contrario le taverne e gli altri disonesti luoghi visitava volentieri ed usavagli. Delle femine era così vago come sono i cani de' bastoni; del contrario più che alcuno altro tristo uomo si dilettava. Imbolato avrebbe e rubato con quella coscienza che un santo uomo offerrebbe. Gulosissimo e bevitor grande, tanto che alcuna volta sconciamente gli facea noia; giucatore e mettitore di malvagi dadi era solenne.

Perché mi distendo io in tante parole? Egli era il piggiore uomo, forse, che mai nascesse. La cui malizia lungo tempo sostenne la potenza e lo stato di messer Musciatto, per cui molte volte e dalle private persone, alle quali assai sovente faceva ingiuria, e dalla corte, a cui tuttavia la facea, fu riguardato. Venuto adunque questo ser Cepparello nell'animo a messer Musciatto, il quale ottimamente la sua vita conosceva, si pensò il detto messer Musciatto, costui dovere esser tale quale la malvagità de' Borgognoni il richiedea; e per ciò, fàttolsi chiamare, gli disse così:

— Ser Ciappelletto, come tu sai, io sono per ritrarmi del tutto di qui, ed avendo tra gli altri a fare co' Borgognoni, uomini pieni d'inganni, non so cui io mi possa lasciare, a riscuotere il mio da loro, più convenevole di te; e per ciò, con ciò sia cosa che tu niente facci al presente, ove a questo vogli intendere, io intendo di farti avere il favore della corte e di donarti quella parte di ciò che tu riscoterai, che convenevole sia.

Ser Ciappelletto, che scioperato si vedea e male agiato delle cose del mondo, e lui ne vedeva andare che suo sostegno e ritegno era lungamente stato, senza niuno indugio o quasi da necessità costretto, si diliberò e disse che volea volentieri. Per che, convenutisi insieme, ricevuta ser Ciappelletto la procura e le lettere favorevoli del re, partitosi messer Musciatto, n'andò in Borgogna, dove quasi niuno il conoscea; e quivi fuori di sua natura benignamente e mansuetamente cominciò a voler riscuotere e fare quello per che andato v'era, quasi si riserbasse l'adirarsi al da sezzo.

the more pleasure he derived. When made party to a murder or any other evil deed, he never refused but went along gladly; often he was happy to wound and kill men with his own hands. He was a very great blasphemer of God and the saints, and on the slightest occasion, because he was more subject to fits of anger than anyone else. He never went to church, and he mocked all its sacraments in filthy language as something vile; on the contrary, he gladly visited and frequented taverns and other lewd places.

He was as fond of women as dogs are of a beating; he took more delight in the contrary pleasure than any other gay man. He would have filched and robbed with the same zeal that a holy man displays in offering alms. A heavy feeder and drinker, so much so that it sometimes made him filthy himself in his distress; as a gambler and manipulator of loaded dice, preeminent!

Why do I waste so many words? He was possibly the worst man ever born. For a long time his evil ways were protected by the commercial and political power of Master Musciatto, thanks to whom he was often spared by the private parties, whom he frequently harmed, and by the courts of law, which he regularly harmed. Well, then, when this Master Cepparello was called to mind by Master Musciatto, who was perfectly well acquainted with his mode of life, the aforesaid Master Musciatto decided he would be just the man the wickedness of the Burgundians called for. Therefore, he had him summoned and addressed him as follows:

"Master Ciappelletto, as you know, I am on the point of leaving this place altogether, and, having to deal, among others, with the Burgundians, men who are full of ruses, I don't know anyone more suitable than you to leave here to collect my money from them. And so, seeing that you are unoccupied at the present time, if you want to take care of this, *I'll* take care of winning the favor of the royal court for you and giving you an appropriate percentage of whatever you collect."

Master Ciappelletto, finding himself idle and poorly supplied with worldly goods, and seeing the man depart who had long been his sponsor and protector, without delay, as if compelled by necessity, made up his mind and said he was willing. And so, after they had agreed on terms, Master Ciappelletto had received the power of attorney and letters patent from the king, and Master Musciatto had departed, Ciappelletto set out for Burgundy, where hardly anyone knew him. There, kindly and gently, unlike his usual self, he began to ask for repayment and to do what he had gone for, almost as if he were reserving fits of anger as his last resort.

E così faccendo, riparandosi in casa di due fratelli fiorentini, li quali quivi ad usura prestavano e lui per amor di messer Musciatto onoravano molto, avvenne che egli infermò; al quale i due fratelli fecero prestamente venir medici e fanti che il servissero ed ogni cosa opportuna alla sua sanità racquistare. Ma ogni aiuto era nullo, per ciò che il buono uomo, il quale già era vecchio e disordinatamente vivuto, secondo che i medici dicevano, andava di giorno in giorno di male in peggio, come colui che aveva il male della morte; di che li due fratelli si dolevan forte, ed un giorno, assai vicini della camera nella quale ser Ciappelletto giaceva infermo, seco medesimi cominciarono a ragionare.

— Che farem noi — diceva l'uno all'altro — di costui? Noi abbiamo de' fatti suoi pessimo partito alle mani: per ciò che il mandarlo fuori di casa nostra così infermo ne sarebbe gran biasimo e segno manifesto di poco senno, veggendo la gente che noi l'avessimo ricevuto prima e poi fatto servire e medicare così sollecitamente, ed ora, senza potere egli aver fatta cosa alcuna che dispiacerci debba, così subitamente di casa nostra, ed infermo a morte, vederlo mandar fuori. D'altra parte, egli è stato sì malvagio uomo, che egli non si vorrà confessare né prendere alcuno sagramento della Chiesa, e morendo senza confessione niuna chiesa vorrà il suo corpo ricevere, anzi sarà gittato a' fossi a guisa d'un cane; e se egli si pur confessa, i peccati suoi son tanti e sì orribili, che il simigliante n'avverrà, per ciò che frate né prete ci sarà che il voglia né possa assolvere; per che, non assoluto, anche sarà gittato a' fossi. E se questo avviene, il popolo di questa terra, il quale sì per lo mestier nostro, il quale loro pare iniquissimo e tutto il giorno ne dicon male, e sì per la volontà che hanno di rubarci, veggendo ciò, si leverà a romore e griderà: «Questi Lombardi cani, li quali a chiesa non sono voluti ricevere, non ci si voglion più sostenere!», e correrannoci alle case e per avventura non solamente l'avere ci ruberanno, ma forse ci torranno oltre a ciò le persone; di che noi in ogni guisa stiam male, se costui muore.

Ser Ciappelletto, il quale, come dicemmo, presso giacea là dove costoro così ragionavano, avendo l'udire sottile, sì come le più volte veggiamo aver gl'infermi, udì ciò che costoro di lui dicevano; li quali egli si fece chiamare, e disse loro:

Acting thus, and living in the house of two Florentine brothers, who lent money on interest there and showed him great honor for the sake of Master Musciatto, he happened to fall ill. Whereupon the two brothers swiftly called in doctors and servants to serve him and do everything conducive to his regaining his health. But all their aid was in vain, and our good man, who was already old and had lived a dissolute life, according to what the doctors said, went from bad to worse daily, his illness being mortal. The two brothers were greatly upset by this, and one day, being very close to the room in which Master Ciappelletto lay ill, they began talking to each other.

"What are we to do with him?" said one to the other. "We're in a really bad situation on his account, because sending him out of our house sick as he is would bring great blame on us and would be a clear sign of stupidity, since the people have seen that first we took him in and then had him waited on and doctored so thoughtfully, and now, without his being able to do anything to displease us, they will see us suddenly drive him out of our house while he's mortally ill. On the other hand, he's been such an evil man that he won't want to make confession or accept any sacrament of the Church; and, if he dies without confession, no church will want to receive his body, but he'll be thrown into the town moat like a dog; and even if he confesses, his sins are so numerous and terrible that the same thing will happen, because no friar or priest will be willing or able to give him absolution, and so, without absolution, he'll still be thrown into the moat. And if that happens, the people of this city, who, both because of our profession, which seems most unjust to them, so that they slander us every day, and because of their wish to plunder us, will start a riot when they see this, yelling: 'These Lombard[2] dogs, who aren't received in church, aren't to be put up with any longer!' They'll run to our houses and perhaps will not only rob us of our wealth but even take our lives besides. So that, any way you look at it, we're in for it if he dies."

Master Ciappelletto, who, as we said, was in bed close to the place where those two were saying this, and whose hearing was keen, as is generally the case with sick people, heard what they were saying about him. He had them called to his side, and said to them:

---

[2]Northern Italians, even Tuscans, were generally called Lombards in other countries, especially when engaged in financial matters. "Lombard" became a term for usurer.

— Io non voglio che voi d'alcuna cosa di me dubitiate né abbiate
paura di ricevere per me danno; io ho inteso ciò che di me ragionato avete e son certissimo che così n'avverrebbe come voi dite,
dove così andasse la bisogna come avvisate; ma ella andrà altramenti. Io ho vivendo tante ingiurie fatte a Domenedio, che, per
farnegli io una in su la mia morte, né più né meno ne farà. E per
ciò procacciate di farmi venire un santo e valente frate, il più che
aver potete, se alcun ce n'è, e lasciate fare a me, ché fermamente
io acconcerò i fatti vostri ed i miei in maniera che starà bene e che
dovrete esser contenti.

I due fratelli, come che molta speranza non prendessono di
questo, nondimeno se n'andarono ad una religione di frati e domandarono alcun santo e savio uomo che udisse la confessione d'un
Lombardo che in casa loro era infermo; e fu lor dato un frate an-
tico di santa e di buona vita, e gran maestro in Iscrittura e molto
venerabile uomo, nel quale tutti i cittadini grandissima e speziale
divozione aveano, e lui menarono. Il quale, giunto nella camera
dove ser Ciappelletto giacea ed allato pòstoglisi a sedere, prima benignamente il cominciò a confortare ed appresso il domandò,
quanto tempo era che egli altra volta confessato si fosse. Al quale
ser Ciappelletto, che mai confessato non s'era, rispose:

— Padre mio, la mia usanza suole essere di confessarmi ogni settimana almeno una volta; senza che, assai sono di quelle che io mi con-
fesso più; è il vero che, poi che io infermai, che son passati da otto dì,
io non mi confessai, tanta è stata la noia che la 'nfermità m'ha data.

Disse allora il frate: — Figliuol mio, bene hai fatto, e così si vuol
fare per innanzi; e veggio che, poi sì spesso ti confessi, poca fatica
avrò d'udire o di domandare.

Disse ser Ciappelletto: — Messer lo frate, non dite così; io non
mi confessai mai tante volte né sì spesso, che io sempre non mi volessi confessare generalmente di tutti i miei peccati che io mi ri-
cordassi dal dì che io nacqui infino a quello che confessato mi sono;
e per ciò vi priego, padre mio buono, che così puntualmente d'ogni
cosa mi domandiate come se mai confessato non mi fossi; e non mi
riguardate perché io infermo sia, ché io amo molto meglio di dis-
piacere a queste mie carni che, faccendo agio loro, io facessi cosa
che potesse essere perdizione dell'anima mia, la quale il mio Salva-
tore ricomperò col suo prezioso sangue.

Queste parole piacquero molto al santo uomo e pàrvongli argo-
mento di bene disposta mente; e poi che a ser Ciappelletto ebbe
molto commendato questa sua usanza, il cominciò a domandare se
egli mai in lussuria con alcuna femina peccato avesse.

"I don't want you to have any worries on my account, or to be afraid of being harmed because of me; I heard what you said about me, and I'm perfectly sure that things would happen as you say if the matter proceeded as you foresee—but it will proceed differently. In my life I've offended God so often that one more instance just before I die won't make any difference. And so, try to fetch me the most holy and competent friar you can find, if there is any such, and leave the rest to me, because I will definitely arrange your business and mine in such a way that all will be well and you'll be contented."

Even though the two brothers failed to derive much hope from this, all the same they went to a friary and asked for a holy and learned man to hear the confession of a Lombard who was ill in their house. They were given an old-time friar of holy and good life, a great master of Scripture and a most venerable man, in whom all the townspeople had very great, special faith, and they took him along. When he arrived in the room where Master Ciappelletto was in bed, and sat down beside him, he first began consoling him kindly and then asked him how long it had been since his last previous confession. Master Ciappelletto, who had never made confession, replied:

"Father, my usual practice is to confess at least once every week, although many weeks I confess more often. But it's true that since I became ill, which is about a week now, I haven't confessed because the illness has troubled me so much."

Then the friar said: "My son, you've been acting properly, and you should continue the same way; and I see that, since you confess so often, I won't have a hard job listening to you or asking you questions."

Master Ciappelletto said: "Father, don't say that. I have never made confession so many times or so often that I didn't want to make a general confession each time of all the sins I could remember from the day I was born to the day of my confession. And so, I beg you, good Father, to ask me about everything in detail as if I had never made confession. Don't spare me because I'm ill, because I much prefer to give grief to this flesh of mine than to indulge it and thus commit an action that could be injurious to my soul, which my Savior redeemed with His precious blood."

These words were greatly pleasing to the holy man, who deemed them a sign of a well-disposed mind; and, after congratulating Master Ciappelletto warmly on this practice of his, he started to ask him whether he had ever committed the sin of lust with any woman.

Al quale ser Ciappelletto sospirando rispose: — Padre mio, di questa parte mi vergogno io di dirvene il vero, temendo di non peccar in vanagloria.

Al quale il santo frate disse: — Di' sicuramente, ché il vero dicendo né in confessione né in altro atto si peccò già mai.

Disse allora ser Ciappelletto: — Poi che voi di questo mi fate sicuro, ed io il vi dirò: io son così vergine come io uscii del corpo della mamma mia.

— O benedetto sii tu da Dio! — disse il frate — come bene hai fatto! E faccendolo hai tanto più meritato, quanto, volendo, avevi più d'arbitrio di fare il contrario che non abbiam noi e qualunque altri son quegli che sotto alcuna regola son costretti.

Ed appresso questo, il domandò se nel peccato della gola aveva a Dio dispiaciuto. Al quale, sospirando forte, ser Ciappelletto rispose del sì, e molte volte, per ciò che, con ciò fosse cosa che egli, oltre alli digiuni delle quaresime che nell'anno si fanno dalle divote persone, ogni settimana almeno tre dì fosse uso di digiunare in pane ed in acqua, con quello diletto e con quello appetito l'acqua bevuta aveva (e spezialmente quando avesse alcuna fatica durata o adorando o andando in pellegrinaggio) che fanno i gran bevitori il vino; e molte volte aveva disiderato d'avere cotali insalatuzze d'erbucce, come le donne fanno quando vanno in villa, ed alcuna volta gli era paruto migliore il mangiare che non pareva a lui che dovesse parere a chi digiuna per divozione, come digiunava egli.

Al quale il frate disse: — Figliuol mio, questi peccati sono naturali, e sono assai leggeri, e per ciò io non voglio che tu ne gravi più la coscienza tua che bisogni. Ad ogni uomo avviene, quantunque santissimo sia, il parergli, dopo lungo digiuno, buono il manicare, e, dopo la fatica, il bere.

— Oh! — disse ser Ciappelletto, — padre mio, non mi dite questo per confortarmi; ben sapete che io so che le cose che al servigio di Dio si fanno, si deono fare tutte nettamente e senza alcuna ruggine d'animo; e chiunque altramenti fa, pecca.

Il frate, contentissimo, disse: — Ed io son contento che così ti cappia nell'animo, e piacemi forte la tua pura e buona coscienza in ciò. Ma dimmi: in avarizia hai tu peccato, disiderando più che il convenevole o tenendo quello che tu tener non dovesti?

— Al quale ser Ciappelletto disse: —Padre mio, io non vorrei che voi guardaste perché io sia in casa di questi usurieri: io non ci ho a far nulla, anzi c'era venuto per dovergli ammonire e gastigare e tôrgli da questo abominevole guadagno; e credo mi sarebbe

At which Master Ciappelletto sighed and answered: "Father, on this subject I'm ashamed to tell you the truth, because I'm afraid of committing the sin of boastfulness."

The holy friar replied: "Speak up, because telling the truth during confession or any other time is no sin."

Then Master Ciappelletto said: "Since you give me assurances about this, I'll tell you: I am as much a virgin as when I came out of my mother's womb."

"Oh, may God bless you!" said the friar. "How well you've behaved! And, acting that way, you've earned even more merit, because, if you had wanted to, you had more leeway to do the opposite than we have, and all others who are bound by some religious rule."

After that, he asked him whether he had offended God through the sin of gluttony. With a loud sigh, Master Ciappelletto said yes, and frequently, because—even though, in addition to the fast days observed by pious people throughout the year, he was accustomed to live on bread and water at least three days out of every week—he had drunk the water with the same pleasure and appetite (especially when he had made some effort either in praying or in going on pilgrimage) that drunkards show when consuming wine. And many a time he had felt desire for those nice little green salads such as women prepare when in their country houses. And, at times, eating had seemed more desirable to him than it seemed to him it should seem to one who fasts out of piety, as he used to fast.

To which the friar replied: "My son, these sins are natural and trivial, and so I don't want you to burden your conscience with them more than you need to. It happens to every man, even the holiest, that he finds eating good after a long fast, and drinking after some effort."

"Oh, Father," said Master Ciappelletto, "don't tell me that to console me; you're well aware that I know that actions performed in the service of God should be done in complete purity and without any soiling of the mind; whoever acts otherwise, sins."

The friar, mightily pleased, said: "And I'm pleased that you think so, and I'm very happy with your pure, good conscience about this. But tell me: have you sinned through avarice, coveting more than was proper or taking what you shouldn't have?"

Master Ciappelletto answered: "Father, I don't want you to get the wrong idea from my being in the house of these usurers. I have nothing to do with their business; in fact, I came here to admonish them, to mend their ways, and to make them give up this abominable

venuto fatto, se Iddio non m'avesse così visitato. Ma voi dovete sapere che mio padre mi lasciò ricco uomo, del cui avere, come egli fu morto, diedi la maggior parte per Dio; e poi, per sostentare la vita mia e per potere aiutare i poveri di Cristo, ho fatte mie piccole mercatantìe ed in quello ho disiderato di guadagnare, e sempre co' poveri di Dio, quello che guadagnato ho, ho partito per mezzo, la mia metà convertendo ne' miei bisogni, l'altra metà dando loro; e di ciò m'ha sì bene il mio Creatore aiutato, che io ho sempre di bene in meglio fatti i fatti miei.

Bene hai fatto, — disse il frate, — ma come ti se' tu spesso adirato?

— Oh! — disse ser Ciappelletto — cotesto vi dico io bene che io ho molto spesso fatto. E chi se ne potrebbe tenere, veggendo tutto il dì gli uomini fare le sconce cose, non servare i comandamenti di Dio, non temere i suoi giudìci? Egli sono state assai volte il dì che io vorrei più tosto essere stato morto che vivo, veggendo i giovani andar dietro alle vanità ed udendogli giurare e spergiurare, andare alle taverne, non visitar le chiese e seguir più tosto le vie del mondo che quella di Dio.

Disse allora il frate: — Figliuol mio, cotesta è buona ira, né io per me te ne saprei penitenza imporre. Ma per alcun caso avrebbeti l'ira potuto inducere a fare alcuno omicidio o a dire villanìa a persona o a fare alcuna altra ingiuria?

A cui ser Ciappelletto rispose: — Oimé! messere, o voi mi parete uomo di Dio: come dite voi coteste parole? O se io avessi avuto pure un pensieruzzo di fare qualunque s'è l'una delle cose che voi dite, credete voi che io creda che Iddio m'avesse tanto sostenuto? Coteste son cose da farle gli scherani ed i rei uomini, de' quali qualunque ora io n'ho mai veduto alcuno, sempre ho detto: «Va', che Iddio ti converta».

Allora disse il frate: — Or mi di', figliuol mio, che benedetto sii tu da Dio: hai tu mai testimonianza niuna falsa detta contra alcuno o detto mal d'altrui o tolte dell'altrui cose senza piacere di colui di cui sono?

— Mai, messer, sì, — rispose ser Ciappelletto, — che io ho detto male d'altri, per ciò che io ebbi già un mio vicino che al maggior torto del mondo non faceva altro che batter la moglie, sì che io dissi una volta male di lui alli parenti della moglie, sì gran pietà mi venne di quella cattivella la quale egli, ogni volta che bevuto avea troppo, conciava come Iddio vel dica.

Disse allora il frate: — Or bene, tu mi di' che se' stato mercatante: ingannasti tu mai persona così come fanno i mercatanti?

livelihood; and I think I would have succeeded if God had not brought this visitation on me. But you ought to know that my father left me a rich man; as soon as he died I gave away most of his wealth as charity. Afterward, to stay alive and to be able to assist the poor of Christ, I carried on my little business dealings; and, in doing so, I wished to make money, and always shared my earnings fifty-fifty with the poor of God, using my half for my needs and giving them the other half. And my Creator has always given me such good help in doing so that my business has constantly improved."

"You've acted well," said the friar, "but how often have you been angry?"

"Oh!" said Master Ciappelletto, "as to that, I can tell you it's been very often. And who could help himself, seeing people doing dirty things all day long, not observing God's commandments, not fearing His judgments? Many times a day I'd rather be dead than alive, when I see young people pursuing vain things and hear them swearing and breaking their oath, going to taverns, staying away from church, and following the ways of the world instead of the way of God."

Then the friar said: "My son, that is justifiable wrath, and I, for one, couldn't impose a penance on you for that. But has anger ever led you to commit murder, to insult anyone, or do people any other injury?"

To which Master Ciappelletto replied: "Woe is me! Father, you strike me as being a man of God: how can you speak such words? If I had had the slightest idea of doing any one of the things you mention, do you believe that I believe that God would have sustained me all this time? Those are things that hardened criminals and evil men do; every time I've ever seen such a person, I've always said: 'Get along with you, may God amend your ways!'"

Then the friar said: "Now tell me, my son, may God bless you: have you ever borne false witness against anyone, or spoken ill of anyone, or taken away anyone's property against the owner's will?"

"Yes, Father, absolutely," Master Ciappelletto replied, "I *have* spoken ill of another, because I once had a neighbor who, without the slightest justification, constantly beat his wife, so that on one occasion I spoke ill of him to his wife's relatives, because I had such great pity for that poor woman, whom he would batter like nobody's business every time he had drunk too much."

Then the friar said: "Well, now, you tell me you've been a merchant. Did you ever cheat anyone the way merchants do?"

— Gnaffe, — disse ser Ciappelletto, — messer sì, ma io non so chi egli si fu: se non che uno avendomi recati denari che egli mi doveva dare di panno che io gli avea venduto, ed io messigli in una mia cassa senza annoverare, ivi bene ad un mese trovai che egli erano quattro pìccioli più che esser non doveano; per che, non riveggendo colui ed avendogli serbati bene uno anno per rendergliele, io gli diedi per l'amor di Dio.

Disse il frate: — Cotesta fu piccola cosa, e facesti bene a farne quello che ne facesti. — Ed oltre a questo, il domandò il santo frate di molte altre cose, delle quali, di tutte, rispose a questo modo.

E volendo egli già procedere all'assoluzione, disse ser Ciappelletto: — Messere, io ho ancora alcun peccato che io non v'ho detto.

Il frate il domandò quale, ed egli disse: — Io mi ricordo che io feci al fante mio, un sabato dopo nona, spazzare la casa e non ebbi alla santa domenica quella reverenza che io dovea.

— Oh! — disse il frate — figliuol mio, cotesta è leggèr cosa.

— No, — disse ser Ciappelletto, — non dite leggèr cosa, ché la domenica è troppo da onorare, però che in così fatto dì risuscitò da morte a vita il nostro Signore.

Disse allora il frate: — O altro hai tu fatto?

— Messer sì, — rispose ser Ciappelletto, — che io, non avvedendomene, sputai una volta nella chiesa di Dio.

Il frate cominciò a sorridere, e disse: — Figliuol mio, cotesta non è cosa da curarsene: noi, che siamo religiosi, tutto il dì vi sputiamo.

Disse allora ser Ciappelletto: — E voi fate gran villania, per ciò che niuna cosa si convien tener netta come il santo tempio, nel quale si rende sacrificio a Dio. — Ed in brieve de' così fatti ne gli disse molti; ed ultimamente cominciò a sospirare ed appresso a piagner forte, come colui che il sapeva troppo ben fare quando volea.

Disse il santo frate: — Figliuol mio, che hai tu?

Rispose ser Ciappelletto: — Oimé! messere, che un peccato m'è rimaso del quale io non mi confessai mai, sì gran vergogna ho di doverlo dire, ed ogni volta che io me ne ricordo piango come voi vedete, e parmi esser molto certo che Iddio mai non avrà misericordia di me per questo peccato.

Allora il santo frate disse: — Va' via, figliuolo, che è ciò che tu di'? Se tutti i peccati che furon mai fatti da tutti gli uomini, o che si deb-

"By my faith," said Master Ciappelletto, "yes, Father, but I don't know who he was, except that he was someone who had brought me money he owed me for cloth I had sold him; I had put it in a strong-box without counting it, and a good month later I discovered that it was four cents over what it should have been. And so, never seeing that man again and having kept the money for about a year to give back to him, I gave it away as charity."

The friar said: "That was a trifling matter, and you disposed of the money in a fine way." And in addition to that, the holy friar asked him about many other things, and in every case he made the same sort of reply.

And when the friar was all set to give him absolution, Master Ciappelletto said: "Father, there are still a few sins I haven't told you."

The friar asked him what they were, and he said: "I recall that, one Saturday after dusk,[3] I made my servant sweep out the house, thus failing to show due reverence to the sacredness of Sunday."

"Oh, my son," said the friar, "that's a trivial matter."

"No," said Master Ciappelletto, "don't call it trivial, because Sunday is to be honored highly, since on that day Our Lord was resurrected from death to life."

Then the friar said: "Did you do anything else?"

"Yes, Father," Master Ciappelletto replied, "once, without realizing it, I spat in God's church."

The friar began to smile, and said: "My son, that is no matter to worry over: we, who are friars, spit in it day in and day out."

Then Master Ciappelletto said: "And it's very wrong of you, too, because nothing should be kept as clean as the holy temple in which sacrifice is made to God." And, in short, he told him many similar things, and, when he had done, he began to sigh and then to weep out loud, being only too able to perform at will.

The holy friar said: "My son, what's wrong?"

Master Ciappelletto replied: "Woe is me! Father, there's one sin left that I've never confessed to, I'm so very ashamed to say it. Every time I think of it I cry as you see me doing. I feel certain that God will never have mercy on me because of this sin."

Then the holy friar said: "Come now, son, what are you saying? Even if all the sins ever committed by all men, or yet to be committed by all men as long as the world lasts, were all contained in

---

[3]Literally, after the part of the day called "none" (3 to 6 P.M.). To observe Sunday as early as Saturday evening was a sign of unusual piety.

bon fare da tutti gli uomini mentre che il mondo durerà, fosser tutti
in uno uom solo, ed egli ne fosse pentuto e contrito come io veggio
te, sì è tanta la benignità e la misericordia di Dio, che, confessandogli
egli, gliele perdonerebbe liberamente; e per ciò dillo sicuramente.
Disse allora ser Ciappelletto, sempre piagnendo forte: — Oimé!
padre mio, il mio è troppo gran peccato, ed appena posso credere,
se i vostri prieghi non ci s'adoperano, che egli mi debba mai da Dio
esser perdonato.

A cui il frate disse: — Dillo sicuramente, ché io ti prometto di
pregare Iddio per te.

Ser Ciappelletto pur piagnea e nol dicea, ed il frate pure il confortava
a dire. Ma poi che ser Ciappelletto piagnendo ebbe una grandissima
pezza tenuto il frate così sospeso, ed egli gittò un gran sospiro e disse:
— Padre mio, poscia che voi mi promettete di pregare Iddio per me,
ed io il vi dirò: sappiate che, quando io era piccolino, io bestemmiai una
volta la mamma mia. — E così detto, ricominciò a piagner forte.

Disse il frate: — O figliuol mio, or pàrti questo così gran peccato? Oh! gli uomini bestemmiano tutto il giorno Iddio, e sì per-
dona egli volentieri a chi si pente d'averlo bestemmiato; e tu non
credi che egli perdoni a te questo? Non piagner, confortati, ché fermamente, se tu fossi stato un di quegli che il posero in croce,
avendo la contrizione che io ti veggio, sì ti perdonerebbe egli.

Disse allora ser Ciappelletto: — Oimé! padre mio, che dite voi?
La mamma mia dolce, che mi portò in corpo nove mesi il dì e la
notte, e portommi in collo più di cento volte! Troppo feci male a
bestemmiarla, e troppo è gran peccato; e se voi non pregate Iddio
per me, egli non mi sarà perdonato.

Veggendo il frate non essere altro restato a dire a ser
Ciappelletto, gli fece l'assoluzione e diedegli la sua benedizione,
avendolo per santissimo uomo, sì como colui che pienamente credeva esser vero ciò che ser Ciappelletto avea detto: e chi sarebbe
colui che nol credesse, veggendo uno uomo in caso di morte dir
così? E poi, dopo tutto questo, gli disse: — Ser Ciappelletto, con
l'aiuto di Dio voi sarete tosto sano; ma se pure avvenisse che Iddio
la vostra benedetta e ben disposta anima chiamasse a sé, piàcevi
egli che il vostro corpo sia sepellito al nostro luogo?

Al quale ser Ciappelletto rispose: — Messer sì, anzi non vorrei io
essere altrove, poscia che voi m'avete promesso di pregare Iddio

a single man, and he were as penitent and contrite as I see that you are, God's kindness and mercy are so great that, whenever that man confessed, He would pardon him freely. And so, speak up!"

Then Master Ciappelletto, still weeping aloud, said: "Woe is me! Father, my sin is too great, and I can scarcely believe that, unless your prayers are added to mine, God can ever forgive me for it."

The friar replied: "Out with it; I promise to pray to God for you."

Master Ciappelletto kept on crying and wouldn't tell it, while the friar kept on urging him to speak. But after Master Ciappelletto, weeping, had kept the friar in suspense that way for a very long time, he heaved a great sigh and said: "Father, since you promise to pray to God for me, I'll tell you: let me inform you that once, when I was a little boy, I cursed my mother." And, having said that, he resumed his loud weeping.

The friar said: "Oh, my son, do you really consider that such a great sin? Oh, men curse God all day long, and He gladly forgives those who repent for having cursed Him. So don't you think He'll forgive you for this? Don't cry, cheer up, because I assure you, even if you had been one of those who placed Him on the Cross, and you were as contrite as I see you are, He would forgive you."

Then Master Ciappelletto said: "Woe is me! Father, what are you saying? My sweet mother, who carried me in her body night and day for nine months and carried me in her arms more than a hundred times! I did too great a wrong when I cursed her, and the sin is too great; if you don't pray to God for me, I won't be forgiven for it."

The friar, seeing that there was nothing left to say to Master Ciappelletto, gave him absolution and his blessing, considering him a most holy man, since he fully believed in the truth of what Master Ciappelletto had told him. And who wouldn't have believed it, seeing a man on the point of death speaking that way? And then, after all that, he said to him: "Master Ciappelletto, with God's help, you[4] will soon be well; but if it should nevertheless happen that God calls your blessed and well-disposed soul to Himself, would you like your body to be buried in our friary?"

Master Ciappelletto replied: "Yes, Father. In fact, I wouldn't want to be anywhere else, ever since your promise to pray to God for me.

---

[4]Beginning here, the friar shows greater respect by using *voi* rather than *tu* for "you."

per me; senza che, io ho avuta sempre spezial divozione al vostro ordine; e per ciò vi priego che, come voi al vostro luogo sarete, facciate che a me venga quel veracissimo corpo di Cristo il quale voi la mattina sopra l'altare consecrate, per ciò che, come che io degno non ne sia, io intendo con la vostra licenza di prenderlo, ed appresso la santa ed ultima unzione, acciò che io, se vivuto son come peccatore, almeno muoia come cristiano.

Il santo uomo disse che molto gli piacea e che egli diceva bene, e farebbe che di presente gli sarebbe apportato; e così fu.

Li due fratelli, li quali dubitavan forte non ser Ciappelletto gl'ingannasse, s'eran posti appresso ad un tavolato, il quale la camera dove ser Ciappelletto giacea dividea da un'altra, ed ascoltando, leggermente udivano ed intendevano ciò che ser Ciappelletto al frate diceva; ed aveano alcuna volta sì gran voglia di ridere, udendo le cose le quali egli confessava d'aver fatte, che quasi scoppiavano, e tra sé talora dicevano:

— Che uomo è costui, il quale né vecchiezza né infermità né paura di morte alla qual si vede vicino, né ancora di Dio, dinanzi al giudicio del quale di qui a piccola ora s'aspetta di dovere essere, dalla sua malvagità l'hanno potuto rimuovere, né far che egli così non voglia morire come egli è vissuto?

Ma pur, veggendo che sì aveva detto, che egli sarebbe a sepoltura ricevuto in chiesa, niente del rimaso si curarono. Ser Ciappelletto poco appresso si comunicò, e peggiorando senza modo, ebbe l'ultima unzione; e poco passato vespro, quel dì stesso che la buona confessione fatta avea, si morì. Per la qual cosa li due fratelli, ordinato di quello di lui medesimo come egli fosse onorevolmente sepellito e mandatolo a dire al luogo de' frati, e che essi si venissero la sera a far la vigilia secondo l'usanza e la mattina per lo corpo, ogni cosa a ciò opportuna disposero.

Il santo frate che confessato l'avea, udendo che egli era trapassato, fu insieme col priore del luogo, e fatto sonare a capitolo, alli frati ragunati in quello mostrò ser Ciappelletto essere stato santo uomo, secondo che per la sua confessione conceputo avea; e sperando per lui Domenedio dovere molti miracoli dimostrare, persuadette loro che con grandissima reverenza e divozione quello corpo si dovesse ricevere.

Alla qual cosa il priore e gli altri frati, creduli, s'accordarono; e la sera, andati tutti là dove il corpo di ser Ciappelletto giacea, sopra esso fecero una grande e solenne vigilia, e la mattina, tutti vestiti co' càmici e co' pieviali, con li libri in mano e con le croci innanzi,

Besides, I've always had a special devotion for your order. And so, I beg of you that, when you're back at your friary, have them send me that most true body of Christ which you consecrate on the altar in the morning, because, all unworthy that I am, I intend by your leave to take it, and then the holy extreme unction, so that, if I have lived as a sinner, I may at least die as a Christian."

The holy man said that it pleased him greatly, and that he had spoken well, and he would see to it that it was brought to him at once; and so it was.

The two brothers, who were greatly afraid that Master Ciappelletto might trick them, had placed themselves by a wooden partition that separated Master Ciappelletto's sickroom from the room adjoining. Listening there, they easily heard and understood what Master Ciappelletto was saying to the friar. And at times they felt such a great urge to laugh, hearing the things he was confessing to, that they nearly burst. And from time to time they said to each other:

"What sort of man is this, if neither his age, nor his illness, nor the fear of death, which he sees approaching, nor the fear of God, before whose tribunal he expects shortly to be standing, has been able to make him swerve from his evil ways or make him desire not to die the way he has lived?"

And yet, seeing that he had spoken in such a way that he would be allowed a religious burial, they cared nothing about the rest. Shortly afterward, Master Ciappelletto received communion, and, his health deteriorating despite all efforts, received extreme unction. A little after Vespers, on the very day on which he had made that valid confession, he died. So that the two brothers, arranging at his own expense for him to be honorably buried, reported his death to the friary, asking them to come that evening to sit up with the body as customary and to collect it in the morning, and took all the necessary steps.

The holy friar who had heard his confession, learning that he had died, reported to the prior of the friary and, ringing for a meeting of the chapter, declared to the friars assembled there that Master Ciappelletto had been a holy man, as he had understood from his confession. Trusting that through his agency God would display many miracles, he persuaded them to receive his body with the greatest reverence and devotion.

To this the prior and the other friars, all gullible, assented. That evening, they all went to where Master Ciappelletto's body was lying and held a great and solemn vigil over him. In the morning, all dressed in albs and copes, chanting with books in hand and crosses going before,

cantando, andaron per questo corpo e con grandissima festa e solennità il recarono alla lor chiesa, seguendo quasi tutto il popolo della città, uomini e donne; e nella chiesa pòstolo, il santo frate che confessato l'avea, salito in sul pergamo, di lui cominciò e della sua vita, de' suoi digiuni, della sua virginità, della sua simplicità ed innocenza e santità, maravigliose cose a predicare, tra l'altre cose narrando quello che ser Ciappelletto per lo suo maggior peccato piagnendo gli avea confessato, e come esso appena gli avea potuto metter nel capo che Iddio gliele dovesse perdonare, da questo volgendosi a riprendere il popolo che ascoltava, dicendo:

— E voi, maladetti da Dio, per ogni fuscello di paglia che vi si volge tra' piedi, bestemmiate Iddio e la Madre e tutta la corte di paradiso! — Ed oltre a queste, molte altre cose disse della sua lealtà e della sua purità, ed in brieve con le sue parole, alle quali era dalla gente della contrada data intera fede, sì il mise nel capo e nella divozion di tutti coloro che v'erano, che, poi che fornito fu l'uficio, con la maggior calca del mondo da tutti fu andato a baciargli i piedi e le mani, e tutti i panni gli furono indosso stracciati, tenendosi beato chi pure un poco di quegli potesse avere; e convenne che tutto il giorno così fosse tenuto, acciò che da tutti potesse essere veduto e visitato.

Poi, la vegnente notte, in un'arca di marmo sepellito fu onorevolmente in una cappella, ed a mano a mano il dì seguente vi cominciarono le genti ad andare e ad accender lumi e ad adorarlo, e per conseguente a botarsi e ad appiccarvi le imagini della cera secondo la promession fatta.

Ed intanto crebbe la fama della sua santità e divozione a lui, che quasi niuno era che in alcuna avversità fosse, che ad altro santo che a lui si botasse, e chiamaronlo e chiamano san Ciappelletto, ed affermano molti miracoli Iddio aver mostrati per lui e mostrare tutto giorno a chi divotamente si raccomanda a lui.

Così adunque visse e morì ser Cepparello da Prato e santo divenne, come avete udito; il quale negar non voglio esser possibile, lui esser beato nella presenza di Dio, per ciò che, come che la sua vita fosse scellerata e malvagia, egli poté in su lo stremo aver sì fatta contrizione, che per avventura Iddio ebbe misericordia di lui e nel suo regno il ricevette; ma, per ciò che questo n'è occulto, secondo quello che ne può apparire ragiono, e dico costui più tosto dovere essere nelle mani del diavolo in perdizione che in paradiso.

E se così è, grandissima si può la benignità di Dio conoscere

they went to get the body and brought it to their church with great pomp and solemnity, almost all the townspeople, men and women, following behind. When it was deposited in the church, the holy friar who had heard his confession climbed into the pulpit and started to speak about him and to preach marvelous things about his way of life, his fasts, his virginity, his simplicity and innocence and sanctity, telling among the other things about what Master Ciappelletto, weeping, had confessed to him as being his greatest sin, and describing how he had barely been able to convince him that God would forgive him. Taking his cue from this to reprimand the people listening, he said:

"And you, accursed of God, for every wisp of straw that blows under your feet, you curse God, His Mother, and the entire assembly of the saints!" In addition to this, he told them many other things about the dead man's faithfulness and purity. In short, with his words, in which the inhabitants of the quarter believed implicitly, he instilled all those present with such a mental image and such devotion for the deceased that, when the service was finished, they all thronged in one mass to kiss the corpse's feet and hands, and all his clothes were torn off him. Everyone who could acquire even a piece of them considered himself fortunate. And it was necessary to leave him there all day long so he could be seen and visited by everybody.

Then, the following night, he was honorably buried in a marble sarcophagus in a chapel, and at once the next day people started to come and light candles and pray to him, afterward making vows and hanging up wax ex-votos in the chapel in accordance with the promises they had made.

And the fame of his sanctity and their devotion to him grew to such an extent that there was almost no one in any sort of distress who made vows to any other saint but him. They called him, and still call him, Saint Ciappelletto, and declare that through him God has displayed, and continues daily to display, many miracles to those who devoutly place themselves under his protection.

And so, that is how Master Cepparello of Prato lived, died, and became a saint, as you have heard. I don't wish to say it's impossible that he is blessed and in the presence of God, because, even though his life was evil and wicked, he might have made such an act of contrition at the very last that perhaps God had pity on him and accepted him into His kingdom. But because that is hidden from us, I speak in accordance with that which meets our eyes, and I say that that man must rather be in the devil's hands in perdition than in paradise.

And, if that is so, God's kindness toward us can be recognized as

verso noi, la quale, non al nostro errore ma alla purità della fè riguardando, così, faccendo noi nostro mezzano un suo nemico, amico credendolo, ci esaudisce, come se ad uno veramente santo per mezzano della sua grazia ricorressimo. E per ciò, acciò che noi per la sua grazia nelle presenti avversità ed in questa compagnia così lieta siamo sani e salvi servati, lodando il suo nome nel quale cominciata l'abbiamo, lui in reverenza avendo, ne' nostri bisogni gli ci raccomanderemo, sicurissimi d'essere uditi.

E si tacque.

I TRE ANELLI [I, 3]

Poi che, commendata da tutti la novella di Neìfile, ella si tacque, come alla reina piacque, Filomena così cominciò a parlare:

La novella da Neìfile detta mi ritorna a memoria il dubbioso caso già avvenuto ad un giudeo; e per ciò che già e di Dio e della verità della nostra fede è assai bene stato detto, il discendere oggimai agli avvenimenti ed agli atti degli uomini non si dovrà disdire, ed a narrarvi quella verrò, la quale udita, forse più caute diverrete nelle risposte alle quistioni che fatte vi fossero.

Voi dovete, amorose compagne, sapere che, sì come la sciocchezza spesse volte trae altrui di felice stato e mette in grandissima miseria, così il senno di grandissimi pericoli trae il savio e ponlo in grande ed in sicuro riposo. E che vero sia che la sciocchezza di buono stato in miseria alcun conduca, per molti esempli si vede, li quali non fia al presente nostra cura di raccontare, avendo riguardo che tutto il dì mille n'appaiano manifesti; ma che il senno di consolazion sia cagione, come premisi, per una novelletta mostrerò brievemente.

Il Saladino, il valore del quale fu tanto, che non solamente di piccolo uomo il fe' di Babilonia soldano, ma ancora molte vittorie sopra li re saracini e cristiani gli fece avere, avendo in diverse guerre ed in grandissime sue magnificenze speso tutto il suo tesoro, e per alcuno accidente sopravvenutogli bisognandogli una buona quantità di denari, né veggendo donde così prestamente come gli bisognavano avergli potesse, gli venne a memoria un ricco giudeo

being very great: having regard not for our mistaken assumption, but for the sincerity of our faith, even when we take an enemy of His as our advocate in the belief he is His friend, His kindness grants our prayers, just as if we were resorting to a truly saintly man as the agent of His grace. Therefore, in order that we may be preserved safe and sound through His grace in our present troubles[5] and in this merry company, praising His name, with which we began our session, holding Him in reverence, we shall commend ourselves to Him in our hour of need, in full confidence that we shall be heard.

And he fell silent.

THE THREE RINGS [I, 3]

After Neifile's story had been praised by everyone and she had stopped speaking, at the "Queen's" pleasure Filomena began:

The story told by Neifile reminds me of the precarious situation in which a Jew once found himself. And because we have already heard fine words about God and the truth of our religion, it should not be unfitting to descend now to human events and actions; and I shall tell you a story that, once you have heard it, may make you more circumspect in answering questions that are put to you.

My charming lady friends, you ought to know that, just as foolishness often changes a person's state from felicity to the direst misery, in the same way good sense leads the wise man out of the greatest dangers into solid, restful security. Many examples show how true it is that foolishness turns happiness into wretchedness; it will not be our concern at present to relate any such examples, seeing that a thousand of them are shown to us clearly all day long. But that good sense is a cause for consolation, as I stated before, I shall demonstrate briefly in a little story.

Saladin, whose valor was such that it not only brought him from humble beginnings to become sultan of Cairo, but also caused him to win many victories over Saracen and Christian kings, had exhausted his entire treasury in various wars and lavish acts of munificence. A certain occasion occurred for which he needed a large sum of money; unable to see how he could obtain it as speedily as necessary, he recalled a rich Jew named Melchizedek who lent money on interest in

---

[5]The plague.

il cui nome era Melchisedech, il quale prestava ad usura in
Alessandria; e pensossi costui avere da poterlo servire, quando volesse, ma sì era avaro, che di sua volontà non l'avrebbe mai fatto, e
forza non gli voleva fare; per che, strignendolo il bisogno, rivòltosi
tutto a dover trovar modo come il giudeo il servisse, s'avvisò di fargli una forza da alcuna ragion colorata, e fattolsi chiamare e
famigliarmente ricevutolo, seco il fece sedere ed appresso gli disse:
— Valente uomo, io ho da più persone inteso che tu se' savissimo
e nelle cose di Dio senti molto avanti; e per ciò io saprei volentieri
da te quale delle tre leggi tu reputi la verace, o la giudaica o la
saracina o la cristiana.

Il giudeo, il quale veramente era savio uomo, s'avvisò troppo
bene che il Saladino guardava di pigliarlo nelle parole per dovergli
muovere alcuna quistione, e pensò non potere alcuna di queste tre
più l'una che l'altre lodare, che il Saladino non avesse la sua intenzione; per che, come colui al qual pareva d'aver bisogno di risposta
per la quale preso non potesse essere, aguzzato lo 'ngegno, gli
venne prestamente avanti quello che dir dovesse; e disse:

— Signor mio, la quistione la qual voi mi fate è bella, ed a voler-
vene dire ciò che io sento, mi vi convien dire una novelletta, qual
voi udirete. Se io non erro, io mi ricordo aver molte volte udito dire
che un grande uomo e ricco fu già, il quale, intra l'altre gioie più
care che nel suo tesoro avesse, era uno anello bellissimo e prezioso;
al quale per lo suo valore e per la sua bellezza volendo fare onore
ed in perpetuo lasciarlo ne' suoi discendenti, ordinò che colui de'
suoi figliuoli appo il quale, sì come lasciatogli da lui, fosse questo
anello trovato, che colui s'intendesse essere il suo erede e dovesse
da tutti gli altri esser come maggiore onorato e reverito; e colui al
quale da costui fu lasciato tenne simigliante ordine ne' suoi discendenti, e così fece come fatto avea il suo predecessore. Ed in brieve
andò questo anello di mano in mano a molti successori, ed ultimamente pervenne alle mani ad uno il quale avea tre figliuoli belli e
virtuosi e molto al padre loro obedienti, per la qual cosa tutti e tre
parimente gli amava; ed i giovani, li quali la consuetudine del-
l'anello sapevano, sì como vaghi ciascuno d'essere il più onorato tra'
suoi, ciascun per sé, come meglio sapeva, pregava il padre, il quale
era già vecchio, che, quando a morte venisse, a lui quello anello la-
sciasse. Il valente uomo, che parimente tutti gli amava, né sapeva
esso medesimo eleggere a quale più tosto lasciarlo volesse, pensò,

Alexandria. He thought that that man could lend him some[1] if he so wished, but that he was so avaricious that he would never do so willingly; nor did Saladin wish to use force on him. And so, his needs becoming more urgent, he devoted all his energy to find a way to make the Jew help him out, and finally decided to put pressure on him under some specious pretext. He summoned him, welcomed him in a friendly way, had him sit next to him, and then said:

"My worthy man, I have heard from several people that you are extremely wise and are deeply studied in the ways of God. Therefore I would like to hear from you which of the three religions you consider the true one, Judaism, Islam, or Christianity."

The Jew, who really *was* a wise man, perceived only too clearly that Saladin was seeking to trap him through his words in order to pick a quarrel with him; he thought that he couldn't praise any of those three above the rest without Saladin's achieving his aim. And so, seeing that he needed to answer in such a way that he wouldn't be caught, he sharpened his wits and quickly discovered what he needed to say:

"My lord, the question you put to me is a fine one. In order to give you my opinion on the subject, I must tell you a brief story, as you shall hear. If I'm not mistaken, I remember having often heard tell that there was once a powerful, rich man who, among the other most costly jewels that were among his treasures, possessed a most beautiful and costly ring. Because of its value and beauty he wished to honor it by leaving it in perpetuity to his descendants; he left instructions that whichever of his sons would be found in possession of the ring as his bequest should be considered to be his heir and should be honored and revered by all the rest as the head of the family. The man who inherited it laid a similar injunction on his own offspring, and acted in the same way as his predecessor. To be brief, this ring passed from hand to hand through many successive generations, finally reaching the hands of a man with three sons who were handsome, virtuous, and very obedient to their father, so that he loved all three equally. The young men were acquainted with the tradition of the ring, and each one of them, desiring to be the most honored among his fellows, did his very best to persuade his father, who was already old, to leave him that ring when he died. The good man, who loved them all equally, was himself unable to decide to whom he preferred to leave it, and devised a way to satisfy all three, after promising the ring to each one. In secret he had

---

[1] *Servire* is here a technical business term for lending money.

avendolo a ciascun promesso, di volergli tutti e tre sodisfare; e segretamente ad un buon maestro ne fece fare due altri, li quali sì
furono simiglianti al primiero, che esso medesimo che fatti gli
aveva fare appena conosceva qual si fosse il vero; e venendo a
morte, segretamente diede il suo a ciascun de' figliuoli. Li quali
dopo la morte del padre volendo ciascuno l'eredità e l'onore occu-
pare, e l'uno negandolo all'altro, in testimonianza di dover ciò ra-
gionevolmente fare, ciascuno produsse fuori il suo anello; e
trovatisi gli anelli sì simili l'uno all'altro, che qual fosse il vero non
si sapeva conoscere, si rimase la quistione, qual fosse il vero erede
del padre, in pendente, ed ancor pende. E così vi dico, signor mio,
delle tre leggi alli tre popoli date da Dio padre, delle quali la quistion proponeste: ciascun la sua eredità, la sua vera legge ed i suoi
comandamenti dirittamente si crede avere e fare, ma chi se l'abbia,
come degli anelli, ancora ne pende la quistione.

Il Saladino conobbe costui ottimamente esser saputo uscire del
laccio il quale davanti a' piedi teso gli aveva, e per ciò dispose
d'aprirgli il suo bisogno e vedere se servire il volesse; e così fece,
aprendogli ciò che in animo avesse avuto di fare, se così discretamente, come fatto avea, non gli avesse risposto. Il giudeo liberamente d'ogni quantità che il Saladino il richiese il servì, ed il
Saladino poi interamente il sodisfece, ed oltre a ciò gli donò grandissimi doni e sempre per suo amico l'ebbe ed in grande ed onorevole stato appresso di sé il mantenne.

LE DISGRAZIE D'ANDREUCCIO [II, 5]

Le pietre da Landolfo trovate — cominciò la Fiammetta, alla quale
del novellare la volta toccava — m'hanno alla memoria tornata una
novella non guari meno di pericoli in sé contenente che la narrata
dalla Lauretta, ma in tanto differente da essa, in quanto quegli
forse in più anni e questi nello spazio d'una sola notte addivennero,
come udirete.

Fu, secondo che io già intesi, in Perugia un giovane il cui nome
era Andreuccio di Pietro, cozzone di cavalli, il quale, avendo inteso
che a Napoli era buon mercato di cavalli, mèssisi in borsa cinquecento fiorin d'oro, non essendo mai più fuori di casa stato, con altri
mercatanti là se n'andò; dove giunto una domenica sera in sul

a goldsmith make two others, which looked so much like the original that even the man who had had them made could hardly pick out the real one. When he was dying, he secretly gave each of his sons a ring of his own. After their father's death, each one wanted to claim the inheritance and the honored status. When each of them denied it to the others, as evidence that they were doing so with justification each one produced his ring. The rings were found to be so much alike that it was impossible to judge which one was the real one. The question as to who was his father's real heir remained pending, and is pending to this day. And I say the same thing to you, my lord, concerning the three religions given to the three nations by God the Father, which were the subject of your question. Each one of them justly believes it possesses[2] His inheritance and His true religion, and is observing His commandments, but as to who really possesses them, just as with the rings, the question is still pending."

Saladin realized that the Jew had been perfectly able to escape the snare he had laid before his feet. Therefore he decided to speak openly to him about his needs and to see whether he was willing to help him. He did so, also revealing what he had intended to do if he hadn't answered him as cleverly as he did. The Jew freely helped Saladin to any amount he wanted, and afterward Saladin not only repaid him in full but also gave him very great gifts, always treated him as a friend, and kept him at his side in a position of high honor.

ANDREUCCIO'S MISHAPS [II, 5]

The stones found by Landolfo (began Fiammetta, whose turn it now was to tell a story) have reminded me of a story that contains scarcely fewer dangerous moments than the one Lauretta told, but is different from hers inasmuch as, in hers, those incidents were spread over several years, perhaps, and in mine they all occurred within a single night, as you will hear.

According to what I once heard, there was a young man in Perugia named Andreuccio son of Pietro, a horse dealer who, having heard there were good horses to be found in the Naples market, put five hundred gold florins in his purse and, never having been away from home, went there with other traders. Arriving there on Sunday

---

[2]Or: "Each one of them believes it possesses in a direct line from God."

vespro, dall'oste suo informato, la seguente mattina fu in sul mercato, e molti ne vide ed assai ne gli piacquero e di più mercato
tenne; né di niuno potendosi accordare, per mostrare che per comperar fosse, sì come rozzo e poco cauto, più volte in presenza di chi
andava e di chi veniva trasse fuori questa sua borsa de' fiorini che
aveva.

Ed in questi trattati stando, avendo esso la sua borsa mostrata,
avvenne che una giovane ciciliana bellissima, ma disposta per piccol pregio a compiacere a qualunque uomo, senza vederla egli,
passò appresso di lui e la sua borsa vide, e subito seco disse: — Chi
starebbe meglio di me se quegli denari fosser miei? — e passò
oltre.

Era con questa giovane una vecchia similmente ciciliana, la
quale, come vide Andreuccio, lasciata oltre la giovane andare, affettuosamente corse ad abbracciarlo; il che la giovane veggendo,
senza dire alcuna cosa, da una delle parti la cominciò ad attendere.
Andreuccio, alla vecchia rivòltosi e conosciutala, le fece gran festa,
e promettendogli essa di venire a lui all'albergo, senza quivi tenere
troppo lungo sermone si partì, ed Andreuccio si tornò a mercatare;
ma niente comperò la mattina.

La giovane, che prima la borsa d'Andreuccio e poi la contezza
della sua vecchia con lui aveva veduta, per tentare se modo alcuno
trovar potesse a dovere aver quegli denari, o tutti o parte, cautamente incominciò a domandare chi colui fosse o donde, e che quivi
facesse e come il conoscesse. La quale ogni cosa così particular-
mente de' fatti d'Andreuccio le disse come avrebbe per poco detto
egli stesso, sì come colei che lungamente in Cicilia col padre di lui
e poi a Perugia dimorata era, e similmente le contò dove tornasse
e perché venuto fosse.

La giovane, pienamente informata e del parentado di lui e de'
nomi, al suo appetito fornire con una sottil malizia, sopra questo
fondò la sua intenzione, ed a casa tornatasi, mise la vecchia in faccenda per tutto il giorno, acciò che ad Andreuccio non potesse
tornare; e presa una sua fanticella la quale essa assai bene a così
fatti servigi aveva ammaestrata, in sul vespro la mandò all'albergo
dove Andreuccio tornava. La qual quivi venuta, per ventura lui
medesimo, e solo, trovò in su la porta, e di lui stesso il domandò:
alla quale dicendole egli che era desso, essa, tiratolo da parte, disse:
— Messere, una gentil donna di questa terra, quando vi piacesse,
vi parlerìa volentieri.

Il quale, veggendola, tutto postosi mente e parendogli essere un

evening about the time of Vespers, he obtained information from the landlord of his inn and the next morning went to the market. He saw many horses, liked a lot of them, and negotiated for several; unable to close any of the deals, in order to show he was ready to buy, and being a tyro and careless, he frequently pulled out that purse full of florins that he had, in the presence of passersby.

As he was occupied in these dealings, having displayed his purse, it happened that a young Sicilian woman, very beautiful but prepared to accommodate any man at a low price, passed by him; he didn't see her, but she saw his purse, and immediately said to herself: "Wouldn't I be the lucky one if that money was mine?" And she walked away.

With that young woman was an old woman, also Sicilian; when she caught sight of Andreuccio, she let the young woman keep walking, while she herself ran over to Andreuccio and hugged him affectionately. When the young woman saw this, she said nothing, but stood on one side waiting for her. Andreuccio, looking at the old woman and recognizing her, greeted her warmly. Promising to visit him at his inn, she left him without entering into a long conversation, and Andreuccio returned to his negotiations. But he made no purchases that morning.

The young woman, who had seen, first Andreuccio's purse, and then the acquaintance between him and her old servant, to try whether she could lay her hands on all or some of that money in any way, cautiously began to ask her who he was and where from, what he was doing there, and how she happened to know him. She told her everything concerning Andreuccio, almost as circumstantially as he would have done himself, since she had lived with his father for a long time in Sicily and then in Perugia. She also told her where he was staying and why he had come.

The young woman, fully informed about his family and their names, conceived a plan on the basis of this knowledge in order to satisfy her greed with a subtle trick. Returning home, she sent the old woman out on errands that would take all day, so she couldn't get back to Andreuccio; and, summoning a young maid whom she had trained very thoroughly for such duties, about the time of Vespers she sent her to the inn where Andreuccio was staying. Arriving there, she happened to meet him himself in the doorway, and asked Andreuccio for Andreuccio. He told her she was speaking to him, and she, drawing him aside, said: "Sir, a noble lady of this city would like to speak with you, if you don't mind."

Seeing her, he took a good, long look at himself; deeming himself

bel fante della persona, s'avvisò questa donna dover di lui essere innamorata, quasi altro bel giovane che egli non si trovasse allora in Napoli, e prestamente rispose che era apparecchiato, e domandolla dove e quando questa donna parlargli volesse. A cui la fanticella rispose: — Messere, quando di venir vi piaccia, ella v'attende in casa sua.

Andreuccio presto, senza alcuna cosa dir nell'albergo, disse: — Or via, mettiti avanti; io ti verrò appresso.

Laonde la fanticella a casa di costei il condusse, la quale dimorava in una contrada chiamata Malpertugio, la quale quanto sia onesta contrada, il nome medesimo il dimostra. Ma esso, niente di ciò sappiendo né suspicando, credendosi in uno onestissimo luogo andare e ad una cara donna, liberamente, andata la fanticella avanti, se n'entrò nella sua casa; e salendo su per le scale, avendo la fanticella già la sua donna chiamata e detto: — Ecco Andreuccio! — la vide in capo della scala farsi ad aspettarlo.

Ella era ancora assai giovane, di persona grande e con bellissimo viso, vestita ed ornata assai orrevolemente. Alla quale come Andreuccio fu presso, essa incòntrogli da tre gradi discese con le braccia aperte, ed avvinghiatogli il collo, alquanto stette senza alcuna cosa dire, quasi da soperchia tenerezza impedita; poi lagrimando gli baciò la fronte, e con voce alquanto rotta disse: — O Andreuccio mio, tu sii il benvenuto!

Esso, maravigliandosi di così tenere carezze, tutto stupefatto rispose: — Madonna, voi siate la ben trovata!

Ella appresso, per la man presolo, suso nella sua sala il menò, e di quella, senza alcuna altra cosa parlare, con lui nella camera se n'entrò, la quale di rose, di fiori d'aranci e d'altri odori tutta oliva, là dove egli un bellissimo letto incortinato e molte robe su per le stanghe, secondo il costume di là, ed altri assai belli e ricchi arnesi vide; per le quali cose, sì come nuovo, fermamente credette lei dovere essere non men che gran donna; e postisi a sedere insieme sopra una cassa che a piè del suo letto era, così gli cominciò a parlare:

— Andreuccio, io sono molto certa che tu ti maravigli e delle carezze le quali io ti fo e delle mie lagrime, sì come colui che non mi conosci e per avventura mai ricordar non m'udisti; ma tu udirai tosto cosa la quale più ti farà forse maravigliare, sì come è che io sia tua sorella; e dicoti che, poi che Iddio m'ha fatta tanta grazia, che io anzi la mia morte ho veduto alcuno de' miei fratelli, come che io disideri di vedervi tutti, io non morrò a quella ora che io consolata non muoia. E se tu forse questo mai più non udisti, io tel vo' dire.

quite a handsome young fellow, he concluded that that lady must be in love with him—as if he were the only good-looking youth in Naples at the time. He quickly replied that he was willing, asking her where and when that lady wanted to speak with him. The young maid replied: "Sir, whenever you feel like coming, she'll be waiting for you at home."

At once Andreuccio, saying no word of all this to anyone in the inn, said: "Come on, start out and I'll follow you."

Whereupon the young maid led him to her mistress' house, which was in a neighborhood called Malpertugio, whose very name, "Evil Hole," shows how respectable that neighborhood is. But he, neither knowing nor suspecting any of this, and believing that he was heading for the very respectable home of a worthy lady, followed the young maid into the house. Climbing the stairs, the maid already having called her mistress with the words "Here's Andreuccio," he saw her at the head of the stairs preparing to greet him.

She was still quite young, tall, with a beautiful face; her attire and jewelry were most dignified. When Andreuccio was near her, she walked down three steps to meet him with open arms. Hugging his neck, she stood silent for a while, as if overcome by the intensity of her affection; then, in tears, she kissed his forehead and said in a somewhat shaky voice: "Oh, my Andreuccio, how glad I am to see you!"

He, marveling at the tenderness of those caresses, replied, dumbfounded: "My lady, how glad I am to find you!"

Then, taking him by the hand, she led him up into her parlor and from there, without saying another word, she brought him into her bedroom, which was fragrant with roses, orange blossoms, and other scents. There he saw a beautiful curtained bed, many dresses hanging from rods, as is the custom there, and other most beautiful and rich furnishings. On that account, being inexperienced, he was positive she must be nothing less than a grand lady. They sat down together on a chest at the foot of the bed, and she began to speak to him:

"Andreuccio, I'm quite sure that you are surprised at both my affectionate greeting and my tears, since you don't know me and perhaps have never heard me mentioned. But you will soon hear something that may surprise you even more: namely, that I am your sister. And I assure you that, now that God has so greatly favored me with a sight of one of my brothers before my death—although I long to see all of you—whenever I die, it will be with consolation! And in case you've never heard this, I'll tell you. Pietro, my father and yours, lived

Pietro, mio padre e tuo, come io credo che tu abbi potuto sapere, dimorò lungamente in Palermo, e per la sua bontà e piacevolezza vi fu ed è ancora da quegli che il conobbero amato assai; ma tra gli altri che molto l'amarono, mia madre, che gentil donna fu ed allora era vedova, fu quella che più l'amò, tanto che, posta giù la paura del padre e de' fratelli ed il suo onore, in tal guisa con lui si dimesticò, che io ne nacqui, e sonne qual tu mi vedi. Poi, sopravvenuta cagione a Pietro di partirsi di Palermo e tornare in Perugia, me con la mia madre, piccola fanciulla, lasciò, né mai, per quello che io sentissi, più né di me né di lei si ricordò; di che io, se mio padre stato non fosse, forte il riprenderei, avendo riguardo alla 'ngratitudine di lui verso mia madre mostrata, (lasciamo stare all'amore che a me come a sua figliuola non nata d'una fante né di vil femina dovea portare); la quale le sue cose e sé parimente, senza sapere altramenti chi egli si fosse, da fedelissimo amor mossa rimise nelle sue mani. Ma che è? Le cose mal fatte e di gran tempo passate sono troppo più agevoli a riprendere che ad emendare; la cosa andò pur così. Egli mi lasciò piccola fanciulla in Palermo, dove, cresciuta quasi come io mi sono, mia madre, che ricca donna era, mi diede per moglie ad un da Gergenti, gentile uomo e da bene, il quale per amor di mia madre e di me tornò a stare in Palermo, e quivi, come colui che è molto guelfo, cominciò ad avere alcuno trattato col nostro re Carlo. Il quale sentito dal re Federigo prima che dare gli si potesse effetto, fu cagione di farci fuggire di Cicilia, quando io aspettava essere la maggior cavalleressa che mai in quella isola fosse. Donde, prese quelle poche cose che prender potemmo (poche dico, per rispetto alle molte le quali avevamo), lasciate le terre e li palazzi, in questa terra ne rifuggimmo, dove il re Carlo verso di noi trovammo sì grato, che, ristoratici in parte li danni li quali per lui ricevuti avevamo, e possessioni e case ci ha date, e dà continuamente al mio marito, e tuo cognato che è, buona provvisione, sì come tu potrai ancor vedere; ed in questa maniera son qui, dove io, la buona mercé di Dio e non tua, fratel mio dolce, ti veggio.

E così detto, da capo il rabbracciò, ed ancora teneramente lagrimando gli baciò la fronte. Andreuccio, udendo questa favola così ordinatamente e così compostamente detta da costei, alla quale in niuno atto moriva la parola tra' denti né balbettava la lingua, e ricordandosi esser vero che il padre era stato in Palermo, e per se

for a long time in Palermo, as I believe you must have learned. There, thanks to his goodness and charm, he was, and still is, greatly loved by all who knew him. But among the others who loved him dearly, my mother, who was a noble lady and a widow at the time, loved him most of all—so much so that, setting aside her fear of her father and brothers and the danger to her honor, she became so intimate with him that I, the person you see before you, was born. Then, when Pietro had to leave Palermo and return to Perugia, he left me there, still a little girl, with my mother, and never again, as far as I heard, gave another thought to either of us. If he hadn't been my father, I would blame him severely for that, in view of the ingratitude he showed my mother (let's not mention the love he should have had for me as a daughter who was not born of a servant or some low woman); for my mother, inspired by the most faithful love, had put into his hands all her affairs and herself as well, without knowing at all who he was. But why dwell on that? Long-past misdeeds are much more easily blamed than amended. That's how things went. He abandoned me as a little girl in Palermo, where, when I was almost as full-grown as I now am, my mother, who was a wealthy woman, married me off to a man from Agrigento, a respectable nobleman, who, out of love for my mother and me, took up residence in Palermo. There, being a thorough Guelf,[1] he entered into secret negotiations with our King Charles. When this was learned by King Frederick before the matter could be concluded, it was the reason we had to escape from Sicily, just when I expected to be the grandest noblewoman who ever lived on that island. And so, snatching the few things we were able to (I say few in comparison with the many that we possessed), abandoning our lands and palaces, we escaped to this city, where we found King Charles so grateful to us that he has partially made up to us the losses we had sustained on his account, giving us property and houses, and giving my husband, your brother-in-law, a substantial ongoing stipend, as you will be able to see. That is why I am here, where, thanks to God and not to you, I have been able to see you, my sweet brother."

Saying this, she embraced him again and, weeping tenderly, once more kissed his forehead. Andreuccio, hearing this cock-and-bull story which she told so neatly and smoothly, the words never faltering on her lips and her tongue never tripping; recalling that his father really had been in Palermo; knowing from his

---

[1] In this case, the term implies that he was on the side of the pope and the pope's ally, King Charles of Naples.

medesimo de' giovani conoscendo i costumi, che volentieri amano nella giovinezza, e veggendo le tenere lagrime, gli abbracciari e gli onesti baci, ebbe ciò che ella diceva più che per vero. E poscia che ella tacque, le rispose:

— Madonna, egli non vi dée parer gran cosa se io mi maraviglio, per ciò che nel vero (o che mio padre, per che che egli si facesse, di vostra madre e di voi non ragionasse già mai, o che, se egli ne ragionò, a mia notizia venuto non sia), io per me niuna conoscenza aveva di voi se non come se non foste; ed èmmi tanto più caro l'avervi qui mia sorella trovata, quanto io ci sono più solo e meno questo sperava. E nel vero, io non conosco uomo di sì alto affare, al quale voi non doveste esser cara, non che a me che un piccolo mercatante sono. Ma d'una cosa vi priego mi facciate chiaro: come sapeste voi che io qui fossi?

Al quale ella rispose: — Questa mattina mel fe' sapere una povera femina la qual molto meco si ritiene, per ciò che con nostro padre, per quello che ella mi dica, lungamente ed in Palermo ed in Perugia stette; e se non fosse che più onesta cosa mi parea che tu a me venissi in casa tua che io a te nell'altrui; egli ha gran pezza che io a te venuta sarei.

Appresso queste parole, ella cominciò distintamente a domandare di tutti i suoi parenti nominatamente; alla quale di tutti Andreuccio rispose, per questo ancora più credendo quello che meno di credere gli bisognava. Essendo stati i ragionamenti lunghi ed il caldo grande, ella fece venire greco e confetti, e fe' dar bere ad Andreuccio; il quale dopo questo partir volendosi, per ciò che ora di cena era, in niuna guisa il sostenne, ma sembianti fatto di forte turbarsi, abbracciandol disse:

— Ahi lassa me! ché assai chiaro conosco come io ti sia poco cara. Che è a pensare che tu sii con una tua sorella mai più da te veduta, ed in casa sua, dove, qui venendo, smontato esser dovresti; e vogli di quella uscire per andare a cenare all'albergo? Di vero tu cenerai con essomeco; e perché mio marito non ci sia, di che forte mi grava, io ti saprò bene, secondo donna, fare un poco d'onore.

Alla quale Andreuccio, non sappiendo altro che rispondersi, disse: — Io v'ho cara quanto sorella si dée avere, ma se io non ne vado, io sarò tutta sera aspettato a cena e farò villania.

Ed ella allora disse: — Lodato sia Iddio, se io non ho in casa per cui mandare a dire che tu non sii aspettato! Benché tu faresti assai maggior cortesia, e tuo dovere, mandare a dire a' tuoi compagni che qui venissero a cenare, e poi, se pure andare te ne volessi, ve ne potreste tutti andar di brigata.

own experience the ways of young men, who readily fall in love in youth; and seeing her tender tears, embraces, and chaste kisses, believed implicitly everything she had said. After she fell silent, he replied:

"My lady, it should be no wonder to you if I'm surprised, because truly (either my father, for whatever reason, never spoke about you and your mother, or, if he did so, it never came to my notice), for my part, I had no more knowledge of you than if you didn't exist. I'm all the happier to have found my sister here because I'm all alone here and wasn't expecting this. And to tell the truth, I know no man, no matter how high his rank, to whom you wouldn't be dear, let alone me, just a petty trader. But please explain one thing to me: how did you know I was here?"

She replied: "I was told of it this morning by a poor woman who spends a lot of time with me because, from what she tells me, she was long with our father in both Palermo and Perugia. And, if it weren't that I thought it more proper for you to visit me in what is your home than for me to visit you in someone else's, I would have come to you long before."

After those words, she began asking about all his relatives individually by name. Andreuccio gave her answers about each one. That made him believe all the more in what he shouldn't have believed. After a long conversation, when it was very hot, she sent for Greek wine and snacks, and made Andreuccio drink. Then, he wanted to leave because it was suppertime. She wouldn't hear of it; pretending to be very upset, she embraced him, saying:

"Ah, woe is me, now I see all too well how little I mean to you! Is it to be believed that here you are with a sister you've never seen, in her house, where you should have come to stay when you arrived, and you want to leave it to go and have supper at an inn? I tell you, you're going to eat with *me*. Even though my husband is away, which I'm very sorry about, I will be able to show you whatever hospitality a lady can."

Andreuccio, not knowing how else to reply, said: "You mean as much to me as any sister could, but if I don't go, they'll expect me for supper all evening, and it will be very rude of me."

Then she said: "Thank God I have people in my house I can send to tell them not to expect you! Although you would show much greater courtesy, and would be doing your duty, to send word to your friends to come here for supper. Later on, if you still wanted to leave, you could all leave together."

Andreuccio rispose che de' suoi compagni non volea quella sera, ma poi che pure a grado l'era, di lui facesse il piacere suo. Ella allora fe' vista di mandare a dire all'albergo che egli non fosse atteso a cena; e poi, dopo molti altri ragionamenti, postisi a cena e splendidamente di più vivande serviti, astutamente quella menò per lungo infino alla notte oscura; ed essendo da tavola levati, ed Andreuccio partir volendosi, ella disse che ciò in niuna guisa sofferrebbe, per ciò che Napoli non era terra da andarvi per entro di notte e massimamente un forestiere, e che, come che egli a cena non fosse atteso aveva mandato a dire, così aveva dell'albergo fatto il simigliante. Egli, questo credendo, e dilettandogli, da falsa credenza ingannato, d'esser con costei, stette.

Furono adunque dopo cena i ragionamenti molti e lunghi, non senza cagione, tenuti; ed essendo della notte una parte passata, ella, lasciato Andreuccio a dormire nella sua camera con un piccol fanciullo che gli mostrasse se egli volesse nulla, con le sue femine in un'altra camera se n'andò.

Era il caldo grande; per la qual cosa Andreuccio, veggendosi solo rimasto, subitamente si spogliò in farsetto e trassesi i panni di gamba ed al capo del letto gli si pose; e richiedendo il naturale uso di dovere diporre il superfluo peso del ventre, dove ciò si facesse domandò quel fanciullo, il quale nell'un de' canti della camera gli mostrò uno uscio, e disse: — Andate là entro.

Andreuccio dentro sicuramente passato, gli venne per ventura posto il pié sopra una tavola la quale, dalla contrapposta parte sconfitta dal travicello sopra il quale era, per la qual cosa capolevando questa tavola, con lui insieme se n'andò quindi giuso; e di tanto l'amò Iddio, che niuno male si fece nella caduta, quantunque alquanto cadesse da alto; ma tutto della bruttura della quale il luogo era pieno, s'imbrattò. Il quale luogo, acciò che meglio intendiate e quello che è detto e ciò che segue, come stesse vi mostrerò.

Egli era in un chiassetto stretto, come spesso tra due case veggiamo; sopra due travicelli tra l'una casa e l'altra posti, alcune tavole eran confitte, ed il luogo da seder posto; delle quali tavole quella che con lui cadde era l'una. Ritrovandosi adunque là giù nel chiassetto Andreuccio, dolente del caso, cominciò a chiamare il fanciullo; ma il fanciullo, come sentito l'ebbe cadere, così corse a dirlo alla donna, la quale, corsa alla sua camera, prestamente cercò se i suoi panni v'erano, e trovati i panni e con essi i denari, li quali esso, non fidandosi, mattamente sempre portava addosso, avendo quello a che ella di Palermo, sirocchia d'un Perugin faccendosi,

Andreuccio replied that he had no need of his friends that evening, but that, since it so pleased her, she should do with him whatever she liked. Then she pretended to send word to the inn not to expect him for supper. Next, after another long conversation, they sat down to supper and were splendidly served a number of courses. She cleverly stretched out the meal until it was pitch dark. When they rose from table, and Andreuccio wished to leave, she said she wouldn't allow it, because Naples was no city to walk around in at night, especially for a stranger; at the same time when she had sent word that he shouldn't be expected for dinner, she had also announced he wouldn't be back for the night. Believing this and enjoying her company because of his unwarranted belief, he stayed.

Well, after supper they had many long conversations, not by accident. When a part of the night had gone by, she left Andreuccio to sleep in her room in the company of a little boy who could help him if he wanted anything, and she and her maids withdrew into another bedroom.

The heat was intense, and so Andreuccio, finding himself alone, immediately stripped down to his doublet, pulling off his hose and breeches and placing them at the head of the bed. Feeling a call of nature to eliminate the excess weight of his bowels, he asked the boy where he could do so. The boy showed him a door in one corner of the room, saying: "Go in there."

When Andreuccio had gone in safely, by chance he placed his foot on a board that, on the side opposite him, had worked itself loose from the beam it was nailed to. It turned over and plunged downward together with him. But God loved him so much that he suffered no harm from the fall, even though it had been from a fair height. He was, however, soiled by the muck the place was full of. So that you can understand better what I have said and what follows, I will describe to you what that place was like.

It was in a narrow alleyway such as we often see between two houses. A few boards had been nailed to two beams placed between the houses, and a place to sit arranged. The board that fell with him was one of those. So then, Andreuccio, finding himself down in the alley, aching from the fall, began to call the boy. But the boy, as soon as he heard the fall, had run to tell his mistress, who ran to her room and immediately began searching to see if his clothes were there. Finding his clothes and, in them, his money, which, not trusting anyone, he foolishly always carried on him, now that she was in possession of what she had laid her snare for, by transforming herself from a

aveva teso il lacciuolo, più di lui non curandosi, prestamente andò a chiuder l'uscio del quale egli era uscito quando cadde.

Andreuccio, non rispondendogli il fanciullo, cominciò più forte a chiamare, ma ciò era niente; per che egli, già sospettando e tardi dello 'nganno cominciandosi ad accorgere, salito sopra un muretto, che quel chiassolino della strada chiudea e nella via disceso, all'uscio della casa, il quale egli molto ben riconobbe, se n'andò, e quivi invano lungamente chiamò, e molto il dimenò e percosse. Di che egli piagnendo, come colui che chiara vedea la sua disavventura, cominciò a dire: — Oimé lasso! in come piccol tempo ho io perduti cinquecento fiorini ed una sorella!

E dopo molte altre parole, da capo cominciò a battere l'uscio ed a gridare; e tanto fece così, che molti de' circostanti vicini, desti, non potendo la noia sofferire, si levarono, ed una delle servigiali della donna, in vista tutta sonnacchiosa, fattasi alla finestra, proverbiosamente disse: — Chi picchia là giù?

— Oh! — disse Andreuccio — o non mi conosci tu? Io sono Andreuccio, fratello di madama Fiordaliso.

Al quale ella rispose: — Buono uomo, se tu hai troppo bevuto, va' dormi e tornerai domattina; io non so che Andreuccio né che ciance son quelle che tu di'; va' in buona ora e lasciaci dormir, se ti piace.

— Come? — disse Andreuccio — non sai che io mi dico? Certo sì sai; ma se pur son così fatti i parentadi di Cicilia, che in sì piccol termine si dimentichino, rendimi almeno i panni miei li quali lasciati v'ho, ed io m'andrò volentier con Dio.

Al quale ella, quasi ridendo, disse: — Buono uomo, el mi par che tu sogni.

Ed il dir questo ed li tornarsi dentro e chiuder la finestra fu una cosa; di che Andreuccio, già certissimo de' suoi danni, quasi per doglia fu presso a convertire in rabbia la sua grande ira, e per ingiuria propose di rivolere quello che per parole riaver non potea; per che da capo, presa una gran pietra, con troppo maggior colpi che prima, fieramente cominciò a percuoter la porta. Per la qual cosa molti de' vicini avanti destisi e levatisi, credendo lui esser alcuno spiacevole il quale queste parole fingesse per noiare quella buona femina, recatosi a noia il picchiare il quale egli faceva, fattisi alle finestre, non altramenti che ad un can forestiere tutti quelli della contrada abbaiano addosso, cominciarono a dire:

— Questa è una gran villania a venire a questa ora a casa [del]le buone femine e dire queste ciance; deh! va' con Dio, buono uomo;

native of Palermo into the sister of a Perugian, she lost all interest in him and immediately went to close the door through which he had exited when he fell.

Andreuccio, when the boy failed to answer, began to yell louder, but to no avail; and so, already growing suspicious and belatedly beginning to realize the fraud, climbed onto a low wall that separated that alley from the street. Stepping down into the street, he went to the house door, which he recognized perfectly, and yelled for a long time in vain there, frequently shaking it and banging on it. And so, weeping, because he now saw his misfortune clearly, he started to say: "Woe is me! In how short a time I've lost five hundred florins and a sister!"

After saying much more, he started hitting the door again and yelling. He did this so long that many of the neighbors were awakened and, unable to stand the racket, got up. One of the young woman's maids, her face all puffy with sleep, showed her face at the window and said reproachfully: "Who's knocking down there?"

"Oh," said Andreuccio, "don't you recognize me? I'm Andreuccio, Monna Fiordaliso's brother."

She replied: "My good fellow, if you've had too much to drink, go to bed and come back in the morning. I don't know what Andreuccio or what nonsense you're talking about. Go away like a nice man and let us sleep, please."

"What?" said Andreuccio. "You don't know what I'm saying? Of course you know. But if this is what Sicilian family relations are like, forgotten in such a little while, at least give me back my clothes that I left with you, and I'll go my way gladly."

She, nearly laughing, replied: "My good man, I think you're dreaming."

And her saying that, her withdrawal inside, and her closing the window were all the work of a moment. So that Andreuccio, now certain of his loss, through grief was close to transforming his great anger into a frenzy; he decided to regain by violence what he was unable to regain by words. And so, picking up a big stone, he resumed banging on the door fiercely, hitting it much harder than before. Because of that, many of the neighbors who had been awakened and had gotten up earlier, thinking he was some nuisance who was making up that excuse in order to bother that "good woman," were annoyed by his knocking, went to their windows, and, just as all the dogs in a neighborhood bark at a strange dog, they started to say:

"It's very rude to come to good women's houses at this hour and talk such nonsense. Please go away, my good man! Let us sleep, please!

lasciaci dormir, se ti piace; e se tu hai nulla a far con lei tornerai domane, e non ci dar questa seccaggine stanotte.

Dalle quali parole forse assicurato uno che dentro dalla casa era,
ruffiano della buona femina, il quale egli né veduto né sentito avea,
si fece alle finestre e con una voce grossa, orribile e fiera disse: —
Chi è là giù?

Andreuccio, a quella voce levata la testa, vide uno il quale, per
quel poco che comprender poté, mostrava di dover essere un gran
bacalare, con una barba nera e folta al volto, e come se del letto o
da alto sonno si levasse, sbadigliava e stropicciavasi gli occhi. A cui
egli, non senza paura, rispose: — Io sono un fratello della donna di
là entro.

Ma colui non aspettò che Andreuccio finisse la risposta, anzi, più
rigido assai che prima, disse: — Io non so a che io mi tengo che io
non vengo là giù, e déati tante bastonate quante io ti veggia muovere,
asino fastidioso ed ebriaco che tu déi essere, che questa notte non ci
lascerai dormire persona! — E tornatosi dentro, serrò la finestra.

Alcuni de' vicini, che meglio conoscìeno la condizion di colui,
umilmente parlando ad Andreuccio dissero: — Per Dio, buono
uomo, vatti con Dio; non volere stanotte essere ucciso costì; vàt-
tene per lo tuo migliore.

Laonde Andreuccio, spaventato dalla voce di colui e dalla vista,
e sospinto da' conforti di coloro, li quali gli pareva che da carità
mossi parlassero, doloroso quanto mai alcuno altro e de' suoi denar
disperato, verso quella parte onde il dì aveva la fanticella seguìta,
senza saper dove s'andasse, prese la via per tornarsi all'albergo. Ed
a se medesimo dispiacendo per lo puzzo che a lui di lui veniva,
disideroso di volgersi al mare per lavarsi, si torse a man sinistra e su
per una via chiamata la Ruga catalana si mise; e verso l'alto della
città andando, per ventura davanti si vide due che verso di lui con
una lanterna in mano venìeno, li quali temendo non fosser della
famiglia della corte o altri uomini a mal far disposti, per fuggirgli,
in un casolare il qual si vide vicino pianamente ricoverò.

Ma costoro, quasi como a quello proprio luogo inviati andassero,
in quel medesimo casolare se n'entrarono; e quivi l'un di loro, scari-
cati certi ferramenti che in collo avea, con l'altro insieme gl'incominciò a guardare, varie cose sopra quegli ragionando. E mentre
parlavano, disse l'uno: — Che vuol dir questo? Io sento il maggior
puzzo che mai mi paresse sentire. — E questo detto, alzata

And if you have any business with her, come back tomorrow and don't bother us like this tonight."

Perhaps made confident by these words, someone from inside the house, the prostitute's pimp, whom Andreuccio had neither seen nor heard, appeared at a window and in a rough, fearsome, and wild voice said: "Who is it down there?"

Andreuccio, raising his head at the sound of that voice, saw a man who, from the little he could make out, seemed to be a person of some authority, with a heavy black beard on his face; he was yawning and rubbing his eyes as if he had just gotten out of bed or arisen from a deep sleep. With some fear, he replied: "I'm a brother of the lady who lives in there."

But the man, even before Andreuccio could finish replying, said, more gruffly than before: "I don't know what's keeping me from going down there and beating you till you can't move, you annoying, drunken donkey who won't let anybody sleep tonight!" And, going back in, he closed the window.

Some of the neighbors, who were more familiar with that man's character, spoke gently[2] to Andreuccio, saying: "For God's sake, young man, go away! Don't stay here tonight to be killed! Go away for your own good!"

Whereupon Andreuccio, frightened by the man's voice and appearance, and influenced by the kind words of those people who seemed to be addressing him in a spirit of charity, as sorrowful as a man has ever been and despairing of ever seeing his money, turned in the direction from which he had followed the young maid the day before without knowing where he was going, and set out to return to his inn. Himself suffering from the stink that came from him, and wishing to head for the seashore to wash, he turned to the left, taking a street called the Via Catalana. As he walked toward the high part of the city, by chance he saw in front of him two men who were approaching him, lantern in hand. Fearing that they belonged to the night watch or were part of another criminal gang, to avoid them he slipped quietly into a hut he saw nearby.

But they, as if they were being guided to that very place, entered the same hut. There one of them, putting down certain tools he had been carrying, started to look at them together with his companion, saying various things about them. And while they were talking, one of them said: "What's this? I smell the worst stink I've ever smelled."

---

[2]Or: "quietly and timorously."

alquanto la lanterna, ebber veduto il cattivel d'Andreuccio, e stupefatti domandâr: — Chi è là?

Andreuccio taceva; ma essi, avvicinatiglisi con lume, il domandarono che quivi così brutto facesse; alli quali Andreuccio ciò che avvenuto gli era narrò interamente. Costoro, imaginando dove ciò gli potesse essere avvenuto, dissero tra sè: — Veramente in casa lo scarabone Buttafuoco fia stato questo. — Ed a lui rivolti, disse l'uno:

— Buono uomo, come che tu abbi perduti i tuoi denari, tu hai molto a lodare Iddio che quel caso ti venne che tu cadesti né potesti poi in casa rientrare; per ciò che, se caduto non fossi, vivi sicuro che, come prima addormentato ti fossi, saresti stato ammazzato e co' denari avresti la persona perduta. Ma che giova oggimai di piagnere? Tu ne potresti così riavere un denaio come avere delle stelle del cielo; ucciso ne potrai tu bene essere, se colui sente che tu mai ne facci parola.

E detto questo, consigliatisi alquanto, gli dissero: — Vedi, a noi è presa compassion di te, e per ciò, dove tu vogli con noi essere a fare alcuna cosa la quale a fare andiamo, egli ci pare esser molto certi che in parte ti toccherà il valere di troppo più che perduto non hai.

Andreuccio, sì come disperato, rispose che era presto. Era quel dì sepellito uno arcivescovo di Napoli, chiamato messer Filippo Minùtolo, ed era stato sepellito con ricchissimi ornamenti e con un rubino in dito il quale valeva oltre a cinquecento fiorin d'oro; il quale costoro volevano andare a spogliare, e così ad Andreuccio fecer veduto. Laonde Andreuccio, più cupido che consigliato, con loro si mise in via; ed andando verso la chiesa maggiore, ed Andreuccio putendo forte, disse l'uno: — Non potremmo noi trovar modo che costui si lavasse un poco dove che sia, ché egli non putisse così fieramente?

Disse l'altro: — Sì, noi siam qui presso ad un pozzo al quale suole sempre esser la carrucola ed un gran secchione; andianne là e laverenlo spacciatamente.

Giunti a questo pozzo, trovarono che la fune v'era, ma il secchione n'era stato levato; per che insieme diliberarono di legarlo alla fune e di collarlo nel pozzo, ed egli là giù si lavasse, e come lavato fosse, crollasse la fune ed essi il tirerebber suso; e così fecero. Avvenne che, avendol costor nel pozzo collato, alcuni della famiglia della signoria, li quali e per lo caldo e perché corsi erano dietro ad alcuno, avendo sete, a quel pozzo venìeno a bere; li quali

Saying this, he raised the lantern a little, and they saw poor Andreuccio. Dumbfounded, they asked: "Who's there?"

Andreuccio kept silent, but they approached him with the light and asked him what he was doing there in such a filthy state. Andreuccio told them every detail of what had happened to him. They realized where that must have happened, and said to themselves: "He must surely have been in the gangleader Buttafuoco's house!" They turned to him, and one of them said:

"My good fellow, even though you lost your money there, you should be very thankful to God that you happened to fall and couldn't get back in; because you can rest assured that, if you hadn't fallen, as soon as you went to sleep you would have been killed, and would have lost your life along with your money. But what's the use of crying over it now? You have the same chance of getting back one penny as of getting a star from the sky. It may well cost you your life if that man ever hears that you've let out a peep about it."

Having said this, they had a short confabulation, and then said to him: "Look, we've taken pity on you, and so, if you agree to join us in a job we're out on, we're pretty sure that your share will be worth much more than what you lost."

Andreuccio, in his state of desperation, replied that he was ready. That day an archbishop of Naples called Filippo Minutolo had been buried, and buried with extremely valuable ornaments, including a ruby ring worth over five hundred gold florins. They were planning to rob the body, and revealed the plan to Andreuccio. Whereupon Andreuccio, more greedy than wise, set out with them. While they were walking toward the cathedral, because Andreuccio stank so badly, one of them said: "Couldn't we find a way for him to wash up a little somewhere, so he won't stink so awfully?"

The other one said: "Yes, we're close to a well where there's usually always a pulley and a big bucket. Let's go there and we'll give him a quick bath."

Arriving at that well, they found that the rope was there, but the bucket had been taken away. And so, together they devised the scheme of tying him to the rope and lowering him into the well; down there he would wash and, once washed, would pull on the rope for them to draw him up; and that's what they did. It fell out that, after they lowered him into the well, some members of the night watch, who were thirsty because it was hot and because they had been chasing someone, came to that well for a drink. When those two saw them,

come quegli due videro, incontanente cominciarono a fuggire. Li
famigliari che quivi venivano a bere non avendogli veduti, essendo
già nel fondo del pozzo Andreuccio lavato, dimenò la fune.
Costoro, assetati, posti giù lor tavolacci e loro armi e lor gonnelle,
cominciarono la fune a tirare, credendo a quella il secchion pien
d'acqua essere appiccato.

Come Andreuccio si vide alla sponda del pozzo vicino, così, lasciata la fune, con le mani si gittò sopra quella; la qual cosa costor
veggendo, da subita paura presi, senza altro dir lasciaron la fune e
cominciarono quanto più poterono a fuggire. Di che Andreuccio si
maravigliò forte, e se egli non si fosse bene attenuto, egli sarebbe
infin nel fondo caduto, forse non senza suo gran danno o morte; ma
pure uscitone e queste armi trovate, le quali egli sapeva che i suoi
compagni non avean portate, ancora più s'incominciò a maravigliare. Ma dubitando e non sappiendo che, della sua fortuna
dolendosi, senza alcuna cosa toccar, quindi diliberò di partirsi; ed
andava senza saper dove.

Così andando, si venne scontrato in que' due suoi compagni, li
quali a trarlo del pozzo venivano; e come il videro, maravigliandosi
forte, il domandarono chi del pozzo l'avesse tratto. Andreuccio
rispose che non sapea, e loro ordinatamente disse come era
avvenuto e quello che trovato aveva fuori del pozzo.

Di che costoro, avvisatisi come stato era, ridendo gli contarono
perché s'eran fuggiti e chi stati eran coloro che sù l'avean tirato; e
senza più parole fare, essendo già mezzanotte, n'andarono alla
chiesa maggiore, ed in quella assai leggermente entrarono, e
furono all'arca, la quale era di marmo e molto grande; e con lor
ferro il coperchio, che era gravissimo, sollevaron tanto quanto uno
uomo vi potesse entrare, e puntellàronlo.

E fatto questo, cominciò l'uno a dire: — Chi entrerà dentro?

A cui l'altro rispose: — Non io.

Né io, — disse colui, — ma èntrivi Andreuccio.

— Questo non farò io — disse Andreuccio; verso il quale am-
menduni costoro rivolti dissero:

— Come non v'entrerai? In fé di Dio, se tu non v'entri, noi ti
darem tante d'un di questi pali di ferro sopra la testa, che noi ti
farem cader morto.

Andreuccio temendo v'entrò, ed entrandovi pensò seco: —
Costoro mi ci fanno entrare per ingannarmi, per ciò che, come io
avrò loro ogni cosa dato, mentre che io penerò ad uscir dell'arca,
essi se n'andranno pe' fatti loro ed io rimarrò senza cosa alcuna.

they immediately took to their heels. The policemen coming there to drink hadn't seen them. Andreuccio, having completed his ablutions at the bottom of the well, tugged on the rope. The parched policemen, putting down their wooden shields, weapons, and tunics, started to draw up the rope, thinking that the bucket, full of water, was attached to it.

As soon as Andreuccio saw he was near the rim of the well, he let go of the rope and leapt for the rim with his hands. The policemen, seeing this, were stricken with sudden fear; without a word, they let go of the rope and started to run away as fast as they could. This surprised Andreuccio greatly, and if he hadn't held on tight, he would have fallen to the very bottom, perhaps being seriously hurt or killed. But, getting out at last and finding those weapons, which he knew his companions hadn't been carrying, his surprise increased. Fearing something but not knowing what, complaining of his ill luck, he touched nothing and decided to leave. He didn't know where he was going.

As he proceeded in that fashion, he met up with those two companions of his, who were on their way to pull him out of the well. When they saw him, they were greatly surprised and asked him who had pulled him out of the well. Andreuccio said he didn't know, and told them in proper sequence what had happened and what he had found outside of the well.

They, realizing what must have happened, laughed and told him why they had run away and who the people were who had pulled him out. Without wasting more words, it now being midnight, they went to the cathedral, entered it easily, and went up to the sarcophagus, which was of marble and very large. With their crowbar they raised the extremely heavy lid far enough for a man to get in, and they propped it up.

After that, one started saying to the other: "Who's going in?"

The other replied: "Not me."

"Not me, either," the first one said. "Let Andreuccio go in."

"Nothing doing," said Andreuccio. Both of them turned toward him and said:

"What do you mean, you won't go in? By my faith in God, if you don't go in, we'll hit you so hard on the head with one of these iron bars that you'll drop dead."

Andreuccio, frightened, went in, and, as he did so, he thought to himself: "These two are making me go in to fool me: as soon as I've handed everything out, while I'm scrambling to get out of the tomb, they'll be on their way, leaving me with nothing."

E per ciò s'avvisò di farsi innanzi tratto la parte sua, e ricordatosi del caro anello che aveva loro udito dire, come fu giù disceso, così di dito il trasse all'arcivescovo e miselo a sé; e poi, dato il pasturale e la mitra ed i guanti, e spogliatolo infino alla camicia, ogni cosa die' loro, dicendo che più niente v'avea. Costoro, affermando che esservi doveva l'anello, gli dissero che cercasse per tutto; ma esso, rispondendo che nol trovava e sembianti faccendo di cercarne, alquanto gli tenne in aspettare.

Costoro che, d'altra parte, erano sì come lui maliziosi, dicendo pur che ben cercasse, preso tempo, tiraron via il puntello che il coperchio dell'arca sostenea, e fuggendosi, lui dentro dall'arca lasciaron racchiuso.

La qual cosa sentendo Andreuccio, quale egli allor divenisse, ciascun sel può pensare. Egli tentò più volte e col capo e con le spalle se alzare potesse il coperchio, ma invano si faticava; per che, da grave dolor vinto, venendo meno, cadde sopra il morto corpo dell'arcivescovo, e chi allora veduti gli avesse, malagevolmente avrebbe conosciuto chi più si fosse morto, o l'arcivescovo o egli.

Ma poi che in sé fu ritornato, dirottissimamente cominciò a piagnere, veggendosi quivi senza dubbio all'un de' due fini dover pervenire: o in quella arca, non venendovi alcuni più ad aprirla, di fame e di puzzo tra' vèrmini del morto corpo convenirgli morire, o venendovi alcuni e trovandovi lui dentro, sì come ladro dovere essere appiccato.

Ed in così fatti pensieri e doloroso molto stando, sentì per la chiesa andar genti e parlar molte persone, le quali, sì come egli avvisava, quello andavano a fare che esso co' suoi compagni avean già fatto; di che la paura gli crebbe forte. Ma poi che costoro ebbero l'arca aperta e puntellata, in quistion caddero chi vi dovesse entrare, e niuno il voleva fare; pur dopo lunga tencione un prete disse: — Che paura avete voi? Credete voi che egli vi manuchi? Li morti non mangian gli uomini; io v'entrerò dentro io.

E così detto, posto il petto sopra l'orlo dell'arca, volse il capo in fuori e dentro mandò le gambe per doversi giuso calare. Andreuccio, questo veggendo, in pié levatosi, prese il prete per l'una delle gambe e fe' sembianti di volerlo giù tirare. La qual cosa sentendo il prete, mise uno strido grandissimo e presto dell'arca si gittò fuori; della qual cosa tutti gli altri spaventati, lasciata l'arca aperta, non altramenti a fuggir cominciaron che se da centomilia diavoli fosser perseguitati.

La qual cosa veggendo Andreuccio, lieto oltre a quello che

And so, he decided to take his share right at the outset; remembering the valuable ring he had heard them mention, as soon as he was down inside he drew it off the archbishop's finger and put it on his own. Then, handing out the crosier, the miter, and the gloves, and stripping the dead man to his shirt, he gave them everything and said there was nothing left. They, declaring that the ring must be there, told him to search everywhere; but he, replying that he couldn't find it, pretended to be looking for it and kept them waiting for a while.

The two men, who, for their part, were just as shrewd as he was, kept telling him to look hard, but, choosing their moment, they pulled away the prop that was holding up the lid of the tomb. Running away, they left him shut inside the tomb.

How Andreuccio felt when he became aware of this, anyone can imagine. He tried several times with his head and shoulders to raise the lid, but his efforts were in vain. And so, overcome by grievous sorrow, he fainted, falling onto the archbishop's dead body. Anyone seeing them then would have had a hard time saying which one was the dead man, the archbishop or Andreuccio.

But after he came to his senses, he started to weep buckets, seeing that he certainly had to come to one of two ends there: either to die of hunger and stench amid the worms from the dead body in that tomb if no one else came to open it, or, if someone came and found him in it, to be hanged as a thief.

And, lost in these thoughts and sunk in sorrow, he heard people walking in the church and the voices of many people, who, as he perceived, were coming to do the same thing he and his companions had done already. And so his fear increased greatly. But once these newcomers had opened the tomb and propped up the lid, they argued over who would go in, and no one wanted to. Finally, after a long altercation, a priest said: "What are you afraid of? Do you think he's going to eat you? The dead don't eat people. I'll go inside myself."

Saying this, he leaned his chest on the rim of the tomb, turned his head toward the outside, and put his legs inside in preparation for dropping to the bottom. Andreuccio, seeing this, stood up straight, seized the priest by one leg, and pretended to be pulling him down. The priest, feeling this, let out a piercing shriek and immediately threw himself out of the tomb. This frightened all the rest; leaving the tomb open, they started running away exactly as if they were being chased by a hundred thousand devils.

Seeing this, Andreuccio, happy beyond anything he had expected,

sperava, subito si gittò fuori e per quella via onde era venuto se n'uscì della chiesa. E già avvicinandosi al giorno, con quello anello in dito andando alla ventura, pervenne alla marina e quindi al suo albergo si rabbatté, dove il suoi compagni e l'albergatore trovò tutta la notte stati in sollecitudine de' fatti suoi.

A' quali ciò che avvenuto gli era raccontato, parve per lo consiglio dell'oste loro che costui incontanente si dovesse di Napoli partire; la qual cosa egli fece prestamente ed a Perugia tornossi, avendo il suo investito in uno anello, dove per comperare cavalli era andato.

UNA SCOMMESSA SULLA VIRTÙ [II, 9]

Avendo Elissa con la sua compassionevole novella il suo dover fornito, Filomena reina, la quale bella e grande era della persona, e nel viso più che altra piacevole e ridente, sopra sé recatasi, disse: — Servar si vogliono i patti a Dionèo, e però, non restandoci altri che egli ed io a novellare, io dirò prima la mia, ed esso, che di grazia il chiese, l'ultimo fia che dirà. — E questo detto, così cominciò:

Suolsi tra' volgari spesse volte dire un cotal proverbio, che lo 'ngannatore rimane a pié dello 'ngannato, il quale non pare che per alcuna ragione si possa mostrare esser vero, se per gli accidenti che avvengono non si mostrasse. E per ciò, seguendo la proposta, questo insiememente, carissime donne, esser vero come si dice, m'è venuto in talento di dimostrarvi: né vi dovrà esser discaro d'averlo udito, acciò che dagl'ingannatori guardarvi sappiate.

Erano in Parigi in uno albergo alquanti grandissimi mercatanti italiani, qual per una bisogna e qual per un'altra, secondo la loro usanza; ed avendo una sera tra l'altre tutti lietamente cenato, cominciarono di diverse cose a ragionare, e d'un ragionamento in altro travalicando, pervennero a dire delle lor donne, le quali alle lor case avevan lasciate; e motteggiando cominciò alcuno a dire: — Io non so come la mia si fa, ma questo so io bene, che, quando qui mi viene alle mani alcuna giovanetta che mi piaccia, io lascio stare dall'un de' lati l'amore il quale io porto a mia mogliere, e prendo di questa qua quel piacere che io posso.

L'altro rispose: — Ed io fo il simigliante, per ciò che, se io credo

immediately jumped out and left the church by the same route he had taken when entering. It was now getting near day. Walking at random, the ring on his finger, he reached the port and then stumbled upon his inn, where he discovered that his friends and the innkeeper had been worried about him all night long.

After he told them what had happened to him, their landlord advised him to leave Naples at once. He did so briskly and went back to Perugia, with his wealth in the form of a ring, whereas he had set out to buy horses.

A WAGER OVER VIRTUE [II, 9]

After Elissa had done her duty, telling that compassion-arousing story, "Queen" Filomena, who was beautiful and tall and had an exceptionally charming and smiling face, reflected for a while, then said: "We want to keep our agreement with Dioneo,[1] and so, there being no one left to tell a story besides him and me, I'll tell mine first, and he, who requested that favor, will be the last to speak." Having said that, she began thus:

The common folk often repeat a proverb to the effect that the man who deceives ultimately falls at the feet of the one he has deceived. The truth of this doesn't seem provable in any other way than through the actual incidents that exemplify it. Therefore, while still following our proposed theme, dearest ladies, I have taken a fancy to prove to you at the same time that this is as true as people say. It won't be displeasing to you to have heard it, so that you can guard yourselves from deceivers.

At an inn in Paris several major Italian merchants were assembled, each pursuing his own business affairs, as their usual practice is. One evening, after a merry supper together, they began talking about various matters; passing from one topic to another, they finally spoke about the wives they had left at home. One of them started to say, jokingly: "I don't know how mine behaves, but this I know: when I'm here and some desirable girl falls into my hands, I set on one side the love I bear my wife, and get all the pleasure I can from the girl."

The next man said: "And I do the same, because if I suspect that my

---

[1]The group of narrators had acceded to his double request: that he should always tell the last story of each day, and that he need not adhere to the stated theme for the day.

che la mia donna alcuna sua ventura procacci, ella il fa, e se io nol credo, sì il fa; e per ciò da fare a far sia: quale asino dà in parete, tal riceve.

Il terzo quasi in questa medesima sentenza parlando pervenne; e brievemente, tutti pareva che a questo s'accordassero, che le donne lasciate da loro non volessero perder tempo.

Un solamente, il quale avea nome Bernabò Lomellin da Genova, disse il contrario, affermando sé, di spezial grazia, da Dio avere una donna per moglie la più compiuta di tutte quelle vertù che donna o ancora cavaliere, in gran parte, o donzello dée avere, che forse in Italia ne fosse un'altra; per ciò che ella era bella del corpo e giovane ancora assai e destra ed atante della persona, né alcuna cosa era che a donna appartenesse, sì come di lavorare lavorii di seta e simili cose, che ella non facesse meglio che alcuna altra. Oltre a questo, niuno scudiere, o famigliare che dir vogliamo, diceva trovarsi il quale meglio né più accortamente servisse ad una tavola d'un signore, che serviva ella, sì come colei che era costumatissima, savia e discreta molto.

Appresso questo, la commendò meglio saper cavalcare un cavallo, tenere uno uccello, leggere e scrivere e fare una ragione che se un mercatante fosse; e da questo, dopo molte altre lode, pervenne a quello di che quivi si ragionava, affermando con saramento niuna altra più onesta né più casta potersene trovar di lei; per la qual cosa egli credeva certamente che, se egli diece anni o sempre mai fuori di casa dimorasse, che ella mai a così fatte novelle non intenderebbe con altro uomo.

Era tra questi mercatanti che così ragionavano un giovane mercatante chiamato Ambruogiuolo da Piagenza, il quale di questa ultima loda che Bernabò avea data alla sua donna cominciò a far le maggior risa del mondo, e gabbando il domandò se lo 'mperadore gli avea questo privilegio più che a tutti gli altri uomini conceduto. Bernabò, un poco turbatetto, disse che non lo 'mperadore, ma Iddio il quale poteva un poco più che lo 'mperadore, gli avea questa grazia conceduta.

Allora disse Ambruogiuolo: — Bernabò, io non dubito punto che tu non ti creda dir vero, ma per quello che a me paia, tu hai poco riguardato alla natura delle cose, per ciò che, se riguardato v'avessi, non ti sento di sì grosso ingegno, che tu non avessi in quella conosciute cose che ti farebbono sopra questa materia più temperatamente parlare. E per ciò che tu non creda che noi, che molto largo abbiamo delle nostre mogli parlato, crediamo avere altra

wife is pursuing some fancy of hers, she does what she wants, and if I don't suspect it, she does it just the same; and so, let us play tricks on each other. When the donkey kicks the wall he gets his own back: tit for tat!"

The third man, in what he had to say, reached practically the same conclusion. In short, it seemed that they all agreed that the wives they had left behind were unwilling to waste time.

Only one man, whose name was Bernabò Lomellin from Genoa, said the opposite, declaring that, by a special grace, he had received as a wife from God a woman who was most perfect in all the good qualities that a woman, or even a knight, in large part, or a young gentleman ought to possess, and perhaps more so than any other woman in Italy; because she was physically beautiful and still quite young and skillful and vigorous of body, and there was nothing pertaining to women, such as doing silk embroidery and the like, that she didn't do better than the rest. In addition, he said there was no servant of any kind who could wait at a lordly table better or more adroitly than she did, since she was highly well-bred, wise, and very clever.

After this, he praised her ability to ride, handle hawks, read, and write, saying she could do accounts better than merchants; then, after many other compliments, he got to the specific subject of the conversation and affirmed with an oath that no woman more modest and chaste could be found than she. Therefore, he said, he believed implicitly that if he were to stay away from home for ten years or forever, she would never indulge in such liberties with any other man.

Among the merchants engaged in this conversation was a young merchant named Ambruogiuolo from Piacenza, who, hearing the last-mentioned praise Bernabò had bestowed on his wife, burst into loud laughter and mockingly asked him whether the Emperor had granted him that privilege over and above all other men. Bernabò, somewhat vexed, said that it wasn't the Emperor but God, who was a little more powerful than the Emperor, who had granted him that favor.

Then Ambruogiuolo said: "Bernabò, I don't doubt at all that you believe you're speaking the truth, but it seems to me that you haven't looked into the nature of things sufficiently, because, if you had, I don't think your wits are so dull that you wouldn't have discovered in that nature things which would make you speak on this subject with greater moderation. And, in order that you don't think that we, who have spoken very freely about our own wives, think we have wives

moglie o altramenti fatta che tu, ma da un naturale avvedimento mossi così abbiàn detto, voglio un poco con teco sopra questa materia ragionare. Io ho sempre inteso l'uomo essere il più nobile animale che tra' mortali fosse creato da Dio, ed appresso la femina; ma l'uomo, sì come generalmente si crede e vede per opere, è più perfetto; ed avendo più di perfezione, senza alcun fallo dée avere più di fermezza, a così ha, per ciò che universalmente le femine sono più mobili, ed il perché si potrebbe per molte ragioni naturali dimostrare, le quali al presente intendo di lasciare stare. Se l'uomo adunque è di maggior fermezza, e non si può tenere che non condiscenda, lasciamo stare ad una che il prieghi, ma pure a non disiderare una che gli piaccia, ed oltre al disidéro, di far ciò che può acciò che con quella esser possa, e questo non una volta il mese, ma mille il giorno avvenirgli, che speri tu che una donna, naturalmente mobile, possa fare a' prieghi, alle lusinghe, a' doni, a mille altri modi che userà uno uom savio che l'ami? Credi che ella si possa tenere? Certo, quantunque tu te l'affermi, io non credo che tu il creda; e tu medesimo di' che la moglie tua è femina e che ella è di carne e d'ossa come son l'altre. Per che, se così è, quegli medesimi disidéri deono essere i suoi o quelle medesime forze che nell'altre sono a resistere a questi naturali appetiti; per che possibile è, quantunque ella sia onestissima, che ella quello che l'altre faccia; e niuna cosa possibile è così acerbamente da negare, o da affermare il contrario a quella, come tu fai.

Al quale Bernabò rispose, a disse: — Io son mercatante e non fisofolo, e come mercatante risponderò; e dico che io conosco ciò che tu di' potere avvenire alle stolte, nelle quali non è alcuna vergogna; ma quelle che savie sono, hanno tanta sollecitudine dell'onor loro, che elle diventan forti più che gli uomini, che di ciò non si curano, a guardarlo; e di queste così fatte è la mia.

Disse Ambruogiuolo: — Veramente, se per ogni volta che elle a queste così fatte novelle attendono, nascesse loro un corno nella fronte, il quale desse testimonianza di ciò che fatto avessero, io mi credo che poche sarebber quelle che v'attendessero; ma, non che il corno nasca, egli non se ne pare, a quelle che savie sono, né pedata né orma, e la vergogna ed il guastamento dell'onore non consiste se non nelle cose palesi; per che, quando possono, occultamente il fanno, o per mattezza lasciano. Ed abbi questo per certo, che colei sola è casta la quale o non fu mai da alcuno pregata, o se pregò, non fu esaudita. E quantunque io conosca per naturali e vere ragioni così dovere essere, non ne parlerei io così appieno, come io fo, se

different or differently made from yours, but, on the contrary, we spoke the way we did out of natural good sense, I want to talk to you a little on this subject. I've always heard that man, the male, was the noblest mortal creature made by God, woman coming next; but the man, as is generally believed and seen through his actions, is more perfect; and, having more perfection, he must indubitably have more constancy, and he does, because women are universally more change-able. The reason for that could be shown through many natural proofs, which I intend to leave aside for the present. And so, if man is of greater constancy, and nevertheless can't resist obliging a woman who asks him to sleep with her, and what's more, can't help yearning for a woman who attracts him, and not just yearning but doing all he can to get together with her—and yearns this way not just once a month, but a thousand times a day—what do you imagine that a woman, changeable by nature, can do against the entreaties, flattery, gifts, and the thousand other ploys that a wise man in love with her will use? Do you think she can resist? In truth, even though you affirm it, I don't believe you believe it. You yourself say your wife is a woman, made of flesh and blood like the rest. And so, if that's the case, she must share the same desires or the same strength that the others have to combat those natural appetites. And so, it is possible that, chaste as she may be, she does what all the others do. And nothing that is pos-sible should be so categorically denied, and the opposite declared to be true, as it is by you."

Bernabò replied: "I'm a merchant, not a philosopher, and I'll an-swer like a merchant: I tell you, I know that what you're talking about can happen to stupid women who have no shame; but those who are wise have so much concern for their honor that they become stronger than men (who don't care about honor in such matters) when it comes to protecting it. And my wife is one of this sort."

Ambruogiuolo said: "To tell the truth, if every time they pursued such adventures a horn grew on their forehead, testifying to what they had done, I think that very few would attempt it. However, not only does no horn grow, but if the woman is smart, not a single sign or trace shows—and shame and loss of honor only occur when things are made public. And so, when they can, they do it in secret or, if they're too dumb, they avoid it. You can be sure that the only chaste woman is one who either was never approached by any man or else made the approach herself and was turned down. And even though I know from natural and true considerations that it must be so, I wouldn't speak of it as positively as I do if I hadn't made the test of it myself many times

io non ne fossi molte volte e con molte stato alla pruova; e dicoti
così, che, se io fossi presso a questa tua così santissima donna, io mi
crederei in brieve spazio di tempo recarla a quello che io ho già del-
l'altre recate.

Bernabò, turbato, rispose: — Il quistionar con parole potrebbe
distendersi troppo: tu diresti ed io direi, ed alla fine niente mon-
terebbe. Ma poi che tu di' che tutte sono così pieghevoli e che il tuo
ingegno è cotanto, acciò che io ti faccia certo dell'onestà della mia
donna, io son disposto che mi sia tagliata la testa se tu mai a cosa
che ti piaccia in cotale atto la puoi conducere; e se tu non puoi, io
non voglio che tu perda altro che mille fiorin d'oro.

Ambruogiuolo, già in su la novella riscaldato, rispose: — Bernabò,
io non so quello che io mi facessi del tuo sangue, se io vincessi; ma
se tu hai voglia di vedere pruova di ciò che io ho già ragionato, metti
cinquemila fiorin d'oro de' tuoi, che meno ti deono essere cari che
la testa, contro a mille de' miei; e dove tu niuno termine poni, io mi
voglio obligare d'andare e Genova ed infra tre mesi dal dì che io mi
partirò di qui avere della tua donna fatta mia volontà, ed in segno di
ciò recarne meco delle sue cose più care e sì fatti e tanti indizi, che
tu medesimo confesserai esser vero, sì veramente che tu mi promet-
terai sopra la tua fede infra questo termine non venire a Genova né
scrivere a lei alcuna cosa di questa materia.

Bernabò disse che gli piacea molto; e quantunque gli altri mercatanti che quivi erano s'ingegnassero di sturbar questo fatto,
conoscendo che gran male ne potea nascere, pure erano de' due
mercatanti sì gli animi accesi, che, oltre al voler degli altri, per belle
scritte di lor mano s'obbligarono l'uno all'altro. E fatta l'obbliga-
gione, Bernabò rimase ed Ambruogiuolo quanto più tosto poté se
ne venne a Genova. E dimoratovi alcun giorno e con molta cautela
informatosi del nome della contrada e de' costumi della donna,
quello e più ne 'ntese che da Bernabò udito n'avea; per che gli
parve matta impresa aver fatta. Ma pure, accontatosi con una
povera femina che molto nella casa usava ed a cui la donna voleva
gran bene, non potendola ad altro inducere, con denari la corruppe
ed a lei in una cassa artificiata a suo modo si fece portare non solamente nella casa, ma nella camera della gentil donna; e quivi, come
se in alcuna parte andar volesse, la buona femina, secondo l'ordine
datole da Ambruogiuolo, la raccomandò per alcun dì.

Rimasa adunque la cassa nella camera e venuta la notte, allora
che Ambruogiuolo avvisò che la donna dormisse, con certi suoi ingegni apertala, chetamente nella camera uscì, nella quale un lume

and with many women. And I tell you, if I ever got near that most holy wife of yours, I'm sure that I'd quickly persuade her to give me what I've gotten from the others."

Bernabò, vexed, replied: "Discussing this with words could go on and on: you would speak your piece and I'd speak mine, and nothing would come of it. But since you say that all women are that pliable and that you're so ingenious, in order to prove my wife's chastity to you I'm willing to have my head cut off if you can ever bring her to do your will in such a way; and, if you can't, all I want you to lose is a thousand gold florins."

Ambruogiuolo, already excited by the argument, replied: "Bernabò, I don't know what I'd do with your blood if I won; but if you want to see the proof of what I've told you, put down five thousand of your gold florins, which ought to be less dear to you than your head, against a thousand of mine. And although you set no time limit, I'm willing to undertake to go to Genoa and have my will of your wife within three months from the day I leave. As a proof of it, I'll bring back some of her dearest possessions and evidence so great and of such a nature that you yourself will admit it's true, as long as you promise me on your faith that you won't go to Genoa within that period or write anything to her on this subject."

Bernabò said it was quite all right with him, and, even though the other merchants there strove to avoid this business, knowing it could lead to great evils, the two merchants' spirits were so aroused that, ignoring the pleas of the others, they both signed a formal agreement. After the agreement was reached, Bernabò remained behind and Ambruogiuolo traveled to Genoa as fast as he could. Residing there for several days while he gathered information on the name of the neighborhood and the woman's character, he learned the same that he had heard from Bernabò, and even more so, so that it now seemed he had made a foolish undertaking. Nevertheless, after meeting a poor woman who frequented the lady's house and was well liked by her, finding himself unable to induce her to do any more, he bribed her to have him placed inside a specially constructed chest and brought, not only inside the house, but into the gentlewoman's bedroom. There the good woman, following Ambruogiuolo's orders, said she was going to make a trip somewhere and entrusted the chest to her for a few days.

And so, the chest remaining in the bedroom, after nightfall, when Ambruogiuolo perceived that the lady was asleep, he opened the chest with certain special tools and quietly stepped out into the room,

acceso avea; per la qual cosa egli il sito della camera, le dipinture
ed ogni altra cosa notabile che in quella era comìnciò a ragguardare
ed a fermare nella sua memoria.

Quindi, avvicinatosi al letto e sentendo che la donna ed una piccola fanciulla che con lei era dormivan forte, pianamente scoper-
tala tutta, vide che così era bella ignuda come vestita, ma niun segnale da poterè rapportare le vide, fuori che uno che ella n'avea
sotto la sinistra poppa, ciò era uno neo dintorno al quale erano
alquanti peluzzi biondi come oro; e ciò veduto, chetamente la ri-
coperse, come che, così bella veggendola, in disidéro avesse di mettere in avventura la vita sua e coricarlesi allato. Ma pure, avendo
udito lei essere così cruda ed alpestra intorno a quelle novelle, non
s'arrischiò, e statosi la maggior parte della notte per la camera a suo
agio, una borsa ed una guarnacca d'un suo forzier trasse, ed alcuno
anello ed alcuna cintura, ed ogni cosa nella cassa sua messa, egli altresì vi si ritornò, e così la serrò come prima stava; ed in questa
maniera fece due notti senza che la donna di niente s'accorgesse.

Vegnente il terzo dì, secondo l'ordine dato, la buona femina
tornò per la cassa sua, e colà la riportò onde levata l'avea; della
quale Ambruogiuolo uscito, e contentata secondo la promessa la
femina, quanto più tosto, con quelle cose si tornò a Parigi avanti il
termine preso. Quivi, chiamati que' mercatanti che presenti erano
stati alle parole ed al metter de' pegni, presente Bernabò, disse sé
aver vinto il pegno tra lor messo, per ciò che fornito aveva quello di
che vantato s'era; e che ciò fosse vero, primieramente disegnò la
forma della camera e le dipinture di quella, ed appresso mostrò le
cose che di lei n'aveva seco recate, affermando da lei averle avute.

Confessò Bernabò così essere fatta la camera come diceva, ed
oltre a ciò, sé riconoscere quelle cose veramente della sua donna
essere state; ma disse, lui aver potuto da alcuno de' fanti della casa
sapere la qualità della camera, ed in simil maniera avere avute le
cose; per che, se altro non dicea, non gli parea che questo bastasse
a dovere aver vinto.

Per che Ambruogiuolo disse: — Nel vero questo doveva bastare; ma
poi che tu vuogli che io più avanti ancora dica, ed io dirò. Dicoti che
madonna Zinevra, tua mogliere, ha sotto la sinistra poppa un neo ben
grandicello, dintorno al quale son forse sei peluzzi biondi come oro.

Quando Bernabò udì questo, parve che gli fosse dato d'un
coltello al cuore, sì fatto dolore sentì, e tutto nel viso cambiato,
eziandio se parola non avesse detta, diede assai manifesto segnale
ciò esser vero che Ambruogiuolo diceva; e dopo alquanto disse: —

in which a lamp was burning, so that he began to observe and fix in his memory the layout of the room, the wall paintings, and every other noteworthy thing it contained.

Next, approaching the bed and seeing that the lady and a little girl who was with her were fast asleep, he uncovered her whole body and saw that she was as beautiful naked as when she was dressed, but found no mark that he could report on except one below her left breast, a mole around which grew a few little hairs as yellow as gold. Seeing this, he quietly covered her up again, even though, seeing how beautiful she was, he felt a yearning to risk his life and lie down beside her. Nevertheless, having heard she was rigid and severe when it came to such doings, he did not venture to do so; having remained in the room at his ease most of the night, he took a purse and a cloak out of a coffer, and a few rings and belts. Placing all of this in the chest, he climbed back into it himself and locked it as it was before. He behaved in this way for two nights without the lady noticing a thing.

When the third day arrived, the good woman came back for her chest in accordance with her instructions, and brought it back to its original location. Ambruogiuolo came out of it, paid the woman what he had promised her, and, as fast as he could, returned to Paris with those items before the deadline. There, calling together the merchants who had been present at the argument and bet, in the presence of Bernabò, he said that he had won their bet because he had made good his boast. As a proof that it was so, he first described the shape of the room and its paintings, and then displayed the items he had brought with him, affirming that he had received them from her.

Bernabò admitted that the room matched his description, and, in addition, that he recognized those items as really belonging to his wife. But he said that his opponent could have learned the appearance of the room from one of the servants, and could have procured the items in a similar manner; so that, if he had no more to say, he didn't think this was enough to declare him the winner.

And so Ambruogiuolo said: "Actually, this should be enough, but since you want me to say more, I will. I say that Monna Zinevra, your wife, has quite a sizable mole under her left breast and, around it, something like six little hairs as yellow as gold."

When Bernabò heard that, it was as if he had been stabbed in the heart, so great was the pain he felt. His face turned colors and, even though he had said not a word, he gave the clearest signs that what Ambruogiuolo had said was true. After a while he said: "Gentlemen,

Signori, ciò che Ambruogiuolo dice è vero, e per ciò, avendo egli vinto, venga qualor gli piace e sì si paghi.

E così fu il dì seguente Ambruogiuolo interamente pagato; e Bernabò, da Parigi partitosi, con fellone animo contro alla donna, verso Genova se ne venne. Ed appressandosi a quella, non volle in essa entrare, ma si rimase ben venti miglia lontano ad essa ad una sua possessione; ed un suo famigliare, in cui molto si fidava, con due cavalli e con sue lettere mandò a Genova, scrivendo alla donna come tornato era e che con lui a lui venisse; ed al famiglio segretamente impose che, come in parte fosse con la donna che miglior gli paresse, senza niuna misericordia la dovesse uccidere ed a lui tornarsene.

Giunto adunque il famigliare a Genova e date le lettere e fatta l'ambasciata, fu dalla donna con gran festa ricevuto; la quale la seguente mattina, montata col famigliare a cavallo, verso la sua possessione prese il cammino; e camminando insieme e di varie cose ragionando, pervennero in un vallone molto profondo e solitario e chiuso d'alte grotte e d'alberi; il quale parendo al famigliare luogo da dovere sicuramente per sé fare il comandamento del suo signore, tratto fuori il coltello e presa la donna per lo braccio, disse:

— Madonna, raccomandate l'anima vostra a Dio, ché a voi, senza passar più avanti, convien morire.

La donna, veggendo il coltello ed udendo le parole, tutta spaventata disse: — Mercé per Dio! anzi che tu m'uccida dimmi di che io t'ho offeso, che tu uccidermi debbi.

— Madonna, — disse il famigliare, — me non avete offeso d'alcuna cosa; ma di che voi offeso abbiate il vostro marito, io nol so, se non che egli mi comandò che, senza alcuna misericordia aver di voi, io in questo cammin v'uccidessi; e se io nol facessi, mi minacciò di farmi impiccar per la gola. Voi sapete bene quanto io gli son tenuto, e come io di cosa che egli m'imponga possa dir di no; sallo Iddio che di voi m'increscie, ma io non posso altro.

A cui la donna piagnendo disse: — Ahi mercé per Dio! non volere divenire micidiale di chi mai non t'offese, per servire altrui. Iddio, che tutto conosce, sa che io non feci mai cosa per la quale io dal mio marito debba così fatto merito ricevere. Ma lasciamo ora star questo; tu puoi, quando tu vogli, ad una ora piacere a Dio ed al tuo signore ed a me in questa maniera: che tu prenda questi miei panni, e donimi solamente il tuo farsetto ed un cappuccio, e con essi torni al mio e tuo signore, e dichi che tu m'abbi uccisa; ed io ti giuro per quella salute la quale tu donata m'avrai, che io mi

what Ambruogiuolo says is true, and so, since he has won, he may come and be paid whenever he likes."

And so, the next day Ambruogiuolo was paid in full; and Bernabò left Paris, filled with hatred for his wife, and traveled toward Genoa. Nearing the city, he didn't enter it but stayed some twenty miles outside it on an estate of his. He sent one of his servants, a man he had great trust in, to Genoa with two horses and a letter; he wrote to his wife that he had returned and that she should come to where he was along with the servant. To the servant he gave secret orders: on his way back with his mistress, in the place he found most suitable, he was to kill her without mercy and then return to him.

And so, when the servant had come to Genoa, handed over the letter, and delivered his message, he was received by the lady most heartily. The next morning she and the servant mounted their horses and headed for the estate; as they traveled together, talking about this and that, they reached a very deep, solitary glen shut in by high cliffs and trees. Since this looked to the servant like a place where he could carry out his master's orders at no risk to himself, he drew out his knife, took the lady by the arm, and said: "My lady, commend your soul to God, because, without proceeding any further, you must die."

The lady, seeing the knife and hearing those words, said in great fright: "Have mercy, for the love of God! Before you kill me, tell me what injury I've done to you to deserve your killing me!"

"My lady," said the servant, "you've done no injury to *me* at all; but you've done one to your husband—I don't know what—except that he ordered me to show you no mercy but to kill you on this journey; he threatened that, if I didn't do it, he would hang me. You know very well how obliged I am to him, so that I can't refuse any order of his. God knows I'm sorry for you, but I have no choice."

Weeping, the lady replied: "Ah, mercy, for God's sake! Don't become the murderer of someone who has never injured you, just to serve somebody else! God, who knows all things, knows that I've never done anything for which I deserve to receive such a reward from my husband. But enough of this! If you're willing, you can, at one and the same time, satisfy God, your master, and me, in this manner: take these clothes of mine, and give me only your doublet and a hooded cape; take the clothes to your master and mine, and say you've killed me. I swear, by that salvation you'll have given me, that I will

dileguerò ed andronne in parte che mai né a lui né a te né in queste contrade di me perverrà alcuna novella. Il famigliare, che mal volentieri l'uccidea, leggermente divenne pietoso; per che, presi i drappi suoi e datole un suo farsettaccio ed un cappuccio, e lasciatile certi denari li quali essa avea, pregandola che di quelle contrade si dileguasse, la lasciò nel vallone a pié ed andonne al signor suo, al quale disse che il suo comandamento non solamente era fornito, ma che il corpo di lei morta aveva tra parecchi lupi lasciato. Bernabò dopo alcun tempo se ne tornò a Genova, e saputosi il fatto, forte fu biasimato.

La donna, rimasa sola e sconsolata, come la notte fu venuta, contraffatta il più che poté, n'andò ad una villetta ivi vicina, e quivi, da una vecchia procacciato quello che le bisognava, racconciò il farsetto a suo dosso, e fattol corto, e fattosi della sua camicia un paio di pannilini ed i capelli tondutisi e trasformatasi tutta in forma d'un marinaro, verso il mare se ne venne, dove per ventura trovò un gentile uom catalano il cui nome era segner En Cararh, il quale d'una sua nave, la quale alquanto di quivi era lontana, in Alba già disceso era a rinfrescarsi ad una fontana; col quale entrata in parole, con lui s'acconciò per servidore, e salissene sopra la nave, faccendosi chiamare Sicuran da Finale. Quivi, di migliori panni rimesso in arnese dal gentile uomo, lo 'ncominciò a servir sì bene e sì acconciamente, che egli gli venne oltre modo a grado.

Avvenne ivi a non guari di tempo che questo Catalano con un suo carico navigò in Alessandria e portò certi falconi pellegrini al soldano, e presentòglile; al quale il soldano avendo alcuna volta dato mangiare e veduti i costumi di Sicurano che sempre a servir l'andava, e piaciutigli, al Catalano il domandò, e quegli, ancora che grave gli paresse, gliele lasciò.

Sicurano in poco di tempo non meno la grazia e l'amor del soldano acquistò, col suo bene adoperare, che quella del Catalano avesse fatto; per che in processo di tempo avvenne che, dovendosi in un certo tempo dell'anno, a guisa d'una fiera, fare una ragunanza di mercatanti e cristiani e saracini in Acri, la quale sotto la signoria del soldano era, ed acciò che i mercatanti e le mercatantìe sicure stessero, era il soldano sempre usato di mandarvi, oltre agli altri suoi uficiali, alcuno de'

disappear and go so far away that no word of me will ever reach him, you, or this part of the world."

The servant, who hadn't been eager to kill her, was easily moved to pity. And so, taking her rich garments, giving her a worn-out doublet of his and a hooded cape, and leaving her with the little money she had on her, he begged her to disappear from that region and he left her on foot in the glen. He rejoined his master, to whom he reported that not only had his orders been carried out, but that he had left her dead body in the midst of a pack of wolves. After some time, Bernabò returned to Genoa; when the incident became known, he was severely blamed for this.

When night fell, the lady, left alone and disconsolate, disguising herself as best she could, went to a little village nearby, where, receiving what she needed from an old woman, she altered the doublet to fit her and shortened it, made herself a pair of breeches out of her shift, cut her hair short, and changed her whole appearance into that of a sailor. She headed for the seacoast, where by good fortune she met at Alba[2] a Catalan gentleman named Senyor En[3] Cararh, who, once disembarked from a ship of his, a little distant from there, had gone to refresh himself at a spring. Entering into conversation with him, she hired herself out to him as a servant and boarded his ship, calling herself Sicurano from Finale.[4] There, fitted out with better clothes by that gentleman, "he" began to serve him so well and so elegantly that "he" found very great favor with him.

Not long afterward, this Catalan happened to sail to Alexandria with a cargo, bringing some peregrine falcons for the sultan and presenting them to him. The sultan, having invited him to meals several times, saw the fine manners of Sicurano, who always served him, took a liking to them, and asked the Catalan for "him." The Catalan, although it grieved him, let the sultan have "him."

Before very long, Sicurano won the favor and love of the sultan by his skillful service just as "he" had won the Catalan's. And so it occurred in the course of time that, an assembly of Christian and Saracen merchants, like a trade fair, being due to be held in Acre at a certain time of the year, and that city being under the sovereignty of the sultan, the sultan was always accustomed to send, among other officials, one of his dignitaries with a corps of guards in order to protect

---

[2]Possibly Albaro, now a suburb of Genoa on the road to Rapallo; or Albisola, near Savona. [3]In Catalan, *en* (feminine: *na*) is a term of respect, like *don* (*doña*) in Castilian. [4]On the Ligurian coast, near the Italian Riviera.

suoi grandi uomini con gente che alla guardia attendesse; nella quale bisogna, sopravvegnendo il tempo, diliberò di mandare Sicurano, il quale già ottimamente la linqua sapeva, e così fece.

Venuto adunque Sicurano in Acri signore e capitano della guardia de' mercatanti e della mercatantìa, e quivi bene e sollecitamente faccendo ciò che al suo uficio appartenea, ed andando da torno veggendo, e molti mercatanti e ciciliani e pisani e genovesi e viniziani ed altri italiani veggendovi, con loro volentieri si dimesticava per rimembranza della contrada sua.

Ora, avvenne tra l'altre volte che, essendo egli ad un fondaco di mercatanti viniziani smontato, gli vennero vedute, tra altre gioie, una borsa ed una cintura le quali egli prestamente riconobbe essere state sue, e maravigliossi; ma senza altra vista fare, piacevolmente domandò di cui fossero e se vendere si voleano. Era quivi venuto Ambruogiuolo da Piagenza con molta mercatantìa in su una nave di Viniziani; il quale, udendo che il capitano della guardia domandava di cui fossero, si trasse avanti e ridendo disse: — Messer, le cose son mie, e non le vendo, ma se elle vi piacciono, io le vi donerò volentieri.

Sicurano, veggendol ridere, suspicò non costui in alcuno atto l'avesse raffigurato; ma pur, fermo viso faccendo, disse: — Tu ridi forse perché vedi me uom d'arme andar domandando di queste cose feminili.

Disse Ambruogiuolo: — Messere, io non rido di ciò, ma rido del modo nel quale io le guadagnai.

A cui Sicuran disse: — Deh! se Iddio ti déa buona ventura, se egli non è disdicevole, diccelo come tu le guadagnasti.

— Messere, — disse Ambruogiuolo, — queste mi donò con alcuna altra cosa una gentil donna di Genova chiamata madonna Zinevra moglie di Bernabò Lomellin, una notte che io giacqui con lei, e pregommi che per suo amore io le tenessi. Ora, risi io per ciò che egli mi ricordò della sciocchezza di Bernabò, il quale fu di tanta follia, che mise cinquemila fiorin d'oro contro a mille che io la sua donna non recherei a' miei piaceri; il che io feci, e vinsi il pegno; ed egli, che più tosto sé della sua bestialità punir dovea che lei d'aver fatto quello che tutte le femine fanno, da Parigi a Genova tornandosene per quello che io abbia poi sentito, la fece uccidere.

Sicurano, udendo questo, prestamente comprese qual fosse la cagione dell'ira di Bernabò verso lei e manifestamente conobbe

the merchants and the merchandise. When the time came, he decided to entrust that task to Sicurano, who by this time knew the language perfectly; and so he did.

So Sicurano went to Acre as master and captain of the guards protecting the merchants and the merchandise. There "he" carried out the duties of his office well and conscientiously. On a tour of inspection, "he" saw many merchants from Sicily, Pisa, Genoa, Venice, and other places in Italy, and took pleasure in their company, fondly recalling "his" own native region.

Now, on one of these occasions, "he" happened to dismount at a warehouse[5] of Venetian merchants, where "he" saw, among other jewelry, a purse and a belt which "he" immediately recognized as having been "his." He was amazed at this, but, without changing "his" expression, "he" pleasantly asked whose they were and if they were for sale. Ambruogiuolo of Piacenza had come there with a lot of goods on a Venetian ship. When he heard that the captain of the guards was asking whose they were, he stepped forward and said with a smile: "Sir, the items are mine, and not for sale, but if you like them, I'll gladly make you a gift of them."

Sicurano, seeing him smile, was afraid he had somehow seen through the disguise; but, keeping "his" expression unchanged, "he" said: "Perhaps you are smiling because you see me, a warrior, asking about these women's things."

Ambruogiuolo said: "Sir, I'm not smiling about that, but about the way I acquired them."

Sicurano said: "Please—so may God give you good fortune!—if you don't mind, tell me how you acquired them."

"Sir," said Ambruogiuolo, "they were given to me, among other things, by a gentlewoman of Genoa called Monna Zinevra, the wife of Bernabò Lomellin, one night when I slept with her; she asked me to keep them for love of her. Now, I smiled because this reminded me of the folly of Bernabò, who was so foolish that he bet five thousand gold florins against a thousand that I wouldn't persuade his wife to do my will. I did and won the bet. And he, who should have punished himself for his own stupidity rather than his wife for doing what all women do, returned home from Paris to Genoa, from what I've heard, and had her killed."

Sicurano, hearing this, immediately understood the reason for Bernabò's anger at her and clearly realized that this man was the

---

[5]Or: "mercantile concession."

costui di tutto il suo male esser cagione; e seco pensò di non la-
sciargliene portare impunità. Mostrò adunque Sicurano d'aver
molto cara questa novella, ed artatamente prese con costui una
stretta dimestichezza, tanto che per gli suoi conforti Ambruogiuolo,
finita la fiera, con essolui e con ogni sua cosa se n'andò in
Alessandria, dove Sicurano gli fece fare un fondaco e misegli in
mano de' suoi denari assai; per che egli, util grande veggendosi, vi
dimorava volentieri.

Sicurano, sollecito a voler della sua innocenza far chiaro
Bernabò, mai non riposò infino a tanto che, con opera d'alcuni gran
mercatanti genovesi che in Alessandria erano, nuove cagioni
trovando, non l'ebbe fatto venire; il quale in assai povero stato essendo, ad alcun suo amico tacitamente il fece ricevere infino che
tempo gli paresse da quel fare che di fare intendea.

Aveva già Sicurano fatta raccontare ad Ambruogiuolo la novella
davanti al soldano, e fattone al soldano prender piacere; ma poi che
vide quivi Bernabò, pensando che alla bisogna non era da dare indugio, preso tempo convenevole, dal soldano impetrò che davanti
venir si facesse Ambruogliuolo e Bernabò, ed in presenza di
Bernabò, se agevolmente fare non si potesse, con severità da
Ambruogiuolo si traesse il vero come stato fosse quello di che egli
della moglie di Bernabò si vantava.

Per la qual cosa, Ambruogiuolo e Bernabò venuti, il soldano in
presenza di molti con rigido viso ad Ambruogiuol comandò che il
vero dicesse come a Bernabò vinti avesse cinquemilia fiorin d'oro;
e quivi era presente Sicurano, in cui Ambruogiuolo più avea di fidanza, il quale con viso troppo più turbato gli minacciava gravissimi
tormenti se nol dicesse. Per che Ambruogiuolo, da una parte e d'altra spaventato, ed ancora alquanto costretto, in presenza di
Bernabò e molti altri, niuna pena più aspettandone che la resti-
tuzione di fiorini cinquemilia d'oro e delle cose, chiaramente, come
stato era il fatto, narrò ogni cosa.

Ed avendo Ambruogiuol detto, Sicurano, quasi esecutore del
soldano in quello, rivolto a Bernabò, disse: — E tu che facesti per
questa bugia alla tua donna?

A cui Bernabò rispose: — Io, vinto dall'ira della perdita de' miei
denari e dall'onta della vergogna che mi parea avere ricevuta dalla
mia donna, la feci ad un mio famigliare uccidere, e secondo che egli
mi rapportò, ella fu prestamente divorata da molti lupi.

Queste cose così nella presenza del soldan dette e da lui tutte
udite ed intese, non sappiendo egli ancora a che Sicurano, che

cause of all her grief. She decided not to let him go unpunished for it. And so, Sicurano gave signs of enjoying that story very much, and artfully struck up a close acquaintance with him, so that, at "his" urging, when the fair was over Ambruogiuolo accompanied "him" with all his possessions to Alexandria. There Sicurano had a warehouse constructed for him and placed a lot of "his" own money in his hands; so that he was glad to reside there, in the expectation of great profits.

Sicurano, eager to prove "his" innocence to Bernabò, knew no rest until, with the aid of some wealthy Genoese merchants who were in Alexandria, "he" hit upon some novel pretexts and got him to come. Bernabò's fortunes were at a very low ebb, and Sicurano secretly had a friend of "his" take him in until "he" thought the time was ripe to do what "he" intended to do.

Sicurano had already made Ambruogiuolo tell his story in the presence of the sultan, and had made the sultan take pleasure in it. But, once "he" saw that Bernabò was there, "he" thought that the affair shouldn't be delayed. Choosing a suitable moment, "he" received the sultan's permission to bring both Ambruogiuolo and Bernabò before him. In Bernabò's presence, if "he" couldn't do it gently, "he" would use violence to get Ambruogiuolo to tell the truth about his boasted encounter with Bernabò's wife.

And so, when Ambruogiuolo and Bernabò had come, the sultan, with many people looking on, ordered Ambruogiuolo with a severe countenance to tell the truth about how he had won five thousand gold florins from Bernabò. Also present was Sicurano, in whom Ambruogiuolo placed most trust. With a face distorted by emotion, "he" threatened him with awful tortures if he didn't confess. And so Ambruogiuolo was frightened by both of them, and after a little more pressure was put on him, he clearly told the whole story, just as it had occurred, in the presence of Bernabò and many others, expecting no other punishment than being made to return the five thousand gold florins and the items he had taken.

When Ambruogiuolo had finished, Sicurano, acting like the sultan's representative in the matter, turned toward Bernabò and said: "And you, what did you do to your wife on account of that lie?"

Bernabò replied: "Overcome by anger at the loss of my money and the disgrace I thought I had received from my wife, I had her killed by a servant of mine, and, according to his report to me, she was immediately devoured by a pack of wolves."

When these things had thus been spoken in the presence of the sultan, and they had all been heard and understood by him, but he did not

questo ordinato avea e domandato, volesse riuscire, gli disse
Sicurano: — Signor mio, assai chiaramente potete conoscere
quanto quella buona donna gloriarsi possa d'amante e di marito;
ché l'amante ad una ora lei priva d'onor con bugie guastando la
fama sua e diserta il marito di lei, ed il marito, più credulo alle altrui falsità che alla verità da lui per lunga esperienza potuta
conoscere, la fa uccidere e mangiare a' lupi; ed oltre a questo, è
tanto il bene e l'amore che l'amico ed il marito le porta, che, con lei
lungamente dimorati, niun la conosce. Ma per ciò che voi ottimamente conoscete quello che ciascun di costoro ha meritato, ove voi
mi vogliate di spezial grazia fare di punire lo 'ngannatore e perdonare allo 'ngannato, io la farò qui in vostra ed in lor presenza
venire.

Il soldano disposto in questa cosa di volere in tutto compiacere a
Sicurano, disse che gli piacea e che facesse la donna venire.
Maravigliavasi forte Bernabò, il quale lei per fermo morta credea;
ed Ambruogiuolo, già del suo male indovino, di peggio avea paura
che di pagar denari, né sapea che si sperare o che più temere, perché quivi la donna venisse, ma più con maraviglia la sua venuta
aspettava.

Fatta adunque la concession dal soldano a Sicurano, esso, piagnendo ed inginocchion dinanzi al soldano gittatosi, quasi ad una
ora la maschil voce ed il più non volere maschio parere si partì, e
disse: — Signor mio, io sono la misera sventurata Zinevra, sei anni
andata tapinando in forma d'uom per lo mondo, da questo traditor
d'Ambruogiuolo falsamente e reamente vituperata, e da questo
crudele ed iniquo uomo data ad uccidere ad uno suo fante ed a
mangiare a' lupi.

E stracciando i panni dinanzi e mostrando il petto, sé esser femina
ed al soldano ed a ciascuno altro fece palese, rivolgendosi poi ad
Ambruogiuolo, ingiuriosamente domandandolo quando mai, secondo che egli avanti si vantava, con lei giaciuto fosse. Il quale, già
riconoscendola e per vergogna quasi mutolo divenuto, niente dicea.
Il soldano, il quale sempre per uomo avuta l'avea, questo veggendo
ed udendo, venne in tanta maraviglia, che più volte quello che egli
vedeva ed udiva credette più tosto esser sogno che vero.

Ma pur, poi che la maraviglia cessò, la verità conoscendo, con
somma laude la vita e la costanza ed i costumi e la vertù della
Zinevra, infino allora stata Sicuran chiamata, commendò. E fattile

yet know what Sicurano, who had arranged and requested this, was trying to accomplish, Sicurano said to him: "My lord, you can clearly see
how proud that good woman can be of her admirer and her husband!
For, at one and the same time, her admirer robs her of her honor with
lies, destroying her reputation, and ruins her husband; and the husband, more disposed to believe other people's false statements than the
truthfulness he had long had the occasion to recognize, has her killed
and eaten by wolves. Besides this, the love and affection that both the
lover and the husband feel for her are so great that neither one recog-
nizes her, even though they associate with her for a long time. But because you know perfectly well what each of them deserves, if you wish
to do me the great favor of punishing the deceiver and pardoning the
deceived, I shall have her brought here into your presence and theirs."

The sultan, willing to oblige Sicurano in every way in this matter,
said that he consented and that "he" should have the woman brought.
Bernabò, who was sure she was dead, was greatly amazed; and
Ambruogiuolo, already guessing his evil fate, was now afraid of worse
than having to repay the money; he didn't know whether he should be
hopeful or rather fearful because the woman was coming, but it was
mainly with amazement that he awaited her arrival.

And so, when the sultan had given his consent to Sicurano, and
"he," weeping, fell to "his" knees before the sultan, almost simultane-
ously "his" masculine voice and "his" desire to continue playing the
man vanished, and "he" said: "My lord, I am the unhappy and unfortunate Zinevra, who in misery has traveled all over in the guise of a
man for six years, falsely and criminally slandered by this villain
Ambruogiuolo, and handed over by this cruel and unjust man to be
killed by his servant and eaten by wolves."

And, tearing her clothes in front and showing her bosom, she made
it clear to the sultan and everybody else that she was a woman. Then,
addressing Ambruogiuolo, she asked him insultingly[6] when he had
ever slept with her, as he had boasted previously. Now recognizing her
and becoming nearly mute from shame, he said nothing. The sultan,
who had always taken her for a man, seeing and hearing this, was sunk
in such amazement that more than once he thought what he was seeing and hearing was rather a dream than reality.

But, when his amazement had worn off, in possession of the truth,
he lauded Zinevra's life, constancy, habits, and virtue with the highest
praise—Zinevra, who until then had been called Sicurano. He

---

[6]Or: "violently."

venire onorevolissimi vestimenti feminili e donne che compagnia le tenessero, secondo la domanda fatta da lei, a Bernabò perdonò la meritata morte; il quale, riconosciutala, a' piedi di lei si gittò piagnendo e domandò perdonanza, la quale ella, quantunque egli mal degno ne fosse, benignamente gli diede, ed in piede il fece levare, teneramente sì come suo marito abbracciandolo.

Il soldano appresso comandò che incontanente Ambruogiuolo in alcuno alto luogo nella città fosse al sole legato ad un palo ed unto di méle, né quindi mai, infino a tanto che per se medesimo non cadesse, levato fosse; e così fu fatto. Appresso questo, comandò che ciò che d'Ambruogiuolo stato era, fosse alla donna donato, che non era sì poco che oltre a diecemilia doble non valesse; ed egli, fatta apprestare una bellissima festa, in quella Bernabò come marito di madonna Zinevra, e madonna Zinevra sì come valorosissima donna onorò, e donolle, che in gioie e che in vasellamenti d'oro e d'ariento e che in denari, quello che valse meglio d'altre diecemilia doble.

E fatto loro apprestare un legno, poi che fatta fu la festa, gli licenziò di potersi tornare a Genova al lor piacere; dove ricchissimi e con grande allegrezza tornarono, e con sommo onore ricevuti furono, e spezialmente madonna Zinevra, la quale da tutti si credeva che morta fosse; e sempre di gran vertù e da molto, mentre visse, fu reputata.

Ambruogiuolo il dì medesimo che legato fu al palo ed unto di méle, con sua grandissima angoscia dalle mosche e dalle vespe e da' tafani, de' quali quel paese è copioso molto, fu non solamente ucciso, ma infino all'ossa divorato; le quali, bianche rimase ed a' nervi appiccate, poi lungo tempo, senza esser mosse, della sua malvagità fecero a chiunque le vide testimonianza. E così rimase lo 'ngannatore a pié dello 'ngannato.

GILETTA DI NARBONA [III, 9]

Restava, non volendo il suo privilegio rompere a Dionèo, solamente a dire alla reina, con ciò fosse cosa che già finita fosse la novella di Lauretta; per la qual cosa essa, senza aspettar d'esser sollecitata da' suoi, così tutta vaga cominciò a parlare:

Chi dirà novella omai che bella paia, avendo quella di Lauretta udita? Certo vantaggio ne fu che ella non fu la primiera, ché poche poi dell'altre ne sarebbon piaciute, e così spero che avverrà di quelle che per questa giornata sono a raccontare. Ma pure, chente

ordered very elegant feminine attire to be brought to her and women to wait on her; and, in compliance with her request, he pardoned Bernabò, who had deserved death. Bernabò, recognizing her, threw himself at her feet, weeping and imploring forgiveness; and she, even though he scarcely deserved it, kindly granted it, and, having him raised to his feet, she embraced him tenderly as her husband.

Next, the sultan ordered Ambruogiuolo to be taken at once to some high place in the city, tied to a stake in the sunshine, and smeared with honey; he was not to be taken away until he collapsed spontaneously; and so it was done. After that, he ordered that what Ambruogiuolo had possessed should be given to the lady; this was so valuable that it was worth over ten thousand doubloons. Having a splendid feast prepared, at which he honored Bernabò as Monna Zinevra's husband, and Monna Zinevra as a woman of great worth, he gave her, partly in jewelry, partly in gold and silver plate, and partly in cash, the equivalent of more than another ten thousand doubloons.

And having a ship made ready for them, after the feast was held, he gave them permission to return to Genoa whenever they liked. They returned there wealthy and most joyful, received with the highest honors, especially Monna Zinevra, who was thought by everyone to be dead. As long as she lived, she was reputed to be highly virtuous and was greatly esteemed.

On the very day that Ambruogiuolo was tied to the stake and smeared with honey, suffering very great tortures, he was not merely killed, but devoured to the bones by the flies, wasps, and gadflies which are so abundant in that land. His bones, having whitened but still attached to the tendons, weren't removed, and for a long time they gave evidence of his viciousness to all who saw them. And thus the man who deceived fell at the feet of the one he deceived.

GILLETTE OF NARBONNE [III, 9]

Not wishing to infringe Dioneo's right (to tell the last story of the day), only the "Queen" had yet to speak, seeing that Lauretta's story was already finished. And so, without waiting to be coaxed by her friends, with great eagerness she began:

Having heard Lauretta's story, who can now tell one that will seem beautiful? It was surely lucky that she wasn't the first to speak, for then not many of the other stories would have been found pleasing. And I fear that will happen with those still to be told today. All the

che ella si sia, quella che alla proposta materia m'occorre vi conterò.

Nel reame di Francia fu un gentile uomo il quale chiamato fu Isnardo, conte di Rossiglione, il quale, per ciò che poco sano era, sempre appresso di sé teneva un medico chiamato maestro Gerardo di Nerbona. Aveva il detto conte un suo figliuol piccolo senza più, chiamato Beltramo, il quale era bellissimo e piacevole, e con lui altri fanciulli della sua età s'allevavano, tra' quali era una fanciulla del detto medico chiamata Giletta, la quale infinito amore ed oltre al convenevole della tenera età fervente, pose a questo Beltramo.

Al quale, morto il conte e lui nelle mani del re lasciato, ne convenne andare a Parigi, di che la giovinetta fieramente rimase sconsolata; e non guari appresso essendosi il padre di lei morto, se o-nesta cagione avesse potuta avere, volentieri a Parigi per vedere Beltramo sarebbe andata, ma essendo molto guardata, per ciò che ricca e sola era rimasta, onesta via non vedea. Ed essendo ella già d'età da marito, non avendo mai potuto Beltramo dimenticare, molti, a' quali i suoi parenti l'avevan voluta maritare, rifiutati n'avea senza la cagion dimostrare.

Ora, avvenne che, ardendo ella dell'amor di Beltramo più che mai, per ciò che bellissimo giovane udiva che era divenuto, le venne sentita una novella, come al re di Francia, per una nascenza che avuta avea nel petto ed era male stata curata, gli era rimasa una fistola la quale di grandissima noia e di grandissima angoscia gli era, né s'era ancor potuto trovar medico, come che molti se ne fossero esperimentati, che di ciò l'avesse potuto guerire, ma tutti l'avean peggiorato; per la qual cosa il re disperatosene, più d'alcun non volea né consiglio né aiuto. Di che la giovane fu oltre modo contenta, e pensossi non solamente per questo aver legittima cagione d'andare a Parigi, ma, se quella infermità fosse che ella credeva, leggermente poterle venir fatto d'aver Beltramo per marito.

Laonde, sì come colei che già dal padre aveva assai cose apprese, fatta sua polvere di certe erbe utili a quella infermità che avvisava che fosse, montò a cavallo ed a Parigi n'andò. Né prima altro fece che ella s'ingegnò di veder Beltramo, ed appresso nel cospetto del re venuta, di grazia chiese che la sua infermità le mostrasse. Il re, veggendola bella giovane ed avvenente, non gliele seppe disdire, e mostrògliele. Come costei l'ebbe veduta, così incontanente si confortò di doverlo guerire, e disse: — Monsignore, quando vi piaccia, senza alcuna noia o fatica di voi, io ho speranza in Dio d'avervi in otto giorni di questa infermità renduto sano.

same, whatever the quality of my story, I shall tell you what came to my mind when I heard the announced theme of the day.

In the kingdom of France there was a gentleman named Isnard, Count of Roussillon, who, because his health was poor, always kept at his side a doctor named Master Gérard of Narbonne. The aforesaid count had a very young son, his only child, named Bertrand, who was very good-looking and charming. With him were raised other children of his own age, among whom was a daughter of the aforesaid doctor, named Gillette. She loved this Bertrand with a mighty love, a love more passionate than befitted her tender years.

When the count died and Bertrand was left as a ward of the king, he was compelled to move to Paris; this left the girl deeply disconsolate. Not long afterward, when her father died, she would gladly have gone to Paris to see Bertrand, had she found some decent pretext; but she was closely guarded because she was wealthy and alone in the world, and she couldn't find an honorable way to do so. When she was of marriageable age, and had never been able to forget Bertrand, she refused many men whom her relatives had wanted her to marry, and she never gave a reason.

Now, loving Bertrand more ardently than ever because she heard he had become an extremely handsome young man, she happened to learn that the king of France, because of a growth he had had in his chest which was improperly treated, had developed a fistula that gave him the greatest annoyance and pain; he had not yet been able to find a doctor who could cure him of it, even though many had tried their hand at it, all of them leaving him even worse off; so that the king, in despair, no longer wanted anyone's advice or aid. The young woman was very pleased to hear this, thinking that it gave her a legitimate reason to go to Paris; what's more, if that illness was what she thought it was, she could easily manage to win Bertrand for her husband.

Whereupon, having in the past learned many things from her father, she made a powder of certain herbs effective for the illness she took the king's to be, mounted a horse, and rode to Paris. The first thing she did was to contrive to get a sight of Bertrand. Next, coming before the king, she asked him to deign to show her his sore spot. The king, seeing she was a beautiful and attractive girl, couldn't refuse, and showed it to her. When she saw it, she was immediately sure she could cure him, and she said: "Sire, whenever you please, with no trouble or annoyance to you, I have hopes, with God's help, of curing you of this illness in a week."

Il re si fece in se medesimo beffe delle parole di costei, dicendo:
— Quello che i maggior medici del mondo non hanno potuto né saputo, una giovane femina come il potrebbe sapere? — Ringraziolla
adunque della sua buona volontà e rispose che proposto avea seco
di più consiglio di medico non seguire; a cui la giovane disse:
— Monsignore, voi schifate la mia arte perché giovane e femina
sono, ma io vi ricordo che io non medico con la mia scienza, anzi
con l'aiuto di Dio e con la scienza del maestro Gerardo nerbonese,
il quale mio padre fu e famoso medico mentre visse.

Il re allora disse seco: — Forse m'è costei mandata da Dio; perché non pruovo io ciò che ella sa fare, poi dice senza noia di me in
piccol tempo guerirmi? — Ed accordatosi di provarlo, disse: —
Damigella, e se voi non ci guerite, faccendoci rompere il nostro
proponimento, che volete voi che ve ne segua?

— Monsignore, — rispose la giovane, — fatemi guardare, e se io
infra otto giorni non vi guerisco, fatemi bruciare. Ma se io vi
guerisco, che merito me ne seguirà?

A cui il re rispose: — Voi ne parete ancora senza marito; se ciò
farete, noi vi mariteremo bene ed altamente.

Al quale la giovane disse: — Monsignore, veramente mi piace
che voi mi maritiate, ma io voglio un marito tale quale io il vi do-
manderò, senza dovervi domandare alcun de' vostri figliuoli o della
casa reale.

Il re tantosto le promise di farlo. La giovane cominciò la sua
medicina ed in brieve anzi il termine l'ebbe condotto a sanità; di
che il re, guerito sentendosi, disse: — Damigella, voi avete ben
guadagnato il marito.

A cui ella rispose: — Adunque, monsignore, ho io guadagnato
Beltramo di Rossiglione, il quale infino nella mia puerizia io co-
minciai ad amare ed ho poi sempre sommamente amato.

Gran cosa parve al re dovergliele dare; ma poi che promesso
l'avea, non volendo della sua fé mancare, sel fece chiamare e sì gli
disse: — Beltramo, voi siete omai grande e fornito; noi vogliamo
che voi torniate a governare il vostro contado e con voi ne meniate
una damigella la quale noi v'abbiamo per moglier data.

Disse Beltramo: — E chi è la damigella, monsignore?

A cui il re rispose: — Ella è colei la quale n'ha con le sue medicine sanità renduta.

Beltramo, il quale la conoscea e veduta l'avea, quantunque molto
bella gli paresse, conoscendo lei non esser di legnaggio che alla sua
nobiltà bene stesse, tutto sdegnoso disse: — Monsignore, adunque

In his mind the king heaped scorn on her words, saying: "How can a young woman know what to do with something that the greatest doctors in the world have been unable to handle?" And so he thanked her for her kind wishes, but replied that he had resolved not to take any doctor's advice henceforth. The young woman replied:

"Sire, you look down on my skill because I'm young and a woman, but I remind you that I don't cure with my own knowledge but with the aid of God and the knowledge of Master Gérard of Narbonne, who was my father and a famous doctor while he was alive."

Then the king said to himself: "Perhaps she has been sent to me by God. Why shouldn't I try out her knowledge, since she says she'll cure me without trouble to me and in a brief period?" And, consenting to try it out, he said: "Young lady, in case you don't cure us, after you've made us break our resolution, what would you want us to do to you?"

"Sire," the young woman replied, "have me kept under guard, and if I don't cure you in a week, have me burned. But if I cure you, what reward will I get?"

The king replied: "It seems you are still unmarried. If you succeed, we shall give you a worthy husband of high rank."

The young woman replied: "Sire, I am truly pleased that you will arrange a marriage for me, but I want the husband that I will designate, although I assure you I won't ask for one of your sons or anyone in the royal family."

The king immediately promised her that. The young woman began her cure and quickly, before the deadline, she restored him to health. And so the king, finding himself cured, said: "Young lady, you have earned your husband well."

She replied: "In that case, sire, I have earned Bertrand of Roussillon, whom I started loving while still a child and whom I have loved mightily ever since."

The king was very reluctant to give him to her, but, since he had promised, he didn't want to break his word; he had him summoned and said to him: "Bertrand, you're now a fully grown and educated man. We want you to go back and govern your county, and to take with you a young lady whom we have given you as a wife."

Bertrand said: "And who is the young lady, sire?"

The king replied: "She is the woman who restored my health with her medicines."

Bertrand, who knew her and had seen her, found her very beautiful, but knowing she was not of a descent befitting his own noble lineage, became very angry and said: "And so, sire, you want me to marry

mi volete voi dar medica per mogliere? Già a Dio non piaccia che io sì fatta femina prenda già mai.

A cui il re disse: — Adunque volete voi che noi vegnamo meno di nostra fede, la qual noi per riaver sanità donammo alla damigella che voi in guiderdon di ciò domandò per marito?

— Monsignore, — disse Beltramo, — voi mi potete tôrre quanto io tengo, e donarmi, sì come vostro uomo, a chi vi piace; ma di questo vi rendo sicuro, che mai io non sarò di tal maritaggio contento.

— Sì sarete, — disse il re, — per ciò che la damigella è bella e savia ed àmavi molto; per che speriamo che molto più lieta vita con lei avrete che con una dama di più alto legnaggio non avreste.

Beltramo si tacque, ed il re fece fare l'apparecchio grande per la festa delle nozze; e venuto il giorno a ciò diterminato, quantunque Beltramo mal volentieri il facesse, nella presenza del re la damigella sposò che più che sé l'amava. E questo fatto, come colui che seco già pensato avea quello che far dovesse, dicendo che al suo contado tornarsi volea e quivi consumare il matrimonio, chiese commiato al re; e montato a cavallo, non nel suo contado se n'andò, ma se ne venne in Toscana. E saputo che i Fiorentini guerreggiavano co' Sanesi, ad essere in lor favor si dispose; dove lietamente ricevuto e con onore, fatto di certa quantità di gente capitano e da loro avendo buona provvisione, al loro servigio si rimase e fu buon tempo.

La novella sposa, poco contenta di tal ventura, sperando di doverlo, per suo bene operare, rivocare al suo contado, se ne venne a Rossiglione, dove da tutti come lor donna fu ricevuta. Quivi trovando ella, per lo lungo tempo che senza conte stato v'era, ogni cosa guasta e scapestrata, sì come savia donna, con gran diligenza e sollecitudine ogni cosa rimise in ordine; di che i suggetti si contentaron molto e lei ebbero molto cara e pòserle grande amore, forte biasimando il conte di ciò che egli di lei non si contentava.

Avendo la donna tutto racconcio il paese, per due cavalieri al conte il significò, pregandolo che, se per lei stesse di non venire al suo contado, gliele significasse ed ella per compiacergli si partirebbe; alli quali esso durissimo disse: — Di questo faccia ella il piacer suo; io per me vi tornerò allora ad esser con lei che ella questo anello avrà in dito ed in braccio figliuolo di me acquistato. — Egli avea l'anello assai caro, né mai da sé il partiva, per alcuna vertù che stato gli era dato ad intendere che egli avea.

I cavalieri intesero la dura condizione posta nelle due quasi

a lady doctor? May it never please God to see me accept a woman of that sort!"

The king replied: "And so you want us to break our word, which we gave the young lady to regain our health, she having asked for your hand as a reward?"

"Sire," said Bertrand, "you can take away everything I own, and, since I am your liege man, give me to anyone you like; but I assure you of this: I will never be pleased with such a marriage."

"Yes, you will be," said the king, "because the young lady is beautiful and learned and deeply in love with you, so that we expect you will have a much happier life with her than you would with a lady of nobler descent."

Bertrand fell silent, and the king made lavish arrangements for the wedding banquet. When the day set for it came, Bertrand, though unwillingly, in the presence of the king married the young lady who loved him better than she loved herself. After this, having already planned what he needed to do, he said he wanted to return to his county and consummate the marriage there; and he asked the king for permission to depart. Mounting a horse, he rode, not to his own county but to Tuscany. Learning that the Florentines were waging war against the Sienese, he decided to fight on their side. He was accepted gladly and with honors, and made captain of a certain number of men. Receiving a good salary from them, he long remained in their service.

The new bride, very unhappy with that turn of events, hoped that by suitable actions on her part she could bring him back to his county. She went to Roussillon, where she was accepted by all as their lady. There she found everything in a state of ruin and disorder because the land had been without its count for so long, and, being a learned woman, with great diligence and care she set everything to rights again. Her subjects were very pleased by this, held her in great esteem, and gave her their genuine love, severely blaming the count for being displeased with her.

After the lady had regulated all local affairs, she sent two knights to the count to inform him about it, asking him to let her know if she was the obstacle to his returning to his county, in which case she would leave to please him. His reply to them was most harsh: "Let her do what she likes about that; for my part, I'll only go back there to be with her when she has this ring on her finger and in her arms a child begotten by me." He was extremely attached to that ring and never took it off because of a certain magic property it had, as he had been given to understand.

The knights understood what difficult terms he had stated by

impossibili cose, e veggendo che per loro parole dal suo proponimento nol potevan muovere, si tornarono alla donna e la sua
risposta le raccontarono; la quale, dolorosa molto, dopo lungo pensiero diliberò di voler sapere se quelle due cose potessero venir fatte
dove che fosse, acciò che per conseguente il marito suo riavesse.

Ed avendo quello che far dovesse avvisato, ragunati una parte de'
maggiori e de' migliori uomini del suo contado, loro assai ordinatamente e con pietose parole raccontò ciò che già fatto avea per amor
del conte, e mostrò quello che di ciò seguiva, ed ultimamente disse
che sua intenzion non era che, per la sua dimora quivi, il conte
stesse in perpetuo esilio, anzi intendeva di consumare il rimanente
della sua vita in pellegrinaggi ed in servigi misericordiosi per salute
dell'anima sua; e pregògli che la guardia ed il governo del contado
prendessero, ed al conte significassero, lei avergli vacua ed espedita
lasciata la possessione, e dileguatasi con intenzione di mai in
Rossiglione non tornare.

Quivi, mentre ella parlava, furon lagrime sparte assai da' buoni
uomini ed a lei pòrti molti prieghi che le piacesse di mutar consiglio e di rimanere; ma niente montarono. Essa, accomandàti loro
a Dio, con un suo cugino e con una sua cameriera, in abito di pellegrini, ben forniti a denari e care gioie, senza sapere alcuno ove
ella s'andasse, entrò in cammino, né mai ristette sì fu in Firenze; e
quivi per ventura in uno alberghetto il quale una buona donna vedova teneva, pianamente a guisa di povera pellegrina si stava,
disiderosa di sentir novelle del suo signore.

Avvenne dunque che il seguente dì ella vide davanti all'albergo
passare Beltramo a cavallo con sua compagnia, il quale quantunque
ella molto ben conoscesse, nondimeno domandò la buona donna
dell'albergo chi egli fosse. A cui l'albergatrice rispose: — Questi è
un gentile uom forestiere il quale si chiama il conte Beltramo,
piacevole e cortese e molto amato in questa città; ed è il più innamorato uom del mondo d'una nostra vicina, la quale è gentil
femina, ma è povera. Vero è che onestissima giovane è, e per
povertà non si marita ancora, ma con una sua madre, savissima e
buona donna, si sta; e forse, se questa sua madre non fosse, avrebbe
ella già fatto di quello che a questo conte fosse piaciuto.

La contessa queste parole intendendo, raccolse bene; e più trita-
mente esaminando venendo ogni particolarità e bene ogni cosa
compresa, formò il suo consiglio; ed apparata la casa ed il nome
della donna e della sua figliuola dal conte amata, un giorno tacitamente, in abito pellegrino, là se n'andò, e la donna e la sua figliuola

requiring these two nearly impossible conditions, and, seeing that their words were unable to change his resolve, they returned to their lady and reported his answer. She, in great sorrow, after long deliberation determined to try and see whether those two conditions could possibly be met, so that as a result she could get her husband back.

And having perceived what she needed to do, she gathered together some of the foremost and best men in her county, told them, in proper sequence and with heartfelt words, what she had already done out of love for the count, and showed what the result of it was. She concluded by saying that she didn't intend to keep the count in permanent banishment by remaining there herself; on the contrary, she intended to spend the rest of her life in pilgrimages and charitable works for the salvation of her soul. And she asked them to take over the defense and the government of the county, and to inform the count that she had left him in free and untrammeled possession of it, and had disappeared with the intention of never returning to Roussillon.

In that place, while she spoke, many tears were shed by those good men, and many requests made of her to deign to change her mind and stay; but they accomplished nothing. She commended them to God and, along with a male cousin and a maid, all dressed as pilgrims, well stocked with money and valuable jewels, she set out, telling no one where she was going; and she never stopped till she reached Florence. There, humbly disguised as a poor pilgrim, by good fortune she stayed at a little inn run by a kindly widow, and anxiously awaited news of her lord.

And so, the next day, she happened to see Bertrand riding past the inn with his company. Even though she recognized him perfectly, she asked her kind landlady who he was. The innkeeper replied: "That is a foreign nobleman called Count Bertrand, friendly and courteous and well loved in this city; and he's as much in love as any man can be with a neighbor of ours who's a gentlewoman, but poor. To tell the truth, she's a most respectable girl, and isn't married yet because of her poverty, but lives with her mother, a very wise and good woman. Perhaps, if it weren't for that mother of hers, she'd already have given that count what he wants of her."

Hearing these words, the countess paid careful heed to them; examining every detail more closely and understanding the whole situation, she laid her plans. Learning the house and the name of the woman and her daughter whom the count loved, one day she went there secretly in her pilgrim's attire. Finding mother and daughter

trovate assai poveramente, salutatele, disse alla donna che, quando le piacesse, le volea parlare.

La gentil donna, levatasi, disse che apparecchiata era d'udirla; ed entratesene sole in una sua camera e postesi a sedere, cominciò la contessa: — Madonna, el mi pare che voi siate delle nemiche della fortuna come sono io, ma dove voi voleste, per avventura voi potreste voi e me consolare.

La donna rispose che niuna cosa disiderava quanto di consolarsi onestamente. Seguì la contessa: — A me bisogna la vostra fede, nella quale se io mi rimetto e voi m'ingannaste, voi guastereste i vostri fatti ed i miei.

— Sicuramente — disse la gentil donna — ogni cosa che vi piace mi dite, ché mai da me non vi troverete ingannata.

Allora la contessa, cominciatasi dal suo primo innamoramento, chi ella era e ciò che intervenuto l'era infino a quel giorno le raccontò per sì fatta maniera, che la gentil donna, dando fede alle sue parole, sì come quella che già in parte udite l'aveva da altrui, cominciò di lei ad aver compassione. E la contessa, i suoi casi raccontati, seguì: — Udite adunque avete tra l'altre mie noie quali sieno quelle due cose che aver mi convenga se io voglio avere il mio marito, le quali niuna altra persona conosco che farlemi possa avere se non voi, se quello è vero che io intendo, cioè che il conte mio marito sommamente ami vostra figliuola.

A cui la gentil donna disse: — Madonna, se il conte ama mia figliuola io nol so, ma egli ne fa gran sembianti; ma che posso io per ciò in questo adoperare che voi disiderate?

— Madonna, — rispose la contessa, — io il vi dirò; ma primieramente vi voglio mostrar quello che io voglio che ve ne segua, dove voi mi serviate. Io veggio vostra figliuola bella e grande da marito, e per quello che io abbia inteso e comprender mi paia, il non aver ben da maritarla la vi fa guardare in casa. Io intendo che, in merito del servigio che mi farete, di darle prestamente de' miei denari quella dote che voi medesima a maritarla onorevolmente stimerete che sia convenevole.

Alla donna, sì come bisognosa, piacque la profferta, ma, tuttavia avendo l'animo gentil, disse: — Madonna, ditemi quello che io possa per voi operare, e se egli sarà onesto a me, io il farò volentieri, e voi appresso farete quello che vi piacerà.

Disse allora la contessa: — A me bisogna che voi per alcuna persona di cui voi vi fidiate, facciate al conte mio marito dire che vostra figliuola sia presta a fare ogni suo piacere, dove ella possa esser

living in very straitened circumstances, she greeted them and told the mother that she wanted to speak to her whenever the mother liked.

The gentlewoman rose and said she was ready to hear her out. They entered a room alone and sat down, and the countess began: "My lady, it seems as if fortune is as hostile to you as it is to me, but if you wished, you might be able to console both of us."

The woman replied that she desired nothing better than to receive honorable comfort. The countess went on: "I need your complete fidelity; if I rely on you and you deceive me, you'd spoil your chances and mine."

The gentlewoman said: "Tell me whatever you like without fear, for you will never find yourself deceived by me."

Then the countess, beginning with the first moment she fell in love, told her who she was and what had happened to her up to that day; she did this in such a way that the gentlewoman, believing her words—for she had already heard part of the story from others—began to take pity on her. And, after the countess had told her adventures, she continued: "And so, among my other causes of distress, you've heard what two things I must have if I'm to win my husband. I don't know anyone who can help me get them except you, if what I hear is true: namely, that my husband the count is deeply in love with your daughter."

The gentlewoman replied: "My lady, I don't know whether the count loves my daughter, but he certainly acts as if he did. But what can I do to help you in this matter because of his love?"

"My lady," the countess replied, "I'll tell you. But first I want to tell you what will follow for you if you assist me. I see that your daughter is beautiful and old enough to be married, and, from what I've heard and think I understand, you keep her at home because you don't have enough money for a marriage. As a reward for the services you will render me, I intend to give her immediately from my funds whatever dowry you yourself deem suitable in order to marry her off honorably."

The woman, being in such straits, was pleased with the offer, but, being so nobleminded, she said: "My lady, tell me what I can do for you, and if I consider it honorable, I'll do it gladly, and then you can do what you like."

Then the countess said: "What I need is for you to send someone you trust to my husband the count to say that your daughter is ready to grant all his wishes, if she can be certain that he loves her as much

certa che egli così l'ami come dimostra, il che ella non crederà mai, se egli non le manda l'anello il quale egli porta in mano e che ella ha udito che egli ama cotanto; il quale se egli vi manda, voi mi donerete; ed appresso gli manderete a dire, vostra figliuola essere apparecchiata di fare il piacer suo, e qui il farete occultamente venire e nascosamente me in iscambio di vostra figliuola gli metterete allato. Forse mi farà Iddio grazia d'ingravidare; e così appresso, avendo il suo anello in dito ed il figliuolo in braccio da lui generato, io il racquisterò e con lui dimorerò come moglie dée dimorar con marito, essendone voi stata cagione.

Gran cosa parve questa alla gentil donna, temendo non forse biasimo ne seguisse alla figliuola; ma pur, pensando che onesta cosa era il dare opera che la buona donna riavesse il suo marito e che essa ad onesto fine a far ciò si mettea, nella sua buona ed onesta affezion confidandosi, non solamente di farlo promise alla contessa, ma infra pochi giorni con segreta cautela, secondo l'ordine dato da lei, ed ebbe l'anello, quantunque gravetto paresse al conte, e lei in iscambio della figliuola a giacer col conte maestrevolmente mise.

Ne' quali primi congiugnimenti affettuosissimamente dal conte cercati, come fu piacer di Dio, la donna ingravidò in due figliuoli maschi, come il parto al suo tempo venuto fece manifesto. Né solamente d'una volta contentò la gentil donna la contessa degli abbracciamenti del marito, ma molte, sì segretamente operando, che mai parola non se ne seppe; credendosi sempre il conte, non con la moglie, ma con colei la quale egli amava essere stato. A cui, quando a partir si venìa la mattina, avea parecchie belle e care gioie donate, le quali tutte diligentemente la contessa guardava.

La quale, sentendosi gravida non volle più la gentil donna gravare di tal servigio, ma le disse: — Madonna, la Dio mercé e la vostra, io ho ciò che io disiderava, e per ciò tempo è che per me si faccia quello che v'aggraderà, acciò che io poi me ne vada.

La gentil donna le disse che, se ella aveva cosa che l'aggradisse, che le piaceva, ma che ciò ella non avea fatto per alcuna speranza di guiderdone, ma perché le pareva doverlo fare a voler ben fare. A cui la contessa disse: — Madonna, questo mi piace bene; e così, d'altra parte, io non intendo di donarvi quello che voi mi domanderete, per guiderdone, ma per far bene, ché mi pare che si debba così fare.

La gentil donna allora, da necessità costretta, con grandissima vergogna cento lire le domandò per maritar la figliuola. La contessa, conoscendo la sua vergogna ed udendo la sua cortese

as he makes out; but she'll never believe it unless he sends her the ring he wears on his finger, which she has heard he is so attached to. If he sends it to you, you'll give it to me. Then you'll send word to him that your daughter is all set to do his pleasure; you'll arrange for him to come here secretly, and surreptitiously you'll put me in bed with him in place of your daughter. Perhaps God will give me the grace to conceive; and so, afterwards, with his ring on my finger and a child begotten by him in my arms, I'll win him back and live with him the way a wife should live with her husband, and all thanks to you."

The gentlewoman was reluctant to do this, fearing that blame might attach to her daughter; but, thinking it was an honorable thing to help that good lady win back her husband, and that she was undertaking this with an honorable purpose, trusting in her good and honorable affection, she not only promised the countess to do it, but a few days later, using secrecy and caution, she followed the countess's instructions, securing the ring, even though the count found it a little hard to part with it, and skillfully putting the countess in bed with the count in place of her daughter.

In those first trysts lovingly sought by the count, as it pleased God the lady conceived two boys, as their birth made clear when it occurred. Nor did the gentlewoman give the countess the pleasure of her husband's embraces only once, but several times, acting so prudently that no one ever heard a thing about it. The whole time, the count thought he had been not with his wife, but with the girl he loved. When he departed in the mornings, he left a number of beautiful and valuable jewels as gifts; all of these the countess carefully kept.

Aware that she was pregnant, she no longer wished to burden the gentlewoman with that service, and said to her: "My lady, thanks to God and to you, I have what I wanted, and so it's time for me to do something pleasurable for you, and then to go away."

The gentlewoman replied that, if the countess had anything that would give her pleasure, she was glad of it, but she hadn't done this with any hope of reward, but had felt she ought to do it as something proper. The countess replied: "My lady, I'm glad to hear that; and, similarly I'm not going to give you what you ask me for as if it were a reward, but as something proper, because I think it's what should be done."

Then the gentlewoman, compelled by necessity, but feeling great shame, asked her for a hundred *lire* to marry off her daughter. The countess, sensing her shame and hearing her courteous request, gave

domanda, ne le donò cinquecento e tanti belli e cari gioielli, che valeano per avventura altrettanto; di che la gentil donna vie più che contenta, quelle grazie che maggior poté alla contessa rendé, la quale, da lei partitasi, se ne tornò all'albergo.

La gentil donna, per tôrre materia a Beltramo di più né mandar né venire a casa sua, insieme con la figliuola se n'andò in contado a casa di suoi parenti; e Beltramo ivi a poco tempo, da' suoi uomini richiamato, a casa sua, udendo che la contessa s'era dileguata, se ne tornò. La contessa, sentendo lui di Firenze partito e tornato nel suo contado, fu contenta assai; e tanto in Firenze dimorò, che il tempo del parto venne, e partorì due figliuoli maschi simigliantissimi al padre loro, e quegli fe' diligentemente nudrire.

E quando tempo le parve, in cammino messasi senza essere da alcuna persona conosciuta, a Monpulier se ne venne; e quivi più giorni riposata, e del conte e dove fosse avendo spiato, e sentendo lui il dì d'ognissanti in Rossiglione dover fare una gran festa di donne e di cavalieri, pure in forma di pellegrina come uscita n'era, là se n'andò.

E sentendo le donne ed i cavalieri nel palagio del conte adunati per dovere andare a tavola, senza mutare abito, con questi suoi figlioletti in braccio salita in su la sala, tra uomo ed uomo là se n'andò dove il conte vide, e gittataglisi a' piedi, disse piagnendo: — Signor mio, io sono la tua sventurata sposa, la quale, per lasciar te tornare e stare in casa tua, lungamente andata son tapinando. Io ti richeggio per Dio che le condizion postemi per li due cavalieri che lo ti mandai, tu me l'osservi: ed ecco nelle mie braccia non un sol figliuolo di te, ma due, ed ecco qui il tuo anello. Tempo è adunque che io debba da te sì come moglie esser ricevuta secondo la tua promessa.

Il conte, udendo questo, tutto misvenne, e riconobbe l'anello ed i figliuoli ancora, sì simili erano a lui; ma pur disse: — Come può questo esser intervenuto?

La contessa, con maraviglia del conte e di tutti gli altri che presenti erano, ordinatamente ciò che stato era e come, raccontò; per la qual cosa il conte, conoscendo lei dire il vero e veggendo la sua perseveranza ed il suo senno, ed appresso due così be' figlioletti, e per servar quello che promesso avea e per compiacere a tutti i suoi uomini ed alle donne, che tutti pregavano che lei come sua legittima sposa dovesse omai accogliere ed onorare, pose giù la sua o-stinata gravezza ed in pié fece levar la contessa, e lei abbracciò e baciò e per sua legittima moglie riconobbe, e quegli per suoi

her five hundred, as well as beautiful and valuable jewels that were perhaps worth the same amount; so that the gentlewoman, more than satisfied, thanked the countess to the best of her ability. The countess, taking leave of her, returned to the inn.

The gentlewoman, to give Bertrand no further reason to send her messages or visit her, departed for the country, to a house belonging to relatives. Soon afterward Bertrand was called back by his liege men and, hearing that the countess had disappeared, he returned home. The countess, learning that he had left Florence and returned to his county, was extremely happy. She remained in Florence until her delivery, when she gave birth to two boys, who greatly resembled their father, and she had them carefully nursed.

When she felt it was time, she set out without being recognized by anyone and traveled to Montpellier. Resting there a few days, she received intelligence about the count and his whereabouts; learning that on All Saints' Day he was to hold a big feast for ladies and knights in Roussillon, she went there, once more in the guise of a pilgrim just as when she had departed.

And learning that the ladies and knights were assembled in the count's palace in readiness to sit down at table, she retained her pilgrim's garb and went up to the great hall, her little children in her arms. Passing among the guests, she proceeded until she saw the count; then, falling at his feet, she said tearfully: "My lord, I am your unhappy wife, who, to allow you to return home and remain there, has long been wandering the world in misery. I ask you in the name of God to keep the terms you set me when I sent those two knights to you: here in my arms is not just one son of yours, but two, and here is your ring. And so it's time for me to be accepted by you as your wife in accordance with your promise."

The count, hearing this, nearly passed out. He recognized the ring and also the boys, because they looked so much like him; but still he said: "How can this have happened?"

The countess, to the amazement of the count and all the others present, told in proper sequence what had happened, and how. And so the count, knowing that she was telling the truth, and observing her perseverance and wisdom, not to mention two such beautiful children, both to keep his promise and to please all his knights and ladies, who were all imploring him to accept her and honor her now as his legitimate wife, set aside his stubborn rigidity. He had the countess rise, hugged and kissed her, and acknowledged her as his legitimate wife and the babies as his sons. Ordering her dressed in attire befitting her

figliuoli; e fattala di vestimenti a lei convenevoli rivestire, con grandissimo piacere di quanti ve n'erano e di tutti gli altri suoi vassalli che ciò sentirono, fece non solamente tutto quel dì, ma più altri grandissima festa, e da quel dì innanzi, lei sempre come sua sposa e moglie onorando, l'amò e sommamente ebbe cara.

RIMETTERE IL DIAVOLO IN INFERNO
[III, 10]

Dionèo, che diligentemente la novella della reina ascoltata avea, sentendo che finita era e che a lui solo restava il dire, senza comandamento aspettare, sorridendo cominciò a dire:

Graziose donne, voi non udiste mai dire come il diavolo si rimetta in inferno, e per ciò, senza partirmi guari dall'effetto che voi tutto questo dì ragionato avete, il vi vo' dire; forse ancora ne potrete guadagnar l'anima avendolo apparato, e potrete anche conoscere che, quantunque Amore i lieti palagi e le morbide camere più volentieri che le povere capanne abiti, non è egli per ciò che alcuna volta esso tra' folti boschi e tra le rigide alpi e nelle diserte spelunche non faccia le sue forze sentire; il perché comprender si può alla sua potenza essere ogni cosa suggetta.

Adunque, venendo al fatto, dico che nella città di Capsa in Barberia fu già un ricchissimo uomo, il quale, tra alcuni altri suoi figliuoli, aveva una figlioletta bella e gentilesca il cui nome fu Alibech, la quale, non essendo cristiana ed udendo a molti cristiani che nella città erano, molto commendare la cristiana fade ed il servire a Dio, un dì ne domandò alcuno, in che maniera e con meno impedimento a Dio si potesse servire. Il quale le rispose che coloro meglio a Dio servivano che più dalle cose del mondo fuggivano, come coloro facevano che nelle solitudini de' diserti di Tebaida andati se n'erano.

La giovane, che semplicissima era e d'età forse di quattordici anni, non mossa da ordinato disidéro ma da un cotal fanciullesco appetito, senza altro farne ad alcuna persona sentire, la seguente mattina ad andare verso il diserto di Tebaida nascosamente tutta sola si mise; e con gran fatica di lei, durando l'appetito, dopo alcun dì a quelle solitudini pervenne, e veduta di lontano una casetta, a quella n'andò, dove un santo uomo trovò sopra l'uscio, il quale, maravigliandosi di quivi vederla, la domandò quello che ella andasse cercando. La quale rispose che, spirata da Dio, andava cercando d'essere al suo servigio, ed ancora chi le 'nsegnasse come servire gli si convenia.

rank, to the very great pleasure of everyone present and all his other vassals who heard about it, he held a magnificent feast not only all that day, but for several days afterward. And from that day forward, always honoring her as his wife and spouse, he loved her and held her extremely dear.

PUTTING THE DEVIL BACK IN HELL
[III, 10]

Dioneo, who had carefully listened to the "Queen's" story, hearing that it was finished and that he alone had yet to tell a story, didn't wait to be prompted, but smiled and began to speak:

Gracious ladies, you have never heard tell how the devil is put back in hell, and so, scarcely departing from the theme you have spoken on all day, I'll tell you. Perhaps, having learned how, you may still be able to save your souls. And you will also be able to learn that, although Love prefers to dwell in happy palaces and comfortable chambers rather than in humble shacks, he nevertheless, for all that, sometimes makes his powers felt amid dense forests, rugged mountains, and wilderness caves; so that it can be understood that all things are subject to his might.

And so, coming to the facts, I say that in the city of Gafsa in Tunisia there was once a very rich man who, among other children, had a beautiful and genteel daughter named Alibec. She, not being a Christian, but hearing many Christians who lived in the city praising the Christian religion and the service of God, asked one of them one day how God could be served in the easiest way. This man replied that God was best served by those who fled worldly things, like those men who had gone into the lonely deserts of the Thebaid.

The girl, about fourteen and very ingenuous, urged on not by a moderate desire but by a childish hankering, said nothing to anyone, but set out alone in secret the next morning for the desert of the Thebaid. With great difficulty, this hankering continuing, some days later she arrived in that wilderness. Seeing a hut in the distance, she went to it and found a holy man standing in the doorway. He, amazed to see her there, asked her what she was looking for. She replied that, inspired by God, she was seeking to enter His service, and was looking for someone who could teach her the proper way to serve Him.

Il valente uomo, veggendola giovane ed assai bella, temendo non il dimonio, se egli la ritenesse, lo 'ngannasse, le commendò la sua buona disposizione, e dandole alquanto da mangiare radici d'erbe e pomi salvatichi e datteri e bere acqua, le disse: — Figliuola mia, non guari lontan di qui è un santo uomo, il quale di ciò che tu vai cercando è molto migliore maestro che io non sono; a lui te n'andrai.

E misela nella via; ed ella, pervenuta a lui ed avute da lui queste medesime parole, andata più avanti, pervenne alla cella d'un romito giovane, assai divota persona e buona, il cui nome era Rustico, e quella domanda gli fece che agli altri aveva fatta.

Il quale, per volere fare della sua fermezza una gran pruova, non come gli altri la mandò via o più avanti, ma seco la ritenne nella sua cella; e venuta la notte, un lettuccio di frondi di palma le fece da una parte, e sopra quello le disse si riposasse. Questo fatto, non preser guari d'indugio le tentazioni a dar battaglia alle forze di costui; il quale, trovandosi di gran lunga ingannato, da quelle senza troppi assalti voltò le spalle e rendessi per vinto; e lasciati stare dall'una delle parti i pensier santi e l'orazioni e le discipline, a recarsi per la memoria la giovanezza e la bellezza di costei incominciò, ed oltre a questo, a pensar che via e che modo egli dovesse con lei tenere, acciò che essa non s'accorgesse lui come uomo dissoluto pervenire a quello che egli di lei disiderava.

E tentato primieramente con certe domande, lei non avere mai uomo conosciuto conobbe, e così esser semplice come parea; per che s'avvisò come, sotto spezie di servire a Dio, lei dovesse recare a' suoi piaceri. E primieramente con molte parole le mostrò quanto il diavolo fosse nemico di Domenedio, ed appresso le diede ad intendere che quel servigio che più si poteva far grato a Dio si era rimettere il diavolo in inferno, nel quale Domenedio l'aveva dannato.

La giovanetta il domandò come questo si facesse; alla quale Rustico disse: — Tu il saprai tosto, e per ciò farai che a me far vedrai.

— E cominciossi a spogliare quegli pochi vestimenti che avea, e rimase tutto ignudo, e così ancora fece la fanciulla; e posesi in ginocchione a guisa che adorar volesse, e di rimpetto a sé fece star lei.

E così stando, essendo Rustico più che mai nel suo disidéro acceso per lo vederla così bella, venne la resurrezion della carne; la quale riguardando Alibech e maravigliatasi, disse: — Rustico, quella che cosa è che io ti veggio, che così si pigne in fuori, e non l'ho io?

— O figliuola mia — disse Rustico — questo è il diavolo di che io t'ho parlato; e vedi tu ora: egli mi dà grandissima molestia, tanto che io appena la posso sofferire.

The worthy man, seeing how young and beautiful she was, feared that, if he kept her with him, the devil might play a trick on him; he praised her good intentions, gave her a little to eat—roots, wild fruit, and dates—and water to drink, and said: "Daughter, not at all far from here there is a holy man who is a much better teacher of the knowledge you seek than I am; you should go to him."

And he showed her the way. When she reached the next man, he told her the same thing, so she continued until she reached the cell of a young hermit, a very devout and kind person named Rustico, and asked him the same thing she had asked the others.

He, in order to put his continence to a severe test, did not send her away or further along the road like the others, but kept her with him in his cell. When night fell, he made her a pallet of palm leaves on one side, and told her to sleep on that. After this, it was scarcely any time before temptations began to wage war on his strength; finding himself vastly overmatched by them, he didn't fight back very hard, but turned tail and surrendered. Setting aside his holy thoughts, his prayers, and his castigations, he began to remember the girl's youth and beauty; moreover, he deliberated on the ways and means of behaving with her in such a way that she wouldn't be aware he was just a dissolute man having his way with her.

First feeling his way with certain questions, he learned that she had never slept with a man and was just as naïve as she looked. And so he planned a way to have her submit to his pleasure under the pretext of serving God. First he told her at length that the devil was the enemy of God; then he gave her to understand that the service most pleasing to God was putting the devil back in hell, to which place God had condemned him.

The girl asked him how that was done, and Rustico replied: "You'll soon know; to make it happen, do what you see me doing." And he began to take off the few garments he was wearing until he was stark naked; and the girl did the same. Then he knelt down as if he were going to pray, and he made her do the same, facing him.

As they knelt there, Rustico's desire flared up more than ever at the sight of her great beauty, and there ensued the resurrection of the flesh. Seeing that and wondering at it, Alibec said: "Rustico, what's that thing I see on you sticking out like that? I don't have one."

"My daughter," said Rustico, "that's the devil I told you about. And now look: he's giving me terrible discomfort, so that I can hardly stand it."

Allora disse la giovane: — O lodato sia Iddio, ché io veggio che io sto meglio che non stai tu, ché io non ho cotesto diavolo io.

Disse Rustico: — Tu di' vero; ma tu hai un'altra cosa che non l'ho io, ed haila in iscambio di questo.

Disse Alibech: — O che?

A cui Rustico disse: — Hai il ninferno, e dicoti che io mi credo che Iddio t'abbia qui mandata per la salute dell'anima mia, per ciò che, se questo diavolo pur mi darà questa noia, ove tu vogli aver di me tanta pietà e sofferire che io in inferno il rimetta, tu mi darai grandissima consolazione ed a Dio farai grandissimo piacere e servigio, se tu per quello fare in queste parti venuta se', che tu di'.

La giovane di buona fede rispose: — O padre mio, poscia che io ho il ninferno, sia pure quando vi piacerà.

Disse allora Rustico: — Figliuola mia, benedetta sii tu! Andiamo adunque e rimettianlovi, sì che egli poscia mi lasci stare.

E così detto, menata la giovane sopra un de' lor letticelli, le 'nsegnò come starsi dovesse a dovere incarcerare quel maladetto da Dio. La giovane, che mai più non aveva in inferno messo diavolo alcuno, per la prima volta sentì un poco di noia; per che ella disse a Rustico: — Per certo, padre mio, mala cosa dée essere questo diavolo, veramente nemico di Dio, ché ancora al ninferno, non che altrui, duole quando egli v'è dentro rimesso.

Disse Rustico: — Figliuola, egli non avverrà sempre così.

E per fare che questo non avvenisse, da sei volte, anzi che di sul letticel si movessero, vel rimisero, tanto che per quella volta gli trassero sì la superbia del capo, che egli si stette volentieri in pace. Ma ritornatagli poi nel seguente tempo più volte, e la giovane obediente sempre a trargliele si disponesse, avvenne che il giuoco le cominciò a piacere, e cominciò a dire a Rustico: — Ben veggio che il vero dicevano que' valenti uomini in Capsa, che il servire a Dio era così dolce cosa; e per certo io non mi ricordo che mai alcuna altra io ne facessi che di tanto diletto e piacer mi fosse, quanto è il rimettere il diavolo in inferno; e per ciò io giudico ogni altra persona, che ad altro che a servire a Dio attende, essere una bestia.

Per la qual cosa essa spesse volte andava a Rustico e gli dicea: — Padre mio, io son qui venuta per servire a Dio, e non per istare oziosa; andiamo a rimettere il diavolo in inferno.

La qual cosa faccendo, diceva ella alcuna volta: — Rustico, io non so perché il diavolo si fugga di ninferno; ché, se egli vi stesse così volentieri come il ninferno il riceve e tiene, egli non se n'uscirebbe mai.

Then the girl said: "Praised be God, for I see that I'm better off than you, because I don't have that devil!"

Rustico said: "It's true, but you have something else that I don't have, and you have it in place of this."

Alibec said: "What is it?"

Rustico replied: "You have hell, and, believe me, I think God has sent you here to save my soul, because, whenever this devil causes me this distress, if you want to take pity on me and let me put him back in hell, you will give me the greatest relief, and you'd be doing God the greatest pleasure and service—if you've really come to this area for that purpose, as you say."

The girl replied in good faith: "Oh, Father, since I have hell, let it be whenever you like."

Then Rustico said: "Bless you, daughter! Let's go put him back so he'll leave me in peace."

Saying that, he led the girl to one of their pallets and taught her how to position herself to imprison that being who was accursed of God. The girl, who had never before put any devil in hell, felt that bit of first-time pain, and said to Rustico: "Really, Father, this devil must be a bad thing, truly an enemy of God, because he even hurts hell, let alone other people, when he's put inside."

Rustico said: "Daughter, it won't always be that way."

And to insure that it wouldn't happen, they put him back some six times before getting up from the pallet, until for that occasion they had so bowed down the pride of the devil's head that he was glad to leave them in peace. But later on, when his pride returned a number of times, and, each time, the obedient girl was willing to bow it down, she happened to start enjoying the game, and said to Rustico: "Now I see that those good people in Gafsa were telling the truth when they said the service of God was so sweet. Really, I can't remember anything else I've done that's given me as much delight and pleasure as putting the devil back in hell. And so I think that anyone engaged in any other pursuit than serving God, is a fool."

She went to Rustico often for it, saying: "Father, I've come here to serve God, not to sit around idle. Let's go put the devil back in hell!"

Doing this, she sometimes said: "Rustico, I don't know why the devil runs away from hell; because, if he enjoyed staying there as much as hell enjoys receiving him and holding onto him, he would never leave."

Così adunque invitando spesso la giovane Rustico ed al servigio di Dio confortandolo, sì la bambagia del farsetto tratta gli avea, che egli a tale ora sentiva freddo che uno altro sarebbe sudato; e per ciò egli incominciò a dire alla giovane che il diavolo non era da gastigare né da rimettere in inferno se non quando egli per superbia levasse il capo: — E noi, per la grazia di Dio, l'abbiamo sì isgannato, che egli priega Iddio di starsi in pace.

E così alquanto impose di silenzio alla giovane; la qual poi che vide che Rustico non la richiedeva a dovere il diavolo rimettere in inferno, gli disse un giorno: — Rustico, se il diavol tuo è gastigato e più non ti dà noia, me il mio ninferno non lascia stare; per che tu farai bene che tu col tuo diavolo aiuti ad attutare la rabbia al mio ninferno, come io col mio ninferno ho aiutato a trarre la superbia al tuo diavolo.

Rustico, che di radici d'erba e d'acqua vivea, poteva male rispondere alle poste, e dissele che troppi diavoli vorrebbero essere a potere il ninferno attutare, ma che egli ne farebbe ciò che per lui si potesse; e così alcuna volta le sodisfaceva, ma sì era di rado, che altro non era che gittare una fava in bocca al leone; di che la giovane, non parendole tanto servire a Dio quanto voleva, mormorava anzi che no.

Ma mentre che tra il diavolo di Rustico ed il ninferno d'Alibech era, per troppo disidéro e per men potere, questa quistione, avvenne che un fuoco s'apprese in Capsa, il quale nella propria casa arse il padre d'Alibech con quanti figliuoli ed altra famiglia avea; per la qual cosa Alibech d'ogni suo bene rimase erede. Laonde un giovane chiamato Neerbale, avendo in cortesia tutte le sue facultà spese, sentendo costei esser viva, messosi a cercarla, e ritrovatala avanti che la corte i beni stati del padre, sì come d'uomo senza erede morto, occupasse, con gran piacere di Rustico e contro al voler di lei la rimenò in Capsa e per moglie la prese, e con lei insieme del gran patrimonio di lei divenne erede.

Ma essendo ella domandata dalle donne di che nel diserto servisse a Dio, non essendo ancora Neerbale giaciuto con lei, rispose che il serviva di rimettere il diavolo in inferno e che Neerbale avea fatto gran peccato d'averla tolta da così fatto servigio. Le donne domandarono: — Come si rimette il diavolo in inferno?

La giovane tra con parole e con atti il mostrò loro; di che esse fecero sì gran risa, che ancor ridono, e dissono: — Non ti dar malinconia, figliuola, no, ché egli si fa bene anche qua; Neerbale ne servirà bene con essoteco Domenedio.

And so, the girl invited Rustico so often, urging him to serve God, that she had "pulled the padding out of his doublet" and he felt cold at times when other men would have sweated. Therefore, he started telling the girl that the devil was only to be chastised and put back in hell when he raised his head in pride: "And we, by the grace of God, have so humbled him that he is praying to God to be left in peace."

And so for a while he got the girl to be still; but, seeing that Rustico wasn't asking her to put the devil back in hell, she said to him one day: "Rustico, if your devil is chastised and no longer bothering you, for my part, my hell gives me no rest. And so you'd be doing a kind thing if, with your devil, you helped me calm down the rage of my hell, just as I helped you with my hell to bow down the pride of your devil."

Rustico, who lived on roots and water, was scarcely able to match her stakes; he told her that it would take too many devils to calm down that hell, but he would do everything in his power. And so he satisfied her once in a while, but so seldom that it was just like throwing one bean in a lion's mouth. So that the girl, believing she wasn't serving God as much as she wanted to, kept on grumbling.

But while this dispute was going on between Rustico's devil and Alibec's hell, because of too much desire and too little power, a fire happened to break out in Gafsa, in the course of which Alibec's father and all his other children and household members were burned in their own home, so that Alibec inherited all his property. Whereupon a young man named Neerbal, who had squandered all his wealth in high living, hearing she was alive, set out in search of her. Finding her before the court could confiscate the property that had been her father's on the grounds that he had died without an heir, to Rustico's great pleasure, but against her will, he brought her back to Gafsa and married her, becoming co-heir to her great inheritance.

But, being asked by the ladies what she had done to serve God in the desert—this was before Neerbal had slept with her—she replied that she had served Him by putting the devil back in hell, and that Neerbal had committed a great sin by taking her away from that service. The ladies asked: "How is the devil put back in hell?"

Partly with words and partly with gestures, the girl showed them how. They laughed so loud at this that they're still laughing, and they said: "Don't fret, youngster, no, because that's done here, too; Neerbal and you will do God good service that way."

Poi l'una all'altra per la città ridicendolo, vi ridussono in volgar motto che il più piacevol servigio che a Dio si facesse era rimettere il diavolo in inferno; il qual motto, passato di qua da mare, ancora dura. E per ciò voi, giovani donne, alle quali la grazia di Dio bisogna, apparate a rimettere il diavolo in inferno, per ciò che egli è forte a grado a Dio e piacere delle parti, e molto bene ne può nascere e seguire.

IL VASO DI BASILICO [IV, 5]

Finita la novella d'Elissa ed alquanto dal re commendata, a Filomena fu imposto che ragionasse; la quale, tutta piena di compassione del misero Gerbino e della sua donna, dopo un pietoso sospiro incominciò:

La mia novella, graziose donne, non sarà di genti di sì alta condizione come costor furono de' quali Elissa ha raccontato, ma ella per avventura non sarà men pietosa; ed a ricordarmi di quella mi tira Messina poco innanzi ricordata, dove l'accidente avvenne.

Erano adunque in Messina tre giovani fratelli e mercatanti, ed assai ricchi uomini rimasi dopo la morte del padre loro, il quale fu da San Gimignano, ed avevano una loro sorella chiamata Lisabetta, giovane assai bella e costumata, la quale, che che se ne fosse cagione, ancora maritata non aveano.

Ed avevano oltre a ciò questi tre fratelli in un lor fondaco un giovanetto pisano chiamato Lorenzo, che tutti i lor fatti guidava e faceva, il quale essendo assai bello della persona e leggiadro molto, avendolo più volte l'Isabetta guatato, avvenne che egli le 'ncominciò stranamente a piacere; di che Lorenzo accortosi ed una volta ed altra, similmente, lasciati suoi altri innamoramenti di fuori, incominciò a porre l'animo a lei; e sì andò la bisogna, che, piacendo l'uno all'altro igualmente, non passò gran tempo che, assicuratisi, fecero di quello che più disiderava ciascuno.

Ed in questo continuando ed avendo insieme assai di buon tempo e di piacere, non seppero sì segretamente fare, che una notte, andando l'Isabetta là dove Lorenzo dormiva, che il maggior de' fratelli, senza accorgersene ella, non se n'accorgesse; il quale per ciò che savio giovane era, quantunque molto noioso gli fosse a ciò sapere, pur mosso da più onesto consiglio, senza far motto o dir cosa alcuna, varie cose tra sé rivolgendo intorno a questo fatto, infino alla mattina seguente trapassò.

Then, after one woman repeated it to another all over town, it became a common expression that the service that most pleased God was putting the devil back in hell. This saying, crossing the sea to our land, is still current. And so, you young ladies, who are in need of God's grace, learn to put the devil back in hell, because it is greatly pleasing to God and enjoyable to the participants, and much good can accrue and come of it.

THE POT OF BASIL [IV, 5]

When Elissa's story was finished and praised for a while by the "King," Filomena was requested to speak. Full of pity for unhappy Gerbino and his lady, she heaved a compassionate sigh and began:

My story, gracious ladies, won't be about people of such high station as those in Elissa's story, but perhaps it will not be less touching; what reminds me of it is the mention of Messina just now, for the incident took place there.

Well, in Messina there were three young brothers, merchants, who had been left great wealth upon the death of their father, a native of San Gimignano. They had a sister named Lisabetta, young, very beautiful and well-bred, whom they had not yet married off for one reason or another.

In addition, these three brothers had in a warehouse of theirs a young man from Pisa, named Lorenzo, who acted as foreman and manager. He was very handsome and attractive, and, Lisabetta having cast eyes on him several times, she happened to conceive a tremendous liking for him. Lorenzo, having noticed this on various occasions, dropped his other outside attachments and likewise began to turn his thoughts toward her. And matters so proceeded that, since they liked each other equally well, before long they felt out of danger and indulged in the activity they both desired.

Continuing to do so, and having a very good time and much pleasure together, they were not sufficiently cautious to prevent Lisabetta's eldest brother from noticing it one night when she had gone to Lorenzo's bedroom; she herself was unaware she had been detected. Because this brother was a sensible young man, even though he was greatly distressed by what he had learned, he was still governed by more prudent counsel; without making a sound or saying anything, he spent the time until the next morning thinking the matter over.

Poi, venuto il giorno, a' suoi fratelli ciò che veduto aveva la passata notte dell'Isabetta e di Lorenzo raccontò, e con loro insieme, dopo lungo consiglio, diliberò di questa cosa, acciò che né a loro né alla sirocchia alcuna infamia ne seguisse, di passarsene tacitamente e d'infignersi del tutto d'averne alcuna cosa veduta o saputa infino a tanto che tempo venisse nel quale essi, senza danno o sconcio di loro, questa vergogna avanti che più andasse innanzi, si potessero tôrre dal viso.

Ed in tal disposizion dimorando, così cianciando e ridendo con Lorenzo come usati erano, avvenne che, sembianti faccendo d'andare fuori della città a diletto tutti e tre, seco menaron Lorenzo, e pervenuti in un luogo molto solitario e rimoto, veggendosi il destro, Lorenzo, che di ciò niuna guardia prendeva, uccisono e sotterrarono in guisa che niuna persona se n'accorse; ed in Messina tornatisi, dieder voce d'averlo per loro bisogne mandato in alcun luogo, il che leggermente creduto fu, per ciò che spesse volte eran di mandarlo da torno usati.

Non tornando Lorenzo, e l'Isabetta molto spesso e sollecitamente i fratei domandandone, sì come colei a cui la dimora lunga gravava, avvenne un giorno che, domandandone ella molto istantemente, che l'un de' fratelli disse: — Che vuol dir questo? Che hai tu a far di Lorenzo, che tu ne domandi così spesso? Se tu ne domanderai più, noi ti faremo quella risposta che ti si conviene.

Per che la giovane dolente e trista, temendo e non sappiendo che, senza più domandarne si stava, ed assai volte la notte pietosamente il chiamava e pregava che ne venisse, ed alcuna volta con molte lagrime della sua lunga dimora si doleva e senza punto rallegrarsi, sempre aspettando, si stava.

Avvenne una notte che, avendo costei molto pianto Lorenzo che non tornava ed essendosi alla fine piagnendo addormentata, Lorenzo l'apparve nel sonno, pallido e tutto rabbuffato e co' panni tutti stracciati e fracidi, e parvele che egli dicesse: — O Lisabetta, tu non mi fai altro che chiamare e della mia lunga dimora t'attristi e me con le tue lagrime fieramente accusi; e per ciò sappi che io non posso più ritornarci, per ciò che l'ultimo dì che tu mi vedesti i tuoi fratelli m'uccisono.

E disegnàtole il luogo dove sotterrato l'aveano, le disse che più nol chiamasse né l'aspettasse, e disparve. La giovane, destatasi e dando fede alla visione, amaramente pianse; poi la mattina levata, non avendo ardire di dire alcuna cosa a' fratelli, propose di volere andare al mostrato luogo e di vedere se ciò fosse vero che nel sonno l'era paruto. Ed avuta la licenza d'andare alquanto fuor della terra

Then, after daybreak, he told his brothers what he had seen between Lisabetta and Lorenzo the night before, and together with them, after a long discussion, he decided to pass over the matter in silence, in order to avoid any scandal to themselves or their sister, and to pretend not to have seen or learned a thing about it until the time came when, without harm or trouble to themselves, they could wipe away that shame before it went any further.

Remaining so resolved, they continued to joke and laugh with Lorenzo just as in the past, until, one day, all three pretended to be going on a pleasurable outing in the country. They took along Lorenzo, and when they had reached a spot that was very solitary and remote, they saw their opportunity and killed Lorenzo, who was not on guard against it. They did such a good job of burying him that no one was aware of it; and, returning to Messina, they spread the word that they had sent him away on business. This was readily believed because they had been accustomed to send him on such errands frequently.

When Lorenzo failed to return, and Lisabetta had very often asked her brothers anxiously about him, since his long absence was grievous to her, one day when she was asking them very insistently, one of her brothers happened to say: "What's the meaning of this? What is Lorenzo to you, that you ask about him so often? If you ask about him again, we'll give you a suitable answer!"

And so the girl, sorrowful and unhappy, fearing she knew not what, asked no more questions, but many times each night she would call him pitifully and beg him to come, and at times she would lament his long absence with many tears, always waiting and never cheering up.

One night, after she had long wept over Lorenzo's failure to return, and had finally cried herself to sleep, Lorenzo happened to appear to her in a dream, pale, completely disheveled, his clothes all torn and decaying, and seemed to say to her: "Lisabetta, you do nothing but call me, you are saddened by my long absence, and you make wild accusations against me with your tears. Therefore, let me tell you that I can no longer come back here because, on the last day you saw me, your brothers killed me."

And, describing the place where they had buried him, he told her to stop calling him and awaiting him, and he vanished. The girl, awakening and believing in the truth of her dream, wept bitterly; when she arose in the morning, she didn't have the courage to say anything to her brothers, but decided to go to the indicated spot and find out whether what she had seen in her dream was true. Receiving

a diporto in compagnia d'una fante che altra volta con loro era stata
e tutti i suoi fatti sapeva, quanto più tosto poté là se n'andò, e tolte
via foglie secche che nel luogo erano, dove men dura le parve la
terra, quivi cavò; né ebbe guari cavato, che ella trovò il corpo del
suo misero amante in niuna cosa ancora guasto né corrotto; per che
manifestamente conobbe essere vera la visione.

Di che più che altra femina dolorosa, conoscendo che quivi non
era da piagnere, se avesse potuto volentier tutto il corpo n'avrebbe
portato per dargli più convenevole sepoltura; ma veggendo che ciò
esser non poteva, con un coltello il meglio che poté gli spiccò dallo
'mbusto la testa, e quella in uno asciugatoio inviluppata e la terra
sopra l'altro corpo gittata, mèssala in grembo alla fante, senza essere stata da alcun veduta, quindi si dipartì e tornossene a casa sua.

Quivi con questa testa nella sua camera rinchiusasi, sopra essa
lungamente ed amaramente pianse, tanto che tutta con le sue lagrime la lavò, mille baci dandole in ogni parte. Poi prese un grande
ed un bel testo, di questi ne' quali si pianta la persa o il basilico, e
dentro la vi mise fasciata in un bel drappo, e poi, messavi sù la
terra, sù vi piantò parecchi piedi di bellissimo basilico salernetano,
e quegli di niuna altra acqua che o rosata o di fior d'aranci o delle
sue lagrime non innaffiava già mai; e per usanza aveva preso di
sedersi sempre a questo testo vicina e quello con tutto il suo
disidéro vagheggiare, sì come quello che il suo Lorenzo teneva
nascoso; e poi che molto vagheggiato l'avea, sopra esso andatasene,
cominciava a piagnere, e per lungo spazio, tanto che tutto il basilico bagnava, piagnea.

Il basilico, sì per lo lungo e continuo studio, sì per la grassezza
della terra procedente dalla terra corrotta che dentro v'era, divenne
bellissimo ed odorifero molto. E servando la giovane questa
maniera del continuo, più volte da' suoi vicin fu veduta; li quali,
maravigliandosi i fratelli della sua guasta bellezza e di ciò che gli
occhi le parevano della testa fuggiti, il disser loro: — Noi ci siamo
accorti che ella ogni dì tiene la cotal maniera.

Il che udendo i fratelli ed accorgendosene, avendonela alcuna
volta ripresa e non giovando, nascosamente da lei fecero portar via
questo testo. Il quale, non ritrovandolo ella, con grandissima i-
stanza molte volte richiese, e non essendole renduto, non cessando
il pianto e le lagrime, infermò, né altro che il testo suo nella 'nfermità domandava.

I giovani si maravigliavan forte di questo addomandare, e per ciò
vollero vedere che dentro vi fosse; e versata la terra, videro il

permission to go a little distance out of town for pleasure, she took along a maid who had been with the lovers and knew all her doings. As fast as she could, she reached the spot, and, brushing away the dry leaves that covered it, she dug where she found the ground least hard. She hadn't dug long before she found the body of her unfortunate lover, not yet decomposed or rotting to any extent. And so she clearly realized the dream had been true.

The saddest of all womankind at this, knowing that that was no place for tears, she would gladly have carried away the entire body, had she been able, in order to bury it more fittingly; but, seeing that this was impossible, she separated the head from the trunk with a knife to the best of her ability. Wrapping the head in a towel, and shoveling back the earth over the rest of the body, she put the head in the folds of her maid's dress, without being seen by anyone, then left and returned home.

There she locked herself into her room with the head and wept over it long and bitterly until she had washed it clean with her tears, giving it a thousand kisses all over. Then she took a large, beautiful flowerpot, of the kind in which marjoram or basil is planted. Into it she placed the head, swathed in a beautiful cloth; then, adding soil on top, she planted in it several stalks of very fine basil from Salerno. These she never watered with any liquid other than rose or orange water or her tears. She had acquired the habit of always sitting next to this pot and gazing at it lovingly with all her heart, since it hid her Lorenzo. And after gazing at it for some time, she would go and lean over it, beginning to weep, and continuing to do so for a long time, until she had completely moistened the basil.

Both because of this long-continued nurturing and because of the richness of the soil, due to the rotting earth that was in it, the basil became very beautiful and exceptionally fragrant. Since the girl kept up these habits constantly, she was often observed by her neighbors, who said to her brothers, when those three were surprised at the loss of her beauty, her eyes being so sunken as to be almost invisible: "We have noticed that she acts that way every day."

Her brothers, hearing and observing this, reprimanded her for it a number of times to no avail; then, unknown to her, they had that pot taken away. When she failed to find it, she frequently asked for it most insistently; when it was not returned, she didn't cease crying and weeping until she fell ill; in her illness she did nothing but ask for the pot.

The young men were greatly amazed by those requests, and so they wanted to see what was inside. Shaking out the soil, they saw the

drappo ed in quello la testa non ancora sì consumata, che essi alla capellatura crespa non conoscessero lei esser quella di Lorenzo. Di che essi si maravigliaron forte e temettero non questa cosa si risapesse; e sotterrata quella, senza altro dire, cautamente di Messina uscitisi ed ordinato come di quindi si ritraessono, se n'andarono a Napoli.

La giovane, non ristando di piagnere e pure il suo testo addomandando, piagnendo si morì, e così il suo disavventurato amore ebbe termine; ma poi a certo tempo divenuta questa cosa manifesta a molti, fu alcun che compose quella canzone la quale ancora oggi si canta, cioè:

> Qual esso fu lo malo cristiano
> che mi furò la grasta, *etc.*

IL CUORE DI GUGLIELMO GUARDASTAGNO [IV, 9]

Essendo la novella di Neìfile finita, non senza aver gran compassion messa in tutte le sue compagne, il re, il quale non intendeva di guastare il privilegio di Dionèo, non essendovi altri a dire, incominciò:

Èmmisi parata dinanzi, pietose donne, una novella alla qual, poi che così degl'infortunati casi d'amore vi duole, vi converrà non meno di compassione avere che alla passata, per ciò che da più furono coloro a' quali ciò che io dirò avvenne, e con più fiero accidente che quegli de' quali è parlato.

Dovete adunque sapere che, secondo che raccontano i Provenzali, in Provenza furon già due nobili cavalieri, de' quali ciascuno e castella e vassalli aveva sotto di sé, ed aveva l'un nome messer Guiglielmo Rossiglione e l'altro messer Guiglielmo Guardastagno; e per ciò che l'uno e l'altro era prod'uomo molto nell'armi, s'amavano assai ed in costume avean d'andar sempre ad ogni torneamento o giostra o altro fatto d'arme insieme e vestiti d'un'assisa.

E come che ciascun dimorasse in un suo castello, e fosse l'un dall'altro ben diece miglia, pure avvenne che, avendo messer Guiglielmo Rossiglione una bellissima e vaga donna per moglie, messer Guiglielmo Guardastagno fuor di misura, nonostante l'amistà e la compagnia che era tra loro, s'innamorò di lei e tanto or con uno atto o con uno altro fece, che la donna se n'accorse; e conoscendolo per valorosissimo cavaliere, le piacque, e cominciò a porre amore a lui, intanto che niuna cosa più che lui disiderava o

cloth and, in it, the head, not yet so decayed that they failed to recognize from the curly hair that it was Lorenzo's. Greatly amazed by this, they feared lest the matter should become known; burying the head and saying nothing else, they quietly slipped out of Messina, leaving instructions for their merchandise to follow, and went to Naples.

The girl, never ceasing to weep and constantly asking for her flowerpot, died of grief; and so her unfortunate love came to an end. But afterward, at a certain time, these events became known to many people, and someone wrote the song that is still sung today:

> Who was the bad Christian
> That stole my flowerpot? . . .

THE HEART OF GUILHEM OF CABESTANY
[IV, 9]

Neifile's story being finished, not without having stirred great pity in all her lady friends, the "King," who didn't wish to infringe Dioneo's privilege, finding himself the only other one yet to speak, began:

Compassionate ladies, I have thought of a story which, since you grieve so much at unhappy love affairs, will surely inspire you with no less pity than the previous one, because the people involved were of higher rank and the misfortune was crueler than the one those others suffered.

And so, you are to hear that, according to what the Provençals tell, there were once in Provence two noble knights, each of them master of castles and vassals. One was named Sir Guilhem of Roussillon, and the other Sir Guilhem of Cabestany. Because both of them were highly skilled in arms, it was their great joy and their practice to participate in every tournament, joust, or other feat of arms together, wearing the same device.

And, although each dwelt in a castle of his own, and these castles were at least ten miles apart, it nevertheless occurred that, Sir Guilhem of Roussillon being married to a most beautiful and charming woman, Sir Guilhem of Cabestany, despite the two men's friendship and companionship, fell wildly in love with her, and by his various actions brought this to the lady's attention. Knowing he was a most worthy knight, she took a liking to him, and began to feel love for him, so much so that she desired and loved nothing more than him, and

amava, né altro attendeva che da lui esser richesta; il che non guari stette che addivenne, ed insieme furono una volta ed altra, amandosi forte.

E men discretamente insieme usando, avvenne che il marito se n'accorse e forte ne sdegnò, intanto che il grande amore che al Guardastagno portava, in mortale odio convertì, ma meglio il seppe tener nascoso che i due amanti non avevan saputo tenere il loro amore; e seco diliberò del tutto d'ucciderlo.

Per che, essendo il Rossiglione in questa disposizione, sopravvenne che un gran torneamento si bandì in Francia; il che il Rossiglione incontanente significò al Guardastagno, e mandògli a dire che, se a lui piacesse, da lui venisse, ed insieme dilibererebbono se andarvi volessono e come. Il Guardastagno lietissimo rispose che senza fallo il dì seguente andrebbe a cenar con lui.

Il Rossiglione, udendo questo, pensò il tempo esser venuto da poterlo uccidere, ed armatosi, il dì seguente con alcun suo famigliare montò a cavallo, e forse un miglio fuori del suo castello in un bosco si ripose in agguato donde doveva il Guardastagno passare; ed avendolo per un buon spazio atteso, venir lo vide disarmato con due famigliari appresso disarmati, sì come colui che di niente da lui si guardava; e come in quella parte il vide giunto dove voleva, fellone e pieno di maltalento, con una lancia sopra mano gli uscì addosso gridando: — Traditor, tu se' morto!

Ed il così dire ed il dargli di questa lancia per lo petto fu una cosa: il Guardastagno, senza potere alcuna difesa fare o pur dire una parola, passato di quella lancia, cadde e poco appresso morì. I suoi famigliari, senza aver conosciuto chi ciò fatto s'avesse, voltate le teste de' cavalli, quanto più poterono si fuggirono verso il castello del lor signore. Il Rossiglione, smontato, con un coltello il petto del Guardastagno aprì e con le proprie mani il cuor gli trasse, e quel fatto avviluppare in un pennoncello di lancia, comandò ad un de' suoi famigliari che nel portasse; ed avendo a ciascun comandato che niun fosse tanto ardito, che di questo facesse parola, rimontò a cavallo, ed essendo già notte, al suo castello se ne tornò.

La donna, che udito aveva il Guardastagno dovervi esser la sera a cena, e con disidéro grandissimo l'aspettava, non veggendol venir si maravigliò forte ed al marito disse: — E come è così, messer, che il Guardastagno non è venuto?

A cui il marito disse: — Donna, io ho avuto da lui che egli non ci può essere di qui domane, — di che la donna un poco turbatetta rimase.

waited impatiently for him to request her favors. It wasn't very long before this occurred, and they spent odd moments together, deeply in love.

Abandoning their caution when together, they allowed her husband to get wind of the affair. Though he became so furious that the great affection he had for Cabestany was changed to mortal hatred, he was able to keep this hidden better than the two lovers had been able to hide their love. He determined that he must definitely kill him.

And so, Roussillon having thus resolved, a grand tournament happened to be announced in France. Roussillon immediately informed Cabestany of this, sending him a message saying that, if he wished, he should visit him and together they would discuss whether to attend and, if so, how. Cabestany replied gladly that the next day he would come to have supper with him without fail.

Hearing this, Roussillon decided that this was his opportunity to kill him. He armed himself the next day, mounted his horse in the company of a few servants, and hid in ambush in a forest about a mile from his castle in a spot Cabestany had to pass. After awaiting him for a long while, he saw him coming unarmed with two unarmed servants after him, unaware that he needed to take any precautions. When he saw him arrive at the desired spot, he was filled with cruelty and hatred, and dashed out toward him with raised lance, shouting: "Traitor, you're a dead man!"

As he said this, he struck him in the chest with the lance. Cabestany, unable to defend himself or even say a word, pierced by that lance, fell and died shortly afterward. His servants, not recognizing the perpetrator, turned their horses' heads around and fled toward their lord's castle as fast as they could. Roussillon dismounted, opened Cabestany's chest with a knife, and extracted his heart with his own hands. Having it wrapped up in a lance pennon, he ordered one of his servants to carry it. Ordering each one not to be so bold as to say a word about this, he mounted his horse again and, night having now fallen, returned to his castle.

His lady, who had heard that Cabestany was expected there for supper that evening, and who was awaiting his arrival with tremendous desire, was greatly surprised at his failure to appear, and said to her husband: "How is it, my lord, that Cabestany hasn't come?"

Her husband replied: "Lady, I've had word from him that he can't be here until tomorrow." This left the lady somewhat disturbed.

Il Rossiglione, smontato, si fece chiamare il cuoco e gli disse: — Prenderai quel cuor di cinghiare e fa' che tu ne facci una vivandetta, la migliore e la più dilettevole a mangiar che tu sai; e quando a tavola sarò, la mi manda in una scodella d'ariento.

Il cuoco, presolo e postavi tutta l'arte e tutta la sollecitudine sua, minuzzatolo e messevi di buone spezie assai, ne fece un manicaretto troppo buono. Messer Guiglielmo, quando tempo fu, con la sua donna si mise a tavola. La vivanda venne, ma egli, per lo maleficio da lui commesso, nel pensiero impedito, poco mangiò. Il cuoco gli mandò il manicaretto, il quale egli fece porre davanti alla donna, sé mostrando quella sera svogliato, e lodòcgliele molto.

La donna, che svogliata non era, ne cominciò a mangiare, e parvele buono; per la qual cosa ella il mangiò tutto. Come il cavaliere ebbe veduto che la donna tutto l'ebbe mangiato, disse: — Donna, chente v'è paruta questa vivanda?

La donna rispose: — Monsignore, in buona fé ella m'è piaciuta molto.

— Se m'aìti Iddio, — disse il cavaliere, — io il vi credo, né me ne meraviglio se morto v'è piaciuto ciò che vivo più che altra cosa vi piacque.

La donna, udito questo, alquanto stette; poi disse: — Come? Che cosa è questa che voi m'avete fatta mangiare?

Il cavalier rispose: — Quello che voi avete mangiato è stato veramente il cuore di messer Guiglielmo Guardastagno, il qual voi come disleal femina tanto amavate; e sappiate di certo che egli è stato desso, per ciò che io con queste mani gliele strappai, poco avanti che io tornassi, del petto.

La donna, udendo questo di colui cui ella più che altra cosa amava, se dolorosa fu non è da domandare; e dopo alquanto disse: — Voi faceste quello che disleale e malvagio cavalier dée fare; ché se io, non isforzandomi egli, l'aveva del mio amor fatto signore e voi in questo oltreggiato, non egli ma io ne doveva la pena portare. Ma unque a Dio non piaccia che, sopra a così nobil vivanda come è stata quella del cuore d'un così valoroso e così cortese cavaliere come messer Guiglielmo Guardastagno fu, mai altra vivanda vada!

E levata in piè, per una finestra la quale dietro a lei era, indietro senza altra diliberazione si lasciò cadere. La finestra era molto alta da terra; per che, come la donna cadde, non solamente morì, ma quasi tutta si disfece. Messer Guiglielmo, veggendo questo, stordì forte, e parvegli aver mal fatto; e temendo egli dei paesani e del conte di Provenza, fatti sellare i cavalli, andò via.

La mattina seguente fu saputo per tutta la contrada come questa

Roussillon dismounted and called for his cook, to whom he said: "Take that boar's heart and see that you make the best and tastiest dish of it that you know how. When I'm at table, send it to me in a silver bowl."

The cook took it and lavished all his skill and care on it; mincing it and adding many flavorful spices, he created an extremely good dish. When the time arrived, Sir Guilhem sat down at table with his lady. The food came, but his thoughts were preoccupied by the crime he had committed and he ate very little. The cook sent him that special dish, which he ordered to be served to his lady, praising it to her highly, although he said he himself had no appetite that evening.

The lady had a fine appetite and, beginning to eat it, found it good and ate the whole thing. When the knight saw that the lady had eaten all of it, he said: "Lady, how did you like that food?"

The lady replied: "My lord, honestly I liked it very much."

"So help me God," said the knight, "I believe you, and I'm not surprised that you liked, when it was dead, the thing you liked best in the world when it was alive."

Hearing this, the lady paused for a moment, then said: "What did you say? What is this thing you've made me eat?"

The knight replied: "What you ate was actually the heart of Sir Guilhem of Cabestany, whom you, as an unfaithful wife, loved so much. Know for a fact that that's what it was, because I ripped it out of his chest with these hands shortly before I came home!"

The lady, hearing this news about the man she loved best in the world, was as unhappy as you can imagine. After a moment, she said: "You have acted like a disloyal and wicked knight; for, if I had made him lord of my love, with no compulsion on his part, and had offended you by so doing, I and not he should have been punished for it. But may it never please God that so noble a dish as the heart of such a worthy and courtly knight as Sir Guilhem of Cabestany should ever be followed by any other food!"

And, rising from table, without any forethought, she let herself fall backward out of the window behind her. The window was very high above the ground, so that, when the lady fell, she was not merely killed but almost totally shattered. Seeing this, Sir Guilhem was altogether stunned, and he realized he had done wrong. In fear of the local people and the count of Provence, he had his horses saddled and departed.

The next morning, these events were bruited throughout the

cosa era stata; per che da quegli del castello di messer Guiglielmo Guardastagno e da quegli ancora del castello della donna, con grandissimo dolore e pianto, furono i due corpi ricolti e nella chiesa del castello medesimo della donna in una medesima sepoltura fûr posti, e sopra essa scritti versi significanti chi fosser quegli che dentro sepolti v'erano, ed il modo e la cagione della lor morte.

LA CACCIA INFERNALE [V, 8]

Come la Lauretta si tacque, così, per comandamento della reina, cominciò Filomena:

Amabili donne, come in noi è la pietà commendata, così ancora in noi è dalla divina giustizia rigidamente la crudeltà vendicata, il che acciò che io vi dimostri e materia vi déa di cacciarla del tutto da voi, mi piace dirvi una novella non meno di compassione piena che dilettevole.

In Ravenna, antichissima città di Romagna, furon già assai nobili e gentili uomini, tra' quali un giovane chiamato Nastagio degli Onesti, per la morte del padre di lui e d'un suo zio, senza stima rimase ricchissimo; il quale, sì come de' giovani avviene, essendo senza moglie, s'innamorò d'una figliuola di messer Paolo Traversaro, giovane troppo più nobile che esso non era, prendendo speranza con le sue opere di doverla trarre ad amar lui.

Le quali, quantunque grandissime, belle e laudevoli fossero, non solamente non gli giovavano, anzi pareva che gli nocessero, tanto cruda e dura e salvatica gli si mostrava la giovanetta amata, forse per la sua singular bellezza o per la sua nobiltà sì altiera e disdegnosa divenuta, che né egli né cosa che gli piacesse, le piaceva, la qual cosa era tanto a Nastagio gravosa a comportare, che per dolore più volte, dopo essersi doluto, gli venne in disidéro d'uccidersi; poi, pur tenendosene, molte volte si mise in cuore di doverla del tutto lasciare stare, o se potesse, d'averla in odio come ella aveva lui.

Ma invano tal proponimento prendeva, per ciò che pareva che quanto più la speranza mancava, tanto più multiplicasse il suo amore. Perseverando adunque il giovane e nell'amare e nello spendere smisuratamente, parve a certi suoi amici e parenti che egli sé ed il suo avere parimente fosse per consumare; per la qual cosa più volte il pregarono e consigliarono che si dovesse di Ravenna partire ed in alcun altro luogo per alquanto tempo andare a dimorare, per ciò che, così faccendo, scemerebbe l'amore e le spese.

region. And so, by those in the castle of Sir Guilhem of Cabestany and by those in the lady's castle the two bodies were picked up, with great sorrow and lamentation, and placed in one tomb in the very castle of the lady. On the tomb were inscribed verses identifying its occupants and telling the nature and cause of their death.

THE WILD HUNT [V, 8]

When Lauretta fell silent, at the "Queen's" command Filomena began:

Charming ladies, just as we are enjoined to be merciful, divine justice punishes us severely for being cruel. In order to prove this to you and give you the wherewithal to eliminate cruelty completely from your mind, I am pleased to tell you a story no less full of compassion than of delight.

In Ravenna, that very ancient city in Romagna, there once lived many noblemen and gentlemen, among them a young man named Nastagio degli Onesti, who was left incalculably rich at the deaths of his father and an uncle. As is the way with young men, being still unmarried, he fell in love with a daughter of Master Paolo Traversari, a young woman of much higher rank than his own, although he hoped he could induce her to love him by his munificence.

Though this was lavish, fine, and laudable, it not only didn't help him but even seemed to harm him, so cruel, hard, and uncivil was the behavior toward him of the girl he loved; perhaps because of her unusual beauty or her high rank, she had become so haughty and scornful that she liked neither him nor anything that *he* liked. Nastagio found this so hard to bear that several times, after lamenting, he felt like killing himself from grief; but, controlling himself, he frequently set his heart on leaving her altogether or, if he could, hating her as she hated him.

But he made such resolutions in vain, because it seemed that the less hope he had, the greater his love grew. And so, as he persevered both in his love and his immoderate expenses, it seemed to some of the young man's friends and relatives that he was on the point of wearing out both himself and his fortune. Therefore they frequently asked and advised him to leave Ravenna and take up residence elsewhere for a while; by so doing, both his love and his outlay would decrease.

Di questo consiglio più volte fece beffe Nastagio; ma pure, essendo da loro sollecitato, non potendo tanto dir di no, disse di farlo, e fatto fare un grande apparecchiamento, come se in Francia o se in Ispagna o in alcuno altro luogo lontano andar volesse, montato a cavallo e da' suoi amici accompagnato, di Ravenna uscì ed andossene ad un luogo fuor di Ravenna forse tre miglia, che si chiama Chiassi, e quivi fatti venir padiglioni e trabacche, disse a color che accompagnato l'aveano che starsi volea e che essi a Ravenna se ne tornassono.

Attendatosi adunque quivi Nastagio, cominciò a fare la più bella vita e la più magnifica che mai si facesse, or questi ed or quegli altri invitando a cena ed a desinare, come usato s'era. Ora, avvenne che uno venerdì, quasi all'entrata di maggio, essendo un bellissimo tempo, ed egli entrato in pensiero della sua crudel donna, comandato a tutta la sua famiglia che solo il lasciassero, per più poter pensare a suo piacere, piede innanzi pié se medesimo trasportò, pensando, infino nella pigneta.

Ed essendo già passata presso che la quinta ora del giorno, ed esso bene un mezzo miglio per la pigneta entrato, non ricordandosi di mangiare né d'altra cosa, subitamente gli parve udire un grandissimo pianto e guai altissimi messi da una donna; per che, rotto il suo dolce pensiero, alzò il capo per veder che fosse, e maravigliossi nella pigneta veggendosi; ed oltre a ciò, davanti guardandosi, vide venire per un boschetto assai folto d'albuscelli e di pruni, correndo verso il luogo dove egli era, una bellissima giovane ignuda, scapigliata e tutta graffiata dalle frasche e da' pruni, piagnendo e gridando forte mercé; ed oltre a questo, le vide a' fianchi due grandi e fieri mastini, li quali duramente appresso correndole, spesse volte crudelmente dove la giugnevano la mordevano, e dietro a lei vide venire sopra un corsier nero un cavalier bruno, forte nel viso crucciato, con uno stocco in mano, lei di morte con parole spaventevoli e villane minacciando.

Questa cosa ad una ora maraviglia e spavento gli mise nell'animo, ed ultimamente compassione della sventurata donna, dalla qual nacque disidéro di liberarla da sì fatta angoscia e morte, se el potesse. Ma senza arme trovandosi, ricorse a prendere un ramo d'albero in luogo di bastone, e cominciò a farsi incontro a' cani e contro al cavaliere. Ma il cavaliere che questo vide, gli gridò di lontano: — Nastagio, non t'impacciare, lascia fare a' cani ed a me quello che questa malvagia femina ha meritato.

E così dicendo, i cani, presa forte la giovane ne' fianchi, la fermarono, ed il cavaliere sopraggiunto smontò da cavallo; al quale

Several times Nastagio laughed at that advice; but, urged by them and unable to keep on refusing, he assented. Making lavish preparations, as if he were going to France, Spain, or some other distant place, he mounted his horse and in the company of his friends left Ravenna and traveled to a spot about three miles outside Ravenna called Classe. Sending for tents and pavilions, he told those who had come with him that he wanted to stay, asking them to return to Ravenna.

And so, Nastagio, setting up tents there, started to lead the finest and most magnificent existence possible, inviting various people for supper or dinner, as he was accustomed to do. Now, it happened that, one Friday near the beginning of May, when the weather was excellent, he started thinking about his cruel lady. Ordering all his servants to leave him alone, so he could pursue his thoughts more freely, he gradually walked into the local pine woods, lost in thought.

The time being nearly eleven in the morning, and he having walked about a half mile into the woods, forgetful of food and everything else, he suddenly thought he heard a loud lament and shrill cries uttered by a woman. And so, abandoning his pleasant thoughts, he raised his head to see what was happening, and was amazed to find himself deep in the forest. Furthermore, looking in front of him, he saw coming through a very dense stand of bushes and brambles, and running in his direction, a very beautiful nude young woman, disheveled and scratched all over by the branches and thorns, weeping and crying aloud for mercy. In addition, he saw beside her two large, fierce mastiffs running hard after her and often cruelly biting her whenever they reached her. And behind her, on a black charger, he saw a dark-haired knight, his features expressing great anger; he was holding a rapier, and threatening her with death in frightening and insulting terms.

This sight inspired Nastagio's mind with amazement, fear, and finally pity for the unfortunate lady; from this pity arose a desire to rescue her from such great pain and death, if he could. But, finding himself unarmed, he ran and broke off a branch to use as a club, and he began to face the dogs and confront the knight. But the knight, seeing this, shouted to him from a distance: "Nastagio, don't meddle in this! Let the dogs and me do what this wicked woman has deserved!"

When he had said this, the dogs seized the young woman's sides, stopping her, and the knight, arriving on the spot, dismounted.

Nastagio avvicinatosi, disse: — Io non so chi tu ti se' che me così conosci, ma tanto ti dico, che gran viltà è d'un cavaliere armato volere uccidere una femina ignuda ed averle i cani alle coste messi come se ella fosse una fiera selvatica; io per certo la difenderò quanto io potrò.

Il cavaliere allora disse: — Nastagio, io fui d'una medesima terra teco, ed eri tu ancora piccol fanciullo quando io, il quale fui chiamato messer Guido degli Anastagi, era troppo più innamorato di costei che tu ora non se' di quella de' Traversari; e per la sua fierezza e crudeltà andò sì la mia sciagura, che io un dì, con questo stocco il quale tu mi vedi in mano, come disperato m'uccisi, e sono alle pene eternali dannato. Né stette poi guari di tempo, che costei, la qual della mia morte fu lieta oltre misura, morì, e per lo peccato della sua crudeltà e della letizia avuta de' miei tormenti, non pentendosene, come colei che non credeva in ciò aver peccato ma meritato, similmente fu ed è dannata alle pene del ninferno; nel quale come ella discese, così ne fu, ed a lei ed a me, per pena dato, a lei di fuggirmi davanti, ed a me, che già cotanto l'amai, di seguitarla come mortal nemica, non come amata donna; e quante volte io la giungo, tante con questo stocco col quale io uccisi me, uccido lei ed àprola per ischiena, e quel cuor duro e freddo nel qual mai né amor né pietà poterono entrare, con l'altre interiora insieme, sì come tu vedrai incontanente, le caccio di corpo, e dolle mangiare a questi cani. Né sta poi grande spazio, che ella, sì come la giustizia e la potenza di Dio vuole, come se morta non fosse stata, risurge e da capo incomincia la dolorosa fugga, ed i cani ed io a seguitarla; ed avviene che ogni venerdì in su questa ora io la giungo qui, e qui ne fo lo strazio che vedrai; e gli altri dì non credere che noi riposiamo, ma giungola in altri luoghi ne' quali ella crudelmente contro a me pensò o operò; ed essendole d'amante divenuto nemico, come tu vedi, la mi conviene in questa guisa tanti anni seguitar quanti mesi ella fu contro a me crudele. Adunque, lasciami la divina giustizia mandare ad esecuzione, né ti volere opporre a quello a che tu non potresti contrastare.

Nastagio, udendo queste parole, tutto timido divenuto e quasi non avendo pelo addosso che arricciato non fosse, tirandosi addietro e riguardando alla misera giovane, cominciò pauroso ad aspettare quei che facesse il cavaliere; il quale, finito il suo ragionare, a guisa d'un cane rabbioso, con lo stocco in mano corse addosso alla giovane, la quale, inginocchiata e da' due mastini tenuta forte, gli gridava mercé, ed a quella con tutta sua forza diede per mezzo il petto e passolla dall'altra parte.

Nastagio came up to him and said: "I don't know who you are or how you know me, but I tell you that it's great cowardice in an armed knight to want to kill a naked woman and to set his dogs upon her as if she were a wild beast; you can be sure that I will do all I can to protect her."

Then the knight said: "I was from your city. You were still a small boy when I, Sir Guido degli Anastagi, was more deeply in love with this woman than you now are with the Traversari girl. Because of her fierceness and cruelty, my unhappiness increased until, one day, with this very rapier you see me holding, I killed myself in despair, and am thus condemned to eternal punishment. Not long afterward, she, who was immoderately happy at my death, died herself; because she had sinned by being so cruel and taking such pleasure in my suffering, and because she made no atonement for this, thinking she had not sinned but earned merit by her behavior, she likewise was and is condemned to the pains of hell. When she descended there, it was given to us, her and me, as punishment, that she should run from me and that I, who once loved her so, should pursue her as my mortal enemy, not as my beloved. Every time I catch up with her, I kill her with this rapier I employed to kill myself with, and I rip her back open, and pull out of her body that hard, cold heart which love and pity could never enter; along with her other internal organs, as you will see right away, I give it to the dogs to eat. But before very long, as God's justice and might prescribe, she arises as if she had never died and resumes her sad race, the dogs and I pursuing her. Every Friday at this hour I catch up with her here, and here I slaughter her as you will see. You mustn't think that we're at rest on the other days; rather, I catch up with her in other places in which she once conceived cruel thoughts or actions against me. Having changed from her lover to her enemy, as you see, I am compelled to pursue her this way for a number of years equal to the number of months that she was cruel to me. And so, allow me to fulfill the commandment of divine justice, and do not oppose something you're unable to prevent."

Hearing these words, Nastagio took fright, and there was hardly a hair on his body that didn't stand on end. Drawing back and looking at the unhappy young woman, he began to wait timidly and see what the knight would do. When the knight had done speaking, he ran up to the young woman, rapier in hand, like a mad dog. She, kneeling and pinned down by the two mastiffs, shouted for mercy. With all his strength he struck her in the middle of her chest and pierced her through.

Il qual colpo come la giovane ebbe ricevuto, così cadde boccone sempre piagnendo e gridando; ed il cavaliere, messo mano ad un coltello, quella aprì nelle reni, e fuori tràttone il cuore ed ogni altra cosa da torno, a' due mastini il gittò, li quali affamatissimi incontanente il mangiarono; né stette guari, che la giovane, quasi niuna di queste cose stata fosse, subitamente si levò in pié e cominciò a fuggire verso il mare, ed i cani appresso di lei, sempre lacerandola, ed il cavaliere, rimontato a cavallo e ripreso il suo stocco, la cominciò a seguitare; ed in piccola ora si dileguarono in maniera, che più Nastagio non gli poté vedere.

Il quale, avendo queste cose vedute, gran pezza stette tra pietoso e pauroso, e dopo alquanto gli venne nella mente, questa cosa dovergli molto poter valere, poi che ogni venerdì avvenia; per che, segnato il luogo, a' suoi famigliari se ne tornò, ed appresso, quando gli parve, mandato per più suoi parenti ed amici, disse loro:

— Voi m'avete lungo tempo stimolato che io d'amare questa mia nemica mi rimanga e ponga fine al mio spendere; ed io son presto di farlo, dove voi una grazia m'impetriate, la quale è questa, che venerdì che viene voi facciate sì che messer Paolo Traversaro e la moglie e la figliuola e tutte le donne lor parenti, ed altre chi vi piacerà, qui sieno a desinar meco. Quello per che io questo voglia, voi il vedrete allora.

A costor parve questa assai piccola cosa a dover fare; ed a Ravenna tornati, quando tempo fu, coloro invitarono li quali Nastagio voleva, e come che dura cosa fosse il potervi menare la giovane da Nastagio amata, pur v'andò con altre insieme. Nastagio fece magnificamente apprestar da mangiare e fece le tavole mettere sotto i pini dintorno a quel luogo dove veduto aveva lo strazio della crudel donna; e fatti metter gli uomini e le donne a tavola, sì ordinò, che appunto la giovane amata da lui fu posta a seder di rimpetto al luogo dove doveva il fatto intervenire.

Essendo adunque già venuta l'ultima vivanda, ed il romor disperato della cacciata giovane da tutti fu cominciato ad udire; di che maravigliandosi forte ciascuno e domandando che ciò fosse, e niuno sappiendol dire, levatisi tutti diritti e riguardando che ciò potesse essere, videro la dolente giovane ed il cavaliere ed i cani, né guari stette che essi tutti furon quivi tra loro.

Il romore fu fatto grande ed a' cani ed al cavaliere, e molti per aiutare la giovane si fecero innanzi, ma il cavaliere, parlando loro come a Nastagio aveva parlato, non solamente gli fece indietro tirare, ma tutti gli spaventò e riempì di maraviglia; e faccendo

As soon as the young woman had received that blow, she fell on her face, still weeping and crying out; the knight, laying hold of a knife, opened her back and, pulling out her heart and everything around it, he threw it to the two mastiffs, who immediately devoured it ravenously. In scarcely a moment, as if none of this had taken place, the young woman suddenly stood up and started running toward the sea with the dogs after her, constantly tearing at her. The knight, remounting and taking up his rapier again, started to pursue her, and before long they had vanished so that Nastagio could no longer see them.

Having viewed all this, he remained there a long while, half in pity and half in fear; after some time it occurred to him that this event could be very useful to him, since it occurred every Friday. And so, making a note of the place, he returned to his servants; later, when he thought the time was right, he sent for his relatives and friends, and said to them:

"For a long time you have urged me to cease loving that enemy of mine and to curb my spending. I'm ready to do so, if you grant me one favor: that, next Friday, you arrange for Paolo Traversari to come and dine with me here with his wife, his daughter, all their female relatives, and any other women you choose. The reason for my request you will see at that time."

They considered this a very small favor to grant; back in Ravenna, when the time came, they invited those whom Nastagio had asked for. Even though they had trouble bringing the girl Nastagio loved, still she did come along with the others. Nastagio had a splendid meal prepared, having the tables laid out under the pine trees around the place where he had witnessed the slaughter of the cruel lady. Having summoned the men and women to table, he arranged to have the girl he loved seated exactly opposite the place where the event was to occur.

And so, after the last course had arrived, they all began to hear the despairing cries of the hunted young woman. Everyone was greatly surprised at this and asked what it could be, but no one could answer. They all stood up and gazed to see what could be going on, when they saw the sorrowful young woman, the knight, and the dogs, who before long were all there in their midst.

They raised a great outcry against both the dogs and the knight, and many men started forward to help the young woman, but the knight, telling them the same thing he had told Nastagio, not only made them draw back but also frightened them all and filled them

quello che altra volta aveva fatto, quante donne v'aveva (ché ve n'aveva assai che parenti erano state e della dolente giovane e del cavaliere, e che si ricordavano dell'amore e della morte di lui), tutte così miseramente piagnevano come se a se medesime quello avesser veduto fare.

La qual cosa al suo termine fornita, ed andata via la donna ed il cavaliere, mise costoro che ciò veduto aveano in molti e vari ragionamenti; ma tra gli altri che più di spavento ebbero, fu la crudel giovane da Nastagio amata, la quale ogni cosa distintamente veduta avea ed udita, e conosciuto che a sé più che ad altra persona che vi fosse queste cose toccavano, ricordandosi della crudeltà sempre da lei usata verso Nastagio; per che già le parea fuggire dinanzi da lui adirato ed avere i mastini a' fianchi.

E tanta fu la paura che di questo le nacque, che, acciò che questo a lei non avvenisse, prima tempo non si vide (il quale quella medesima sera prestato le fu) che ella, avendo l'odio in amor tramutato, una sua fida cameriera segretamente a Nastagio mandò, la quale da parte di lei il pregò che gli dovesse piacere d'andare a lei, per ciò che ella era presta di far tutto ciò che fosse piacer di lui.

Alla qual Nastagio fece rispondere che questo gli era a grado molto, ma che, dove le piacesse, con onor di lei volea il suo piacere, e questo era sposandola per moglie. La giovane, la qual sapeva che da altrui che da lei rimaso non era che moglie di Nastagio stata non fosse, gli fece risponder che le piacea; per che, essendo ella medesima la messaggera, al padre ed alla madre disse che era contenta d'essere sposa di Nastagio, di che essi furon contenti molto; e la domenica seguente Nastagio sposatala e fatte le sue nozze, con lei più tempo lietamente visse. E non fu questa paura cagione solamente di questo bene, anzi sì tutte le ravignane donne paurose ne divennero, che sempre poi troppo più arrendevoli a' piaceri degli uomini furono che prima state non erano.

FEDERIGO E IL SUO FALCONE [V, 9]

Era già di parlar ristata Filomena, quando la reina, avendo veduto che più niuno a dover dire se non Dionèo, per lo suo privilegio, v'era rimaso, con lieto viso disse:

A me omai appartiene di ragionare; ed io, carissime donne, d'una novella simile in parte alla precedente il farò volentieri, non acciò solamente che conosciate quanto la vostra vaghezza possa ne' cuor

with awe. When he proceeded to do what he had done the last time, all the women present (for many of them were relatives of both the afflicted young woman and the knight, and recalled his love and death) wept as bitterly as if they had seen it happening to themselves.

When the procedure was completed, and the woman and the knight were gone, those who had seen this had a long, varied discussion about it. But among those who were most frightened by it was the cruel young woman whom Nastagio loved. She had seen and heard everything distinctly, and realized that those events were more relevant to her than to anyone else there, recalling the cruelty with which she had always treated Nastagio. And so she already had visions of running away from his angry pursuit with the mastiffs at her side.

This instilled such great fear in her that, to avoid having it happen to her, she seized the earliest opportunity (which was offered to her that very evening) to change her hatred to love, and to send a trustworthy maid to Nastagio in secret, to ask him on her behalf to be so good as to come and see her, since she was ready to do anything he liked.

Nastagio replied that he was very happy to do so, but that, if she liked, he wanted his pleasure to redound to her honor; that is, he wanted to marry her. The young woman, aware that only she was to blame for not already being Nastagio's wife, replied that she was willing. And so, acting as her own marriage broker, she told her father and mother that she would gladly become Nastagio's bride, and they were very pleased. The next Sunday, Nastagio married her and celebrated his wedding; he lived with her happily for many years. And not only was that scene of terror the cause of that glad event, but, in addition, all the women in Ravenna became so alarmed by it that forever afterward they were much more compliant to the menfolk's wishes than they had been previously.

FEDERIGO AND HIS FALCON [V, 9]

Filomena had already finished speaking when the "Queen," seeing that no one had yet to speak but [herself and] Dioneo, thanks to his privilege, said with a cheerful face:

It now behooves me to speak; and I, dearest ladies, will gladly do so, telling a story partially similar to the last one, not merely so that you may learn what power your charm wields over noble hearts, but

gentili, ma perché apprendiate d'essere voi medesime, dove si
conviene, donatrici de' vostri guiderdoni senza lasciarne sempre
esser la fortuna guidatrice, la qual non discretamente, ma, come
s'avviene, smoderatamente il più delle volte dona.

Dovete adunque sapere che Coppo di Borghese Domenichi, il
quale fu nella nostra città e forse ancora è, uomo di grande e di re-
verenda autorità ne' dì nostri, e per costumi e per vertù molto più
che per nobiltà di sangue chiarissimo e degno d'eterna fama, ed essendo già d'anni pieno, spesse volte delle cose passate co' suoi
vicini e con altri si dilettava di ragionare; la qual cosa egli meglio e
con più ordine e con maggior memoria ed ornato parlare che altro
uom seppe fare; ed era usato di dire tra l'altre sue belle cose che in
Firenze fu già un giovane chiamato Federigo di messer Filippo
Alberighi, in opera d'arme ed in cortesia pregiato sopra ogni altro
donzel di Toscana.

Il quale, sì come, il più, de' gentili uomini avviene, d'una gentil
donna chiamata monna Giovanna s'innamorò, ne' suoi tempi
tenuta delle più belle donne e delle più leggiadre che in Firenze
fossero; ed acciò che egli l'amor di lei acquistar potesse, giostrava,
armeggiava, faceva feste e donava, ed il suo senza alcun ritegno
spendeva; ma ella, non meno onesta che bella, niente di queste
cose per lei fatte né di colui si curava che le faceva.

Spendendo adunque Federigo oltre ad ogni suo potere molto e
niente acquistando, sì come di leggeri addiviene, le ricchezze man-
carono, ed esso rimase povero, senza altra cosa che un suo
poderetto piccolo essergli rimasa, delle rendite del quale strettissi-
mamente vivea, ed oltre a questo, un suo falcone de' miglior del
mondo; per che, amando più che mai né parendogli più potere essere cittadino come disiderava, a Campi, là dove il suo poderetto
era, se n'andò a stare. Quivi, quando poteva, uccellando e senza alcuna persona richiedere, pazientemente la sua povertà compor-
tava.

Ora, avvenne un dì che, essendo così Federigo divenuto allo
stremo, che il marito di monna Giovanna infermò, e veggendosi
alla morte venire, fece testamento; ed essendo ricchissimo, in
quello lasciò suo erede un suo figliuolo già grandicello, ed appresso
questo, avendo molto amata monna Giovanna, lei, se avvenisse che
il figliuolo senza erede legittimo morisse, suo erede sostituì e
morissi. Rimasa adunque vedova monna Giovanna, come usanza è

also so that you may learn to be the bestowers of your own rewards, when this is proper, and not always let Fortune be the guide, for most of the time she makes her gifts not prudently but, as it happens, without moderation.

Well, then, let me tell you that Coppo Domenichi, son of Borghese Domenichi, was, and perhaps still is,[1] a man of great and reverend authority in our city in our time. Very distinguished and worthy of eternal fame because of his ways and virtue much more than because of the nobility of his blood, when already full of years he often enjoyed talking about events of the past with his neighbors and others. He surpassed all others in this by his narrative skill, his good memory, and the elegance of his diction. Among his other good stories, he was accustomed to tell that there once lived in Florence a young man named Federigo Alberighi, son of Master Filippo Alberighi; in feats of arms and courtly manners Federigo was esteemed as the leading young nobleman in Tuscany.

As is the case with most young noblemen, he fell in love with a noblewoman named Monna Giovanna, who in her day was reputed to be one of the most beautiful and attractive women in Florence. In order to win her love, he used to participate in jousts and other warlike spectacles, and gave parties and made gifts, spending his wealth without restraint. But she, no less chaste than beautiful, cared nothing about those things or the man who did them.

And so, as Federigo continued to practice extravagance a great deal beyond his means, gaining nothing thereby, his money gave out, as so readily happens, and he was left poor, retaining only a very small country estate, from the proceeds of which he lived in very straitened circumstances; besides this, he owned a falcon, one of the very best. And so, more in love than ever but feeling he could no longer afford to live in town as he liked, he went to live at Campi,[2] where his property was located. There, hunting with his falcon whenever he could, and asking no one for assistance, he patiently bore his poverty.

Now, it happened one day, when Federigo had thus reached rock bottom, that Monna Giovanna's husband fell ill, and seeing himself close to death, made a will. Being extremely wealthy, in that will he left as his heir his son, who was already a fairly big boy; then, since he had greatly loved Monna Giovanna, he named her as his heir in the event that his son should die without a legitimate heir of his own. Then her husband died. And so, Monna Giovanna, left widowed,

---

[1]If not killed off by the plague. [2]A village not far from Florence.

delle nostre donne, l'anno di state con questo suo figliuolo se n'andava in contado ad una sua possessione assai vicina a quella di
Federigo; per che avvenne che questo garzoncello s'incominciò a
dimesticare con Federigo ed a dilettarsi d'uccelli e di cani; ed
avendo veduto molte volte il falcon di Federigo volare, stranamente piacendogli, forte disiderava d'averlo, ma pure non s'attentava di domandarlo, veggendolo a lui essere cotanto caro.

E così stando la cosa, avvenne che il garzoncello infermò, di che
la madre dolorosa molto, come colei che più non n'avea e lui amava
quanto più si poteva, tutto il dì standogli dintorno, non ristava di
confortarlo e spesse volte il domandava se alcuna cosa era la quale
egli disiderasse, pregandolo gliele dicesse, ché per certo, se possibile fosse ad avere, procaccerebbe come l'avesse. Il giovanetto,
udite molte volte queste profferte disse: — Madre mia, se voi fate
che io abbia il falcone di Federico, io mi credo prestamente guerire.

La donna, udendo questo, alquanto sopra sé stette, e cominciò a
pensar quello che far dovesse. Ella sapeva che Federigo lungamente l'aveva amata, né mai da lei una sola guatatura aveva avuta;
per che ella diceva: — Come manderò io o andrò a domandargli
questo falcone, che è, per quel che io oda, il migliore che mai
volasse, ed oltre a ciò, il mantien nel mondo? E come sarò io sì
sconoscente, che ad un gentile uomo al quale niuno altro diletto è
più rimaso, io questo gli voglia tôrre?

Ed in così fatto pensiero impacciata, come che ella fosse certissima d'averlo se il domandasse, senza sapere che dover dire, non
rispondeva al figliuolo, ma si stava. Ultimamente, tanto la vinse
l'amor del figliuolo, che ella seco dispose, per contentarlo, che che
esserne dovesse, di non mandare, ma d'andare ella medesima per
esso e di recargliele, e risposegli: — Figliuol mio, confòrtati e pensa
di guerire di forza, che io ti prometto che la prima cosa che io farò
domattina, io andrò per esso e sì il ti recherò.

Di che il fanciullo lieto, il dì medesimo mostrò alcun migliora-
mento. La donna la mattina seguente, presa un'altra donna in compagnia, per modo di diporto se n'andò alla piccola casetta di
Federigo e fecelo addomandare. Egli, per ciò che non era tempo,
né era stato a quei dì, d'uccellare, era in un suo orto e faceva certi
suoi lavorietti acconciare; il quale, udendo che monna Giovanna il
domandava alla porta, maravigliandosi forte, lieto là corse, la quale
veggendol venire, con una donnesca piacevolezza levatagli incontro, avendola già Federigo reverentemente salutata, disse: — Bene
stea Federigo!

followed the custom of our women by going to the country with her son every summer. The estate she occupied was very close to Federigo's, and so that boy struck up a friendship with Federigo and took delight in hunting with hawk and hound. Having often seen Federigo's falcon fly, he took an extreme fancy to it and wanted very much to own it, and yet didn't venture to ask for it, seeing how dear it was to its owner.

And, things being thus, the boy happened to fall ill. His mother, extremely sorrowful because she had no other children and loved him as much as possible, remained at his side all day long, never ceasing to comfort him. She frequently asked him whether there was anything he wanted, urging him to tell her, because, if it could possibly be acquired, she would definitely make sure he got it. The boy, hearing that offer so frequently, said: "Mother, if you arrange to get Federigo's falcon for me, I think I'll get well right away."

Hearing this, the lady felt a jolt, but then began to plan what she should do. She knew that Federigo had long loved her but had never won even a kind look from her. And so she said: "How can I send someone, or go myself, to ask him for that falcon, which, from what I hear, is the best that ever flew, and, besides that, keeps him alive with its hunting? And how can I be so ungrateful as to take away a worthy man's sole remaining pleasure?"

And, entangled in such thoughts, even though she was sure she'd get it if she asked for it, she didn't know what to say; she didn't answer her son, but waited. Finally her love for her son got the upper hand, and she determined, in order to satisfy him no matter what the outcome, to go for the falcon personally, not sending a messenger, and to bring it back for him. And so she replied: "Son, cheer up and think about getting well and strong, because I promise you that, first thing tomorrow morning, I'll go for it and bring it back for you."

The boy, happy to hear that, showed some improvement that very day. The next morning, the lady, taking another lady as a companion, as if on an outing, went to Federigo's little house and asked for him. Because the weather wasn't right for hawking, and hadn't been for a few days, he was in his vegetable garden attending to various chores. Hearing that Monna Giovanna was asking for him at the door, he was very surprised and ran over cheerfully. Seeing him come, she went up to meet him with courtly charm and, after Federigo had greeted her reverently, she said: "Good health to you, Federigo!"

E seguitò: — Io son venuta a ristorarti de' danni li quali tu hai già avuti per me, amandomi più che stato non ti sarebbe bisogno; ed il ristoro è cotale, che io intendo con questa mia compagna insieme desinar teco dimesticamente stamane.

Alla qual Federigo umilmente rispose: — Madonna, niun danno mi ricorda mai avere ricevuto per voi, ma tanto di bene che, se io mai alcuna cosa valsi, per lo vostro valore e per l'amore che portato v'ho addivenne; e per certo questa vostra liberale venuta m'è troppo più cara che non sarebbe se da capo mi fosse dato da spendere quanto per addietro ho già speso, come che a povero oste siate venuta.

E così detto, vergognosamente dentro alla sua casa la ricevette, e di quella nel suo giardino la condusse, e quivi non avendo a cui farle tener compagnia ad altrui, disse: — Madonna, poi che altri non c'è, questa buona donna, moglie di questo lavoratore, vi terrà compagnia tanto che io vada a far metter la tavola.

Egli, con tutto che la sua povertà fosse strema, non s'era ancor tanto avveduto quanto bisogno gli facea che egli avesse fuor d'ordine spese le sue ricchezze; ma questa mattina, niuna cosa trovandosi di che potere onorar la donna, per amore della quale egli già infiniti uomini onorati avea, il fe' ravvedere.

Ed oltre modo angoscioso, seco stesso maladicendo la sua fortuna, come uomo che fuor di sé fosse, or qua ed or là trascorrendo, né denari né pegno trovandosi, essendo l'ora tarda ed il disidéro grande di pure onorar d'alcuna cosa la gentil donna, e non volendo, non che altrui, ma il lavorator suo stesso richiedere, gli corse agli occhi il suo buon falcone, il quale nella sua saletta vide sopra la stanga; per che, non avendo a che altro ricorrere, presolo e trovatolo grasso, pensò lui esser degna vivanda di cotal donna. E però, senza pensare, tiràtogli il collo, ad una sua fanticella il fe' prestamente, pelato ed acconcio, mettere in uno schedone ed arrostir diligentemente; e messa la tavola con tovaglie bianchissime, delle quali alcuna ancora avea, con lieto viso ritornò alla donna nel suo giardino, ed il desinare che per lui far si potea, disse essere apparecchiato.

Laonde la donna con la sua compagna levatasi, andarono a tavola, e senza saper che si mangiassero, insieme con Federigo il quale con somma fede le serviva, mangiarono il buon falcone. E levate da tavola, ed alquanto con piacevoli ragionamenti con lui dimorate, parendo alla donna tempo di dire quello per che andata era, così benignamente verso Federigo cominciò a parlare:

— Federigo, ricordandoti tu della tua preterita vita e della mia

Then she continued: "I've come to make things up to you for the harm you've suffered on my account because you loved me more than you should have. And my reparation is as follows: my companion and I intend to have an informal meal with you this noon."

Federigo humbly replied: "My lady, I can't recall ever suffering harm on your account; on the contrary, I've received such benefits that, if I ever possessed any worth, it was only thanks to *your* worth and the love I bore you. This kind visit of yours definitely means much more to me than if I could spend again everything I spent in the past—though you've come to a penniless host."

Saying this, he welcomed her to his house timidly and humbly. From the house he led her into his ornamental garden, where, having no one else to keep her company, he said: "My lady, since there's no one else, this good woman, the wife of my farmer, will keep you company while I go see to the meal."

Even though his poverty was extreme, he had not yet noticed as much as he should have that he had spent his wealth immoderately. But that morning, this was made plain to him by his inability to find anything with which to entertain the lady, out of love for whom he had once given hospitality to an infinite number of people.

Distressed beyond measure, silently cursing his fortune, like a man beside himself he ran back and forth, finding neither money nor anything to pawn. The hour was late, and his desire was great to find something to serve to the noblewoman. Not wishing to ask anyone, not even his own farmer, for assistance, his eyes fell on his good falcon, which he saw on its perch in its little room. And so, having no other recourse, he picked it up, and finding it plump, imagined it would be a worthy dish for so great a lady. And so, without further thought, he wrung its neck and had his maid quickly pluck and clean it, put it on a spit, and carefully roast it. Setting the table with gleaming white cloths, of which he still owned some, he returned to the lady in his garden with a cheerful expression and told her that whatever dinner he had been able to prepare was ready.

Whereupon the lady and her companion arose, went to the table, and, not knowing what they were eating, together with Federigo, who served her most devotedly, ate the good falcon. The woman rose from table and spent a while with him in pleasant conversation. Then, thinking it was time to tell him what she had come for, the lady began addressing Federigo kindly in these words:

"Federigo, when you recall your past life and my chastity, which

onestà, la quale per avventura tu hai reputata durezza e crudeltà, io non dubito punto che tu non ti debbi maravigliare della mia presunzione, sentendo quello per che principalmente qui venuta sono; ma se figliuoli avessi o avessi avuti, per li quali potessi conoscere di quanta forza sia l'amor che lor si porta, mi parrebbe esser certa che in parte m'avresti per iscusata. Ma come che tu non n'abbia, io che n'ho uno, non posso però le leggi comuni dell'altre madri fuggire; le cui forze seguir convenendomi, mi conviene, oltre al piacer mio ed oltre ad ogni convenevolezza e dovere, chiederti un dono il quale io so che sommamente t'è caro; ed è ragione, per ciò che niuno altro diletto, niuno altro diporto, niuna consolazione lasciata t'ha la tua strema fortuna; e questo dono è il falcon tuo, del quale il fanciul mio è sì forte invaghito, che, se io non gliele porto, io temo che egli non aggravi tanto nella 'nfermità la quale ha, che poi ne segua cosa per la quale io il perda. E per ciò ti priego, non per l'amore che tu mi porti, al quale tu di niente se' tenuto, ma per la tua nobiltà la quale in usar cortesia s'è maggiore che in alcuno altro mostrata, che ti debba piacere di donàrlomi, acciò che io per questo dono possa dire d'avere ritenuto in vita il mio figliuolo, e per quello avèrloti sempre obligato.

Federigo, udendo ciò che la donna addomandava e sentendo che servir non ne la potea, per ciò che mangiar gliele avea dato, cominciò in presenza di lei a piagnere anzi che alcuna parola risponder potesse: il qual pianto la donna prima credette che da dolore di dover da sé dipartire il buon falcon divenisse, più che da altro, e quasi fu per dire che nol volesse; ma pur sostenutasi, aspettò dopo il pianto la risposta di Federigo. Il qual così disse:

— Madonna, poscia che a Dio piacque che io in voi ponessi il mio amore, in assai cose m'ho reputata la fortuna contraria e sonmi di lei doluto, ma tutte sono state leggére a rispetto di quello che ella mi fa al presente, di che io mai pace con lei aver non debbo, pensando che voi qui alla mia povera casa venuta siete, dove, mentre che ricca fu, venir non degnaste, e da me un piccol don vogliate, ed ella abbia sì fatto, che io donar nol vi possa; e perché questo esser non possa, vi dirò brievemente. Come io udii che voi, la vostra mercé, meco desinar volevate, avendo riguardo alla vostra eccellenza ed al vostro valore, reputai degna e convenevole cosa che con più cara vivanda, secondo la mia possibilità, io vi dovessi onorare, che con quelle che generalmente per l'altre persone s'usano; per che, ricordandomi del falcon che mi domandate e della sua bontà, degno cibo da voi il reputai; e questa mattina arrostito l'avete avuto

you may have looked on as hardness and cruelty, I have no doubt that you will be amazed at my presumptuousness when you hear the main reason for my visit. But if you had ever had children, now or in the past, so that you could know how strong one's love for them is, I think you would surely excuse me in part. But even though you have none, I, who do have one, cannot escape the natural feelings common to all mothers; being obliged to obey the strength of those feelings, I am obliged, though it goes against my wishes and against all propriety and duty, to ask you to make a gift of something that I know is extremely precious to you—and rightly so, because the severity of your fortune has left you with no other pleasure, relaxation, or consolation. That gift is your falcon, of which my boy is so enamored that, if I don't bring it to him, I'm afraid his illness will get so bad that something will happen to make me lose him. And so I implore you, not for the love you bear me, which doesn't bind you in any way, but out of your nobility, which in the practice of courtliness has been seen to be greater than anyone else's, to have the goodness to offer it to me, so that, by means of that gift, I will be able to say I saved my son's life, thereby making him eternally obliged to you."

Federigo, hearing the lady's request and knowing he couldn't help her, because he had given her the falcon to eat, started to weep right there in front of her before he could say a word in reply. At first the lady thought he was crying for grief at having to part with the falcon, more than for any other reason, and she was on the point of saying she didn't want it; but she restrained herself and waited for Federigo to stop crying and answer her. He said:

"My lady, ever since it pleased God to have me fall in love with you, I have thought Fortune to be hostile to me on many occasions, and I've complained of her, but all those occasions were trivial compared to the blow she is dealing me now, for which I shall never forgive her when I think that you have come here to my humble home, which you didn't condescend to visit when it was wealthy, and are requesting a small gift of me—and Fortune has so arranged things that I can't give it to you! And I shall tell you briefly why it's impossible. When I heard that you graciously wished to dine with me, in consideration of your excellence and worth I deemed it fitting and proper to entertain you with finer food (within my limits) than is generally served to other people. And so, remembering the falcon you are asking me for, and its good qualities, I deemed it was a dish worthy of you. And this noon you had it, roasted, served to you on its platter. I believed I had made

in sul tagliere, il quale io per ottimamente allogato avea, ma veggendo ora che in altra maniera il disideravate, m'è sì gran duolo che servire non ve ne posso, che mai pace non me ne credo dare.
E questo detto, le penne ed i piedi ed il becco le fe' in testimonianza di ciò gittare avanti. La qual cosa la donna veggendo ed udendo, prima il biasimò d'aver per dar mangiare ad una femina ucciso un tal falcone, e poi la grandezza dell'animo suo, la quale la povertà non avea potuto né potea rintuzzare, molto seco medesima commendò; poi, rimasa fuori della speranza d'avere il falcone, e per quello della salute del figliuolo entrata in forse, tutta malinconosa si dipartì e tornossi al figliuolo.

Il quale, o per malinconia che il falcone aver non potea, o per la 'nfermità che pur a ciò il dovesse aver condotto, non trapassâr molti giorni che egli, con grandissimo dolor della madre, di questa vita passò.

La quale, poi che piena di lagrime e d'amaritudine fu stata alquanto, essendo rimasa ricchissima ed ancora giovane, più volte fu da' fratelli costretta a rimaritarsi; la quale, come che voluto non avesse, pur veggendosi infestare, ricordatasi del valore di Federigo e della sua magnificenza ultima, cioè d'avere ucciso un così fatto falcone per onorarla, disse a' fratelli: — Io volentieri, quando vi piacesse, mi starei; ma se a voi pur piace che io marito prenda, per certo io non ne prenderò mai alcun altro, se io non ho Federigo degli Alberighi.

Alla quale i fratelli, faccendosi beffe di lei, dissero: — Sciocca, che è ciò che tu di'? Come vuoi tu lui che non ha cosa del mondo?

A' quali ella rispose: — Fratelli miei, io so bene che così è come voi dite; ma io voglio avanti uomo che abbia bisogno di ricchezza che ricchezza che abbia bisogno d'uomo.

Li fratelli, udendo l'animo di lei e conoscendo Federigo da molto, quantunque povero fosse, sì come ella volle, lei con tutte le sue ricchezze gli donarono; il quale, così fatta donna e cui egli amata avea, per moglie veggendosi, ed oltre a ciò ricchissimo, in letizia con lei, miglior massaio fatto, terminò gli anni suoi.

IL FANCIULLO AMATO [V, 10]

Il ragionare della reina era alla sua fine venuto, essendo lodato da tutti Iddio che degnamente aveva guiderdonato Federigo, quando Dionèo, che mai comandamento non aspettava, incominciò:
Io non so se mi dica che sia accidental vizio e per malvagità di

the best possible use of it, but now that I see you wanted it for another purpose, I am so grieved at being unable to assist you, by giving it to you, that I don't believe I'll ever forgive myself."

Saying this, as evidence of his words he had its feathers, feet, and beak placed in front of her. Seeing and hearing this, the lady first upbraided him for killing such a fine falcon as food for a woman, and then, in her own mind, highly praised his nobility of soul, which poverty hadn't been able to diminish, either then or earlier. After that, seeing that her hopes of acquiring the falcon were gone, and therefore feeling insecure about her son's well-being, she left in deep melancholy and rejoined her son.

The boy, either because he was despondent at not getting the falcon, or because the illness would have led to it anyway, died not many days later, to his mother's extreme grief.

She remained a while full of tears and bitter sorrow; then, since she had now become very rich and was still young, she was frequently pressured by her brothers to remarry. Although she hadn't wanted to, nevertheless, finding herself so harassed, she remembered Federigo's worth and his last munificent gesture: killing so fine a falcon in order to offer her hospitality. She said to her brothers: "If you don't mind, I'd prefer to stay as I am, but if you insist that I take a husband, I will definitely never take anyone but Federigo degli Alberighi."

The brothers, laughing at her, said: "Silly woman, what are you saying? Why do you want a man who possesses nothing?"

She replied: "Brothers, I'm well aware it's as you say. But I'd rather have a real man who's short of wealth than a wealthy one who's short of manhood."

When her brothers heard her choice, knowing that Federigo was very worthy although poor, they let her have her way, giving her to him with all her riches. He, finding himself married to such a fine woman, whom he had loved for so long, and a wealthy man to boot, ended his days in happiness with her, having become a better manager of his money.

THE BELOVED BOY [V, 10]

The "Queen's" story had come to an end, all present praising God for having rewarded Federigo worthily, when Dioneo, who never waited to be asked, began:

I don't know whether to call it an acquired vice which has befallen

costume ne' mortali sopravvenuto, o se pure è della natura peccato,
il rider più tosto delle cattive cose che delle buone opere, e spezialmente quando quelle cotali a noi non pertengono. E per ciò che la
fatica la quale altra volta ho impresa, ed ora son per pigliare, a
niuno altro fine riguarda se non a dovervi tôrre malinconia, e riso
ed allegrezza porgervi, quantunque la materia della mia seguente
novella, innamorate giovani, sia in parte men che onesta, però che
diletto può porgere, la vi dirò; e voi, ascoltandola, quello ne fate che
usate di fare quando ne' giardini entrate, che, distesa la dilicata
mano, cogliete le rose e lasciate le spine stare; il che farete lasciando il cattivo uomo con la mala ventura stare con la sua disonestà, e liete riderete degli amorosi inganni della sua donna, compassione avendo all'altrui sciagure dove bisogna.

Fu in Perugia, non è ancora molto tempo passato, un ricco uomo
chiamato Pietro di Vinciolo, il quale, forse più per ingannare altrui
e diminuire la generale oppinion di lui avuta da tutti i Perugini che
per vaghezza che egli n'avesse, prese moglie; e fu la fortuna con-
forme al suo appetito in questo modo, che la moglie la quale egli
prese era una giovane compressa, di pel rosso ed accesa, la quale
due mariti più tosto che uno avrebbe voluti, là dove ella s'avvenne
ad uno che molto più ad altro che a lei l'animo avea disposto.

Il che ella in processo di tempo conoscendo, e veggendosi bella
e fresca, sentendosi gagliarda e poderosa, prima se ne cominciò
forte a turbare e ad averne col marito di sconce parole alcuna volta
e quasi di continuo mala vita; poi, veggendo che questo, suo con-
sumamento più tosto che ammendamento della cattività del marito
potrebbe essere, seco stessa disse:

— Questo dolente abbandona me per volere con le sue disonestà
andare in zoccoli per l'asciutto; ed io m'ingegnerò di portare altrui
in nave per lo piovoso. Io il presi per marito e diedigli grande e
buona dota sappiendo che egli era uomo e credendol vago di quello
che sono e deono essere vaghi gli uomini; e se io non avessi creduto
che fosse stato uomo, io non l'avrei mai preso. Egli, che sapeva che
io era femina, perché per moglie mi prendeva, se le femine contro
all'animo gli erano? Questo non è da sofferire. Se io non avessi voluto essere al mondo, io mi sarei fatta monaca; e volendoci essere,
come io voglio e sono, se io aspetterò diletto o piacer di costui, io
potrò per avventura, invano aspettando, invecchiare; e quando io
sarò vecchia ravveggendomi, indarno mi dorrò d'avere la mia

mortals because of their evil ways, or a natural sin, when we prefer to laugh over nasty things than over good actions, especially when the nasty things don't directly affect us. And because the labors I have already undergone, and am now about to undertake, have no other purpose than to free you of melancholy and offer you laughter and joy— even though, amorous young ladies, the subject of my next story is to some extent indecent, I shall tell it because it may provide delight. When you listen to it, do the same thing you normally do when you visit gardens: stretching out your delicate hand, pick the roses and leave the thorns. That's what you'll do if you leave the perverted man and his vices to his evil fortune, and laugh merrily at his wife's amorous ruses, feeling compassion for people's misfortunes when necessary.

In Perugia not long ago there was a rich man named Pietro di Vinciolo who, perhaps more to deceive people and palliate the bad impression everyone in Perugia had about him, rather than because he had a desire to, got married. And fortune complied with his desire in this way: the woman he married was young, physically firm and compact, redheaded, and florid; she could have used two husbands instead of one, whereas she had hit upon a man whose preferences lay elsewhere, and not so much with her.

When she had realized this in the course of time, seeing herself beautiful and vigorous, and feeling herself lively and ardent, first she became quite upset and began to speak insultingly to her husband about it at some times, and to lead an unhappy life at almost all times. Then, finding that this could sooner result in her exhaustion than in a change in her husband's perversion, she said to herself:

"This miserable creature deserts me so he can live indecently and 'walk in clogs over dry spots.' Well, I'll just contrive to 'ship people through rainy territory!'[1] I took him as a husband and gave him a nice big dowry in the knowledge he was a man and in the belief he liked what men do and should like. If I hadn't thought he was a man, I'd never have taken him. Why did he, knowing I was a woman, take me as his wife if women weren't to his taste? This is unbearable! If I had wanted to withdraw from the world, I'd have become a nun. But if I want to remain in society—which I'm in, and want to be in—if I wait till I get pleasure or satisfaction from him, I may very well grow old waiting for nothing. And when I take stock as an old woman, I'll lament in vain for having wasted my youth. If I want to indulge my

---

[1] The two phrases stand for homosexual and heterosexual lovemaking, respectively.

giovanezza perduta, alla qual dover consolare m'è egli assai buon
maestro e dimostratore, in farmi dilettare di quello che egli si
diletta; il quale diletto fia a me laudevole, dove biasimevole è forte
a lui: io offenderò le leggi sole, dove egli offende le leggi e la
natura.

Avendo adunque la buona donna così fatto pensiero avuto, e
forse più d'una volta, per dare segretamente a ciò effetto, si dimesticò con una vecchia che pareva pur santa Verdiana che dà beccare
alle serpi, la quale sempre co' paternostri in mano andava ad ogni
perdonanza, né mai d'altro che della vita de' santi Padri ragionava
e delle piaghe di san Francesco, e quasi da tutti era tenuta una
santa; e quando tempo le parve, l'aperse la sua intenzion compiutamente.

A cui la vecchia disse: — Figliuola mia, sallo Iddio, che sa tutte
le cose, che tu molto ben fai; e quando per niuna altra cosa il
facessi, sì il dovresti far tu e ciascuna giovane per non perdere il
tempo della vostra giovanezza, per ciò che niun dolore è pari a
quello, a chi conoscimento ha, che è ad avere il tempo perduto. E
da che diavol siam noi poi, da che noi siam vecchie, se non da
guardar la cenere intorno al focolare? Se niuna il sa o ne può render testimonianza, io sono una di quelle; ché ora che vecchia
sono, non senza grandissime ed amare punture d'animo conosco,
e senza prò, il tempo che andar lasciai; e ben che io nol perdessi
tutto, ché non vorrei che tu credessi che io fossi stata una milensa,
io pur non feci ciò che io avrei potuto fare; di che quando io mi
ricordo, veggendomi fatta come tu mi vedi, che non troverei chi
mi desse fuoco a cencio, Iddio il sa che dolore io sento. Degli uomini non avvien così: essi nascono buoni a mille cose, non pure a
questa, e la maggior parte sono da molto più vecchi che giovani;
ma le femine a niuna altra cosa che a fare questo e figliuoli, ci
nascono, e per questo son tenute care. E se tu non te n'avvedessi
ad altro, sì te ne déi tu avvedere a questo, che noi siam sempre
apparecchiate a ciò, che degli uomini non avviene; ed oltre a
questo, una femina stancherebbe molti uomini, dove molti uomini non possono una femina stancare; e per ciò che a questo
siam nate, da capo ti dico che tu fai molto bene a rendere al marito tuo pan per focaccia, sì che l'anima tua non abbia in vecchiezza che rimproverare alle carni. Di questo mondo ha ciascun

youth, he himself is a very good teacher and guide, showing me I should take pleasure in the very thing that gives *him* pleasure.[2] That kind of pleasure will be praiseworthy for me, whereas it's highly blameworthy for him: I will only be violating the law, whereas he violates the law and nature."

So, when the good woman had conceived that idea (and maybe more than once), in order to put it into effect secretly, she struck up an acquaintance with an old woman who looked just like Saint Verdiana[3] feeding her snakes. She went to every Church indulgence service, rosary in hand; never spoke of anything but the lives of the Fathers and Saint Francis's stigmata; and was herself considered a saint by almost everyone. When Pietro's wife thought the right time had come, she revealed her entire plan to her.

The old woman said: "Daughter, God, who knows all things, knows that you are very right to do this. Even if you did it for no other reason, you and every young woman should do it in order not to waste your youthful years; because, to anyone in the know, there's no sorrow equal to that of having wasted your time. And what the hell are we good for, after we become old, except for watching the ashes around the hearth? If there's anyone who knows this and can testify to it, it's me; because now that I'm old, I realize, with enormous and bitter mental pangs, but to no advantage, how much time I let slip by. Even though I didn't waste it all, because I wouldn't want you to think I was a dimwit, all the same I didn't do everything I could have. When I think about that, and I see myself in the state you see me in, a person for whom nobody would lift a finger,[4] only God knows how bad I feel. That doesn't happen to men: by birth, they're good for a thousand things, not just sex, and most of them are more highly skilled when old than when young; but women are born for nothing but bed and children, and they're cherished only for that. And even if you didn't recall any other proof, you ought to recall this: we're always prepared for the act, which isn't the case with men. Besides, one woman can tire out many men, whereas many men can't tire out one woman. So, because we're born to do it, I tell you again that you're very right to give your husband tit for tat, 'bread for cake,' so that your soul won't have to upbraid your flesh when you're old. In this world everyone gets only what he grabs, and

---

[2]Boys.   [3]A local saint whose iconography included snakes, which had once attacked her.   [4]Literally: "nobody would give me fire on a rag" (considered to be the most trivial favor). Women used to borrow a light from neighbors who had already kindled their fire, the borrower using a rag or a spill to carry it home.

tanto quanto egli se ne toglie e spezialmente le femine, alle quali si convien troppo più d'adoperare il tempo quando l'hanno che agli uomini, per ciò che tu puoi vedere che, quando c'invecchiamo, né marito né altri ci vuol vedere, anzi ci cacciano in cucina a dir favole con la gatta e ad annoverare le pentole e le scodelle; e peggio, che noi siamo messe in canzone, e dicono: «Alle giovani i buon bocconi — ed alle vecchie gli stranguglioni», ed altre lor cose assai ancora dicono. Ed acciò che io non ti tenga più in parole, ti dico infino da ora che tu non potevi a persona del mondo scoprire l'animo tuo che più utile ti fosse di me, per ciò che egli non è alcun sì forbito, al quale io non ardisca di dire ciò che bisogna, né sì duro o zotico, che io non ammorbidisca bene e rèchilo a ciò che io vorrò. Fa' pure che tu mi mostri qual ti piace, e lascia poscia fare a me; ma una cosa ti ricordo, figliuola mia, che io ti sia raccomandata, per ciò che io son povera persona, ed io voglio infino da ora che tu sii partefice di tutte le mie perdonanze e di quanti paternostri io dirò, acciò che Iddio gli faccia lume e candela a' morti tuoi. — E fece fine.

Rimase adunque la giovane in questa concordia con la vecchia, che, se veduto le venisse un giovanetto il quale per quella contrada molto spesso passava, del quale tutti i segni le disse, che ella sapesse quello che avesse a fare; e datole un pezzo di carne salata, la mandò con Dio. La vecchia, non passâr molti dì, occultamente le mise colui di cui ella detto l'aveva, in camera, ed ivi a poco tempo uno altro, secondo che alla giovane donna ne venivan piacendo; la quale, in cosa che far potesse intorno a ciò, sempre del marito temendo, non ne lasciava a far tratto.

Avvenne che, dovendo una sera andare a cena il marito con un suo amico, il quale aveva nome Ercolano, la giovane impose alla vecchia che facesse venire a lei un garzone che era dei più belli e de' più piacevoli di Perugia; la quale prestamente così fece. Ed essendosi la donna col giovane posti a tavola per cenare, ed ecco Pietro chiamò all'uscio che aperto gli fosse.

La donna, questo sentendo, si tenne morta; ma pur volendo, se potuto avesse, celare il giovane, non avendo accorgimento di mandarlo o di farlo nascondere in altra parte, essendo una sua loggetta vicina alla camera nella quale cenavano, sotto una cesta da polli che v'era il fece ricoverare, e gittovvi suso un pannaccio d'un saccone

especially women, whom it behooves much more than men to use their time when they have it. Because you can see that, when we get old, neither husbands nor anyone else wants to look at us, but instead they chase us into the kitchen to tell stories to the cat and to count the pots and pans. Even worse, they make up songs about us, saying: 'The tasty tidbits for young women, and for old women the tough pieces.'[5] And they have many other such sayings. And, in order not to waste your time with more words, I tell you now that you couldn't have revealed your plan to anyone in the world more useful to you than I am, because there's no man so refined that I'm not brave enough to tell him his business, and no one so rough and uncouth that I can't soften him up and bring him around to do what I want. Go right ahead and show me what you fancy, and then leave the rest to me. But I remind you of one thing, daughter: keep my needs in mind, because I'm a poor person, and from now on I'll mention you at all my indulgence services and in every Our Father I say, so that God will shine upon your dead relatives."[6] And so she concluded.

Therefore the young woman made this compact with the old one: if the latter should happen to see a certain young man who passed through that neighborhood very often (and she gave her a full description of him), then she knew what she was to do. She gave her a piece of salted meat and sent her on her way. Not many days later, the old woman clandestinely sent the youngster she had mentioned to her bedroom, and, not long after, another and another, according to the young woman's preference of the moment. Although always afraid of her husband, the young woman didn't cease taking advantage of every opportunity.

It so happened that, one evening when her husband was due to have supper with a friend named Ercolano, the young woman ordered the old woman to send her a boy who was among the handsomest and most charming in Perugia. The old woman quickly did so. When the young woman and the boy had sat down to supper, suddenly Pietro was at the door, shouting to be let in.

Hearing this, the woman thought her end had come. She wanted to conceal the boy's presence if she could, but unable to think of sending him to, or hiding him in, any other place, she made him take refuge under a chicken coop located in a shed next to the room in which they were eating. She threw onto the coop a burlap sack that

---

[5]Or: "hiccups."   [6]Or: "so that God will chalk them up to the merit of your dead relatives just as if you had lit candles for them."

che fatto aveva il dì vôtare; e questo fatto, prestamente fece aprire al marito. Al quale entrato in casa ella disse: — Molto tosto l'avete voi trangugiata, questa cena.

Pietro rispose: — Non l'abbiam noi assaggiata.

— E come è stato così? — disse la donna.

Pietro allora disse: — Dirolti. Essendo noi già posti a tavola, Ercolano e la moglie ed io, e noi sentimmo presso di noi starnutire, di che noi né la prima volta né la seconda ce ne curammo; ma quegli che starnutito aveva starnutendo ancora la terza volta e la quarta e la quinta e molte altre, tutti ci fece maravigliare; di che Ercolano, che alquanto turbato con la moglie era, per ciò che gran pezza ci avea fatti stare all'uscio senza aprirci, quasi con furia disse: — Questo che vuol dire? Chi è questi che così starnutisce?

— E levatosi da tavola andò verso una scala la quale assai vicina n'era, sotto la quale era un chiuso di tavole, vicino al pié della scala, da riporvi, chi avesse voluto, alcuna cosa, come tutto dì veggiamo che fanno far coloro che le lor case acconciano; e parendogli che di quindi venisse il suono dello starnuto, aperse uno usciuolo il qual v'era, e come aperto l'ebbe, subitamente n'uscì fuori il maggior puzzo di solfo del mondo, benché, davanti essendocene venuto puzzo e ramaricaticene, aveva detto la donna: — Egli è che dianzi io imbiancai miei veli col solfo, e poi la tegghiuzza sopra la quale sparto l'avea, perché il fummo ricevessero, io la misi sotto quella scala, sì che ancora ne viene. — E poi che Ercolano aperto ebbe l'usciuolo e sfogato fu alquanto il puzzo, guardando dentro, vide colui il quale starnutito aveva ed ancora starnutiva, a ciò la forza del solfo strignendolo; e come che egli starnutisse, gli aveva già il solfo sì il petto serrato, che poco a stare avea che né starnutito né altro non avrebbe mai. Ercolano, vedutolo, gridò: — Or veggio, donna, quello per che poco avanti, quando ce ne venimmo, tanto tenuti fuor della porta, senza esserci aperto, fummo; ma non abbia io mai cosa che mi piaccia se io non te ne pago. — Il che la donna udendo, e veggendo che il suo peccato era palese, senza alcuna scusa fare, levatasi da tavola, si fuggì, né so ove se n'andasse. Ercolano, non accorgendosi che la moglie si fuggìa, più volte disse a colui che starnutiva che egli uscisse fuori, ma quegli, che già più non potea, per cosa che Ercolano dicesse, non si movea; laonde Ercolano, presolo per l'un de' piedi, nel tirò fuori, e correva per un coltello per ucciderlo; ma io, temendo per me medesimo la signoria, levatomi, non lo lasciai uccidere né fargli alcun male, anzi gridando e difendendolo, fui cagione che quivi

she had had emptied that day. Then she quickly opened the door for her husband. When he had come in, she said: "You really gulped down that supper fast!"

Pietro replied: "We didn't even taste it!"

"How was that?" the woman asked.

Then Pietro said: "I'll tell you. When we were already sitting at the table, Ercolano, his wife, and I, we heard a sneeze right near us. We paid no mind to it the first time or the second; but when the one who had sneezed did it again for the third time, the fourth, the fifth, and many more, he made us all amazed. And so, Ercolano, who was a little on the outs with his wife because she had kept us waiting at the door a long time before opening it, said, almost in a rage: 'What's the meaning of this? Who is it that's sneezing that way?' He got up from the table and went over to a staircase very close by, under which there was a wooden enclosure close to the foot of the stairs, for storing things when necessary, as we see people do every day when they straighten up their house. Thinking that the sneezing sounds were coming from there, he opened up the little door there; when he opened, suddenly the most awful stench of sulphur came out—although, when we had felt some stench earlier and had complained about it, his wife had said: 'It's because during the day I bleached my kerchiefs with sulphur, and then I took the pan into which I had sprinkled it so the fumes could reach the cloth, and put it under the stairs there, so that there's still some smell.' After Ercolano had opened the door, and the stench had dissipated somewhat, he looked inside and saw the man who had been sneezing and was still sneezing, compelled to do so by the strength of the sulphur. Even though he was sneezing, the sulphur had already so constricted his chest that it wouldn't have been long before he ceased sneezing or ever doing anything else again. When Ercolano saw him, he shouted: 'Now, woman, I see why, a little while ago, when we arrived, we were kept in front of the door so long without being let in. But may I never enjoy anything in life again if I don't pay you back for this!' When his wife heard that, and realized that her sin had been revealed, she made no further excuses but got up from the table and ran away, I don't know where to. Ercolano, not noticing that his wife was running away, several times told the sneezing man to come out, but he was unable to, and, no matter what Ercolano said, he didn't move. And so Ercolano grabbed him by one foot and dragged him out; then he ran to get a knife to kill him with. But I, who was afraid of the police on my own account, got up and prevented him from killing him or doing him any other harm;

de' vicini traessero, li quali, preso il già vinto giovane, fuori della casa il portarono non so dove; per le quali cose la nostra cena turbata, io non solamente non l'ho trangugiata, anzi non l'ho pure assaggiata, come io dissi.

Udendo la donna queste cose, conobbe che egli erano dell'altre così savie come ella fosse, quantunque talvolta sciagura ne cogliesse ad alcuna, e volentieri avrebbe con parole la donna d'Ercolano difesa; ma per ciò che col biasimare il fallo altrui le parve dovere a' suoi far più libera via, cominciò a dire:

— Ecco belle cose! ecco buona e santa donna che costei dée essere! ecco fede d'onesta donna, che mi sarei confessata da lei, sì spirital mi parea! e peggio, che, essendo ella oggimai vecchia, dà molto buono esemplo alle giovani! Che maladetta sia l'ora che ella nel mondo venne, ed ella altresì che viver si lascia, perfidissima e rea femina che ella dée essere, universal vergogna e vitupéro di tutte le donne di questa terra; la quale, gittata via la sua onestà e la fede promessa al suo marito e l'onor di questo mondo, lui, che è così fatto uomo e così onorevole cittadino e che così ben la trattava, per uno altro uomo non s'è vergognata di vituperare, e se medesima insieme con lui. Se Iddio mi salvi, di così fatte femine non si vorrebbe avere misericordia; elle si vorrebbero uccidere, elle si vorrebbon vive vive mettere nel fuoco e farne cenere!

Poi, del suo amante ricordandosi, il quale ella sotto la cesta assai presso di quivi aveva, cominciò a confortar Pietro che s'andasse a letto, per ciò che tempo n'era. Pietro, che maggior voglia aveva di mangiare che di dormire, domandava pure se da cena cosa alcuna vi fosse; a cui la donna rispondeva: — Sì, da cena ci ha! Noi siamo molto usate di far da cena, quando tu non se'! Sì, che io sono la moglie d'Ercolano! Deh! ché non vai dormi per istasera? Quanto farai meglio!

Avvenne che, essendo la sera certi lavoratori di Pietro venuti con certe cose dalla villa, ed avendo messi gli asini loro, senza dar loro bere, in una stalletta la quale allato alla loggetta era, l'un degli asini, che grandissima sete avea, tratto il capo del capestro, era uscito della stalla ed ogni cosa andava fiutando se forse trovasse dell'acqua; e così andando, s'avvenne per mei la cesta sotto la quale era il giovanetto; il quale avendo, per ciò che carpone gli convenìa stare, alquanto le dita dell'una mano stese in terra fuori della cesta, tanta fu la sua ventura, o sciagura che vogliam dire, che questo asino ve gli pose sù piede, laonde egli, grandissimo dolor sentendo, mise un grande strido.

instead, I yelled and defended him, so that it was thanks to me that some neighbors arrived. They picked up the young man, who was already out cold, and carried him out of the house somewhere or other. Since our supper was interrupted by these events, not only did I not gulp it down, I didn't even taste it, as I said."

When the woman heard all this, she realized there were other women as clever as she was, even though one of them might sometimes meet with an unfortunate accident. She would have liked to say something in defense of Ercolano's wife; but, because she thought that by blaming other people's faults she could smooth the path for her own, she began to say:

"Those are fine goings-on for you! What a good, saintly woman she must be! What a faithful and chaste wife! I would have made my confession to her, she seemed so pious! Even worse, at her advanced age, she's setting young women a fine example! Cursed be the hour she came into the world, and a curse on her for staying alive, treacherous and evil woman that she must be, a general disgrace and a source of shame to every woman in this city! Throwing away her chastity, the faith she pledged to her husband, and the honor of this world, she wasn't ashamed, for another man's sake, to heap dishonor on such a fine man and respected citizen, who treated her so well—and to dishonor herself at the same time! So help me God, no decent women should have mercy on such women; they ought to be killed, they ought to be thrown onto the fire alive and burned to ashes!"

Then, remembering her lover, whom she had placed under the coop no distance away, she began urging Pietro to go to bed, because it was time to. Pietro, who felt more like eating than sleeping, kept asking her whether there was anything for supper. His wife replied: "Sure, we've got supper! I never fail to make a big supper when you're not home! Sure, I'm just like Ercolano's wife! Say, why don't you go to bed for the night? You'd be much better off!"

It so happened that some of Pietro's farmers had brought a few things from the country during the evening and had stalled their donkeys in a little stable next to that shed, without watering them. One of the donkeys, being very thirsty, drew its head out of the halter, left the stable, and was going around smelling at everything in search of water. As it went, it walked up to the coop under which the boy was hiding. Because the boy had to remain on his hands and knees, he had stretched out the fingers of one hand on the ground outside the coop. Such was his luck, or, rather, misfortune, that the donkey stepped on them, so that, in his enormous pain, he let out a loud yell.

Il quale udendo Pietro, si maravigliò, ed avvidesi ciò esser dentro alla casa; per che, uscito della camera e sentendo ancora costui ramaricarsi, non avendogli ancora l'asino levato il pié d'in su le dita ma premendol tuttavia forte, disse: — Chi è là? — e corso alla cesta, e quella levata, vide il giovanetto, il quale, oltre al dolore avuto delle dita premute dal pié dell'asino, tutto di paura tremava che Pietro alcun male non gli facesse.

Il quale essendo da Pietro riconosciuto, sì come colui a cui Pietro per le sue cattività era andato lungamente dietro, essendo da lui domandato: — Che fai tu qui? — niente a ciò gli rispose, ma pregollo che per l'amor di Dio non gli dovesse far male.

A cui Pietro disse: — Lieva sù, non dubitare che io alcun mal ti faccia; ma dimmi come tu se' qui e perché.

Il giovanetto gli disse ogni cosa; il quale Pietro, non men lieto d'averlo trovato che la sua donna dolente, presolo per mano, con seco nel menò nella camera, nella quale la donna con la maggior paura del mondo l'aspettava.

Alla quale Pietro postosi a seder di rimpetto, disse: — Or tu maladicevi così testé la moglie d'Ercolano e dicevi che arder si vorrebbe e che ella era vergogna di tutte voi; come non dicevi di te medesima? O se di te dir non volevi, come ti sofferiva l'animo di dir di lei, sentendoti quel medesimo aver fatto che ella fatto avea? Certo niuna altra cosa vi t'induceva, se non che voi siete tutte così fatte, e con l'altrui colpe guatate di ricoprire i vostri falli; che venir possa fuoco da cielo che tutte v'arda, generazion pessima che voi siete!

La donna, veggendo che egli nella prima giunta altro male che di parole fatto non l'avea, e parendole conoscere lui tutto gongolare per ciò che per man tenea un così bel giovanetto, prese cuore e disse:

— Io ne son molto certa che tu vorresti che fuoco venisse da cielo che tutte ci ardesse, sì come colui che se' così vago di noi come il can delle mazze; ma alla croce di Dio egli non ti verrà fatto. Ma volentieri farei un poco ragione con essoteco per sapere di che tu ti ramarichi; e certo io starei pur bene, se tu alla moglie d'Ercolano mi volessi aguagliare, la quale è una vecchia picchiapetto spigolistra ed ha da lui ciò che ella vuole, e tienla cara come si dée tener moglie, il che a me non avviene. Ché, posto che io sia da te ben vestita e ben calzata, tu sai bene come io sto d'altro e quanto tempo egli ha che tu non giacesti con meco; ed io vorrei innanzi andar con gli stracci indosso e scalza, ed esser ben trattata da te nel letto, che aver tutte queste cose, trattandomi come tu mi

When Pietro heard that, he was amazed, and realized it came from inside the house. And so, leaving the room and hearing the victim still complaining, because the donkey still had not released his fingers, but was still bearing down hard on him, he asked who was there and ran over to the coop. Raising it, he saw the boy, who, in addition to the pain from his fingers that the donkey had stepped on, was trembling all over in fear that Pietro would do him some harm.

He was recognized by Pietro, who for his own evil purposes had long stalked him; and, when asked what he was doing there, he didn't answer the question, but begged him, for God's sake, not to hurt him.

Pietro said: "Get up, don't worry about my hurting you in any way! But tell me how you got here, and why!"

The boy told him everything. Pietro, just as happy to find him as his wife was sad about it, took him by the hand and led him into the bedroom, where his wife was awaiting him in a state of extreme fright.

Sitting down opposite her, Pietro said: "Now, just a while ago you were cursing Ercolano's wife, saying she ought to be burned, and that she was a disgrace to all you women. Why didn't you say that about yourself? Or, if you didn't want to accuse yourself, how did your conscience allow you to accuse her, knowing you had done the same thing? Certainly, nothing induced you to do it, except that you're all alike, seeking to cover up your own misdeeds by blaming others. May fire descend from heaven and burn you all up, you generation of vipers!"

His wife, seeing that, in the first flush of his anger, he hadn't gone beyond verbal insults, and feeling sure that he was tickled pink at holding hands with such a pretty boy, took heart and said:

"I can well believe that you want fire to come down from heaven and burn up all women, because you're as fond of us as dogs are of a beating! But, by God's Cross, it won't happen! But I'd gladly have a little chat with you to find out what you're complaining about. I'd come off really well if you equated me with Ercolano's wife! She's an old sanctimonious hypocrite and gets whatever she wants from him; he holds her dear, as a wife deserves, which is not my situation. Because, even though you provide me with good dresses and footwear, you know very well how I'm fixed in other ways, and how long it's been since you slept with me. I'd rather go around wearing rags and barefoot, but have you treat me well in bed, than have all this, and be treated the way you treat me. Get this into your head, Pietro: I'm just

tratti. Ed intendi sanamente, Pietro, che io son femina come l'altre, ed ho voglia di quel che l'altre, sì che, perché io me ne procacci, non avendone da te, non è da dirmene male; almeno ti fo io cotanto d'onore, che io non mi pongo né con ragazzi né con tignosi.

Pietro s'avvide che le parole non erano per venir meno in tutta notte; per che, come colui che poco di lei curava, disse: — Or non più, donna: di questo ti contenterò io bene; farai tu gran cortesia di fare che noi abbiamo da cena qualche cosa, ché mi pare che questo garzone, altresì ben come io, non abbia ancor cenato.

— Certo no, — disse la donna, — che egli non ha ancor cenato, ché quando tu nella tua malora venisti, ci ponevàm noi a tavola per cenare.

— Or va' dunque, — disse Pietro, — fa' che noi ceniamo, ed appresso io disporrò di questa cosa in guisa che tu non t'avrai che ramaricare.

La donna, levata sù, udendo il marito contento, prestamente fatta rimetter la tavola, fece venir la cena la quale apparecchiata avea, ed insieme col suo cattivo marito e col giovane lietamente cenò.

Dopo la cena, quello che Pietro si divisasse a sodisfacimento di tutti e tre, m'è uscito di mente; so io ben cotanto, che la mattina vegnente infino in su la piazza fu il giovane, non assai certo qual più stato si fosse la notte o moglie o marito, accompagnato. Per che così vi vo' dire, donne mie care, che, chi la ti fa, fagliele; e se tu non puoi, tien'loti a mente fin che tu possa, acciò che quale asino dà in parete tal riceva.

LA GRU CON UNA SOLA GAMBA [VI, 4]

Tacevasi già la Lauretta e da tutti era stata sommamente commendata la Nonna, quando la reina a Neìfile impose che seguitasse; la qual disse:

Quantunque il pronto ingegno, amorose donne, spesso parole presti ed utili e belle, secondo gli accidenti, a' dicitori, la fortuna ancora, alcuna volta aiutatrice de' paurosi, sopra la lor lingua subitamente di quelle pone che mai, ad animo riposato, per lo dicitore si sarebber saputo trovare; il che io per la mia novella intendo di dimostrarvi.

Currado Gianfigliazzi, sì come ciascuna di voi ed udito e veduto puote avere, sempre della nostra città è stato notabile cittadino, liberale e magnifico, e vita cavalleresca tenendo, continuamente in

as much a woman as any other, with the same need that the others have, so that if I don't get it from you and look for it elsewhere, I'm not to be blamed. At least I do you the honor of avoiding stableboys and lowlifes!"

Pietro realized that she could go on talking like that all night. And so, since she didn't matter much to him, he said: "No more now, woman. I'll satisfy you on that score. Be so very kind as to prepare us something to eat, because it seems to me that, just like me, this boy hasn't had any supper yet."

His wife replied: "Of course he hasn't had any supper, because we were just sitting down to eat when you arrived in an unlucky hour!"

"Well, go now," said Pietro, "and make us something to eat; and, later on, I'll arrange this matter so that you'll have nothing to complain about."

The woman, hearing that her husband was contented, got up, quickly reset the table, and dished out the supper she had prepared earlier. In the company of her perverted husband and the boy, she supped merrily.

After supper, I have forgotten what it was that Pietro contrived in order to give all three of them satisfaction. This, however, I know well: the next morning, the boy, not quite sure whether that night he had been more frequently active or passive, was escorted all the way to the main square. And so, my dear ladies, I wish to say to you: give tit for tat; and, if you can't, keep it in mind until you can, so that "the donkey who kicks the wall gets his own back."

THE ONE-LEGGED CRANE [VI, 4]

Lauretta was already silent, and [her heroine] Nonna had been highly praised by all, when the "Queen" ordered Neifile to tell the next story, and she said:

Although readiness of wit, enamored ladies, often supplies speakers with sayings both useful and elegant according to the specific occasion, Fortune too sometimes aids the timorous, unexpectedly placing on their tongue words which the speaker would never have been able to come up with if his mind were calm. I wish to demonstrate this to you in my story.

As each one of you ladies may have heard and seen, Currado Gianfigliazzi has always been a notable citizen of our town, open-handed and munificent; leading a courtly life, he has always delighted

cani ed in uccelli s'è dilettato, le sue opere maggiori al presente lasciando stare.

Il quale con un suo falcone avendo un dì presso a Perétola una gru ammazzata, trovandola grassa e giovane, quella mandò ad un suo buon cuoco il quale era chiamato Chichibìo ed era viniziano, e sì gli mandò dicendo che a cena l'arrostisse e governassela bene.

Chichibìo, il quale, come nuovo bèrgolo era, così pareva, acconcia la gru, la mise a fuoco e con sollecitudine a cuocerla cominciò. La quale essendo già presso che cotta e grandissimo odor venendone, avvenne che una feminetta della contrada, la quale Brunetta era chiamata e di cui Chichibìo era forte innamorato, entrò nella cucina, e sentendo l'odor della gru e veggendola, pregò caramente Chichibìo che ne le desse una coscia.

Chichibìo le rispose cantando, e disse: — Voi non l'avrì da mi, donna Brunetta, voi non l'avrì da mi.

Di che donna Brunetta essendo turbata, gli disse: — In fé di Dio, se tu non la mi dài, tu non avrai mai da me cosa che ti piaccia.

Ed in brieve le parole furon molte; alla fine Chichibìo, per non crucciar la sua donna, spiccata l'una delle cosce alla gru, gliele diede.

Essendo poi davanti a Currado e ad alcun suo forestiere messa la gru senza coscia, e Currado maravigliandosene, fece chiamare Chichibìo, e domandollo che fosse divenuta l'altra coscia della gru.

Al quale il Vinizian bugiardo subitamente rispose: — Signor mio, le gru non hanno se non una coscia ed una gamba.

Currado allora turbato disse: — Come diavol non hanno che una coscia ed una gamba? Non vidi io mai più gru che questa?

Chichibìo seguitò: — Egli è, messer, come io vi dico; e quando vi piaccia, io il vi farò veder ne' vivi.

Currado, per amore de' forestieri che seco avea, non volle dietro alle parole andare, ma disse: — Poi che tu di' di farmelo veder ne' vivi, cosa che io mai più non vidi né udii dir che fosse, ed io il voglio veder domattina, e sarò contento; ma io ti giuro in sul corpo di Cristo che, se altramenti sarà, che io ti farò conciare in maniera, che tu con tuo danno ti ricorderai, sempre che tu ci viverai, del nome mio.

Finite adunque per quella sera le parole, la mattina seguente, come il giorno apparve, Currado, a cui non era per lo dormire l'ira cessata, tutto ancor gonfiato si levò e comandò che i cavalli gli fossero menati; e fatto montar Chichibìo sopra un ronzino, verso una

in hawks and hounds, not to mention his more important accomplishments for the moment.

One day, having killed a crane with a falcon of his near Peretola,[1] and finding it young and plump, he sent it to a skillful cook of his named Chichibio, a Venetian; when he sent it, he said he wanted it roasted and well prepared for supper.

Chichibio, who was as great a ninny and chatterbox as he looked, dressed the crane, put it over the fire, and began cooking it carefully. When it was nearly done, and a wonderful aroma was coming from it, a local girl called Brunetta, with whom Chichibio was very much in love, came into the kitchen. Smelling the aroma from the crane and seeing it, she asked Chichibio sweetly to give her a drumstick.

Chichibio replied in a singsong, saying: "You won't get it from me, Miss Brunetta, you won't get it from me!"[2]

Miss Brunetta, vexed at this, said: "By my faith, if you don't give it to me, you'll never get anything you like from *me*!"

In short, they exchanged many words, but finally, so as not to make his lady angry, Chichibio detached one of the crane's legs and gave it to her. When the one-legged crane was set before Currado and several guests of his, Currado was surprised. He sent for Chichibio and asked him what had become of the crane's other leg.

The mendacious Venetian swiftly replied: "My lord, cranes have only one leg and one foot."

Then Corrado, vexed, said: "What the hell do you mean, only one leg and one foot? Is this the first crane I've ever seen?"

Chichibio went on: "It's as I tell you, sir. If you like, I'll show you on live birds."

Currado, out of respect for his guests, didn't wish to go on bandying words, and said: "Since you say you want to show me on live birds something I've never seen or heard tell about, I agree to see it tomorrow morning, and I'll be satisfied. But I swear to you on the body of Christ that, if you're wrong, I'll punish you in such a way that, as long as you live, you'll remember my name to your regret!"

And so, the words being over for that evening, on the next morning at daybreak, Currado, whose anger hadn't vanished overnight, got up, still puffed up with rage, and ordered the horses to be brought out. Having Chichibio mount a nag, he led him toward a river by whose

---

[1]A village near Florence.   [2]This line, in the original, is meant to be tinged with Venetian dialect.

fiumana, alla riva della quale sempre soleva in sul far del dì vedersi delle gru, nel menò, dicendo: — Tosto vedremo chi avrà iersera mentito, o tu o io.

Chichibìo, veggendo che ancora durava l'ira di Currado e che far gli conveniva pruova della sua bugia, non sappiendo come potèrlasi fare, cavalcava appresso a Currado con la maggior paura del mondo, e volentieri, se potuto avesse, si sarebbe fuggito; ma non potendo, ora innanzi ed ora addietro e da lato si riguardava, e ciò che vedeva credeva che gru fossero che stessero in due piè.

Ma già vicini al fiume pervenuti, gli venner, prima che ad alcun, vedute sopra la riva di quello ben dodici gru, le quali tutte in un piè dimoravano, sì come quando dormono soglion fare. Per che egli, prestamente mostratele a Currado, disse: — Assai bene potete, messer, vedere che iersera vi dissi il vero, che le gru non hanno se non una coscia ed un piè, se voi riguardate a quelle che colà stanno.

Currado veggendole disse: — Aspéttati, che io ti mostrerò che elle n'hanno due! — E fattosi alquanto più a quelle vicino, gridò: — Hohò!

Per lo qual grido le gru, mandato l'altro piè giù, tutte dopo alquanti passi cominciarono a fuggire; laonde Currado, rivolto a Chichibìo, disse: — Che ti par, ghiottone? Pàrti che elle n'abbian due?

Chichibìo quasi sbigottito, non sappiendo egli stesso donde si venisse, rispose: — Messer sì, ma voi non gridaste «hohò!» a quella d'iersera: chè se così gridato aveste, ella avrebbe così l'altra coscia e l'altro piè fuor mandato come hanno fatto queste.

A Currado piacque tanto questa risposta, che tutta la sua ira si convertì in festa e riso, e disse: — Chichibìo, tu hai ragione: ben lo doveva fare. — Così adunque con la sua pronta e sollazzevol risposta Chichibìo cessò la mala ventura e pac, e pacificossi col suo signore.

LA PENNA DELL'ARCANGELO
GABRIELE [VI, 10]

Essendo ciascuno della brigata della sua novella riuscito, conobbe Dionèo che a lui toccava il dover dire; per la qual cosa, senza troppo solenne comandamento aspettare, imposto silenzio a quegli che il sentito motto di Guido lodavano, incominciò:

Vezzose donne, quantunque io abbia per privilegio di poter di quel che più mi piace parlare, oggi io non intendo di volere da quella materia separarmi della quale voi tutte avete assai acconciamente

bank cranes could always be seen at dawn, and he said: "We shall soon see who lied last night, you or I."

Chichibio, seeing that Currado was still angry and that it behooved him to prove his lie, though he didn't know how to do so, was riding behind Currado in a state of extreme fright. If he could, he would gladly have escaped; but, unable to do so, he kept looking around, ahead of him, in back of him, and off to the sides. Everything he saw looked like cranes standing on two feet.

But when they had come near the river, he saw, before anyone else, that about twelve cranes were standing on the bank, all on one foot, which is their way when sleeping. And so, quickly showing them to Currado, he said: "Sir, you can see quite clearly that I told you the truth last night when I said cranes have only one leg and one foot, if you look at the ones standing there."

Currado saw them and said: "Wait and I'll show you they have two!" And approaching them a little, he shouted: "Hey! Hey!"

At that outcry all the cranes put down their other feet, took a few steps, and started to fly away. Then Currado, turning toward Chichibio, said: "What do you think, you scoundrel? Do you think they have two?"

Chichibio, almost paralyzed with fear, not knowing himself where his inspiration came from, replied: "Yes, sir, but you didn't yell 'Hey! Hey!' at the one last night. If you had yelled like that, it would have let down its other leg and foot the way these did."

Currado was so pleased by that reply that his anger was completely transformed into amusement and laughter, and he said: "Chichibio, you're right; that's what I should have done!" And so, with his prompt and entertaining reply, Chichibio avoided being punished and returned to his master's good graces.

ARCHANGEL GABRIEL'S FEATHER
[VI, 10]

The stories of everyone else in the group being finished, Dioneo realized it was his turn to speak; and so, without awaiting any very formal order, he requested silence of those who were praising Guido's clever retort, and he began:

Pretty ladies, even though I have the privilege of speaking about whatever I like, today I don't intend to diverge from the theme you have all treated so appropriately; but, following in your footsteps, I

parlato; ma seguitando le vostre pedate, intendo di mostrarvi quanto cautamente con subito riparo un de' frati di santo Antonio fuggisse uno scorno che da due giovani apparecchiato gli era. Né vi dovrà esser grave perché io, per ben dir la novella compiuta, alquanto in parlar mi distenda, se al sol guarderete il quale è ancora a mezzo il cielo.

Certaldo, come voi forse avete potuto udire, è un castel di Valdelsa posto nel nostro contado, il quale, quantunque piccol sia, già di nobili uomini e d'agiati fu abitato; nel quale, per ciò che buona pastura vi trovava, usò un lungo tempo d'andare ogni anno una volta a ricoglier le limosine fatte loro dagli sciocchi un de' frati di santo Antonio, il cui nome era frate Cipolla, forse non meno per lo nome che per altra divozione vedutovi volentieri, con ciò sia cosa che quel terreno produca cipolle famose per tutta Toscana.

Era questo frate Cipolla di persona piccolo, di pelo rosso e lieto nel viso, ed il miglior brigante del mondo; ed oltre a questo, niuna scienza avendo, sì ottimo parlatore e pronto era, che chi conosciuto non l'avesse, non solamente un gran rettorico l'avrebbe estimato, ma avrebbe detto esser Tullio medesimo o forse Quintiliano; e quasi di tutti quegli della contrada era compare o amico o benvogliente.

Il quale, secondo la sua usanza, del mese d'agosto, tra l'altre, v'andò una volta, ed una domenica mattina, essendo tutti i buoni uomini e le femine delle ville da torno venuti alla messa nella calonica, quando tempo gli parve, fattosi innanzi, disse:

— Signori e donne, come voi sapete, vostra usanza è di mandare ogni anno a' poveri del baron messer santo Antonio del vostro grano e delle vostre biade, chi poco e chi assai, secondo il podere e la divozion sua, acciò che il beato santo Antonio vi sia guardia de' buoi e degli asini e de' porci e delle pecore vostre; ed oltre a ciò, solete pagare, e spezialmente quegli che alla nostra compagnia scritti sono, quel poco debito che ogni anno si paga una volta. Alle quali cose ricogliere io sono dal mio maggiore, cioè da messer l'abate, stato mandato; e per ciò, con la benedizion di Dio, dopo nona, quando udirete sonare le campanelle, verrete qui di fuori della chiesa, là dove io al modo usato vi farò la predicazione, e bacerete la croce; ed oltre a ciò, per ciò che divotissimi tutti vi conosco del barone messer santo Antonio, di spezial grazia vi mostrerò una santissima e bella reliquia, la quale io medesimo già recai dalle sante terre d'oltremare; e questa è una delle penne dell'agnol Gabriello, la quale nella camera della Vergine Maria rimase quando egli la venne ad annunziare in Nazarette.

intend to show you how prudently, and with how prompt a counter-measure, a friar of Saint Anthony avoided the ridicule that two young men had planned for him. And don't be troubled if, to tell the complete story, I take my time somewhat; look at the sun, and you'll see it's still only halfway across the sky.

Certaldo, as you may have heard, is a walled town on the river Elsa, situated in the Florentine countryside. Though small, it was once inhabited by noble and well-to-do people. Because the pickings were good for him there, over a long period a friar of Saint Anthony was accustomed to go there once every year to collect the alms given to his order by fools. He was called Friar Cipolla (Onion), and that name may have been the reason for his local popularity no less than the people's piety, because of the onions grown there, which are famous all over Tuscany.

This Friar Cipolla was short of stature, redheaded, and merry-faced, and was the best boon companion in the world. Besides, although he had no learning, he was such a good speaker and so glib that anyone who didn't know him would not only have taken him for a great orator, but would have said he was Cicero himself, or maybe Quintilian. He was a godfather, friend, or well-wisher of nearly everyone in the area.

Following his custom, he went there one August, and one Sunday morning, when all the good men and women from the surrounding farms had gathered in the main church for Mass, he came forward at a suitable moment, and said:

"Ladies and gentlemen, as you know, it is your custom to send some of your grain and fodder every year for the poor followers of our master Saint Anthony. Some of you give more, and some less, depending on your ability and the degree of your devotion, in order that blessed [Saint Anthony may pro]tect your oxen, donkeys, pigs, and sheep. In addition, [you are accusto]med to pay those small dues that are owed once [a year, thos]e of you who are inscribed in our confraternity. [I was sent by m]y superior, that is, my lord abbot, to collect this. [And so, with God's] blessing, after three o'clock, when you hear the [bells ring toget]her outside the church here, and, as is my prac[tice, I'll preach a s]ermon and you will kiss the Cross. What's more, [since I know you] all share a deep devotion for our master Saint [Anthony, as a special] favor I'll show you a most holy and beautiful relic [that I brough]t back personally from the Holy Land overseas: [one of the feathers of th]e angel Gabriel, which was left behind in the [Virgin Mary's room w]hen he came to Nazareth for the Annunciation."

E questo detto, si tacque e ritornossi alla messa. Erano, quando
frate Cipolla queste cose diceva, tra gli altri molti nella chiesa due
giovani astuti molto, chiamato l'uno Giovanni del Bragoniera e l'altro Biagio Pizzini, li quali, poi che alquanto tra sé ebbero riso della
reliquia di frate Cipolla, ancora che molto fossero suoi amici e di
sua brigata, seco proposero di fargli di questa penna alcuna beffa.

Ed avendo saputo che frate Cipolla la mattina desinava nel
castello con un suo amico, come a tavola il sentirono, così se ne sce-
sero alla strada, ad all'albergo dove il frate era smontato se n'andarono, con questo proponimento, che Biagio dovesse tenere a parole il fante di frate Cipolla, e Giovanni dovesse tra le cose del frate
cercare di questa penna, chente che ella si fosse, e tôrgliele, per
vedere come egli di questo fatto poi dovesse al popol dire.

Aveva frate Cipolla un suo fante, il quale alcuni chiamavano
Guccio Balena ed altri Guccio Imbratta, e chi gli diceva Guccio
Porco; il quale era tanto cattivo, che egli non è vero che mai Lippo
Topo ne facesse alcun cotanto. Di cui spesse volte frate Cipolla era
usato di motteggiare con la sua brigata e di dire: — Il fante mio ha
in sé nove cose tali, che, se qualunque è l'una di quelle fosse in
Salamone o in Aristotile o in Seneca, avrebbe forza di guastare ogni
lor vertù, ogni lor senno, ogni lor santità. Pensate adunque che uom
dée essere egli, nel quale né vertù né senno né santità alcuna è,
avendone nove! — Ed essendo alcuna volta domandato, quali fossero queste nove cose, ed egli avendole in rima messe, rispondeva:

— Dirolvi. Egli è tardo, sugliardo e bugiardo; negligente, disubidente e maldicente; trascutato, smemorato e scostumato; senza
che, egli ha alcune altre teccherelle con queste, che si taccion per
lo migliore. E quello che sommamente è da rider de' fatti suoi è
che egli in ogni luogo vuol pigliar moglie e tôr casa a pigione, ed
avendo la barba grande e nera ed unta, gli par sì forte esser bello e
piacevole, che egli s'avvisa che quante femine il veggiono tutte di
lui s'innamorino, ed essendo lasciato, a tutte andrebbe dietro per-
dendo la coreggia. È il vero che egli m'è d'un grande aiuto, per ciò
che mai niun non mi vuol sì segreto parlare, che egli non voglia la
sua parte udire, e se avviene che io d'alcuna cosa sia domandato, ha
sì gran paura che io non sappia rispondere, che prestamente
risponde egli e sì e no, come giudica si convenga.

After saying this, he stopped and went back to the Mass. While Friar Cipolla was speaking of these things, among the many others in church were two very foxy young men named Giovanni del Bragoniera and Biagio Pizzini. After they had laughed together for a time over Friar Cipolla's relic, even though they were among his friends and members of his jolly crew, they decided to play a practical joke on him with regard to that feather.

Having learned that Friar Cipolla was to dine with a friend in the citadel that noon, when they knew he was at table they went down to the street and proceeded toward the inn where the friar was staying. Their plan was this: Biagio was to keep Friar Cipolla's servant busy talking while Giovanni was to search through the friar's things for that feather, whatever it might actually be, and take it away, to see what he would say to the people when faced with the situation.

Friar Cipolla had a servant whom some called Guccio[1] the Whale; others, Guccio the Slob; and others, Guccio the Pig. He was so bizarrely dumb that Lippo Topo[2] truly never matched his doings. Friar Cipolla used to joke about him frequently with his cronies, saying: "My servant has nine characteristics of such a sort that, if Solomon, Aristotle, or Seneca possessed any single one of them, it would be powerful enough to ruin all their virtue, wisdom, and sanctity. Just imagine what a man he must be, possessing no virtue, no wisdom, and no sanctity, and yet having all nine!" When once asked what those nine characteristics were, he put them into rhyme, saying:

"I'll tell you. He fibs and jibs; he slanders and meanders; he's fretful and forgetful; and he's rude, crude, and lewd.[3] In addition, he has some other little faults that it's better not to mention. But the most laughable thing about him is that everywhere we go he wants to get married and rent a house; and, because he has a big, black, greasy beard, he thinks he's so handsome and charming that he imagines every woman who sees him falls in love with him; and, if he were turned loose, he'd chase after all of them even if his pants were falling down. To tell the truth, he's a big help to me because there's never a private conversation I'm engaged in on which he doesn't eavesdrop; and, if I happen to be asked something, he's so afraid I won't be able to answer that he immediately says yes or no, as he sees fit."

---

[1] Guccio is short for Arriguccio (ultimately from German Heinrich).   [2] A proverbial bizarre character, probably imaginary.   [3] An attempt at reproducing the jingles in the original Italian. The literal translation of the list is: "He's lazy, dirty, and a liar; careless, disobedient, and slanderous; impudent (or: negligent), forgetful, and immoral."

A costui, lasciandolo all'albergo, aveva frate Cipolla comandato che ben guardasse che alcuna persona non toccasse le cose sue, e spezialmente le sue bisacce, per ciò che in quelle erano le cose sacre; ma Guccio Imbratta, il quale era più vago di stare in cucina che sopra i verdi rami l'usignuolo, e massimamente se fante vi sentiva niuna, avendone in quella dell'oste una veduta, grassa e grossa e piccola e mal fatta, con un paio di poppe che parean due ceston da letame e con un viso che parea de' Baronci, tutta sudata, unta ed affumicata, non altramenti che si gitti l'avoltoio alla carogna, lasciata la camera di frate Cipolla aperta e tutte le sue cose in abbandono, là si calò; ed ancora che d'agosto fosse, postosi presso al fuoco a sedere, cominciò con costei, che Nuta aveva nome, ad entrar in parole e dirle che egli era gentile uomo per procuratore e che egli aveva de' fiorini più di millantanove, senza quegli che egli aveva a dare altrui, che erano anzi più che meno, e che egli sapeva tante cose fare e dire, che domine pure unquanche. E senza riguardare ad un suo cappuccio sopra il quale era tanto untume, che avrebbe condito il calderon d'Altopascio, e ad un suo farsetto rotto e ripezzato, ed intorno al collo e sotto le ditella smaltato di sudiciume, con più macchie e di più colori che mai drappi fossero tartereschi o indiani, ed alle sue scarpette tutte rotte ed alle calze sdrucite, le disse, quasi stato fosse il siri di Ciastiglione, che rivestirla voleva e rimetterla in arnese e trarla di quella cattività di star con altrui, e senza gran possession d'avere, ridurla in isperanza di miglior fortuna, ed altre cose assai, le quali, quantunque molto affettuosamente le dicesse, tutte in vento convertite, come le più delle sue imprese facevano, tornarono in niente.

Trovarono adunque i due giovani Guccio Porco intorno alla Nuta occupato; della qual cosa contenti, per ciò che mezza la lor fatica era cessata, non contraddicendolo alcuno, nella camera di frate Cipolla, la quale aperta trovarono, entrati, la prima cosa che venne lor presa per cercare fu la bisaccia nella quale era la penna, la quale aperta, trovarono in un gran viluppo di zendado fasciata una piccola cassettina, la quale aperta, trovarono in essa una penna di quelle della coda d'un pappagallo, la quale avvisarono dovere esser quella che egli promessa avea di mostrare a' Certaldesi.

It was with this servant that Friar Cipolla, on leaving the inn, had left orders to take good care that no one touched his belongings, especially his saddlebags, because they contained his holy relics. But Guccio the Slob was fonder of hanging around kitchens than nightingales are of "haunting the green spray," especially when he thought a wench might be there. In the present innkeeper's kitchen he had seen one, fat, hefty, short, and ill-built, with a pair of breasts that looked like two baskets of manure, and with a face like one of the Baronci family's.[4] She was all sweaty, greasy, and sooty. Just as a vulture swoops down on a carcass, Guccio, leaving Friar Cipolla's room open and all his belongings unguarded, descended to the kitchen. Even though it was August, he sat down next to the fire and struck up a conversation with this woman, who was named Nuta,[5] telling her he was a nobleman by proxy[6] and that he owned more than umpty-nine florins, not counting what he owed to others, which was more than that rather than less. He told her he could do and say more things than the Lord[7] could. Paying no attention to his hooded cape, which had so much grease on it that it could have flavored the cauldron at Altopascio,[8] his doublet, which was ripped and patched and encrusted with grime around the neck and under the armpits, with more numerous and more multicolored spots than any Tartar or Indian textile, his tattered shoes, and his threadbare stockings, he spoke as if he were the feudal lord of Châtillon. He said he would give her dresses and a new wardrobe, freeing her from her servile condition of waiting on others; although he didn't have great possessions, he could give her hopes of a better lot in life. He said much more, but, although he spoke with great feeling, his words were just air, like most of his ventures, and came to nothing.

And so, the two young men found Guccio the Pig occupied with Nuta. Pleased at this, because half their job was thus done for them, with no one stopping them, they entered Friar Cipolla's room, which they found open. The first thing they thought to search for was the saddlebag containing the feather. Opening it, they found a little box wrapped up in a big length of fine silk. Opening the box, they found in it a feather from a parrot's tail, which they realized must be the one he had promised to show to the people of Certaldo.

---

[4]A proverbially ugly Florentine family, mentioned elsewhere in the *Decameron*. [5]Short for Benvenuta. [6]An ambiguous expression: if not just doubletalk, either he meant he could prove his noble status by means of documents, or else he could stand proxy for a nobleman. [7]Or: "his master." [8]Near Lucca; site of an abbey famous for its soup kitchen.

E certo egli il poteva a que' tempi leggermente far credere, per ciò che ancora non erano le morbidezze d'Egitto se non in piccola quantità trapassate in Toscana, come poi in grandissima copia con disfacimento di tutta Italia son trapassate; e dove che elle poco conosciute fossero, in quella contrada quasi in niente erano dagli abitanti sapute; anzi, durandovi ancora la rozza onestà degli antichi, non che veduti avessero pappagalli, ma di gran lunga la maggior parte mai uditi non gli avea ricordare.

Contenti adunque i giovani d'aver la penna trovata, quella tolsero, e per non lasciare la cassetta vòta, veggendo carboni in un canto della camera, di quegli la cassetta empierono; e richiusala ed ogni cosa racconcia come trovata avevano, senza essere stati veduti, lieti se ne vennero con la penna e cominciarono ad aspettare quello che frate Cipolla, in luogo della penna trovando carboni, dovesse dire.

Gli uomini e le femine semplici che nella chiesa erano, udendo che veder dovevano la penna dell'agnol Gabriello dopo nona, detta la messa, si tornarono a casa; e dèttolo l'un vicino all'altro e l'una comare all'altra, come desinato ebbero ogni uomo, tanti uomini e tante femine concorsono nel castello, che appena vi capèano, con disidèro aspettando di veder questa penna.

Frate Cipolla, avendo ben desinato e poi alquanto dormito, un poco dopo nona levatosi e sentendo la moltitudine grande esser venuta di contadini per dovere la penna vedere, mandò a Guccio Imbratta che là sù con le campanelle venisse e recasse le sue bisacce. Il quale, poi che con fatica dalla cucina e dalla Nuta si fu divelto, con le cose addomandate con fatica là sù n'andò, dove ansando giunto, per ciò che il ber dell'acqua gli avea molto fatto crescere il corpo, per comandamento di frate Cipolla, andatone in su la porta della chiesa, forte incominciò le campanelle a sonare.

Dove poi che tutto il popolo fu ragunato, frate Cipolla, senza es- sersi avveduto che niuna sua cosa fosse stata mossa, cominciò la sua predica, ed in acconcio de' fatti suoi disse molte parole; e dovendo venire al mostrar della penna dell'agnol Gabriello, fatta prima con gran solennità la confessione, fece accender due torchi, e soave- mente sviluppando il zendado, avendosi prima tratto il cappuccio, fuori la cassetta ne trasse; e dette primieramente alcune parolette a laude ed a commendazione dell'agnolo Gabriello e della sua reliquia, la cassetta aperse.

La quale come piena di carboni vide, non suspicò che ciò Guccio Balena gli avesse fatto, per ciò che nol conosceva da tanto, né il maladisse del male aver guardato che altri ciò non facesse; ma

And, truly, he could easily make them believe it in those days, because the fleshpots of Egypt had not yet been imported into Tuscany, except to a slight degree, as they have been since then in enormous quantities, to the undoing of all of Italy. And, if they were little known in general, in that region the people had hardly any inkling of them. On the contrary, the homespun honesty of the ancients still held sway there, and not only had they never seen a parrot, but most of them by far had never heard one mentioned.

And so, the young men, happy that they had found the feather, took it away; in order not to leave the box empty, seeing some pieces of charcoal in a corner of the room, they filled the box with them. Closing it again and rearranging everything as they had found it, at no time having been seen, they merrily made off with the feather and began to wait and see what Friar Cipolla would say when he found coals in place of the feather.

The ingenuous men and women in the church, hearing that they were to see the angel Gabriel's feather after three, went home after Mass. One neighbor telling it to another, and one housewife to another, when everyone had dined so many men and women assembled within the citadel grounds that they could hardly fit, all intent on seeing that feather.

Friar Cipolla, having dined well and then napped for a while, got up a little after three. Finding that a great multitude of farmers had come to see the feather, he sent word to Guccio the Slob to come up there with his handbells and carry up his saddlebags. After Guccio was torn away with difficulty from Nuta and the kitchen, he ascended laboriously with the items requested. Arriving there out of breath, because the water he had drunk had made his body swell up, he followed Friar Cipolla's orders, going up to the church door and starting to ring his bells loudly.

When all the people were assembled, Friar Cipolla, who hadn't noticed that any of his belongings had been touched, began his sermon, saying many things in support of his coming exhibition. When the moment came for displaying the angel Gabriel's feather, he first recited the Confiteor with great solemnity, and had two candles lit. Gently unfurling the silk wrapper, after previously lowering his cowl, he uncovered the box. First saying a few words in praise and commendation of the angel Gabriel and his relic, he opened the box.

When he saw that it was filled with coals, he was sure it wasn't Guccio the Whale who had done it, because he knew he wasn't up to it; nor did he curse him for not having stood guard and prevented anyone else

bestemmiò tacitamente sé, che a lui la guardia delle sue cose aveva commessa, conoscendol, come faceva, negligente, disubidente, trascutato e smemorato; ma nonpertanto, senza mutar colore, alzato il viso e le mani al cielo, disse sì forte che da tutti fu udito: — O Iddio, lodata sia sempre la tua potenza! — Poi, richiusa la cassetta ed al popolo rivolto, disse:

— Signori e donne, voi dovete sapere che, essendo io ancora molto giovane, io fui mandato dal mio superiore in quelle parti dove apparisce il sole, e fummi commesso con espresso comandamento che io cercassi tanto che io trovassi i privilegi del Porcellana, li quali, ancora che a bollar niente costassero, molto più utili sono ad altrui che a noi; per la qual cosa, messomi io in cammino, di Vinegia partendomi ed andandomene per lo Borgo de' Greci e di quindi per lo reame del Garbo cavalcando e per Baldacca, pervenni in Parione, donde, non senza sete, dopo alquanto pervenni in Sardigna. Ma perché vi vo io tutti i paesi cerchi da me divisando? Io capitai, passato il Braccio di san Giorgio, in Truffia ed in Buffia, paesi molto abitati e con gran popoli, e di quindi pervenni in Terra di menzogna, dove molti de' nostri frati e d'altre religioni trovai assai, li quali tutti il disagio andavan per l'amor di Dio schifando, poco dell'altrui fatiche curandosi dove la loro utilità vedessero seguitare, nulla altra moneta spendendo che senza conio per que' paesi; e quindi passai in terra d'Abruzzi, dove gli uomini e le femine vanno in zoccoli su pe' monti, rivestendo i porci delle lor busecchie medesime, e poco più là trovai gente che portano il pan nelle mazze ed il vin nelle sacca, da' quali alle montagne de' Baschi pervenni, dove tutte l'acque corrono alla 'ngiù. Ed in brieve tanto andai addentro, che io pervenni mei infino in India Pastinaca, là dove io vi giuro per l'abito che io porto addosso che io vidi volare i pennati, cose incredibile a chi non gli avesse veduti; ma di ciò non mi lasci mentire Maso del Saggio, il quale gran mercatante io trovai

from doing it. Instead he silently cursed himself for having entrusted the protection of his property to him, knowing as he did that he was careless, disobedient, impudent, and forgetful. Despite his situation, he kept control of his features, lifted his face and hands to heaven, and said so loud that he was heard by everyone: "O God, may Your might be ever blessed!" Then, closing the box again and facing the people, he said:

"Ladies and gentlemen, I'd like you to know that, when I was still very young, I was sent by my superior into those parts where the sun is visible, and I was given the express order to search until I found them for the investitures of the Porcellana,[9] which, even though there is no charge to have them officially stamped, are much more useful to others than to us; and so, setting out, I left Vinegia and traveled through the Borgo de' Greci, and from there I rode through the kingdom of Garbo and through Baldacca until I arrived at Parione, from where, not without suffering from thirst, I shortly afterward reached Sardigna.[10] But why do I enumerate all the lands I traveled through? After passing the Arm of Saint George,[11] I found myself in Scamland and Laughland, densely populated countries with numerous inhabitants, and from there I reached Fibland, where I found many of our friars and those of other religious orders, all of whom avoided discomfort in the service of God, little concerned with the labors of others where they saw profit ensuing to themselves, and spending no other money than unminted coin[12] in those countries. From there I went to the land of Abruzzi, where men and women wear clogs on the mountains and dress their pigs in the pigs' own intestines.[13] Not far from there I found people who carry their bread on sticks and their wine in sacks.[14] From there I traveled to the mountains of the Basques, where all the water runs downhill. And, in short, I journeyed so far that I even reached Parsnippian India, where I swear by the habit I wear that I saw flying billhooks,[15] something incredible if you've never seen it. But may Maso del

---

[9]A designation of the Hospital of Saint Philip in Florence. [10]All these proper nouns are names of streets and neighborhoods in Florence that sound deceptively like other places in the world: Vinegia is Venice, Borgo de' Greci means "Greektown," Garbo was the name of a kingdom in Africa, and Baldacca suggests Baghdad. Throughout the sermon, Friar Cipolla uses ambiguity to suggest that local, commonplace things are exotic and unusual. Many of his utterances must be read in two ways. [11]The Bosphorus. [12]Supporting themselves with their lying stories. [13]An ambiguous way of saying they make sausages; the "clogs on the mountain" may be a sexual joke. [14]Wineskins. The "bread on sticks" may refer to bread rings carried on sticks, or to part of the male anatomy, or both. [15]*Pennati* can also mean "feathered."

là, che schiacciava noci e vendeva gusci a ritaglio. Ma non potendo quello che io andava cercando trovare, per ciò che da indi in là si va per acqua, indietro tornandomene, arrivai in quelle sante terre dove l'anno di state vi vale il pan freddo quattro denari ed il caldo v'è per niente; e quivi trovai il venerabile padre messer Non-mi-blasmate-se-voi-piace, degnissimo patriarca di Ierusalem, il quale, per reverenza dell'abito che io ho sempre portato del baron messer santo Antonio, volle che io vedessi tutte le sante reliquie le quali egli appresso di sé aveva; e furon tante, che, se io le vi volessi tutte contare, io non ne verrei a capo in parecchie miglia; ma pure per non lasciarvi sconsolate, ve ne dirò alquante. Egli primieramente mi mostrò il dito dello Spirito santo così intero e saldo come fu mai, ed il ciuffetto del serafino che apparve a san Francesco, e una dell'unghie de' cherubini, ed una delle coste del Verbum-caro-fàtti-alle-finestre, e de' vestimenti della santa Fé catolica, ed alquanti de' raggi della stella che apparve a' tre Magi in Oriente, ed un'ampolla del sudore di san Michele quando combatté col diavolo, e la mascella della morte di san Lazzero ed altre. E per ciò che io liberamente gli feci copia delle piagge di Montemorello in volgare e d'alquanti capitoli del Caprezio li quali egli lungamente era andato cercando, mi fece egli partefice delle sue sante reliquie, e donommi un de' denti della santa Croce ed in un'ampolletta alquanto del suono delle campane del tempio di Salamone e la penna dell'agnol Gabriello, della quale già detto v'ho, e l'un de' zoccoli di san Gherardo da Villamagna, il quale io, non ha molto, a Firenze donai a Gherardo de' Bonsi, il quale in lui ha grandissima divozione; e diedemi de' carboni co' quali fu il beatissimo martire san Lorenzo arrostito; le quali cose io tutte di qua con meco divotamente le recai, ed holle tutte. È il vero che il mio maggiore non ha mai sofferto che io l'abbia mostrate infino a tanto che certificato non s'è se desse sono o no, ma ora che per certi miracoli fatti da esse e per lettere ricevute dal patriarca fatto n'è certo, m'ha conceduta licenza che io le mostri; ma io, temendo di fidarle altrui, sempre le porto meco. Vera cosa è che io porto la penna dell'agnolo

Saggio,[16] whom I met there as a great merchant, cracking nuts and selling the shells at retail, not allow me to lie about it! But, unable to find what I was seeking, because from that point on the journey is by water,[17] I turned back and arrived in the Holy Land, where every summer the cold bread costs four cents and the hot[18] is for nothing. And there I met the venerable Father Don't-blame-me-please, the very worthy patriarch of Jerusalem. Out of reverence for the habit of master Saint Anthony that I have always worn, he allowed me to see all the holy relics he had with him. There were so many that, if I wanted to count them all, I wouldn't finish for miles and miles. Nevertheless, so as not to disappoint you, I'll tell you a few of them. First he showed me the finger of the Holy Spirit, just as intact and firm as ever; then the forelock of the Seraph who appeared to Saint Francis, and one of the fingernails of the Cherubim, and one of the ribs of the Word-made-flash-your-face-at-the-window, as well as some vestments of the Holy Catholic Faith, and some of the rays of the star that appeared to the three wise men of the East, and a vial of Saint Michael's sweat from the time he fought the devil, the jawbone from Saint Lazarus's death,[19] and more. And because I generously made him a copy[20] of *The Slopes of Montemorello*[21] in the vernacular and a few chapters of Capretius,[22] which he had long sought for,[23] he made me a sharer in his holy relics, giving me one of the teeth of the Holy Cross and, in a little vial, some of the ringing of the bells of Solomon's temple, and the feather from the angel Gabriel, which I've already mentioned, and one of the clogs of Saint Gherardo of Villamagna, which not long ago in Florence I gave to Gherardo de' Bonsi, who feels a very great devotion to him.[24] He also gave me some of the coals over which the most blessed martyr Saint Lawrence was grilled. All of these things I piously brought back here with me, and they're all in my possession. To tell the truth, my superior never allowed me to display them before there was a certificate of their authenticity, but now that they're verified, thanks to several miracles they've performed and letters received from the patriarch, he's given me permission to display them. Being afraid to entrust them to

---

[16]A Florentine wag who reappears in the story "The Stone of Invisibility" later in this volume.   [17]Or: "from that point on, people go out to fetch water."   [18]Can also be read: "the heat."   [19]Pictured as a skeleton.   [20]Or: "gave him a generous supply."   [21]A mountain of that name is near Florence.   [22]A ribald mangling of Lucretius?   [23]The whole sentence up to this point is obscure; it has been suggested that it is slang for: "I gave him plenty of gay sex."   [24]Both Gherardos are historical figures.

Gabriello, acciò che non si guasti, in una cassetta, ed i carboni co' quali fu arrostito san Lorenzo in un'altra; le quali son sì simiglianti l'una all'altra, che spesse volte mi vien presa l'una per l'altra, ed al presente m'è avvenuto: per ciò che, credendomi io qui avere arrecata la cassetta dove era la penna, io ho arrecata quella dove sono i carboni. Il quale io non reputo che stato sia errore, anzi mi pare esser certo che volontà sia stata di Dio e che egli stesso la cassetta de' carboni ponesse nelle mie mani, ricordandomi io pur testé che la festa di san Lorenzo sia di qui a due dì: e per ciò, volendo Iddio che io, col mostrarvi i carboni co' quali esso fu arrostito, raccenda nelle vostre anime la divozione che in lui aver dovete, non la penna che io voleva, ma i benedetti carboni spenti dall'omor di quel santissimo corpo mi fe' pigliare. E per ciò, figliuoli benedetti, trarretevi i cappucci e qua divotamente v'appresserete a vedergli. Ma prima voglio che voi sappiate che chiunque da questi carbon in segno di croce è tócco, tutto quello anno può viver sicuro che fuoco nol cocerà che non si senta.

E poi che così detto ebbe, cantando una lauda di san Lorenzo, aperse la cassetta e mostrò i carboni, li quali poi che alquanto la stolta moltitudine ebbe con ammirazione reverentemente guardati, con grandissima calca tutti s'appressarono a frate Cipolla, e migliori offerte dando che usati non erano, che con essi gli dovesse toccare il pregava ciascuno. Per la qual cosa frate Cipolla, recatisi questi carboni in mano, sopra li lor camicion bianchi e sopra i farsetti e sopra li veli delle donne cominciò a fare le maggior croci che vi capèvano, affermando che tanto quanto essi scemavano a far quelle croci, poi ricrescevano nella cassetta, sì come egli molte volte aveva provato. Ed in cotal guisa, non senza sua grandissima utilità avendo tutti crociati i Certaldesi, per presto accorgimento fece coloro rimanere scherniti, che lui, togliendogli la penna, avevan creduto schernire.

Li quali, stati alla sua predica ed avendo udito il nuovo riparo preso da lui, e quanto da lungi fatto si fosse e con che parole, avevan tanto riso, che s'eran creduti smascellare; e poi che partito si fu il vulgo, a lui andatisene, con la maggior festa del mondo ciò che fatto avean gli discoprirono, ed appresso gli renderono la sua penna, la quale l'anno seguente gli valse non meno che quel giorno gli fosser valuti i carboni.

anyone else, I always carry them along with me. It's true that, to avoid its being damaged, I carry the angel Gabriel's feather in one box, and the coals over which Saint Lawrence was grilled in another. The two boxes look so much alike that I often mistake one for the other, and this has happened to me now. And so, thinking I had brought here the box with the feather in it, I brought the one with the coals. But I don't look upon this as an error; rather, I'm fairly sure it was the will of God, and that He Himself placed the box of coals in my hands, recalling, as I did just now, that the feast of Saint Lawrence is two days from now.[25] Therefore, since God intended me, by showing you the coals over which he was grilled, to rekindle in your souls the devotion you ought to feel for him, He made me take, not the feather I had in mind, but the blessed coals that were extinguished by the fluids from that most holy body. And so, my blessed children, pull down your hoods and devoutly approach this spot to see them! But first I want you to know that whoever is marked in the form of a cross by these coals can rest assured for a full year that fire won't burn him without his feeling it."

And after he had said all this, he sang a hymn in praise of Saint Lawrence, opened the box, and displayed the coals. After the foolish crowd had reverently gazed on them with awe for a while, they all approached Friar Cipolla in a dense throng and, giving more alms than they usually did, begged him to mark them with the coals. And so, Friar Cipolla, picking up the coals, began to draw the biggest crosses that would fit on their white smocks and their doublets and on the women's kerchiefs. He declared that all the substance the coals lost in drawing those crosses they regained inside the box, as he had experienced many times. And in this way, having drawn crosses on everyone in Certaldo to his own great profit, through his readiness of wit he turned the tables on those who thought they were mocking him by stealing the feather from him.

Those two, who had attended his sermon and had heard what a novel countermeasure he had taken, how far-fetched his ideas were, and how humorous his wording, had laughed so hard they thought they dislocated their jaws. After the mob left, they went up to him and, as merrily as possible, revealed what they had done. Then they gave him back his feather, which the following year brought him in as much profit as the coals had done that day.

---

[25] It falls on August 10.

LO SPAGHETTO [VII, 8]

Stranamente pareva a tutti madonna Beatrice essere stata maliziosa in beffare il suo marito, e ciascuno affermava dovere essere stata la paura d'Anichino grandissima quando, tenuto forte dalla donna, l'udì dire che egli d'amore l'aveva richesta. Ma poi che il re vide Filomena tacersi, verso Neìfile vòltosi, disse: — Dite voi. — La qual, sorridendo prima un poco, cominciò:

Belle donne, gran peso mi resta se io vorrò con una bella novella contentarvi, come quelle che davanti hanno detto contentate v'hanno; del quale con l'aiuto di Dio io spero assai bene scaricarmi.

Dovete adunque sapere che nella nostra città fu già un ricchissimo mercatante chiamato Arriguccio Berlinghieri, il quale scioccamente, sì come ancora oggi fanno tutto il dì i mercatanti, pensò di volere ingentilire per moglie, e prese una giovane gentil donna male a lui convenièntesi, il cui nome fu monna Sismonda.

La quale, per ciò che egli, sì come i mercatanti fanno, andava molto da torno e poco con lei dimorava, s'innamorò d'un giovane chiamato Ruberto, il quale lungamente vagheggiata l'avea; ed avendo presa sua dimestichezza, e quella forse men discretamente usando, per ciò che sommamente le dilettava, avvene, o che Arriguccio alcuna cosa ne sentisse o come che s'andasse, che egli ne diventò il più geloso uomo del mondo e lascionne stare l'andar da torno ed ogni altro suo fatto, e quasi tutta la sua sollecitudine aveva posta in guardar ben costei, né mai addormentato si sarebbe se lei primieramente non avesse sentita entrar nel letto; per la qual cosa la donna sentiva gravissimo dolore, per ciò che in guisa niuna col suo Ruberto esser poteva.

Or pure, avendo molti pensieri avuti a dover trovare alcun modo d'esser con essolui, e molto ancora da lui essendone sollecitata, le venne pensato di tener questa maniera, che, con ciò fosse cosa che la sua camera fosse lungo la via, ed ella si fosse molte volte accorta che Arriguccio assai ad addormentarsi penasse, ma poi dormiva saldissimo, avvisò di dover far venire Ruberto in su la mezzanotte all'uscio della casa e d'andargli ad aprire ed a starsi alquanto con essolui mentre il marito dormiva forte.

Ed a fare che ella il sentisse quando venuto fosse, in guisa che persona non se n'accorgesse, divisò di mandare uno spaghetto fuori della finestra della camera, il quale con l'un de' capi vicino alla terra aggiugnesse, e l'altro capo mandatol basso infin sopra il palco e conducendolo al letto suo, quello sotto i panni mettere, e quando

THE STRING [VII, 8]

Everyone thought Monna Beatrice had been exceptionally cunning in tricking her husband, and they all declared that Anichino's fear must have been great indeed when, held tight by the lady, he heard her say he had made advances to her. But when the "King" saw that Filomena was silent, he turned to Neifile and said: "Your turn!" She first smiled a little, then began:

Beautiful ladies, I'm quite worried about whether I can please you with a fine story, as those who spoke before me have pleased you; but, with God's help, I hope to acquit myself well.

And so, I want to tell you that in our city there once lived a very rich merchant named Arriguccio Berlinghieri. Foolishly, just as merchants are still doing every day, he thought he could become a nobleman by marriage, and he wed a young noblewoman who was a bad match for him in character. Her name was Monna Sismonda.

Because he, like merchants in general, was often away on business and didn't spend much time with her, she fell in love with a young man named Ruberto, who had long courted her. They began an affair, but she was perhaps insufficiently cautious because she liked him so much; so that, either because Arriguccio heard something about it, or however it came about, he finally became violently jealous. Abandoning his travels and all his other business affairs, he was all but exclusively concerned with guarding her carefully. He never allowed himself to go to sleep before being sure she had come to bed, too. And so the lady was extremely sorrowful because there was no way for her to enjoy Ruberto's company.

Now, having expended much thought on ways and means to be with him, especially since he was begging her for a tryst, she hit upon the following idea. Because her bedroom faced the street and she had often noticed that, if Arriguccio struggled against falling asleep, he slept very soundly once he did, she planned to have Ruberto come to her house door around midnight, when she would go down to open the door and spend some time with him while her husband was fast asleep.

In order to be informed of his arrival without anyone else becoming aware of it, her plan was to lower a string from the bedroom window; one end of it would nearly reach the ground, while she would lower the other end onto the floor all the way to the bed, hide it under

essa nel letto fosse, legarlosi al dito grosso del piede; ed appresso, mandato questo a dire a Ruberto, gl'impose che, quando venisse, dovesse lo spago tirare, ed ella, se il marito dormisse, il lascerebbe andare ed andrebbegli ad aprire, e se egli non dormisse, ella il terrebbe fermo e tirerebbelo a sé, acciò che egli non aspettasse. La qual cosa piacque a Ruberto; ed assai volte andatovi, alcuna gli venne fatto d'esser con lei ed alcuna no. Ultimamente, continuando costoro questo artificio così fatto, avvenne una notte che, dormendo la donna, ed Arriguccio stendendo il pié per lo letto, gli venne questo spago trovato; per che, postavi la mano e trovatolo al dito della donna legato, disse seco stesso: — Per certo questo dée essere qualche inganno.

Ed avvedutosi poi che lo spago usciva fuori per la finestra, l'ebbe per fermo; per che, pianamente tagliatolo dal dito della donna, al suo il legò, e stette attento per vedere quel che questo volesse dire. Né stette guari che Ruberto venne, e tirato lo spago, come usato era, Arriguccio si sentì; e non avendoselo ben saputo legare, e Ruberto avendo tirato forte ed essendogli lo spago in man venuto, intese di doversi aspettare; e così fece. Arriguccio, levatosi prestamente e prese sue armi, corse all'uscio per dover vedere chi fosse costui e per fargli male.

Ora, era Arriguccio, con tutto che fosse mercatante, un fiero uomo ed un forte; e giunto all'uscio, e non aprendolo soavemente come soleva far la donna, e Ruberto che aspettava, sentendolo, s'avvisò esser ciò che era, cioè che colui che l'uscio apriva fosse Arriguccio; per che prestamente cominciò a fuggire, ed Arriguccio a seguitarlo. Ultimamente, avendo Ruberto un gran pezzo fuggito e colui non cessando di seguitarlo, essendo altresì Ruberto armato, tirò fuori la spada e rivolsesi, ed incominciarono l'uno a volere offendere e l'altro a difendersi.

La donna, come Arriguccio aprì la camera, svegliatasi, e trovatosi tagliato lo spago dal dito, incontanente s'accorse che il suo inganno era scoperto; e sentendo Arriguccio esser corso dietro a Ruberto, prestamente levatasi, avvisandosi ciò che doveva potere avvenire, chiamò la fante sua, la quale ogni cosa sapeva, e tanto la predicò, che ella in persona di sé nel suo letto la mise, pregandola che, senza farsi conoscere, quelle busse pazientemente ricevesse che Arriguccio le desse, per ciò che ella ne le renderebbe sì fatto merito, che ella non avrebbe cagione donde dolersi. E spento il lume che nella camera ardeva, di quella s'uscì, e nascosa in una parte della casa cominciò ad aspettare quello che dovesse avvenire.

Essendo tra Arriguccio e Ruberto la zuffa, i vicini della contrada,

the bedclothes, and, once she was in bed, tie it to her big toe. Later, sending word of this to Ruberto, she told him to pull the string when he came; if her husband was asleep, she'd let it go and come down to open the door; if he wasn't asleep, she'd hold the string tight and give it a tug in her direction, so that he shouldn't wait.

Ruberto liked this idea; he visited her often, sometimes being admitted and sometimes not. Finally, as they kept using this stratagem, one night the lady was asleep and Arriguccio, stretching out his leg in bed, discovered that string. Grasping it and finding it was tied to his wife's toe, he said to himself: "This must surely be some deception!"

Then, observing that the string hung out the window, he was sure of it. And so, quietly cutting it off his wife's toe, he tied it to his own and waited eagerly to see what it all meant. Before very long Ruberto came and pulled the string as usual, and Arriguccio felt it. He hadn't tied it very firmly and Ruberto had pulled hard. Now Ruberto, left with the string in his hand, thought it was a signal to wait, and did. Arriguccio got up quickly and armed himself, then he ran to the door to see who was there and inflict some injury on him.

Now, though he was a merchant, Arriguccio was a fierce, strong man. When he got to the door, he didn't open it quietly the way his wife usually did. When the waiting Ruberto heard it, he understood the situation: that it was Arriguccio opening the door. And so he immediately started running away, with Arriguccio at his heels. Finally, after Ruberto had run a good long way but was still being followed, he, being armed as well, drew his sword and turned around. They began to fight, one on the offensive and the other on the defensive.

When Arriguccio opened the bedroom door, his wife woke up. Finding that the string had been cut away from her toe, she realized at once that her ruse had been uncovered. In the knowledge that Arriguccio was chasing Ruberto, she quickly got out of bed. Realizing what the consequences could be, she called her lady's maid, who knew all about her affair, and persuaded her with difficulty to take her place in bed, asking her not to reveal her identity, but to accept patiently whatever blows Arriguccio might give her. She would reward her so handsomely for such a great favor that she'd have no cause for complaint. She extinguished the lamp that was burning in the bedroom, went out, and hid in another part of the house, waiting to see what would happen.

While Arriguccio and Ruberto were skirmishing, the neighbors

sentendola e levatisi, cominciarono loro a dir male, ed Arriguccio, per tema di non esser conosciuto, senza aver potuto sapere chi il giovane si fosse o d'alcuna cosa offenderlo, adirato e di maltalento, lasciatolo stare, se ne tornò verso la casa sua; e pervenuto nella camera, adiratamente cominciò a dire: — Ove se' tu, rea femina? Tu hai spento il lume perché io non ti truovi, ma tu l'hai fallita!

Ed andatosene al letto, credendosi la moglie pigliare, prese la fante, e quanto egli poté menare le mani ed i piedi, tante pugna e tanti calci le diede, che tutto il viso l'ammaccò, ed ultimamente la tagliò i capelli, sempre dicendole la maggior villania che mai a cattiva femina si dicesse. La fante piagneva forte, come colei che aveva di che, ed ancora che ella alcuna volta dicesse: — Oimé! mercé per Dio! — o — Non più! — era sì la voce dal pianto rotta ed Arriguccio impedito dal suo furore, che discerner non poteva più quella esser d'un'altra femina che della moglie.

Battutala adunque di santa ragione e tagliatile i capelli, come dicemmo, disse: — Malvagia femina, io non intendo di toccarti altramenti, ma io andrò per li tuoi fratelli e dirò loro le tue buone opere; ed appresso, che essi vengan per te e fàccianne quello che essi credono che loro onor fia e mènintene, ché per certo in questa casa non istarai tu mai più. — E così detto, uscito della camera, la serrò di fuori ed andò tutto sol via.

Come monna Sismonda, che ogni cosa udita aveva, sentì il marito essere andato via, così, aperta la camera e racceso il lume, trovò la fante sua tutta pesta che piagneva forte; la quale come poté il meglio racconsolò, e nella camera di lei la rimise, dove poi chetamente fattala servire e governare, sì di quel d'Arriguccio medesimo la sovvenne, che ella si chiamò per contenta.

E come la fante nella sua camera rimessa ebbe, così prestamente il letto della sua rifece, e quella tutta racconciò e rimise in ordine, come se quella notte niuna persona giaciuta vi fosse, e raccese la lampana, e sé rivestì e racconciò, come se ancora a letto non si fosse andata; ed accesa una lucerna e presi suoi panni, in capo della scala si pose a sedere, e cominciò a cucire e ad aspettare quello a che il fatto dovesse riuscire.

Arriguccio, uscito di casa sua, quanto più tosto poté, n'andò alla casa de' fratelli della moglie, e quivi tanto picchiò, che fu sentito e fugli aperto. Li fratelli della donna, che eran tre, e la madre di lei, sentendo che Arriguccio era, tutti si levarono, e fatto accendere de' lumi, vennero a lui e domandaronlo quello che egli a quella ora e così solo andasse cercando.

heard them, got out of bed, and started to fling curses at them. Arriguccio, afraid of being recognized, let the young man alone before he could learn who he was or do him any harm. Angry and full of hatred, he set out for home. When he reached his bedroom, he began to say in his anger: "Where are you, slut? You've put out the light so I can't find you, but it won't work!"

Approaching the bed and thinking he was seizing his wife, he seized her maid and gave her so many punches and kicks, as long as his hands and feet held out, that he bruised her entire face. As a final measure he cut her hair short, continuing all the while to heap on her the vilest insults ever bestowed on an erring wife. The maid was weeping loudly, as she had good reason to do, and even though from time to time she said "Woe is me! Mercy, for the love of God!" or "Stop!," her voice was so shaken by weeping, and Arriguccio's mind so clouded with rage, that he could no longer distinguish that different voice from his wife's.

And so, after beating the daylights out of her and cutting her hair, as we stated, he said: "Rotten woman, I won't do you any other harm, but I'm off to your brothers to tell them about your good deeds. Then I'll tell them to come for you, to do whatever they think their honor calls for, and to get you out of here, because you can be sure your days in this house are over!" Saying this, he left the room, locked the door from the outside, and departed alone.

As soon as Monna Sismonda, who had heard everything, was sure her husband had left, she unlocked the bedroom door, relit the lamp, and found her maid thoroughly battered and weeping loudly. She comforted her to the best of her ability and brought her back to her own room, where she then had her secretly waited on and tended to, repaying her with so much of Arriguccio's own money that she said she was satisfied.

And as soon as she had brought her maid back to her room, she quickly remade the bed in her own room. She tidied up the room and put it all back in shape, as if no one had slept there that night. She rekindled the lamp, and put on her clothes and jewelry again as if she had not yet gone to bed. Lighting a portable lamp and taking her sewing, she sat down at the head of the stairs and began to sew, waiting to see what would ensue.

After Arriguccio left his house, he went to the house of his wife's brothers as fast as he could. There he knocked until he was heard and let in. His wife's three brothers and her mother, hearing that the visitor was Arriguccio, all got up, had lamps lit, went down to see him, and asked him what he wanted, all alone at that hour.

A' quali Arriguccio, cominciandosi dallo spago che trovato aveva legato al dito del piè di monna Sismonda infino all'ultimo di ciò che trovato e fatto avea, narrò loro; e per fare loro intera testimonianza di ciò che fatto avesse, i capelli che alla moglie tagliati aver credeva, lor pose in mano, aggiugnendo che per lei venissero e quel ne facessero che essi credessero che al loro onore appartenesse, per ciò che egli non intendeva di mai più in casa tenerla. I fratelli della donna, crucciati forte di ciò che udito avevano e per fermo tenendolo, contro a lei inanimati, fatti accender de' torchi, con intenzione di farle un mal giuoco, con Arriguccio si misero in via ed andàronne a casa sua.

Il che veggendo la madre di loro, piagnendo gl'incominciò a seguitare, or l'uno ed or l'altro pregando che non dovessero queste cose così subitamente credere senza vederne altro o saperne, per ciò che il marito poteva per altra cagione esser crucciato con lei ed averle fatto male, ed ora apporle questo per iscusa di sé, dicendo ancora che ella si maravigliava forte come ciò potesse essere avvenuto, per ciò che ella conosceva ben la sua figliuola, sì come colei che infino da piccolina l'aveva allevata, e molte altre parole simiglianti.

Pervenuti adunque a casa d'Arriguccio ed entrati dentro, cominciarono a salir le scale; li quali monna Sismonda sentendo venir, disse: — Chi è là?

Alla quale l'un dei fratelli rispose: — Tu il saprai bene, rea femina, chi è.

Disse allora monna Sismonda: — Ora che vorrà dir questo? Domine, aiutaci! — e levatasi in piè, disse: — Fratelli miei, voi siate ben venuti; che andate voi cercando a questa ora tutti e tre?

Costoro, avendola veduta seder e cucire e senza alcuna vista nel viso d'essere stata battuta, dove Arriguccio aveva detto che tutta l'aveva pesta, alquanto nella prima giunta si maravigliarono e rifrenarono l'impeto della loro ira, e domandaronla come stato fosse quello di che Arriguccio di lei si doleva, minacciandola forte se ogni cosa non dicesse loro. La donna disse: — Io non so ciò che io mi vi debba dire, né di che Arriguccio di me vi si debba esser doluto.

Arriguccio, veggendola, la guatava come smemorato, ricordandosi che egli l'aveva dati forse mille punzoni per lo viso e graffiatogliele, e fattole tutti i mali del mondo, ed ora la vedeva come se di ciò niente fosse stato. In brieve i fratelli le dissero ciò che Arriguccio loro aveva detto e dello spago e delle battiture e di tutto.

La donna, rivolta ad Arriguccio, disse: — Oimé! marito mio, che è quel che io odo? Perché fai tu tener me rea femina con tua gran vergogna, dove io non sono, e te malvagio uomo e crudele di quello

Arriguccio told them everything, from the string he had found tied to Monna Sismonda's toe down to the last things he had learned and done. As full evidence of what he had done, he placed in their hands the hair he thought he had cut off his wife's head, adding that they should come to get her and do with her whatever they thought their honor demanded, because he didn't intend to keep her in his house any longer. His wife's brothers, enraged at what they had heard, and furious at her because they believed what he said, had torches lit. With the intention of doing her some physical harm, they set out with Arriguccio and proceeded to his house.

When their mother saw this, she burst into tears and began to follow them, begging one after the other not to believe those accusations so readily without hearing or learning anything else: her husband might have become angry with her and beaten her for other reasons, and might now be accusing her of this to exonerate himself. In addition, she said that she was amazed at such a happening because she was well acquainted with her daughter, having raised her from infancy. She added many other similar objections.

Well, when they reached Arriguccio's house and went in, they started to go upstairs. Hearing them come, Monna Sismonda asked: "Who is it?"

One of her brothers answered: "You know very well who it is, slut!"

Then Monna Sismonda said: "Now, what's the meaning of this? Lord help us!" And, standing up, she said: "Welcome, brothers! What are the three of you after at this hour?"

Seeing her sitting there with her sewing, her face showing no signs of a beating, whereas Arriguccio said he had beaten her black and blue, at first her brothers were a little surprised. They moderated the intensity of their rage, and asked her for her view of Arriguccio's complaint against her, uttering severe threats if she didn't tell them everything. The lady said: "I don't know what I'm supposed to tell, or what Arriguccio had to complain about concerning me."

Seeing her, Arriguccio looked at her like a man who had lost his mind; he remembered having given her maybe a thousand punches in the face and having scratched it, and doing her extreme injury, and now she looked as if none of that had happened. In short, her brothers told her what Arriguccio had told *them*, about the string, the beating, and everything.

The lady, facing Arriguccio, said: "Woe is me, husband, what's this I hear? Why are you giving me the reputation of a slut, to your own great disgrace, when I'm not one, and giving yourself the reputation

che tu non se'? E quando fostù questa notte più in questa casa, non che con meco? o quando mi battesti? Io per me non me ne ricordo.

Arriguccio cominciò a dire: — Come, rea femina, non ci andammo noi a letto insieme? Non ci tornai io, avendo corso dietro all'amante tuo? Non ti diedi io dimolte busse e taglia'ti i capelli?

La donna rispose: — In questa casa non ti coricasti tu iersera; ma lasciamo stare di questo, ché non ne posso altra testimonianza fare che le mie vere parole, e vegnamo a quello che tu di', che mi battesti e tagliasti i capelli. Me non battestù mai, e quanti n'ha qui, e tu altressì, mi ponete mente se io ho segno alcuno per tutta la persona di battitura; né ti consiglierei che tu fossi tanto ardito, che tu mano addosso mi ponessi, ché, alla croce di Dio, io ti sviserei. Né i capelli altressì mi tagliasti, che io sentissi o vedessi, ma forse il facesti che io non me n'avvidi; lasciami vedere se io gli ho tagliati o no.

E levatisi suoi veli di testa, mostrò che tagliati non gli avea, ma interi; le quali cose e veggendo ed udendo i fratelli e la madre, cominciarono verso d'Arriguccio a dire: — Che vuoi tu dire, Arriguccio? Questo non è già quello che tu ne venisti a dire che avevi fatto; e non sappiam noi come tu ti proverai il rimanente.

Arriguccio stava come trasognato e voleva pur dire; ma veggendo che quello che egli credeva poter mostrare non era così, non s'attentava di dir nulla. La donna, rivolta verso i fratelli, disse:

— Fratei miei, io veggio che egli è andato cercando che io faccia quello che io non volli mai fare, cioè che io vi racconti le miserie e le cattività sue; ed io il farò. Io credo fermamente che ciò che egli v'ha detto gli sia intervenuto ed abbial fatto, ed udite come. Questo valente uomo, al qual voi nella mia malora per moglie mi deste, che si chiama mercatante, e che vuole esser creduto, e che dovrebbe esser più temperato che un religioso e più onesto che una donzella, son poche sere che egli non si vada inebriando per le taverne, ed or con questa cattiva femina ed or con quella rimescolando; ed a me si fa infino a mezzanotte e talora infino a matutino aspettare nella maniera che mi trovaste. Son certa che, essendo bene ebbro, si mise a giacere con alcuna sua trista ed a lei, destandosi, trovò lo spago al piede e poi fece tutte quelle sue gagliardie che egli dice, ed ultimamente tornò a lei e battella e tagliolle i capelli; e non essendo ancora ben tornato in sé, si credette, e son certa che egli crede ancora, queste cose aver fatte a me: e se voi il porrete ben mente nel viso, egli è ancora mezzo ebbro. Ma tuttavia, che egli s'abbia di me detto, io non voglio che voi il vi rechiate se non come da uno ebriaco; e poscia che io gli perdono io, gli perdonate voi altressì.

La madre di lei, udendo queste parole, cominciò a far romore ed

of a mean, cruel man, which *you're* not? When were you in the house tonight, much less with me? When did you beat me? For my part, I don't remember it."

Arriguccio began to speak: "What, slut, didn't we go to bed together? Didn't I come back here again after chasing your lover? Didn't I give you a good knocking around, and didn't I cut off your hair?"

The lady replied: "You didn't go to bed in this house tonight—but let that go, because I can't give any other proof of it than my own true statement. Let's come to what you say: that you beat me and cut off my hair. You never beat me; let everyone here, you included, take a good look at me and see if I have any sign of a beating anywhere on me. And I'd advise you not to be so rash as ever to lay a hand on me, because, by God's Cross, I'd disfigure your face! Nor did you cut off my hair, either, for all I felt or saw, but maybe you did it without my noticing. Let me see whether it's been cut or not!"

And, taking off her kerchief, she showed that it was not cut, but intact. When her brothers and her mother saw and heard all this, they began to address Arriguccio: "What do you mean, Arriguccio? This isn't what you told us you had done when you came to see us. And we don't know how you intend to prove the rest of what you said!"

Arriguccio stood there like a daydreamer; he wanted to say something but, seeing that what he thought he could prove wasn't so, he didn't venture to say a word. His wife, facing her brothers, said:

"Brothers, I see that he's gone out of his way to make me do something I never wanted to do: to tell you about his terrible and evil ways; now I'll do it. I firmly believe that what he told you about did happen and that he did do it, but like this: This worthy gentleman, to whom you married me to my misfortune, who calls himself a merchant and wants people to believe him (as he ought to be) more temperate than a monk and more honorable than a young maiden, gets drunk in taverns almost every night, rubbing elbows with one prostitute after another. He makes me sit up waiting the way you found me as late as midnight and sometimes even till morning. I'm sure that he got good and drunk and went to bed with one of his loose women. It was on *her* foot that he found the string when he woke up, after which he performed all those valiant feats he says he did, then finally returned to her, beat her, and cut off her hair. Not yet sobered up, he thought, and still thinks, I'm sure, that he did all that to me. If you take a good look at his face, you'll see he's still half drunk. But, all the same, whatever he said about me I want you to consider as merely the words of a drunk; since I forgive him, I want you to forgive him, too."

Hearing this, her mother started to raise a ruckus, saying: "By God's

a dire: — Alla croce di Dio, figliuola mia, cotesto non si vorrebbe fare, anzi si vorrebbe uccidere questo can fastidioso e sconoscente, che egli non ne fu degno d'avere una figliuola fatta come se' tu. Frate, bene sta! basterebbe se egli t'avesse ricolta del fango! Col malanno possa egli essere oggimai, se tu déi stare al fracidume delle parole d'un mercatantuzzo di feccia d'asino, che venutici di contado ed usciti delle troiate vestiti di romagnuolo, con le calze a campanile e con la penna in culo, come egli hanno tre soldi, vogliono le figliuole de' gentili uomini e delle buone donne per moglie, e fanno arme e dicono: «Io son de' cotali» e «Que' di casa mia fecer così»! Ben vorrei che i miei figliuoli n'avesser seguito il mio consiglio, che ti potevano così orrevolmente acconciare in casa i conti Guidi con un pezzo di pane; ed essi vollon pur darti a questa bella gioia, che, dove tu se' la miglior figliuola di Firenze e la più onesta, egli non s'è vergognato di mezzanotte di dir che tu sii puttana, quasi noi non ti conoscessimo; ma alla fé di Dio, se me ne fosse creduto, el se ne gli darebbe sì fatta gastigatoia, che gli putirebbe.

E rivolta a' figliuoli, disse: — Figliuoli miei, io il vi dicea bene che questo non doveva potere essere. Avete voi udito come il buon vostro cognato tratta la sirocchia vostra, mercatantuolo di quattro denari che egli è? Ché, se io fossi come voi, avendo detto quello che egli ha di lei e faccendo quello che egli fa, io non mi terrei mai né contenta né appagata se io nol levassi di terra; e se io fossi uomo come io son femina, io non vorrei che altri che io se ne 'mpacciasse. Domine, fallo tristo, ebriaco doloroso che non si vergogna!

I giovani, vedute ed udite queste cose, rivoltisi ad Arriguccio, gli dissero la maggior villania che mai a niun cattivo uom si dicesse, ed ultimamente dissero: — Noi ti perdoniam questa sì come ad ebbro, ma guarda che per la vita tua da quinci innanzi simili novelle noi non sentiamo più, ché per certo, se più nulla ce ne viene agli orecchi, noi ti pagheremo di questa e di quella. — E così detto, se n'andarono.

Arriguccio, rimaso come uno smemorato, seco stesso non sappiendo se quello che fatto avea era stato vero o se egli aveva sognato, senza più farne parola, lasciò la moglie in pace; la qual non solamente con la sua sagacità fuggì il pericolo soprastante, ma s'aperse la via a poter fare nel tempo avvenire ogni suo piacere, senza paura alcuna più aver del marito.

Cross, daughter, there should be no forgiveness; rather, this mangy, ungrateful dog should be killed, because he didn't deserve to have a girl like you! Bless me, this would be too much even if he had lifted you out of the mud by marrying you! The hell with him now! You don't have to take such filthy language from a little donkey-manure peddler! These people come here from the sticks dressed in homespun, right out of their gangs of highwaymen, with a hick's short, turned-up pants and a pen sticking out of their ass;[1] and as soon as they've scraped together a little money, they want to marry the daughters of noblemen and gentlewomen; they have a coat-of-arms designed and say: "I belong to the So-and-so family" and "my ancestors did such-and-such"! I wish my sons had followed my advice, because they could have settled you honorably in the house of the Counts of Guidi for just a crust of bread![2] But no, they insisted on giving you to this true jewel of a man, who, though you're the finest and most chaste girl in Florence, wasn't ashamed to come at midnight and call you a whore, as if we didn't know you for what you are. But, by my faith in God, if they listened to me, he'd get such a punishment for it, it would stink out of his ears!"

Addressing her sons, she said: "Boys, I warned you not to let this happen. Did you hear how your good brother-in-law treats your sister, little two-bit tradesman that he is? I tell you, if I were you, and he said what he did about her, and behaved the way he does, I'd never be contented or satisfied if I didn't rid the earth of him. And if I, a weak woman, were a man, I wouldn't want anyone else but me to have a hand in it. God curse him, that miserable, shameless sot!"

When the young men had seen and heard all this, they confronted Arriguccio and insulted him as foully as any unfortunate man has ever been. Finally they said: "We forgive you this, as you were drunk, but, if you value your life, take care that we never hear anything like this from now on, because, you can be sure, if we hear anything else, we'll pay you back for this time and that one!" Saying this, they left.

Arriguccio remained there totally bewildered. He himself didn't know whether the things he had done were true or whether he had dreamed them. Saying not one word more about it, he left his wife in peace; and she not only escaped the impending danger through her wisdom, but also cleared the path for doing whatever she liked in the future, without any further fear of her husband.

---

[1]Merchants carried pencases in their back pockets.   [2]That is, with a minimal dowry. A marriage with the Counts of Guidi seems to have been a proverbial term for a good match. This line of Boccaccio's has a close parallel in one of Dante's satirical sonnets.

L'ELITROPIA [VIII, 3]

Finita la novella di Pànfilo, della quale le donne avevan tanto riso, che ancora ridono, la reina ad Elissa commise che seguitasse; la quale, ancora ridendo, incominciò:

Io non so, piacevoli donne, se egli mi si verrà fatto di farvi con una mia novelletta non men vera che piacevole tanto ridere quanto ha fatto Pànfilo con la sua: ma io me ne 'ngegnerò.

Nella nostra città, la qual sempre di varie maniere e di nuove genti è stata abbondevole, fu, ancora non è gran tempo, un dipintore chiamato Calandrino, uom semplice e di nuovi costumi, il quale il più del tempo con due altri dipintori usava, chiamati l'un Bruno e l'altro Buffalmacco, uomini sollazzevoli molto, ma per altro avveduti e sagaci, li quali con Calandrino usavan, per ciò che de' modi suoi e della sua simplicità sovente gran festa prendevano.

Era similmente allora in Firenze un giovane di maravigliosa piacevolezza, in ciascuna cosa che far voleva astuto ed avvenevole, chiamato Maso del Saggio, il quale, udendo alcune cose della simplicità di Calandrino, propose di voler prender diletto de' fatti suoi col fargli alcuna beffa o fargli credere alcuna nuova cosa; e per ventura trovandolo un dì nella chiesa di San Giovanni e veggendolo stare attento a riguardare le dipinture e gl'intagli del tabernaculo il quale è sopra l'altare della detta chiesa, non molto tempo davanti postovi, pensò essergli dato luogo e tempo alla sua intenzione.

Ed informato un compagno di ciò che fare intendeva, insieme s'accostarono là dove Calandrino solo si sedeva, e faccendo vista di non vederlo, insieme incominciarono a ragionare delle vertù di diverse pietre, delle quali Maso così efficacemente parlava come se stato fosse un solenne e gran lapidario; a' quali ragionamenti Calandrino posto orecchi, e dopo alquanto levatosi in piè, sentendo che non era credenza, si congiunse con loro, il che forte piacque a Maso.

Il quale seguendo le sue parole, fu da Calandrin domandato dove queste pietre così virtuose si trovassero. Maso rispose che le più si trovavano in Berlinzone, terra de' Baschi, in una contrada che si chiamava Bengodi, nella quale si legano le vigne con le salsicce,

THE STONE OF INVISIBILITY [VIII, 3]

After Panfilo had finished his story, at which the ladies had laughed so much that they are laughing yet, the "Queen" ordered Elissa to follow. Still laughing, she began:

I don't know, charming ladies, if my little story, which is no less true than amusing, will succeed in making you laugh as much as Panfilo's did, but I'll do my best.

In our city, which has always abounded in odd customs and unusual people, there was not very long ago a painter called Calandrino, a naïve man of bizarre ways who spent most of his time in the company of two other painters, one called Bruno and the other Buffalmacco. These men, who clearly liked a joke but were otherwise well informed and clever, frequented Calandrino because they often got a lot of fun out of his habits and his naïveté.

There was also in Florence at the time a young man of outstanding charm, shrewd and successful in everything he undertook, his name being Maso del Saggio. When he heard some reports about Calandrino's naïveté, he decided to derive enjoyment from his doings by playing some trick on him or making him believe some outlandish thing. Happening to run across him one day in the church of San Giovanni, and seeing him engrossed in viewing the paintings and reliefs of the tabernacle on the altar of that church, which was a recent installation, he thought he had found the right time and place for his plan.

He informed a companion of his intentions, and together they approached Calandrino where he was sitting alone. Pretending not to see him, they began discussing the special properties of various stones, Maso speaking about them as professionally as if he were a singularly eminent expert on the subject. Calandrino lent an ear to this conversation; after a while, realizing it wasn't meant to be secret, he stood up and joined them, to Maso's great glee.

Maso, continuing his discourse, was asked by Calandrino where those stones with such wonderful powers were to be found. Maso replied that most of them were located in Berlinzone,[1] in Basque country, in a region called Liveitup, where vines were tied with

---

[1]The Italian words suggested by this fictitious name connote merry feasting, ruddy complexions, and good times in general. The Basques occur as exotic folk in Friar Cipolla's sermon in the story "Archangel Gabriel's Feather," above, which also mentions the soon-to-be-cited Abruzzi.

ed avevavisi una oca a denaio ed un pàpero giunta, ed eravi una
montagna tutta di formaggio parmigiano grattugiato sopra la quale
stavan genti che niuna altra cosa facevano che far maccheroni e ra-
viuoli e cuocergli in brodo di capponi, e poi gli gittavan quindi
giù; e chi più ne pigliava più se n'aveva; ed ivi presso correva un fiu-
micel di vernaccia, della migliore che mai si bevve, senza avervi
entro gocciola d'acqua.

— Oh! — disse Calandrino, — cotesto è buon paese; ma dimmi,
che si fa de' capponi che cuocon coloro?

Rispose Maso: — Màngianglisi i Baschi tutti.

Disse allora Calandrino: — Fòstivi tu mai?

A cui Maso rispose: — Di' tu se io vi fu' mai? Sì, vi sono stato così
una volta come mille!

Disse allora Calandrino: — E quante miglia ci ha?

Maso rispose: — Hàccene più di millanta, che tutta notte canta.

Disse Calandrino: — Adunque dée egli essere più là che Abruzzi.

— Sì bene, — rispose Maso, — si è cavelle.

Calandrino semplice, veggendo Maso dir queste parole con un
viso fermo e senza ridere, quella fede vi dava che dar si può a
qualunque verità è più manifesta, e così l'aveva per vere; e disse: —
Troppo c'è di lungi a' fatti miei; ma se più presso ci fosse, ben ti
dico che io vi verrei una volta con essoteco pur per veder fare il
tómo a que' maccheroni e tôrmene una satolla. Ma dimmi, che
lieto sii tu: in queste contrade non se ne truova niuna di queste
pietre così virtuose?

A cui Maso rispose: — Sì, due maniere di pietre ci si truovano di
grandissima vertù. L'una sono i macigni da Settignano e da
Montisci, per vertù de' quali, quando son macine fatti, se ne fa la
farina, e per ciò si dice egli in que' paesi di là che da Dio vengon le
grazie e da Montisci le macine; ma ècci di questi macigni sì gran
quantità, che appo noi è poco prezzata, come appo loro gli
smeraldi, de' quali v'ha maggior montagne che Montemorello, che
rilucon di mezzanotte vatti con Dio; e sappi che chi facesse le
macine belle e fatte legare in anella prima che si forassero e por-
tassele al soldano, n'avrebbe ciò che volesse. L'altra si è una pietra,
la quale noi altri lapidari appelliamo elitropia, pietra di troppo gran
vertù, per ciò che qualunque persona la porta sopra di sé, mentre
la tiene, non è da alcuna altra persona veduto dove non è.

sausages. In that place you could buy a goose for a penny and get a gosling thrown in, and there was a mountain all made of grated Parmesan cheese on which there stood people whose sole activity was to make gnocchi and ravioli, cook them in capon broth, and then cast them down to the foot of the mountain, where they were free for the taking. Nearby there flowed a stream of fine dry white wine, of the best quality ever drunk, unmixed with even a drop of water.

"Oh," said Calandrino, "that's a good country! But tell me, what happens to the capons they cook there?"

Maso replied: "The Basques eat them all."

Then Calandrino said: "Were you ever there?"

Maso replied: "You ask if I was ever there? Yes, I was there a thousand times if I was there once!"

Then Calandrino said: "How many miles away is it?"

Maso replied: "More than a hundredy, more than a thousandy."[2]

Calandrino said: "So it must be farther away than Abruzzi."

"Yes, indeed," Maso replied, "or very little."

Ingenuous Calandrino, seeing Maso say all this with a straight face and without laughing, believed it as men can believe the most evident truths, and trusted him implicitly. He said: "That's too far away for me. But, if it were closer, I assure you I'd go there with you sometime if only to see them hurling down those gnocchi and to get a bellyful of them. But tell me, God bless you: aren't any of those wonder-working stones found hereabouts?"

Maso replied: "Yes, two kinds of stones with marvelous powers are found around here. One kind is the sandstones from Settignano and Montisci, which have the power of creating flour when they're turned into millstones. And for that reason the saying goes in those areas that grace comes from God and millstones from Montisci. But we have such a great quantity of those sandstones that they're little prized around here, just as emeralds are with them, because they've got mountains of them bigger than Montemorello, and they shine at midnight-so-go-home. Let me tell you: if a man could take fine, finished millstones and set them in rings before they're perforated, and then take them to the Sultan, he'd get whatever he asked for them. The other kind is a stone we experts call heliotrope,[3] a stone with exceptional powers: anyone carrying it on his person, as long as he's got it, can't be seen by anyone else where he's not standing."

---

[2] The second clause of Maso's nonsense reply literally means: "which sings all night."
[3] Also called bloodstone, a dark stone with red streaks.

Allora Calandrin disse: — Gran vertù son queste; ma questa seconda dove si truova?
A cui Maso rispose che nel Mugnone se ne solevan trovare. Disse Calandrino: — Di che grossezza è questa pietra o che colore è il suo? Rispose Maso: — Ella è di varie grossezze, ché alcuna n'è più, alcuna meno; ma tutte son di colore quasi come nero.
Calandrino, avendo tutte queste cose seco notate, fatto sembianti d'avere altro a fare, si partì da Maso e seco propose di volere cercare di questa pietra; ma diliberò di non volerlo fare senza saputa di Bruno e di Buffalmacco, li quali spezialissimamente amava. Diessi adunque a cercar di costoro, acciò che senza indugio e prima che alcuno altro, n'andassero a cercare, e tutto il rimanente di quella mattina consumò in cercargli.
Ultimamente, essendo già l'ora della nona passata, ricordandosi egli che essi lavoravano nel monistero delle donne di Faenza, quantunque il caldo fosse grandissimo, lasciata ogni altra sua faccenda, quasi correndo n'andò a costoro, e chiamatigli, così disse loro:
— Compagni, quando voi vogliate credermi, noi possiamo divenire i più ricchi uomini di Firenze, per ciò che io ho inteso da uomo degno di fede che in Mugnone si truova una pietra, la qual chi la porta sopra non è veduto da niuna altra persona; per che a me parrebbe che noi, senza alcuno indugio, prima che altra persona v'andasse, v'andassimo a cercare. Noi la troverem per certo, per ciò che io la conosco; e trovata che noi l'avremo, che avrem noi a fare altro se non mèttercela nella scarsella ed andare alle tavole de' cambiatori, le quali sapete che stanno sempre cariche di grossi e di fiorini, e tôrcene quanti noi ne vorremo? Niuno ci vedrà; e così potremo arricchire subitamente senza avere tuttodì a schiccherare le mura a modo che fa la lumaca.
Bruno e Buffalmacco, udendo costui, tra se medesimi cominciarono a ridere; e guatando l'un verso l'altro, fecer sembianti di maravigliarsi forte e lodarono il consiglio di Calandrino; ma domandò Buffalmacco come questa pietra avesse nome. A Calandrino che era di grossa pasta, era già il nome uscito di mente; per che egli rispose: — Che abbiam noi a fare del nome, poi che noi sappiamo la vertù? A me parrebbe che noi andassimo a cercare senza star più.
— Or ben, — disse Bruno, — come è ella fatta?
Calandrin disse: — Egli ne son d'ogni fatta, ma tutte son quasi nere; per che a me pare che noi abbiamo a ricogliere tutte quelle che noi vedrem nere, tanto che noi ci abbattiamo ad essa: e per ciò non perdiam tempo, andiamo.
A cui Bruno disse: — Or t'aspetta. — E vòlto a Buffalmacco,

Then Calandrino said: "Those are mighty powers, but where is that second stone located?"

Maso replied that they were usually found in the Mugnone. Calandrino said: "How big is that stone and what color is it?"

Maso replied: "It comes in different sizes; some are bigger, some are smaller; but they're all nearly black."

Calandrino, having made a mental note of all this, pretended he had some other business, said good-bye to Maso, and resolved to go looking for that stone. But he decided not to do so without informing Bruno and Buffalmacco, the dearest of his friends. So he set out to hunt them up, so that they could institute their search without delay and ahead of anyone else. He spent the rest of that morning looking for them.

Finally, when it was already after three, he remembered that they were working in the convent outside the Faenza gate. Even though it was extremely hot, he dropped all else and nearly ran to join them. Calling them, he said:

"Friends, if you trust what I'm going to tell you, we can become the richest men in Florence, because I've learned from a reliable man that in the Mugnone there's a stone that makes its bearer invisible to anyone else. And so I think it would be a good idea if we went to look for it without delay, before anyone else does. We're sure to find it because I know what it looks like. Once we've found it, all we have to do is put it in our belt pouch and take it to the moneychangers' benches. You know they're always loaded with silver and gold coins, of which we'll be able to take all we want. No one will see us; and that way we'll be able to get rich at once without having to smear walls every day the way snails do!"

When Bruno and Buffalmacco heard this, they started to laugh on the inside. Giving each other significant looks, they pretended to be greatly amazed, and they approved of Calandrino's advice. But Buffalmacco asked what that stone was called. Calandrino, who was dull-witted, had already forgotten its name, and so he replied: "What use is the name to us if we know what it can do? I think we should go out looking for it this minute!"

"Well, then," said Bruno, "what's it like?"

Calandrino said: "It comes in different sizes and shapes, but it's always nearly black. And so I think we should collect all the black stones we find until we come across the right one. So let's not waste time, let's go!"

Bruno replied: "Wait a minute!" Addressing Buffalmacco, he said:

disse: — A me pare che Calandrino dica bene; ma non mi pare che questa sia ora da ciò, per ciò che il sole è alto e dà per lo Mugnone entro ed ha tutte le pietre rasciutte; per che tali paion testé bianche, delle pietre che vi sono, che la mattina, anzi che il sole l'abbia rasciutte, paion nere; ed oltre a ciò, molta gente per diverse cagioni è oggi, che è dì da lavorare, per lo Mugnone, li quali, veggendoci, si potrebbono indovinare quello che noi andassimo faccendo e forse farlo essi altressì; e potrebbe venire alle mani a loro, e noi avremmo perduto il trotto per l'ambiadura. A me pare, se pare a voi, che questa sia opera da dover far da mattina, che si conoscon meglio le nere dalle bianche, ed in dì di festa che non vi sarà persona che ci veggia.

Buffalmacco lodò il consiglio di Bruno, e Calandrino vi s'accordò, ed ordinarono che la domenica mattina vegnente tutti e tre fossero insieme a cercar di questa pietra; ma sopra ogni altra cosa gli pregò Calandrino che essi non dovesser questa cosa con persona del mondo ragionare, per ciò che a lui era stata posta in credenza. E ragionato questo, disse loro ciò che udito avea della contrada di Bengodi, con saramenti affermando che così era. Partito Calandrino da loro, essi quello che intorno a questo avessero a fare ordinarono tra se medesimi.

Calandrino con disidéro aspettò la domenica mattina; la qual venuta, in sul far del dì si levò, e chiamati i compagni, per la porta a San Gallo usciti e nel Mugnon discesi, cominciarono ad andare ingiù, della pietra cercando. Calandrino andava, come più volenteroso, avanti, e prestamente or qua ed or là saltando, dovunque alcuna pietra nera vedeva, si gittava, e quella ricogliendo si metteva in seno.

I compagni andavano appresso, e quando una e quando un'altra ne ricoglievano; ma Calandrino non fu guari di via andato, che egli il seno se n'ebbe pieno; per che, alzandosi i gheroni della gonnella, che all'analda non era, e faccendo di quegli ampio grembo, bene avendogli alla coreggia attaccati d'ogni parte, non dopo molto gli empiè, e similmente, dopo alquanto spazio, fatto del mantello grembo, quello di pietre empiè. Per che, veggendo Buffalmacco e Bruno che Calandrino era carico e l'ora del mangiare s'avvicinava, secondo l'ordine da sé posto, disse Bruno a Buffalmacco: — Calandrino dove è?

Buffalmacco, che ivi presso sel vedea, volgendosi intorno ed or qua ed or là riguardando, rispose: — Io non so, ma egli era pur poco fa qui dinanzi da noi.

"I think Calandrino's right, but I don't think this is the right time to do it, because the sun is high in the sky and beating directly down on the Mugnone, so that it's dried all the stones. And so, of the stones that are there, some look white right now that look black in the morning before the sun has dried them. Besides, many people have many reasons to be on the Mugnone today, which is a working day. If they see us, they might guess what we were doing there, and might perhaps do the same thing. The stone might fall into their hands, and we would have 'made our horse forget how to trot by trying to teach him to amble.' I think that, if you agree, this is a task to be done in the morning, when it's easier to tell the black and white stones apart, and on a day off, when there won't be anyone to see us."

Buffalmacco approved of Bruno's advice, and Calandrino consented. They decided that on the coming Sunday morning all three would go look for that stone together. Calandrino implored them above all not to tell a soul about it, because he had been told about it in secret. After all this talk about the stone, he also told them what he had heard about the land Liveitup, affirming the truth of it with oaths. After Calandrino departed, the other two planned their future course of action together.

Calandrino anxiously awaited Sunday morning. When it came, he got up at daybreak and called his companions. They left the city by the San Gallo gate and descended into the valley of the Mugnone, where they began to walk along the stream, looking for the stone. Being more eager, Calandrino walked ahead, hopping nimbly on all sides, wherever he saw a black stone. He would pick up each one and put it inside his shirt.

His companions followed, picking up an occasional stone. But Calandrino had gone hardly any distance before there was no more room in his shirt. So, raising the hems of his tunic, which wasn't cut in the [new, tight and short] Hainaut fashion, and creating a capacious sack by fastening them firmly to his belt all around, he filled up that, too, before very long. Shortly thereafter he made another sack out of his cape and filled *it* with stones as well. And so, when Buffalmacco and Bruno saw that Calandrino was fully loaded and that it was nearly mealtime, they followed their plan, and Bruno said to Buffalmacco: "Where's Calandrino?"

Buffalmacco, who could see him a short distance away, turned around in all directions looking for him, and replied: "I don't know, but he was definitely right here in front of us not long ago."

Disse Bruno: — Benché fa poco, a me pare egli esser certo che egli è ora a casa a desinare, e noi ha lasciati nel farnetico d'andar cercando le pietre nere giù per lo Mugnone. — Deh! come egli ha ben fatto — disse allor Buffalmacco — d'averci beffati e lasciati qui, poscia che noi fummo sì sciocchi, che noi gli credemmo. Sappi, chi sarebbe stato sì stolto, che avesse creduto che in Mugnone si dovesse trovare una così virtuosa pietra, altri che noi!

Calandrino, queste parole udendo, imaginò che quella pietra alle mani gli fosse venuta e che, per la vertù d'essa, coloro, ancor che loro fosse presente, nol vedessero. Lieto adunque oltre modo di tal ventura, senza dir loro alcuna cosa, pensò di tornarsi a casa; e vòlti i passi indietro, se ne cominciò a venire. Veggendo ciò Buffalmacco, disse a Bruno: — Noi che faremo? Ché non ce n'andiam noi?

A cui Bruno rispose: — Andianne; ma io giuro a Dio che mai Calandrino non me ne farà più niuna; e se io gli fossi presso come stato sono tutta mattina, io gli darei tale di questo ciotto nelle calcagna, che egli si ricorderebbe forse un mese di questa beffa! — Ed il dir le parole e l'aprirsi ed il dar del ciotto nel calcagno a Calandrino fu tutto uno.

Calandrino, sentendo il duolo, levò alto il piè e cominciò a soffiare, ma pur si tacque ed andò oltre. Buffalmacco, recatosi in mano un de' codoli che raccolti avea, disse a Bruno: — Deh! vedi bel codolo: così giugnesse egli testé nelle reni a Calandrino! — E lasciato andare, gli die' con esso nelle reni una gran percossa; ed in brieve in cotal guisa, or con una parola ed or con un'altra, su per lo Mugnone infino alla porta a San Gallo il vennero lapidando; quindi, in terra gittate le pietre che ricolte aveano, alquanto con le guardie de' gabellieri si ristettero, le quali, prima da loro informate, faccendo vista di non vedere, lasciarono andar Calandrino con le maggior risa del mondo.

Il quale senza arrestarsi se ne venne a casa sua, la quale era vicina al Canto alla macina; ed intanto fu la fortuna piacevole alla beffa, che, mentre Calandrino per lo fiume ne venne e poi per la città, niuna persona gli fece motto, come che pochi ne scontrasse, per ciò che quasi a desinare era ciascuno.

Entròssene adunque Calandrino così carico in casa sua. Era per ventura la moglie di lui, la quale ebbe nome monna Tessa, bella e

Bruno said: "Even though it wasn't long ago,[4] I'm sure that he's at home right now having dinner, and he's left us here crazily looking for black stones along the Mugnone."

Buffalmacco then said: "Well! How right he was to trick us and leave us here, if we were so foolish as to believe him! Listen, who but us would have been so stupid as to believe there was such a powerful stone in the Mugnone?"

Hearing this, Calandrino imagined that the stone had fallen into his hands and that, through its power, they couldn't see him even though he was right there. And so, pleased as Punch at such good fortune, he decided to return home without telling them anything. Turning around, he started to go. When Buffalmacco saw that, he said to Bruno: "What should we do? Why don't we leave, too?"

Bruno replied: "Let's go! But I swear to God that Calandrino will never fool me like this again! If I were as close to him as I was all morning, I'd give him such a blow in the heels with this pebble that he'd remember his practical joke for maybe a month!" And, at the exact moment of saying this, he stretched out his arm, flinging the pebble at Calandrino's heel.

Feeling the pain, Calandrino lifted his foot high in the air and started to puff, but he kept silent and continued walking. Buffalmacco, taking in his hand one of the rocks he had collected, said to Bruno: "Say, isn't this a nice pebble? I wish it would hit Calandrino in the small of the back right now!" And, flinging it, he landed him a mighty blow in the back. In short, in this way, saying different things each time, they kept stoning him all along the Mugnone until they reached the San Gallo gate. There, throwing the stones they had collected to the ground, they lingered a while with the customs guards, who, previously instructed by those two, pretended not to see Calandrino and let him pass, while they laughed to their heart's content.

Calandrino, never stopping, reached his house, which was near Millstone Corner; Fortune so favored the joke that, all the while Calandrino proceeded along the river and through the city, no one said a word to him, although it's true he met very few people because almost everyone was having dinner.

And so Calandrino entered his house, loaded with stones as he was. His wife, who was called Monna Tessa, a good-looking, capable

---

[4]Or, with a slightly different reading of the Italian: "What do you mean, not long ago?"

valente donna, in capo della scala; ed alquanto turbata della sua lunga dimora, veggendol venire, cominciò proverbiando a dire: — Mai, frate, il diavol ti ci reca! Ogni gente ha già desinato quando tu torni a desinare. Il che udendo Calandrino e veggendo che veduto era, pieno di cruccio e di dolore cominciò a gridare: — Oimé! malvagia femina, o eri tu costì? Tu m'hai diserto. Ma in fè di Dio io te ne pagherò!

E salito in una saletta e quivi scaricate le molte pietre che recate avea, niquitoso corse verso la moglie, e presala per le trecce, la si gittò a' piedi, e quivi, quanto egli poté menar le braccia ed i piedi, tanto le die' per tutta la persona pugna e calci, senza lasciarle in capo capello o osso addosso che macero non fosse, niuna cosa valendole il chieder mercé con le mani in croce.

Buffalmacco e Bruno, poi che co' guardiani della porta ebbero alquanto riso, con lento passo cominciarono, alquanto lontani, a seguitar Calandrino; e giunti a pié dell'uscio di lui, sentirono la fiera battitura la quale alla moglie dava, e faccendo vista di giugnere pure allora, il chiamarono. Calandrino tutto sudato, rosso ed affannato si fece alla finestra e pregògli che suso a lui dovessero andare. Essi, mostrandosi alquanto turbati, andarono suso e videro la sala piena di pietre, e nell'un de' canti la donna scapigliata, stracciata, tutta livida e rossa nel viso, dolorosamente piagnere, e d'altra parte, Calandrino, scinto ed ansando a guisa d'uom lasso, sedersi.

Dove come alquanto ebbero riguardato dissero: — Che è questo, Calandrino? Vuoi tu murare, ché noi veggiamo qui tante pietre? — Ed oltre a questo soggiunsero: — E monna Tessa che ha? El par che tu l'abbi battuta; che novelle son queste?

Calandrino, faticato dal peso delle pietre e dalla rabbia con la quale la donna aveva battuta e dal dolore della ventura la quale perduta gli pareva avere, non poteva raccoglier lo spirito a formare intera la parola alla risposta; per che soprastando, Buffalmacco ricominciò: — Calandrino, se tu avevi altra ira, tu non ci dovevi per ciò straziare come fatto hai; ché, poi sodotti ci avesti a cercar teco della pietra preziosa, senza dirci a Dio né a diavolo, a guisa di due becconi nel Mugnon ci lasciasti e venìstitene, il che noi abbiamo forte per male; ma per certo questa fia la sezzaia che ci farai mai.

A queste parole Calandrino, sforzandosi, rispose: — Compagni, non vi turbate: l'opera sta altramenti che voi non pensate. Io, sventurato, aveva quella pietra trovata; e volete udire se io dico il vero?

woman, happened to be at the head of the stairs. A little vexed by his long absence, she started to upbraid him when she saw him arrive, saying: "Well, friend, the devil has finally brought you home! Everyone's already finished eating when you come home to eat!"

When Calandrino heard that, and saw he had been seen, he was filled with anger and grief, and started shouting: "Woe is me, you wicked woman, were you over there? You've ruined me! But, by my faith, I'll pay you back for it!"

He went upstairs to a small room, where he unloaded all the stones he had collected. Then, furious, he ran over to his wife, seized her by her braids, and threw her to the ground, where he punched and kicked her all over her body until his arms and feet gave out, leaving not a hair on her head or a bone in her body unharmed. It did her no good to cry for mercy with her hands clasped.

After Buffalmacco and Bruno had exchanged a few laughs with the guards at the town gate, they began to follow Calandrino at a slow pace, and at a little distance. Arriving at his house door on foot, they heard the severe beating he was giving his wife. Pretending they had just arrived, they called him. Calandrino showed his face at the window, all sweaty, flushed, and breathless, and asked them to come up and join him. With a slightly vexed expression, they came up and saw the room full of stones, and, in one corner, his wife, disheveled, her clothes ripped, all black and blue, and red in the face, weeping sorrowfully. Opposite her sat Calandrino, his clothes in disarray, panting like an exhausted man.

After they had looked at all this briefly, they said: "What's going on, Calandrino? Are you planning to build a wall with all these stones we see?" And they added: "What's wrong with your wife Tessa? It looks as if you've beaten her. What does all this mean?"

Calandrino, worn out by the weight of the stones, by the frenzy in which he had beaten his wife, and by his sorrow at losing his seeming good luck, couldn't pull himself together sufficiently to enunciate a clear answer. While he hesitated, Buffalmacco resumed: "Calandrino, even if you had some cause to be angry, you shouldn't have fooled us the way you did: after inducing us to look for the valuable stone with you, you didn't say a blessed word of farewell, but left us in the Mugnone like two idiots and decamped. We're very sore over it, but this will be the last joke you ever play on us!"

Calandrino, making an effort, replied: "Friends, don't be annoyed! Things are not the way they look to you. Unlucky man that I am, I did find that stone; do you want to hear whether I'm telling the truth?

Quando voi primieramente di me domandaste l'un l'altro, io v'era presso a men di diece braccia, e veggendo che voi ve ne venivate e non mi vedevate, v'entrai innanzi, e continuamente poco innanzi a voi me ne son venuto.

E cominciandosi dall'un de' capi, infino alla fine raccontò loro ciò che essi fatto e detto aveano, e mostrò loro il dosso e le calcagna come i ciotti conci gliel'avessero, e poi seguitò: — E dicovi che, entrando alla porta con tutte queste pietre in seno che voi vedete qui, niuna cosa mi fu detta, ché sapete quanto esser sogliano spiacevoli e noiosi que' guardiani a volere ogni cosa vedere; ed oltre a questo ho trovato per la via più miei compari ed amici, li quali sempre mi soglion far motto ed invitarmi a bere, né alcun fu che parola mi dicesse né mezza, sì come quegli che non mi vedeano. Alla fine, giunto qui a casa, questo diavolo di questa femina maladetta mi si parò dinanzi ed ebbemi veduto, per ciò che, come voi sapete, le femine fanno perder la vertù ad ogni cosa; di che io, che mi poteva dire il più avventurato uom di Firenze, sono rimaso il più sventurato; e per questo l'ho tanto battuta quanto io ho potuto menar le mani, e non so a quello che io mi tengo che io non le sego le veni, che maladetta sia l'ora che io prima la vidi e quando ella mai venne in questa casa!

E raccesosi nell'ira, si voleva levare per tornare a batterla da capo. Buffalmacco e Bruno, queste cose udendo, facevan vista di maravigliarsi forte e spesso affermavano quello che Calandrino diceva, ed avevano sì gran voglia di ridere, che quasi scoppiavano; ma, veggendolo furioso levare per battere un'altra volta la moglie, levatiglisi allo 'ncontro, il ritennero, dicendo di queste cose niuna colpa aver la donna, ma egli, che sapeva che le femine facevano perdere la vertù alle cose, e non l'aveva detto che ella si guardasse d'apparirgli innanzi quel giorno; il quale avvedimento Iddio gli aveva tolto o per ciò che la ventura non doveva esser sua o perché egli aveva in animo d'ingannare i suoi compagni, a' quali, come s'avvedeva d'averla trovata, il dovea palesare. E dopo molte parole, non senza gran fatica la dolente donna riconciliata con essolui, e lasciandol malinconoso con la casa piena di pietre, si partirono.

LA GRAVIDANZA DI CALANDRINO [IX, 3]

Poi che Elissa ebbe la sua novella finita, essendo da tutti rendute grazie a Dio, che la giovane monaca aveva con lieta uscita tratta de' morsi dell'invidiose compagne, la reina a Filòstrato comandò che seguitasse; il quale, senza più comandamento aspettare, incominciò:

When you first asked each other where I was, I was less than ten yards away from you. Seeing that you were leaving and couldn't see me, I moved up front and continued walking just a little ahead of you."

And he recounted what they had said and done, from the very beginning to the very end. He showed them the injuries their rocks had done to his back and heels, and then went on: "And I tell you that, when I entered town through the gate carrying all these stones you see here, not a word was said to me, and you know how unpleasant and bothersome those guards usually are, wanting to inspect everything! Besides, as I went I met several neighbors and friends, who always chat with me and invite me for a drink, but today none of them spoke even half a word to me, because they couldn't see me. Finally, when I got home, this devil of a cursed woman loomed up in front of me and SAW me, because, as you know, women make everything lose its magic powers. Whereupon, from being able to call myself the luckiest man in Florence, I became the unluckiest. That's why I beat her as long as I could move my hands. And I don't know what's keeping me from cutting her throat! I curse the hour I first saw her and the hour she first set foot in this house!"

His anger flaring up again, he wanted to get up and resume beating her. Hearing all this, Buffalmacco and Bruno pretended to be extremely surprised; several times they confirmed what Calandrino was saying. They felt so much like laughing that they almost exploded. But seeing him stand up in a rage to beat his wife again, they got up to stop him. They restrained him, saying that all of this was no fault of his wife's, but his own fault: he knew that women make things lose their special powers, and yet he hadn't instructed her to be sure not to come into his presence that day. God had robbed him of that foresight, either because that good luck wasn't destined to be his, or else because he had schemed to hoodwink his friends, to whom he should have reported at once his discovery of the stone. After a great deal of talk, with great difficulty they made peace between him and his aching wife, and departed, leaving him melancholy, with his house full of stones.

CALANDRINO'S PREGNANCY [IX, 3]

When Elissa finished her story, everyone thanked God for having successfully rescued the young nun from the backbiting of her jealous companions. Then the "Queen" ordered Filostrato to continue. Without awaiting further prompting, he began:

Bellissime donne, lo scostumato giudice marchigiano di cui
ieri vi novellai, mi trasse di bocca una novella di Calandrino la
quale io era per dirvi; e per ciò che ciò che di lui si ragiona non
può altro che multiplicar la festa, benché di lui e de' suoi compagni assai ragionato si sia, ancor pur quella che ieri aveva in
animo vi dirò.

Mostrato è di sopra assai chiaro chi Calandrin fosse e gli altri de'
quali in questa novella ragionar debbo, e per ciò, senza più dirne,
dico che egli avvenne che una zia di Calandrin si morì e lasciògli
dugento lire di piccioli contanti; per la qual cosa Calandrino cominciò a dire che egli voleva comperare un podere, e con quanti
sensali aveva in Firenze, come se da spendere avesse avuti diecemilia fiorin d'oro, teneva mercato, il qual sempre si guastava
quando al prezzo del poder domandato si perveniva.

Bruno e Buffalmacco, che queste cose sapevano, gli avevan più
volte detto che egli farebbe il meglio a goderglisi con loro insieme,
che andar comperando terra come se egli avesse avuto a far pallot-
tole; ma, non che a questo, essi non l'aveano mai potuto conducere
che egli loro una volta desse mangiare.

Per che un dì dolendosene, ed essendo a ciò sopravvenuto un lor
compagno che aveva nome Nello, dipintore, diliberâr tutti e tre di
dover trovar modo da ugnersi il grifo alle spese di Calandrino; e
senza troppo indugio darvi, avendo tra sé ordinato quello che a fare
avessero, la seguente mattina, appostato quando Calandrino di casa
uscisse, non essendo egli guari andato, gli si fece incontro Nello e
disse: — Buon dì, Calandrino.

Calandrino gli rispose che Iddio gli desse il buon dì ed il buon
anno. Appresso questo, Nello, rattenutosi un poco, lo 'ncominciò a
guardar nel viso; a cui Calandrino disse: — Che guati tu?

E Nello disse a lui: — Haiti tu sentita stanotte cosa niuna? Tu
non mi par' desso.

Calandrino incontanente cominciò a dubitare, e disse: — Oimé!
come? che ti pare egli che io abbia?

Disse Nello: — Deh! io nol dico per ciò; ma tu mi pari tutto cambiato; fia forse altro — e lasciollo andare.

Calandrino tutto sospettoso, non sentendosi per ciò cosa del
mondo, andò avanti. Ma Buffalmacco, che guari non era lontano,
veggendol partito da Nello, gli si fece incontro, e salutatolo, il

Beautiful ladies, the rude judge from the Marches whom I told you about yesterday kept me from telling a story about Calandrino that I was on the point of narrating. Since any story about him can't fail to increase our merriment, even though we've spoken a lot about him and his friends, nevertheless I'll tell you the story I had in mind yesterday.

In the earlier stories it's been made quite clear who Calandrino was, and who the others were that figure in the following tale. And so, saying no more of that, I tell you that an aunt of Calandrino's happened to die and leave him two hundred *lire di piccioli*[1] in cash. This made Calandrino start to say that he wanted to buy some real estate and to enter into negotiations with every broker in Florence, as if he had ten thousand gold florins to spend. The deals always fell through whenever the price of the desired property came up.

Knowing all this, Bruno and Buffalmacco had told him several times that he'd be better off using the money on good times with them, rather than buying land as if he needed to make baked-clay pellets for crossbows. But not only had they failed to persuade him to do that: they hadn't even managed to get a free dinner out of him.

And so, while they were lamenting over this one day, they were joined by a painter friend named Nello, and all three plotted ways of filling their belly[2] at Calandrino's expense. After planning what they were to do, they didn't delay very long. The very next morning, Nello lurked outside Calandrino's house, waiting for him to come out. Before Calandrino had walked any distance, Nello came up to him and said: "Good day, Calandrino."

In reply, Calandrino wished that God would give Nello a good day and a good year. Thereupon Nello paused a bit and started to examine his face. So Calandrino said: "What are you looking at?"

And Nello replied: "Did you notice anything wrong with you last night? Somehow you're not yourself today."

Immediately Calandrino began worrying, and said: "Woe is me! How so? What do you think is the matter with me?"

Nello said: "Oh, I don't mean anything by it. Only you look so different! Maybe it's something else." And he allowed him to proceed on his way.

Calandrino, though he didn't notice anything unusual in himself, was filled with doubt as he walked on. But when Buffalmacco, who wasn't very far away, saw Nello leave him, he came up to him, greeted

---

[1]In contrast to *lire di grossi*, which were a significantly greater denomination.
[2]Literally: "greasing their ugly mugs."

domandò se egli si sentisse niente. Calandrino rispose: — Io non so, pur testé mi diceva Nello che io gli pareva tutto cambiato; potrebbe egli essere che io avessi nulla?

Disse Buffalmacco: — Sì, potrestù aver cavelle, non che nulla: tu par' mezzo morto.

A Calandrino pareva già aver la febbre; ed ecco Bruno sopravvenne, e prima che altro dicesse, disse: — Calandrino, che viso è quello? El par che tu sii morto: che ti senti tu?

Calandrino, udendo ciascun di costoro così dire, per certissimo ebbe seco medesimo d'esser malato, e tutto sgomentato gli domandò: — Che fo?

Disse Bruno: — A me pare che tu te ne torni a casa e vaditene in sul letto e facciti ben coprire, e che tu mandi il segnal tuo al maestro Simone, che è così nostra cosa come tu sai. Egli ti dirà incontanente ciò che tu avrai a fare, e noi ne verrem teco; e se bisognerà far cosa niuna, noi la faremo.

E con loro aggiuntosi Nello, con Calandrino se ne tornarono a casa sua; ed egli entratosene tutto affaticato nella camera, disse alla moglie: — Vieni e cuoprimi bene, ché io mi sento un gran male.

Essendo adunque a giacer posto, il suo segnale per una fanticella mandò al maestro Simone, il quale allora a bottega stava in Mercato Vecchio alla 'nsegna del mellone. E Bruno disse a' compagni: — Voi vi rimarrete qui con lui, ed io voglio andare a sapere che il medico dirà, e se bisogno sarà, a menarloci.

Calandrino allora disse: — Deh! sì, compagno mio, vavvi e sappimi ridire come il fatto sta, ché io mi sento non se che dentro.

Bruno, andatosene al maestro Simone, vi fu prima che la fanticella che il segno portava, ed ebbe informato maestro Simon del fatto; per che, venuta la fanticella ed il maestro veduto il segno, disse alla fanticella: — Vattene e di' a Calandrino che egli si tenga ben caldo, ed io verrò a lui incontanente e dirògli ciò che egli ha e ciò che egli avrà a fare.

La fanticella così rapportò; né stette guari che il medico e Brun vennero, e pòstoglisi il medico a sedere allato, gl'incominciò a toccare il polso, e dopo alquanto, essendo ivi presente la moglie, disse: — Vedi, Calandrino, a parlarti come ad amico, tu non hai altro male se non che tu se' pregno.

Come Calandrino udì questo, dolorosamente cominciò a gridare

him, and asked him whether he was suffering from anything. Calandrino replied: "I don't know. Just a moment ago Nello told me I looked so different to him. Could I have something wrong with me?"

Buffalmacco said: "Yes, you might have whatever, not just something. You look half dead."

By this time Calandrino thought he had fever; and now Bruno joined them, and the first thing he said was: "Calandrino, why is your face like that? You look dead: how do you feel?"

After Calandrino heard all three of them saying the same thing, he was absolutely positive in his mind that he was sick. In high alarm he asked: "What should I do?"

Bruno said: "My opinion is that you should go home, go to bed, have yourself covered up nice and warm, and send a urine sample to Master Simone, who, as you know, is such a good chum of ours. He'll tell you right away what you should do. We'll come with you and, if you need anything, we'll do it for you."

With Nello joining in, they accompanied Calandrino back home. Going into his bedroom in a state of exhaustion, he said to his wife: "Come cover me up properly, because I feel just awful."

And so, after lying down, he gave a urine sample to a maid to take to Master Simone, whose apothecary shop was in the Old Market at the time, at the sign of the melon.[3] Bruno said to his friends: "You stay here with him, while I go find out what the doctor has to say and bring him back here if necessary."

Then Calandrino said: "Yes, yes, my friend, go and find out so you can tell me how things stand, because I feel all peculiar inside!"

Heading off for Master Simone's place, Bruno got there before the maid who was bringing the urine, and he let Master Simone into the whole plan. And so, after the maid arrived and the master had looked at the urine, he said to her: "Go back and tell Calandrino to keep good and warm, and I'll come right away to tell him what's wrong with him and what he must do."

The maid reported this, and before very long Bruno and the doctor arrived. The doctor sat down beside Calandrino's bed, and started to take his pulse. After a while, in the presence of Calandrino's wife, he said: "Look, Calandrino, speaking to you as a friend, the only thing wrong with you is that you're pregnant."

When Calandrino heard that, he began to cry out in sorrow, saying:

---

[3]"Melon" was slang for "fool."

ed a dire: — Oimé! Tessa, questo m'hai fatto tu, che non vuogli stare altro che di sopra; io il ti diceva bene!

La donna, che assai onesta persona era, udendo così dire al marito, tutta di vergogna arrossò, ed abbassata la fronte, senza risponder parola s'uscì della camera. Calandrino, continuando il suo ramarichìo, diceva:

— Oimé, tristo me! come farò io? Come partorirò io questo figliuolo? Onde uscirà egli? Ben veggio che io son morto per la rabbia di questa mia moglie, che tanto la faccia Iddio trista quanto io voglio esser lieto; ma così fossi io sano come io non sono, ché io mi leverei e dare'le tante busse, che io la romperei tutta, avvegna che egli mi stea molto bene, ché io non la doveva mai lasciar salir di sopra; ma per certo, se io scampo di questa, ella se ne potrà ben prima morir di voglia.

Bruno e Buffalmacco e Nello avevano sì gran voglia di ridere, che scoppiavano, udendo le parole di Calandrino, ma pur se ne tenevano; ma il maestro Scimmione rideva sì squaccheratamente, che tutti i denti gli si sarebber potuti trarre. Ma pure, a lungo andare, raccomandandosi Calandrino al medico e pregandolo che in questo gli dovesse dar consiglio ed aiuto, gli disse il maestro: — Calandrino, io non voglio che tu ti sgomenti, ché, lodato sia Iddio, noi ci siamo sì tosto accorti del fatto, che con poca fatica ed in pochi dì ti dilibererò; ma conviensi un poco spendere.

Disse Calandrino: — Oimé! maestro mio, sì, per l'amor di Dio; io ho qui da dugento lire di che io volea comperare un podere: se tutti bisognano, tutti gli togliete, pur che io non abbia a partorire, ché io non so come io mi facessi; ch' io odo fare alle femine un sì gran romore quando son per partorire, con tutto che elle abbiano buon cotal grande donde farlo, che io credo, se io avessi quel dolore, che io mi morrei prima che io partorissi.

Disse il medico: — Non aver pensiero: io ti farò fare una certa bevanda stillata molto buona e molto piacevole a bere, che in tre mattine risolverà ogni cosa, e rimarrai più sano che pesce; ma farai che tu sii poscia savio, e più non incappi in queste sciocchezze. Ora, ci bisogna per quella acqua tre paia di buon capponi e grossi, e per altre cose che bisognano, darai ad un di costoro cinque lire di piccioli, che le comperi, e fara'mi ogni cosa recare alla bottega; ed io, al nome di Dio, domattina ti manderò di quel beveraggio stillato, e comincera'ne a bere un buon bicchier grande per volta.

Calandrino, udito questo, disse: — Maestro mio, ciò siane in voi.

"Woe is me! Tessa, you're the one who's done this to me, because you always want to be on top! I told you something would happen!"

When the lady, who was a very respectable person, heard her husband say that, she turned bright red with shame, lowered her head, and left the room without making any reply. Calandrino, continuing his lament, was saying:

"Woe is me, how miserable I am! How will I be able? How will I give birth to this child? Where will he come out? I can see I'll end up dead, thanks to the lustful frenzy of this wife of mine—may God make her as wretched as I wish to be happy! But if I were healthy, which unfortunately I'm not, I'd get up and give her such a hiding that I'd break all of her bones—even though I'm only getting what's coming to me, because I should never have let her climb up on top. You can be sure that, if I get over this, she'll die of wanting it before I allow it!"

Hearing Calandrino's words, Bruno, Buffalmacco, and Nello had such a great urge to laugh, they were bursting; but they contained themselves. On the other hand, Master Simian was laughing so raucously and "juicily" that all of his teeth could have been extracted. Finally, Calandrino put himself in the doctor's hands, begging him for his advice and assistance in this matter. The master replied: "Calandrino, I don't want you to get panicky, because, God be praised, we have become aware of the situation at such an early stage that I can rid you of your trouble easily and in just a few days. But you'll have to lay out a little money."

Calandrino said: "Woe is me! Yes, master, for the love of God! I've got two hundred *lire* here that I wanted to buy property with. If you need it all, take it all, just so long as I don't need to give birth, because I don't know how I'd go about it! You know, I hear women making such a racket when they're about to give birth—and they have such a nice big thing to do it with!—that I'm sure if I had that much pain I'd die before the baby was born!"

The doctor said: "Don't worry. I'll make you a certain distilled medicine that's very effective and very pleasant to drink. In three mornings it will fix everything, and afterward you'll be healthier than a fish. But take care to be sensible in the future, and not let yourself in for such foolish behavior. Now, to make that medicine, we need three pairs of nice fat capons. For other necessary ingredients, give one of these men five *lire* to buy them with, and have everything brought to my shop. Tomorrow, in God's name, I'll send you some of that distilled medicine, and you'll start drinking a nice big glass of it each time."

When Calandrino heard this, he said: "Master, that's all up to you."

E date cinque lire a Bruno e denari per tre paia di capponi, il
pregò che in suo servigio in queste cose durasse fatica. Il medico,
partitosi, gli fece fare un poco di chiarea, e mandògliele. Bruno,
comperati i capponi e altre cose necessarie al godere, insieme col
medico e co' compagni suoi gli si mangiò. Calandrino bevve tre
mattine della chiarea; ed il medico venne da lui, ed i suoi compagni; e toccatogli il polso, gli disse: — Calandrino, tu se' guerito
senza fallo, e però sicuramente oggimai va' a fare ogni tuo fatto, né
per questo star più in casa.

Calandrino lieto, levatosi, s'andò a fare i fatti suoi, lodando
molto, ovunque con persona a parlar s'avveniva, la bella cura che di
lui il maestro Simone aveva fatta, d'averlo fatto in tre dì senza alcuna pena spregnare; e Bruno e Buffalmacco e Nello rimaser contenti d'aver con ingegni saputa schernire l'avarizia di Calandrino,
quantunque monna Tessa, avveggendosene, molto col marito ne
brontolasse.

IL MASNADIERE E L'ABATE [X, 2]

Lodata era già stata la magnificenza del re Anfonso nel fiorentin
cavaliere usata, quando il re, al quale molto era piaciuta, ad Elissa
impose che seguitasse; la quale prestamente incominciò:

Dilicate donne, l'essere stato un re magnifico e l'avere la sua
magnificenza usata verso colui che servito l'avea non si può dire che
laudevole e gran cosa non sia; ma che direm noi se si racconterà un
cherico aver mirabil magnificenza usata verso persona che, se ini-
micato l'avesse, non ne sarebbe stato biasimato da persona? Certo
non altro, se non che quella del re fosse vertù e quella del cherico
miracolo, con ciò sia cosa che essi tutti avarissimi troppo più che le
femine sieno, e d'ogni liberalità nemici a spada tratta; e quantunque ogni uomo naturalmente appetisca vendetta delle ricevute
offese, i cherici, come si vede, quantunque la pazienza prèdichino
e sommamente la remission dell'offese commendino, più focosa-
mente che gli altri uomini a quella discorrono. La qual cosa, cioè
come un cherico magnifico fosse, nella seguente novella potrete
conoscere aperto.

Ghino di Tacco, per la sua fierezza e per le sue ruberie uomo
assai famoso, essendo di Siena cacciato e nemico de' conti di

He gave five *lire* to Bruno, along with money for three pairs of capons, and begged him to run those errands as a favor to him. The doctor, back home, prepared a little bland medicine[4] for him and sent it to him. When Bruno had bought the capons and other items necessary for their banquet, all three companions and the doctor devoured them. Calandrino drank the potion three mornings. The doctor came to see him, along with his companions. Taking his pulse, he said: "Calandrino, you're definitely cured, and, starting today, you can go about your business free from worry. This doesn't have to keep you home anymore."

Overjoyed, Calandrino got out of bed and went about his business; wherever he got into a conversation with anyone, he heaped praise on the wonderful way that Master Simone had handled his case, aborting his pregnancy painlessly in three days. Bruno, Buffalmacco, and Nello were pleased at the clever way in which they had circumvented Calandrino's tightfistedness. But when Monna Tessa saw through it all, she grumbled to her husband about it for some time.

THE HIGHWAYMAN AND THE ABBOT [X, 2]

The listeners had already praised the generosity that King Alfonso had shown to the Florentine knight, when the "King," who had enjoyed the story very much, ordered Elissa to tell the next one, and she immediately began:

Delicate ladies, that a king was munificent, and showed his munificence to a man who had served him, is a great and praiseworthy thing, it cannot be denied; but what are we to say to a story of an ecclesiastic who showed extraordinary munificence to someone whom no one would have blamed him for attacking hostilely? Surely, we could only say that the king's action was a virtuous deed, but the churchman's action was a miracle, seeing that all men of the cloth are much more grasping than women, and enemies at daggers drawn to all generosity. And, while all men naturally seek revenge for injuries done to them, we see that churchmen, even though they preach patience and commend the forgiveness of injuries in the strongest terms, have recourse to vengeance more ardently than other men. This matter—that is, the munificence of an ecclesiastic—you will see clearly in the following story.

Ghino di Tacco, a man notorious for his savagery and his highway robberies, on being banished from Siena as an enemy of the Counts of

---

[4]*Chiarea* has also been interpreted as spiced wine or an emollient.

Santafiore, ribellò Radicòfani alla Chiesa di Roma, ed in quel dimorando, chiunque per le circostanti parti passava rubar faceva a' suoi masnadieri. Ora, essendo Bonifazio papa ottavo in Roma, venne a corte l'abate di Clignì il quale si crede essere un de' più ricchi prelati del mondo; e quivi guastàtoglisi lo stomaco, fu da' medici consigliato che egli andasse a' bagni di Siena, e guerirebbe senza fallo; per la qual cosa, concedutogliele il papa, senza curar della fama di Ghino, con gran pompa d'arnesi e di some e di cavalli e di famiglia entrò in cammino.

Ghino di Tacco, sentendo la sua venuta, tese le reti, e senza perderne un sol ragazzetto, l'abate con tutta la sua famiglia e le sue cose in uno stretto luogo racchiuse; e questo fatto, un de' suoi il più saccente, bene accompagnato, mandò all'abate, al quale da parte di lui assai amorevolmente gli disse che gli dovesse piacere d'andare a smontare con esso Ghino al castello. Il che l'abate udendo, tutto furioso rispose che egli non ne voleva far niente, sì come quegli che con Ghino niente aveva a fare, ma che egli andrebbe avanti e vorrebbe veder chi l'andar gli vietasse.

Al quale l'ambasciadore umilmente parlando disse: — Messer, voi siete in parte venuto dove, dalla forza di Dio in fuori, di niente ci si teme per noi, e dove le scomunicazioni e gl'interdetti sono scomunicati tutti; e per ciò piacciavi per lo migliore di compiacere a Ghino di questo. — Era già, mentre queste parole erano, tutto il luogo di masnadieri circondato; per che l'abate, co' suoi preso veggendosi, disdegnoso forte, con l'ambasciadore prese la via verso il castello, e tutta la sua brigata e li suoi arnesi con lui.

E smontato, come Ghino volle, tutto solo fu messo in una cameretta d'un palagio assai oscura e disagiata, ed ogni altro uomo secondo la sua qualità per lo castello fu assai bene adagiato, ed i cavalli e tutto l'arnese messo in salvo senza alcuna cosa toccarne.

E questo fatto, se n'andò Ghino all'abate e dissegli: — Messer, Ghino, di cui voi siete oste, vi manda pregando che vi piaccia di significargli dove voi andavate e per qual cagione.

L'abate che, come savio, aveva l'altierezza giù posta, gli significò dove andasse e perché. Ghino, udito questo, si partì e pensossi di volerlo querire senza bagno; e faccendo nella cameretta sempre ardere un gran fuoco e ben guardarla, non tornò a lui infino alla seguente mattina, ed allora in una tovagliuola bianchissima gli portò due fette di pane arrostito ed un gran bicchiere

Santafiora, incited the people of Radicofani to revoke their allegiance to the Church of Rome. Residing there, he had his gang rob everyone who passed through the surrounding countryside. Now, Boniface VIII being pope in Rome, the papal court was visited by the abbot of Cluny, who is thought to be one of the richest prelates in the world. While he was there, he developed a stomach ailment, and his doctors advised him to visit the spa in Siena, where he was sure to be cured. And so, with the pope's permission, and not worried by Ghino's notoriety, he set out with a rich train of belongings, pack animals, horses, and servants.

When Ghino di Tacco learned of his approach, he laid his ambush and, not allowing even the humblest stable boy to escape, he encircled the abbot, with his entire household and possessions, in a tight corner. Then he sent the cleverest of his men, well accompanied, to the abbot. With the greatest courtesy this man asked the abbot on Ghino's behalf to be so good as to enjoy Ghino's hospitality in the castle. When the abbot heard this, he became enraged, replying that he would do nothing of the sort, because he had no dealings with Ghino; instead, he would proceed on his way and he'd like to see who'd stop him.

In reply the emissary said gently: "My lord, you have come to a place where nothing is feared except the power of God, and where all excommunications and interdicts are themselves excommunicated. Therefore, be so kind as to oblige Ghino in this for your own good." While this parley was going on, the whole spot had already been surrounded by highwaymen; and so the abbot, finding himself and his men in captivity, took his way, filled with wrath, toward the castle with the emissary, his whole company and all his possessions following after.

Entering the castle, in obedience to Ghino's orders, he was placed all alone in a very dark and uncomfortable small room in one building. All the others were assigned very decent quarters in various parts of the castle according to rank, and the horses and all the baggage were put in a safe place without being rifled to the slightest degree.

After this was done, Ghino visited the abbot and said: "My lord, Ghino, whose guest you are, sends me to ask you to be so good as to inform him where you were going and for what reason."

The abbot, who in his wisdom had put off his haughty bearing, informed him where he had been going and why. When Ghino heard this, he left and thought of a way to cure him without medicinal baths. He had a good fire kept going constantly in the small room, which he ordered to be carefully guarded. He didn't come back to see the abbot until the following morning, when he brought him in a gleaming-white

di vernaccia da Corniglia di quella dell'abate medesimo; e sì disse
all'abate:

— Messer, quando Ghino era più giovane, egli studiò in medicine, e dice che apparò, niuna medicina al mal dello stomaco esser
miglior che quella che egli vi farà; della quale queste cose che io vi
reco sono il cominciamento, e per ciò prendètele e confortàtevi.

L'abate, che maggior fame aveva che voglia di motteggiare, ancora che con isdegno il facesse, si mangiò il pane e bevve la vernaccia, e poi molte cose altiere disse e di molte domandò e molte
ne consigliò, ed in ispezialtà chiese di poter veder Ghino.

Ghino, udendo quelle, parte ne lasciò andar sì come vane e ad
alcuna assai cortesemente rispose, affermando che, come Ghino
più tosto potesse, il visiterebbe; e questo detto, da lui si partì, né
prima vi tornò che il seguente dì, con altrettanto pane arrostito e
con altrettanta vernaccia; e così il tenne più giorni, tanto che egli
s'accorse l'abate aver mangiate fave secche, le quali egli studiosa-
mente e di nascoso portate v'aveva e lasciate. Per la qual cosa egli
il domandò da parte di Ghino come star gli pareva dello stomaco;
al quale l'abate rispose: — A me parrebbe star bene, se io fossi
fuori delle sue mani; ed appresso questo, niuno altro talento ho
maggiore che di mangiare, sì ben m'hanno le sue medicine guerito.

Ghino adunque, avendogli de' suoi arnesi medesimi ed alla
sua famiglia fatta acconciare una bella camera, e fatto apparecchiare un gran convito, al quale, con molti uomini del castello,
fu tutta la famiglia dell'abate, a lui se n'andò la mattina seguente
e dissegli: — Messer, poi che voi ben vi sentite, tempo è d'uscire d'infermeria.

E per la man prèsolo, nella camera apparecchiàtagli nel menò,
ed in quella co' suoi medesimi lasciatolo, a far che il convito fosse
magnifico attese. L'abate co' suoi alquanto si ricreò, e qual fosse la
sua vita stata narrò loro, dove essi in contrario tutti dissero sé essere
stati maravigliosamente onorati da Ghino; ma l'ora del mangiar
venuta, l'abate e tutti gli altri ordinatamente e di buone vivande e
di buoni vini serviti furono, senza lasciarsi Ghino ancora all'abate
conoscere.

Ma poi che l'abate alquanti dì in questa maniera fu dimorato,
avendo Ghino in una sala tutti gli suoi arnesi fatti venire, ed in una
corte che di sotto a quella era, tutti i suoi cavalli infino al più misero ronzino, all'abate se n'andò e domandollo come star gli pareva

cloth two slices of toast and a big glass of fine dry white wine from Corniglia[1] out of the abbot's own stores. And he said to the abbot:

"My lord, when Ghino was younger, he studied medicine, and he says he learned that no cure is better for stomach ailments than the one he intends to give you. These things I now bring you are the first steps in the cure, so take them and be optimistic."

The abbot, whose hunger was greater than his desire to bandy words, ate the bread and drank the wine, though with anger in his heart; then he made a long, haughty speech, asking and giving advice about a number of things. His chief request was to be able to meet Ghino.

When Ghino heard all this, he dismissed some of it as being futile, but replied courteously to part of it, assuring the abbot that Ghino would visit him as soon as he could. Saying this, he left him, not to return until the following day, with the same amount of toast and wine. He kept this up for several days, until he became aware that the abbot had eaten the dry beans that Ghino had intentionally brought in secretly and left there. And so he asked him on Ghino's behalf how his stomach seemed to be feeling. The abbot replied: "I would consider myself to be feeling good, if only I were out of his hands. Aside from that, my greatest wish is to have a good meal, because his cure has worked so well for me."

Therefore Ghino, ordering the abbot's own servants to furnish a beautiful, large room for him with his own belongings, also had a grand banquet prepared, to be attended by the abbot's entire household as well as many men from the castle. He visited him the next morning and said: "My lord, since you are feeling well, it's time to leave sickbay."

He respectfully took his hand and led him to the room that had been prepared for him, leaving him there with his own people, and then attending to the magnificent banquet preparations. The abbot enjoyed the company of his followers for a while, telling them what his living conditions had been like; they all told him that, quite to the contrary, they had been wonderfully well entertained by Ghino. When mealtime arrived, the abbot and all the others were elegantly served good food and wine, but Ghino did not yet reveal his identity to the abbot.

But after the abbot had spent several days in this manner, Ghino had all his belongings brought together in one room, and assembled all the abbot's horses, down to the most miserable nag, in a courtyard below that room. Then he visited the abbot, and asked how he was

---

[1]Probably the place of that name near La Spezia in Liguria.

e se forte si credeva essere da cavalcare; a cui l'abate rispose che forte era egli assai e dello stomaco ben guerito, e che starebbe bene qualora fosse fuori delle mani di Ghino. Menò allora Ghino l'abate nella sala dove erano i suoi arnesi e la sua famiglia tutta, e fàttolo ad una finestra accostare, donde egli poteva tutti i suoi cavalli vedere, disse:

— Messer l'abate, voi dovete sapere che l'esser gentile uomo e cacciato di casa sua e povero, ed avere molti e possenti nemici hanno, per potere la sua vita difendere e la sua nobiltà, e non malvagità d'animo, condotto Ghino di Tacco, il quale io sono, ad essere rubatore delle strade e nemico della corte di Roma. Ma per ciò che voi mi parete valente signore, avendovi io dello stomaco guerito come io ho, non intendo di trattarvi come uno altro farei, a cui, quando nelle mie mani fosse come voi siete, quella parte delle sue cose mi farei che mi paresse; ma io intendo che voi a me, il mio bisogno considerato, quella parte delle vostre cose facciate che voi medesimo volete. Elle sono interamente qui dinanzi da voi tutte, ed i vostri cavalli potete voi da cotesta finestra nella corte vedere; e per ciò e la parte ed il tutto, come vi piace, prendete, e da questa ora innanzi sia e l'andare e lo stare nel piacer vostro.

Maravigliossi l'abate che in un rubator di strada fosser parole sì libere e piacendogli molto, subitamente la sua ira e lo sdegno caduti, anzi in benivolenza mutatisi, col cuore amico di Ghino divenuto, il corse ad abbracciar dicendo: — Io giuro a Dio che, per dover guadagnar l'amistà d'uno uomo sì fatto come omai io giudico che tu sii, io sofferrei di ricevere troppo maggiore ingiuria che quella che infino a qui paruta m'è che tu m'abbi fatta. Maladetta sia la fortuna, la quale a sì dannevole mestier ti costrigne!

Ed appresso questo, fatto delle sue molte cose pochissime ed opportune prendere, e de' cavalli similmente, e l'altre lasciategli tutte, a Roma se ne tornò. Aveva il papa saputa la presura dell'abate, e come che molto gravata gli fosse, veggendolo il domandò come i bagni fatto gli avessero prò; al quale l'abate sorridendo rispose: — Santo padre, io trovai più vicino che i bagni un valente medico, il quale ottimamente guerito m'ha.

E contògli il modo, di che il papa rise; al quale l'abate, seguitando il suo parlare, da magnifico animo mosso, domandò una grazia. Il papa, credendo lui dover domandare altro, liberamente offerse di far ciò che domandasse. Allora l'abate disse:

— Santo padre, quello che io intendo domandarvi è che voi rendiate la grazia vostra a Ghino di Tacco mio medico, per ciò che tra

feeling and whether he felt strong enough to ride again. The abbot replied that he felt very strong, that his stomach was completely settled, and that his health would be perfect as soon as he was out of Ghino's hands. Then Ghino led the abbot to the room containing all his belongings and his entire household. Leading him up to a window from which he could see all his horses, he said:

"My lord abbot, I'd like you to know that it was his being a nobleman banished from his home as a pauper with numerous powerful enemies, and not any inborn wickedness, that led Ghino di Tacco—myself!—to become a highwayman and an enemy of the papal court, in order to save his life and safeguard his noble status. But because I consider you to be a worthy lord, now that I have healed your stomach, I don't intend to treat you the way I would others, of whose belongings I would take any share I chose, if they were in my hands as you are. Instead, I want you to consider my needs and give me whatever part of your goods you yourself choose. They are all here in front of you, and you can see your horses in the courtyard from this window. And so, just as you like, take some of them or all of them; and, from this moment on, the decision whether to stay or go is entirely yours."

The abbot was amazed to hear such generous terms from a highway robber; very pleased, he abandoned his anger and rage and, in fact, transformed them into kindly feelings. Having become Ghino's heartfelt friend, he ran up and embraced him, saying: "I swear to God that, in order to gain the friendship of a man such as I now take you to be, I would submit to receiving much greater harm than any I seem to have received from you up to now. Cursed be Fortune, who forces such a blameworthy occupation on you!"

Then he selected from his numerous goods only a very few and the most necessary, doing the same with the horses; leaving all the rest for Ghino, he returned to Rome. The pope had learned about the abbot's capture and, although he was greatly grieved by it, he first asked him upon seeing him what good the spa had done him. Smiling, the abbot replied: "Holy Father, even before I got to the spa I found a capable doctor, who has cured me completely."

And he told him the manner of the cure, at which the pope laughed. The abbot, following the train of his speech, and in a magnanimous frame of mind, requested a favor of him. The pope, thinking he would ask for something else, promised unconditionally to do whatever he requested. Then the abbot said:

"Holy Father, what I have in mind to request of you is to shed your grace upon my physician, Ghino di Tacco, because he is certainly one

gli altri uomini valorosi e da molto che io accontai mai, egli è per
certo un de' più, e quel male il quale egli fa, io il reputo molto maggior peccato della fortuna che suo; la qual se voi, con alcuna cosa,
dandogli donde egli possa secondo lo stato suo vivere, mutate, io
non dubito punto che in poco di tempo non ne paia a voi quello che
a me pare.

Il papa, udendo questo, sì come colui che di grande animo fu e
vago de' valenti uomini, disse di farlo volentieri se da tanto fosse
come diceva, e che egli il facesse sicuramente venire. Venne
adunque Ghino, fidato, come all'abate piacque, a corte; né guari
appresso del papa fu, che egli il reputò valoroso, e riconciliatolsi, gli
donò una gran prioria di quelle dello Spedale, di quello avendol
fatto far cavaliere; la quale egli, amico e servidore di santa Chiesa e
dell'abate di Clignì, tenne mentre visse.

UNA GARA DI LIBERALITÀ [X, 3]

Simil cosa a miracolo per certo pareva a tutti avere udito, cioè che
un cherico alcuna cosa magnificamente avesse operata; ma ri-
posandosene già il ragionare delle donne, comandò il re a
Filòstrato che procedesse; il quale prestamente incominciò:

Nobili donne, grande fu la magnificenza del re di Spagna e forse
cosa più non udita già mai quella dell'abate di Clignì, ma forse non
meno maravigliosa cosa vi parrà l'udire che uno per liberalità usare ad
uno altro che il suo sangue, anzi il suo spirito disiderava, cautamente
a dargliele si disponesse; e fatto l'avrebbe se colui prender l'avesse voluto, sì come io in una mia novelletta intendo di dimostrarvi.

Certissima cosa è, se fede si può dare alle parole d'alcuni
Genovesi e d'altri uomini che in quelle contrade stati sono, che
nelle parti del Cattaio fu già uno uomo di legnaggio nobile, e ricco
senza comparazione, per nome chiamato Natan, il quale, avendo
un suo ricetto vicino ad una strada per la qual quasi di necessità
passava ciascuno che di Ponente verso Levante andar voleva o di
Levante in Ponente, ed avendo l'animo grande e liberale e
disideroso che fosse per opera conosciuto, quivi avendo molti
maestri, fece in piccolo spazio di tempo fare un de' più belli e de'
maggiori e de' più ricchi palagi che mai fosse stato veduto, e quello
di tutte quelle cose che opportune erano a dovere gentili uomini
ricevere ed onorare fece ottimamente fornire.

Ed avendo grande e bella famiglia, con piacevolezza e con festa

of the most worthy and eminent men I've ever met; and I deem the wrong he does to be Fortune's crime much more than it is his. If you change his fortune by somehow giving him the means to live in accordance with his rank, I have no doubt that before long you will think as highly of him as I do."

Hearing this, the pope, who was of a lofty spirit and who was fond of worthy men, said he would gladly do so if Ghino was as fine a man as the abbot claimed. He asked the abbot to arrange a safe-conduct for Ghino. And so, under a pledge of security, Ghino came to the papal court at the abbot's bidding. He wasn't long in the pope's presence before his worth was recognized and the pope made peace with him, giving him a large priory belonging to the Hospitalers, first making him a knight of that order. And Ghino, as a friend and servant of the Holy Church and of the abbot of Cluny, possessed that benefice as long as he lived.

A CONTEST OF GENEROSITY [X, 3]

They all thought they had heard something very much like a miracle: a churchman who had performed a generous action! But after the ladies had finished discussing the story, the "King" ordered Filostrato to proceed. He began at once:

Noble ladies, great was the munificence of the king of Spain, and that of the abbot of Cluny possibly altogether unheard of, but you may perhaps find it no less amazing to hear about a man who, in order to be generous to one that desired his blood—no, his life!—prudently prepared to make him a gift of them. And so he would have done, had the other man wished to take them, as I intend to show you in my little story.

It is a proven fact, if one may believe the reports of some Genovese and others who have traveled in those realms, that in the region of Cathay there once was a man of noble lineage, rich beyond compare, named Nathan. He resided near a highway that was almost obligatory for anyone wishing to pass from west to east or from east to west. Possessed of a lofty and generous spirit, and eager to make it known through his actions, he ordered the numerous local architects to build, in a very short time, one of the largest, most beautiful, and richest palaces ever seen; and he had it splendidly furnished with everything suitable for welcoming and entertaining wellborn guests.

Having a large, fine household staff, with pleasure and joy he

chiunque andava e veniva faceva ricevere ed onorare; ed intanto perseverò in questo laudevol costume, che già non solamente il Levante, ma quasi tutto il Ponente per fama il conoscea. Ed essendo egli già d'anni pieno, né però del corteseggiar divenuto stanco, avvenne che la sua fama agli orecchi pervenne d'un giovane chiamato Mitridanes, di paese non guari al suo lontano, il quale, sentendosi non meno ricco che Natan fosse, divenuto della sua fama e della sua vertù invidioso, seco propose con maggior liberalità quella o annullare o offuscare; e fatto fare un palagio simile a quello di Natan, cominciò a fare le più smisurate cortesie che mai facesse alcuno altro, a chi andava o veniva per quindi, e senza dubbio in piccol tempo assai divenne famoso.

Ora avvenne un giorno che, dimorando il giovane tutto solo nella corte del suo palagio, una feminella, entrata dentro per una delle porti del palagio gli domandò limosina ed ebbela; e ritornata per la seconda porta pure a lui, ancora l'ebbe, e così successivamente infino alla duodecima; e la tredicesima volta tornata, disse Mitridanes: — Buona femina, tu se' assai sollecita a questo tuo domandare! — E nondimeno le fece limosina.

La vecchierella, udita questa parola, disse: — O liberalità di Natan, quanto se' tu maravigliosa! ché per trentadue porti che ha il suo palagio, sì come questo, entrata e domandatagli limosina, mai da lui, che egli mostrasse, riconosciuta non fui, e sempre l'ebbi; e qui non venuta ancora se non per tredici, e riconosciuta e proverbiata sono stata. — E così dicendo, senza più ritornarvi si dipartì.

Mitridanes, udite le parole della vecchia, come colui che ciò che della fama di Natan udiva, diminuimento della sua estimava, in rabbiosa ira acceso, cominciò a dire: — Ahi lasso a me! quando aggiugnerò io alla liberalità delle gran cose di Natan, non che io il trapassi, come io cerco, quando nelle piccolissime io non gli mi posso avvicinare? Veramente io mi fatico invano, se io di terra nol tolgo, la quale cosa, poscia che la vecchiezza nol porta via, convien senza alcun indugio che io faccia con le mie mani.

E con questo impeto levatosi, senza comunicare il suo consiglio ad alcuno, con poca compagnia montato a cavallo, dopo il terzo dì, dove Natan dimorava pervenne; ed a' compagni imposto che sembianti facessero di non esser con lui né di conoscerlo, e che di stanza si procacciassero infino che da lui altro avessero, quivi in sul fare della sera pervenuto e solo rimaso, non guari lontano al bel palagio trovò Natan tutto solo, il quale, senza alcuno abito

welcomed and entertained all who passed in either direction. And he persisted in that laudable practice so long that not only the eastern lands, but almost the entire Occident as well, had heard about him. When he was already full of years, though not yet weary of providing hospitality, his reputation happened to reach the ears of a young man named Mithridanes, whose country was not too distant from Nathan's. Perceiving himself as being no less wealthy than Nathan, he grew envious of his reputation for nobility, and determined to put that reputation to an end, or at least in the shade, by his own greater generosity. He had a palace built similar to Nathan's, and began to bestow the most spendthrift hospitality ever known on everyone passing by in either direction. Without a doubt, he very soon made a name for himself.

Now, one day, while the young man was all alone in the courtyard of his palace, a little old lady happened to come in by one of the palace gates. She asked him for alms, which she received. Coming back in by the second gate, she sought him out again and was given alms. She did this twelve times in a row. When she returned for the thirteenth time, Mithridanes said: "My good woman, you're very importunate in your begging!" All the same, he gave her alms.

The little old lady, hearing these words, said: "O generosity of Nathan, how wonderful you are! For, when I entered in quest of alms through the thirty-two gates his palace has, like this one, he never gave a sign of recognizing me, and I received my alms each time. Here, having entered through a mere thirteen gates, I've been recognized and scolded!" And with these words she left, never to return.

When Mithridanes heard what the old woman said, because he considered that everything he heard to Nathan's credit amounted to a loss of his own, he became wildly angry and started to say: "Ah, woe is me! When will I ever equal the generosity of Nathan's great deeds, let alone surpass him, as I am striving to do, if I can't get near him in even the smallest things? Truly, I'm wearing myself out for nothing, unless I rid the earth of him! Since old age refuses to carry him off, I must do this with my own hands without delay."

Driven by this idea, he arose. Informing no one of his decision, he took horse with a few companions and arrived at Nathan's home three days later. He ordered his companions to pretend they weren't with him and didn't even know him; they were to seek lodging until they had further instructions from him. After arriving there at dusk and being left alone, he found Nathan all alone not far from his beautiful palace. He was strolling for pleasure, dressed in very plain clothes.

pomposo, andava a suo diporto; cui egli, non conoscendolo, domandò se insegnargli sapesse dove Natan dimorasse.

Natan lietamente rispose: — Figliuol mio, niuno è in questa contrada che meglio di me cotesto ti sappia mostrare, e per ciò, quando ti piaccia, io vi ti menerò.

Il giovane disse che questo gli sarebbe a grado assai, ma che, dove esser potesse, egli non voleva da Natan esser veduto né conosciuto; al qual Natan disse: — E cotesto ancora farò, poi che ti piace.

Smontato adunque Mitridanes, con Natan, che in piacevolissimi ragionamenti assai tosto il mise, infino al suo bel palagio n'andò. Quivi Natan fece ad un de' suoi famigliari prendere il caval del giovane, ed accostatoglisi agli orecchi, gl'impose che egli prestamente con tutti quegli della casa facesse che niuno al giovane dicesse lui esser Natan; e così fu fatto. Ma poi che nel palagio furono, mise Mitridanes in una bellissima camera, dove alcuno nol vedeva, se non quegli che egli al suo servigio diputati avea; e sommamente faccendolo onorare, esso stesso gli tenea compagnia.

Col quale dimorando Mitridanes, ancora che in reverenza come padre l'avesse, pur lo domandò chi el fosse; al quale Natan rispose: — Io sono un piccol servidor di Natan, il quale dalla mia fanciullezza con lui mi sono invecchiato, né mai ad altro che tu mi veggi mi trasse; per che, come che ogni altro uomo molto di lui si lodi, io me ne posso poco lodare io.

Queste parole posero alcuna speranza a Mitridanes di potere con più consiglio e con più salvezza dare effetto al suo perverso intendimento; il qual Natan assai cortesemente domandò chi egli fosse e qual bisogno per quindi il portasse, offerendo il suo consiglio ed il suo aiuto in ciò che per lui si potesse. Mitridanes soprastette alquanto al rispondere, ed ultimamente, diliberando di fidarsi di lui, con una lunga circuizion di parole la sua fede richiese, ed appresso, il consiglio e l'aiuto; e chi egli era e perché venuto e da che mosso, interamente gli discoperse.

Natan, udendo il ragionare ed il fiero proponimento di Mitridanes, in sé tutto si cambiò; ma senza troppo stare, con forte animo e con fermo viso gli rispose: — Mitridanes, nobile uomo fu il tuo padre, dal quale tu non vuogli degenerare, sì alta impresa avendo fatta come hai, cioè d'essere liberale a tutti; e molto la 'nvidia che alla vertù di Natan porti, commendo, per ciò che, se di così fatte fossero assai, il mondo, che è miserissimo, tosto buon

Mithridanes, not knowing who he was, asked him to point out where Nathan could be found.

Nathan gladly replied: "My son, there's no one in this area better able to show you that than I am; and so, whenever you like, I'll lead you there."

The young man said he'd greatly appreciate that; but, if at all possible, he didn't want Nathan to see him or know he was there. Nathan replied: "I'll do that for you, too, since you wish it."

And so Mithridanes dismounted and accompanied Nathan, who immediately struck up an agreeable conversation, all the way to his beautiful palace. Here Nathan had one of his servants take the young man's horse, whispering orders in the servant's ear to the effect that he and everyone else in the house should take care that no one tell the young man that he was Nathan; and so it was done. Once they were inside the palace, he showed Mithridanes to a beautiful room, where no one saw him except the servants he had assigned to wait on him. Showing him exquisite hospitality, he himself kept him company.

While they were together, Mithridanes, though revering him as a father, nevertheless asked him who he was. Nathan replied: "I have been a lowly servant of Nathan's since my childhood, and I've grown old in his service without his ever promoting me beyond what you see. And so, even if everyone else thinks highly of him, I can't very well do so."

These words gave Mithridanes some hope of achieving his evil intentions more advisedly and with greater safety. Nathan asked him very courteously who he was and for what purpose he had come; and he offered him his advice and assistance in doing whatever he could for him. Mithridanes hesitated a moment before replying, but finally, deciding to trust him, in an extremely roundabout way he asked him for his confidence and then for his advice and assistance. He revealed entirely his identity, his purpose in coming, and the spirit that prompted his actions.

When Nathan heard Mithridanes' speech and his savage intentions, he was severely shaken in mind, but he pulled himself together quickly, and replied with a brave spirit, showing no emotions: "Mithridanes, your father was a noble man, and you obviously don't wish to fall short of his standards, since you have made such a high resolve: to be generous to everyone. I highly commend the envy you bear toward Nathan's good qualities, because, if there were many cases of a similar envy, the world, which is a vile place, would soon

diverrebbe. Il tuo proponimento mostratomi senza dubbio sarà occulto, al quale io più tosto util consiglio che grande aiuto posso donare; il quale è questo. Tu puoi di quinci vedere, forse un mezzo miglio vicin di qui, un boschetto, nel quale Natan quasi ogni mattina va tutto solo prendendo diporto per ben lungo spazio; quivi leggér cosa ti fia il trovarlo e farne il tuo piacere; il quale se tu uccidi, acciò che tu possa senza impedimento a casa tua ritornare, non per quella via donde tu qui venisti, ma per quella che tu vedi a sinistra uscir fuor del bosco, n'andrai, per ciò che, ancora che un poco più salvatica sia, ella è più vicina a casa tua e per te più sicura.

Mitridanes ricevuta la 'nformazione, e Natan da lui essendo partito, cautamente a' suoi compagni, che similmente là entro erano, fece sentire dove aspettare il dovessero il dì seguente. Ma poi che il nuovo dì fu venuto, Natan, non avendo animo vario al consiglio dato a Mitridanes, né quello in parte alcuna mutato, solo se n'andò al boschetto a dover morire. Mitridanes, levatosi e preso il suo arco e la sua spada, ché altra arme non avea, e montato a cavallo, n'andò al boschetto, e di lontano vide Natan tutto soletto andar passeggiando per quello; e diliberato, avanti che l'assalisse, di volerlo vedere e d'udirlo parlare, corse verso lui, e presolo per la benda la quale in capo avea, disse: — Vegliardo, tu se' morto!

Al quale niuna altra cosa rispose Natan se non: — Adunque, l'ho io meritato.

Mitridanes, udita la voce e nel viso guardatolo, subitamente riconobbe lui esser colui che benignamente l'avea ricevuto e famigliarmente accompagnato e fedelmente consigliato; per che di presente gli cadde il furore, e la sua ira si convertì in vergogna. Laonde egli, gittata via la spada, la qual già per fedirlo aveva tirata fuori, da caval dismontato, piagnendo corse ai piè di Natan e disse:

— Manifestamente conosco, carissimo padre, la vostra liberalità, riguardando con quanta cautela venuto siate per darmi il vostro spirito, del quale io, niuna ragione avendo, a voi medesimo disideroso mostra'mi; ma Iddio, più al mio dover sollecito che io stesso, a quel punto che maggior bisogno è stato, gli occhi m'ha aperto dello 'ntelletto, li quali misera invidia m'avea serrati; e per ciò, quanto voi più pronto stato siete a compiacermi, tanto più mi conosco debito alla penitenza del mio errore: prendete adunque di me quella vendetta che convenevole estimate al mio peccato.

Natan fece levar Mitridanes in piede, e teneramente l'abbracciò e baciò, e gli disse: — Figliuol mio, alla tua impresa chente che tu la vogli chiamare o malvagia o altramenti, non bisogna di domandar

become good. Rest assured that the purpose you have revealed to me will remain a secret, although I can more readily give you useful advice than any great assistance. And the advice is this: From here you can see, about a half mile away, a grove in which nearly every morning Nathan takes quite a long walk all alone for pleasure. There you can easily find him and do whatever you want with him. If you kill him, in order to be able to return home unimpeded, don't leave the grove by the path you took to enter it, but by the one you see issuing from the grove at the left; even though it's a little more rugged, it's closer to your home and safer for you."

After Mithridanes had received this information and had seen Nathan depart, he cautiously sent word to his companions, who were also in the palace, as to where they were to await him on the following day. When the new day came, Nathan, in strict conformity with his advice to Mithridanes, and making no change in the arrangement, went off alone to the grove and his death. Mithridanes got up, took his bow and his sword, the only weapons he had, mounted his horse, rode to the grove, and from a distance saw Nathan walking in it all alone. Deciding to see him and hear him speak before he attacked him, he galloped up to him, seized him by the turban on his head, and said: "Old man, you're going to die!"

Nathan's only reply was: "If so, I've deserved it."

When Mithridanes heard his voice and looked him in the face, he immediately recognized him as the man who had welcomed him kindly, kept him friendly company, and given him loyal advice. And so his frenzy abated at once, his wrath changing to shame. Then, throwing away his sword, which he had already drawn to strike him a blow, he dismounted, fell at Nathan's feet in tears, and said:

"Dearest father, I clearly recognize your generosity now that I realize with what great prudence you have come to offer me your life, which I had personally revealed to you I was eager to take, though I had no good reason. But God, more concerned about my duty than I was, has opened the eyes of my mind at the moment when that was most needful—those eyes which my wretched envy had sealed shut! And so, if you were so ready to oblige me, I want to be even readier to accept the penalty for my crime; therefore, give me the punishment you feel appropriate to my sin."

Nathan made Mithridanes get up, and hugged and kissed him tenderly, saying: "My son, your undertaking, however you wish to characterize it, wicked or otherwise, does not call for the asking or giving of

né di dar perdono, per ciò che non per odio la seguivi, ma per poter
esser tenuto migliore. Vivi adunque di me sicuro, ed abbi di certo
che niuno altro uom vive il quale te, quanto io, ami, avendo
riguardo all'altezza dell'animo tuo, il quale non ad ammassar
denari, come i miseri fanno, ma ad ispender gli ammassati s'è dato;
né ti vergognare d'avermi voluto uccidere per divenir famoso, né
credere che io me ne maravigli. I sommi imperadori ed i grandissimi re non hanno quasi con altra arte che d'uccidere, non uno
uomo, come tu volevi fare, ma infiniti, ed ardere paesi ed abbattere
le città, li loro regni ampliati, e per conseguente la fama loro; per
che, se tu, per più farti famoso, me solo uccider volevi, non maravigliosa cosa né nuova facevi, ma molto usata.

Mitridanes, non iscusando il suo disidéro perverso, ma commendando l'onesta scusa da Natan trovata ad esso, ragionando pervenne
a dire sé oltre modo maravigliarsi come a ciò si fosse Natan potuto
disporre, ed a ciò dargli modo e consiglio; al quale Natan disse:

— Mitridanes, io non voglio che tu del mio consiglio né della mia
disposizione ti maravigli, per ciò che, poi che io nel mio arbitrio fui
e disposto a fare quel medesimo che tu hai a fare impreso, niun fu
che mai a casa mia capitasse, che io nol contentassi a mio potere di
ciò che da lui mi fu domandato. Venìstivi tu vago della mia vita; per
che, sentendolati domandare, acciò che tu non fossi solo colui che
senza la sua domanda di qui si partisse, prestamente diliberai di
donàrlati, ed acciò che tu l'avessi, quel consiglio ti diedi che io cre-
detti che buon ti fosse ad aver la mia e non perder la tua; e per ciò
ancora ti dico e priego che, se ella ti piace, che tu la prenda e te
medesimo ne sodisfaccia; io non so come io la mi possa meglio
spendere. Io l'ho adoperata già ottanta anni, e ne' miei diletti e
nelle mie consolazioni usata, e so che, seguendo il corso della
natura, come gli altri uomini fanno e generalmente tutte le cose,
ella mi può omai piccol tempo esser lasciata; per che io giudico
molto meglio esser quella donare, come io ho sempre i miei tesori
donati e spesi, che tanto volerla guardare che ella mi sia contro a
mia voglia tolta dalla natura. Piccol dono è donare cento anni;
quanto adunque è minor donarne sei o otto che io a starci abbia?
Prendila adunque, se ella t'aggrada, io te ne priego, per ciò che,
mentre vivuto ci sono, niuno ho ancor trovato che disiderata l'abbia, né so quando trovarmene possa veruno, se tu non la prendi che
la domandi; e se pure avvenisse che io ne dovessi alcun trovare,
conosco che, quanto più la guarderò, di minor pregio sarà; e però,
anzi che ella divenga più vile, prendila, io te ne priego.

pardon, because you were not pursuing it out of hatred, but in order to be considered a better man. And so, have no fears on my account, and rest assured that no other man alive loves you as much as I do, when I consider the loftiness of your spirit, which is dedicated not to accumulating money, as misers do, but to spending what has been accumulated. And don't be ashamed at wanting to kill me in order to acquire a good reputation; nor should you think I'm surprised by your plan. The mightiest emperors and the greatest kings have increased their realms, and consequently their reputations, by hardly any other means than by killing not one man, as you intended to do, but an infinite number, burning entire lands and destroying cities. So that, if you, in order to gain a good reputation, wanted to kill just me, you weren't doing a strange or novel thing, but a very commonplace one."

Mithridanes, not excusing his evil intentions but appreciating the honorable excuse Nathan had found for them, went on to say that he was utterly amazed at Nathan's ability to consent to it, even supplying advice and showing him how to do it. Nathan replied:

"Mithridanes, I don't want you to be amazed at my advice or my complaisance, because, ever since I became my own master and determined to achieve the same lofty aim that you are pursuing, no one has ever arrived at my home whose requests I failed to grant to the best of my ability. You came desiring my life, and so, when I heard you ask for it, I decided at once to give it to you, so you wouldn't be the only man who ever left here without getting his wish. In order for you to get it, I gave you the advice I thought you ought to have if you were to take my life without losing yours. Therefore, I still say to you and beseech you that, if you want it, you should take it and content yourself with it. I don't know how I could better spend it. I've made use of it for eighty years now, consuming it in my pleasures and comforts, and I know that, in the course of nature, as is the case with all other men and with all things in general, only a very little of it may still be left to me. And so I consider that it's much better to give it away, just as I've always given and spent my treasures, rather than to try to hold onto it until nature takes it away from me against my will. The gift of even a hundred years is a small one; so isn't it doing much less to give away the six or eight I may have left to me? Take my life, then, if it suits you, I beg you to, because, all the time I've lived here, I've never found anyone who wanted it, and I don't know when I'll ever be able to find such a person if you, who request it, don't take it. Even if I happen to find somebody, I know that, the longer I keep it, the less valuable it will be. And so, before it becomes more, take it, I beg you."

Mitridanes, vergognandosi forte, disse: — Tolga Iddio che così cara cosa come la vostra vita è, non che io, da voi dividendola, la prenda, ma pur la disideri, come poco avanti faceva; alla quale, non che io diminuissi gli anni suoi, ma io l'aggiugnerei volentier de' miei, se io potessi.

A cui prestamente Natan disse: — E se tu puoi, vuo'nele tu aggiugnere? E farai a me fare verso di te quello che mai verso alcuno altro non feci, cioè delle tue cose pigliare, che mai, dell'altrui non pigliai.

— Sì, — disse subitamente Mitridanes.

— Adunque, — disse Natan, — farai tu come io ti dirò. Tu rimarrai, giovane come tu se', qui nella mia casa ed avrai nome Natan, ed io me n'andrò nella tua e farommi sempre chiamar Mitridanes.

Allora Mitridanes rispose: — Se io sapessi così bene operare come voi sapete ed avete saputo, io prenderei senza troppa diliberazione quello che m'offerete; ma per ciò che egli mi pare esser molto certo che le mie opere sarebbon diminuimento della fama di Natan, ed io non intendo di guastare in altrui quello che in me io non so acconciare, nol prenderò.

Questi e molti altri piacevoli ragionamenti stati tra Natan e Mitridanes, come a Natan piacque, insieme verso il palagio se ne tornarono, dove Natan più giorni sommamente onorò Mitridanes, e lui con ogni ingegno e saper confortò nel suo alto e grande proponimento. E volendosi Mitridanes con la sua compagnia ritornare a casa, avendogli Natan assai ben fatto conoscere che mai di liberalità nol potrebbe avanzare, il licenziò.

SALADINO MERCANTE [X, 9]

Aveva alle sue parole già Filomena fatta fine, e la magnifica gratitudine di Tito da tutti parimente era stata commendata molto, quando il re, il deretano luogo riserbando a Dionèo, così cominciò a parlare.

Vaghe donne, senza alcun fallo Filomena, in ciò che dell'amistà dice, racconta il vero, e con ragione nella fine delle sue parole si dolfe, lei oggi così poco da' mortali esser gradita. E se noi qui per dover correggere i difetti mondani o per riprendergli fossimo, io seguiterei con diffuso sermone le sue parole; ma per ciò che altro è il nostro fine, a me è caduto nell'animo di dimostrarvi forse con una istoria assai lunga ma piacevol per tutto, una delle magnificenze del Saladino, acciò che per le cose che nella mia novella

Mithridanes, deeply ashamed, said: "God forbid that, let alone my depriving you of such a precious life as yours by taking it, I should even so much as desire to do so, as I did a while ago! Not only do I refuse to take years away from it: I'd gladly add some of my own years onto it if I could!"

Nathan promptly replied: "And if you can, you wish to add them on? That would be making me do to you something I've never done to anyone else: to take your possessions away from you—I who have never taken a thing from others!"

"Yes, I do," Mithridanes replied at once.

"In that case," Nathan said, "do as I'm about to tell you. Young as you are, remain here in my house, calling yourself Nathan, while I go to your house, calling myself Mithridanes from now on."

Then Mithridanes replied: "If I were able to do good deeds as readily as you can, and always have been able to, I wouldn't hesitate long to accept your offer. But, because I'm quite sure that my deeds would cause Nathan's reputation to dwindle, and because I don't intend to spoil for others that which I can't attain for myself, I won't accept."

After this and much other agreeable discourse between Nathan and Mithridanes, in compliance with Nathan's wishes they returned together to the palace, where for several days Nathan showed Mithridanes splendid hospitality, encouraging him in his great and lofty purpose with all his wisdom and skill. When Mithridanes wished to return home with his companions, Nathan having completely proved to him that he could never outdo him in generosity, the old man gave him leave to depart.

SALADIN AS A MERCHANT [X, 9]

Filomena had finished her story, and the generous gratitude of Titus had been highly praised by one and all, when the "King," reserving the final turn for Dioneo, began to speak thus:

Pretty ladies, without a doubt Filomena speaks the truth in what she says about friendship, and she did right to lament in her final words that friendship is so little cherished by mortals nowadays. And if we were assembled here for the purpose of amending social wrongs, or even of reproaching them, I would follow her words with a lengthy speech. But, seeing that our goal is a different one, the idea has occurred to me to relate to you, in a tale that is perhaps on the long side and yet entertaining, one of the munificent deeds of Saladin, so that,

udirete, se pienamente l'amicizia d'alcuno non si può per li nostri vizi acquistare, almeno diletto prendiamo del servire, sperando che, quando che sia, di ciò merito ci debba seguire.

Dico adunque che, secondo che alcuni affermano, al tempo dello 'mperador Federigo primo, a racquistar la Terrasanta si fece per li cristiani un general passaggio; la qual cosa il Saladino, valentissimo signore ed allora soldano di Babilonia alquanto dinanzi sentendo, seco propose di voler personalmente vedere gli apparecchiamenti de' signori cristiani a quel passaggio, per meglio poter provvedersi.

Ed ordinato in Egitto ogni suo fatto, sembianti faccendo d'andare in pellegrinaggio, con due de' suoi maggiori e più savi uomini e con tre famigliari solamente, in forma di mercatante si mise in cammino; ed avendo cerche molte province cristiane, e per Lombardia cavalcando per passare oltre a' monti, avvenne che, andando da Melano a Pavia ed essendo già vespro, si scontrarono in un gentile uomo il cui nome era messer Torello di Strà da Pavia, il quale con suoi famigliari e con cani e con falconi se n'andava a dimorare ad un suo bel luogo il quale sopra il Tesino aveva.

Li quali come messer Torel vide, avvisò che gentili uomini e stranier fossero, e disiderò d'onorargli; per che, domandando il Saladino un de' suoi famigliari quanto ancora avesse di quivi a Pavia e se ad ora giugner potesser d'entrarvi, non lasciò rispondere al famigliar, ma rispose egli: — Signori, voi non potrete a Pavia pervenire ad ora che dentro possiate entrare.

— Adunque, — disse il Saladino, — piacciavi d'insegnarne, per ciò che stranier siamo, dove noi possiamo meglio albergare.

Messer Torello disse: — Questo farò volentieri. Io era testé in pensiero di mandare un di questi miei infino vicin di Pavia per alcuna cosa; io nel manderò con voi, ed egli vi conducerà in parte dove voi albergherete assai convenevolmente.

Ed al più discreto de' suoi accostatosi, gl'impose quello che egli avesse a fare, e mandòl con loro; ed egli al suo luogo andatosene, prestamente, come si poté il meglio, fece ordinare una bella cena e metter le tavole in un suo giardino; e questo fatto, sopra la porta se ne venne ad aspettargli. Il famigliare, ragionando co' gentili uomini di diverse cose, per certe strade gli trasviò ed al luogo del suo signore, senza che essi se n'accorgessero, condotti gli ebbe; li quali come messer Torel vide, tutto a pié fattosi loro incontro, ridendo disse: — Signori, voi siate i molto ben venuti.

Il Saladino, il quale accortissimo era, s'avvide che questo cavaliere aveva dubitato che essi non avesser tenuto lo 'nvito se, quando

taking to heart the things you will hear in my story, even though we are unable to win someone's undiluted friendship because of our faults, we may at least find delight in being of service to others, in the hope that, whenever it may be, we shall gain merit thereby.

And so, I say that, according to the report of some people, at the time of Emperor Frederick I, Christians engaged in a universal crusade to reconquer the Holy Land. Learning of this somewhat in advance, Saladin, a most capable lord who was then sultan of Cairo, determined to observe personally the preparations being made by the Christian lords for that crusade, in order to defend himself the better.

He settled all his business in Egypt and, pretending to be going on pilgrimage, he took only two of his highest-ranking and wisest men and three servants, and set out in the guise of a merchant. Having traveled through many Christian provinces, and riding through Lombardy before crossing the Alps, while on the way from Milan to Pavia he happened, when evening fell, to meet a gentleman named Torello da Strada of Pavia, who was on his way, with servants, hounds, and hawks, to a beautiful estate that he owned on the river Ticino.

When Torello saw them, he realized they were well-born foreigners, and he wished to show them hospitality. So, when Saladin asked one of his servants how far it still was to Pavia and whether they could get there before the gates were closed, Torello didn't allow the servant to reply, but answered personally: "Gentlemen, you won't be able to reach Pavia in time to get in."

"In that case," Saladin said, "please inform us, since we're strangers here, where is the best place for us to lodge."

Torello said: "Gladly! I was just now planning to send one of my people almost all the way to Pavia on some errand. I'll send him along with you, and he'll guide you to a place where you'll find very suitable accommodations."

And, drawing near to his most intelligent servant, he gave him instructions on how to proceed, and sent him off with them. Journeying on to his estate, he quickly had his people prepare the best supper he could arrange, setting out the tables in a garden. Then he took his stand at the entrance gate to await his guests. That servant, discussing this and that with the gentlemen, led them over certain roundabout roads until they reached his master's estate, without the strangers' knowledge. When Torello saw them, he walked ahead to meet them, and said with a smile: "Gentlemen, you are most welcome!"

Saladin, who was very perceptive, realized that this knight had feared they might not have accepted his invitation if he had made it at

gli trovò, invitati gli avesse, e per ciò, acciò che negar non potessero
d'esser la sera con lui, con ingegno a casa sua gli aveva condotti; e
risposto al suo saluto, disse:

— Messer, se de' cortesi uomini l'uom si potesse ramaricare, noi
ci dorremmo di voi il quale, lasciamo star del nostro cammino che
impedito alquanto avete, ma senza altro essere stata da noi la vostra
benivolenza meritata che d'un sol saluto, a prender sì alta cortesia
come la vostra è, n'avete quasi costretti.

Il cavalier, savio e ben parlante, disse: — Signori, questa che voi
ricevete da me, a rispetto di quella che vi converrebbe, per quello
che io ne' vostri aspetti comprenda, fia povera cortesia; ma nel vero
fuor di Pavia voi non potreste essere stati in luogo alcun che buon
fosse, e per ciò non vi sia grave l'avere alquanto la via traversata per
un poco men di disagio avere.

E così dicendo, la sua famiglia venuta da torno a costoro, come
smontati furono, i cavalli adagiarono, e messer Torello i tre gentili
uomini menò alle camere per loro apparecchiate, dove gli fece
scalzare e rinfrescare alquanto con freschissimi vini, ed in ragionamenti piacevoli infino all'ora di poter cenar gli ritenne.

Il Saladino ed i compagni ed i famigliari tutti sapevan latino, per
che molto bene intendevano ed erano intesi, e pareva a ciascun di
loro che questo cavalier fosse il più piacevole ed il più costumato
uomo e quegli che meglio ragionasse che alcuno altro che ancora
n'avesser veduto. A messer Torello, d'altra parte, pareva che costoro fossero magnifichi uomini e da molto più che avanti stimato
non avea, per che seco stesso si dolea che di compagnia e di più
solenne convito quella sera non gli poteva onorare; laonde egli
pensò di volere la seguente mattina ristorare, ed informato un de'
suoi famigli di ciò che far volea, alla sua donna, che savissima era e
di grandissimo animo, nel mandò a Pavia assai quivi vicina e dove
porta alcuna non si serrava.

Ed appresso questo, menati i gentili uomini nel giardino,
cortesemente gli domandò chi e' fossero; al quale il Saladino
rispose: — Noi siamo mercatanti cipriani e di Cipri vegnamo, e per
nostre bisogne andiamo a Parigi.

Allora disse messer Torello: — Piacesse a Dio che questa nostra
contrada producesse così fatti gentili uomini, chenti io veggio che
Cipri fa mercatanti!

E di questi ragionamenti in altri trapassando, stati alquanto, fu di
cenar tempo; per che a loro l'onorarsi alla tavola commise, e quivi
secondo cena sprovveduta, furono assai bene ed ordinatamente

the moment he met them, and had therefore led them to his house by a ruse so they couldn't refuse to spend the evening with him. Responding to his greeting, Saladin said:

"Sir, if it were possible to complain of people's courtesy, we would do so about you. I don't mean because you have briefly interrupted our journey, but because, without our deserving your benevolence by any deed other than a single greeting, you have virtually compelled us to accept such outstanding courtesy as yours is."

The knight, wise and eloquent, said: "Gentlemen, the courtesy you receive from me, compared with that which would befit you, to judge by your appearance, will be very modest. But, to tell the truth, you couldn't have found any good lodgings outside of Pavia. Therefore, don't be annoyed at having gone somewhat out of your way to be a little more comfortable."

After he said this, his servants swarmed around the guests. When they dismounted, their horses were cared for, and Torello led the three gentlemen to the bedrooms that had been prepared for them. There he had them relieved of their traveling footgear and refreshed a little with very cool wines, and he engaged in pleasant conversation with them until suppertime.

Saladin, his companions, and his servants all knew Italian, so that they understood and made themselves understood very well. Each of them thought that this knight was the most pleasant and well-bred man, as well as the finest conversationalist, they had ever come across. Torello, for his part, thought they were men of eminence, of much higher rank than he had imagined at first, so that he was inwardly grieved at being unable to offer them better company and a more formal meal that evening. Therefore he decided to make it up to them the following noon. Informing one of his servants of his intentions, he sent him to his wife, a very wise and nobleminded woman, who was in Pavia; the city was very close, and its gates were never shut.

After that, he led his noble guests into the garden and courteously asked them who they were. Saladin replied: "We are Cypriot merchants who have come from Cyprus on business that takes us to Paris."

Then Torello said: "May it please God for our part of the world to produce gentlemen of the same quality I now find in Cypriot merchants!"

Moving on to other subjects, they kept talking until suppertime. Torello asked them all to take their places at table, where, even though the meal had been improvised, they were served very well and

serviti; né guari dopo, le tavole levate, stettero che, avvisandosi messer Torello loro essere stanchi, in bellissimi letti gli mise a riposare, ed esso similmente poco appresso s'andò a dormire.

Il famigliar mandato a Pavia fe' l'ambasciata alla donna, la quale, non con feminile animo ma con reale, fatti prestamente chiamar degli amici e de' servidori di messer Torello assai, ogni cosa opportuna a grandissimo convito fece apparecchiare, ed a lume di torchio molti de' più nobili cittadini fece al convito invitare, e fe' tôrre panni e drappi e vai, e compiutamente mettere in ordine ciò che dal marito l'era stato mandato a dire.

Venuto il giorno, i gentili uomini si levarono, co' quali messer Torello montato a cavallo, e fatti venire i suoi falconi, ad un guazzo vicin gli menò, e mostrò loro come essi volassero; ma domandando il Saladino d'alcuno che a Pavia ed al migliore albergo gli conducesse, disse messer Torello: — Io sarò desso, per ciò che esser mi vi conviene.

Costoro, credendolsi, furon contenti ed insieme con lui entrarono in cammino; ed essendo già terza, ed essi alla città pervenuti, avvisando d'essere al migliore albergo inviati, con messer Torello alle sue case pervennero, dove già ben cinquanta de' maggior cittadini eran venuti per ricevere i gentili uomini, a' quali subitamente furon dintorno a' freni ed alle staffe.

La qual cosa il Saladino ed i compagni veggendo, troppo ben s'avvisaron ciò che era, e dissono: — Messer Torello, questo non è ciò che noi v'avevam domandato: assai n'avete questa notte passata fatto, e troppo più che noi non vagliamo; per che acconciamente ne potevate lasciare andare al cammin nostro.

A' quali messer Torello rispose: — Signori, di ciò che iersera vi fu fatto so io grado alla fortuna più che a voi, la quale ad ora vi colse in cammino che bisogno vi fu di venire alla mia piccola casa; di questo di stamattina sarò io tenuto a voi, e con meco insieme tutti questi gentili uomini che dintorno vi sono, a' quali se cortesia vi par fare il negare di voler con lor desinare, farlo potete, se voi volete.

Il Saladino ed i compagni, vinti, smontarono, e ricevuti da' gentili uomini lietamente, furono alle camere menati, le quali ricchissimamente per loro erano apparecchiate; e posti giù gli arnesi da camminare e rinfrescatisi alquanto, nella sala, dove splendidamente era apparecchiato, vennero; e data l'acqua alle mani ed a tavola messi con grandissimo ordine e bello, di molte vivande magnificamente furon serviti, intanto che, se lo 'mperadore venuto vi fosse, non si sarebbe più potuto fargli d'onore.

E quantunque il Saladino ed i compagni fossero gran signori ed

properly. And not long after the tables had been removed, Torello noticed they were tired and sent them off to rest in excellent beds, shortly thereafter going to bed himself.

The servant sent to Pavia gave his message to his mistress, who, with a more-than-womanly, royal spirit, immediately assembled numerous friends and servants of Torello's, and had everything needful prepared for a magnificent banquet. She sent invitations by torchlight to many of the most eminent townspeople, chose woolens, silks, and furs as gifts, and fulfilled her husband's instructions to the letter.

At daybreak, Torello's wellborn guests arose. Torello mounted a horse in their company, sent for his hawks, and took them to a nearby pond to show them how well the birds were trained. But when Saladin asked for someone to lead him to Pavia and the best inn there, Torello said: "I'll be your guide, because I have some business there myself."

Believing him, they were pleased and set out in his company. It was already nine when they reached town, thinking they were being directed to the best inn; but it was at Torello's own residence that they arrived along with him. There some fifty of the leading citizens had assembled to welcome the gentlemen, who immediately were assisted in dismounting by people who held their bridles and stirrups.

When Saladin and his companions saw this, they realized the true situation with perfect clarity, and said: "Messer Torello, this is not what we asked you for. You did enough for us last night, much more than our station calls for. And so it would have been only proper for you to allow us to proceed on our way."

Torello replied: "Gentlemen, for what was done for you last night I give thanks not so much to you as to Fortune, who overtook you on your journey just at the time when it was necessary for you to visit my humble abode; for this noon's events I shall be obliged to *you* personally, as will all these gentlemen around you. If you think it's courteous behavior to refuse to dine with them, you can do so if you wish."

Saladin and his companions, unable to refuse, dismounted. Joyously welcomed by the local gentlemen, they were led to the rooms that had been opulently prepared for them. After removing their traveling gear and taking some refreshment, they entered the great hall. They had water poured over their hands, and were seated with extreme elegance and etiquette. Many splendid courses were served, and, if the Emperor himself had come, he couldn't have been more honorably entertained.

Though Saladin and his companions were great lords, accustomed

usi di veder grandissime cose, nondimeno si maravigliarono essi molto di questa, e lor pareva delle maggiori, avendo rispetto alla qualità del cavaliere, il qual sapevano che era cittadino e non signore.

Finito il mangiare e le tavole levate, avendo alquanto d'alte cose parlato, essendo il caldo grande, come a messer Torel piacque, i gentili uomini di Pavia tutti s'andarono a riposare; ed esso con li suoi tre rimase e con loro in una camera entratosene, acciò che niuna sua cara cosa rimanesse che essi veduta non avessero, quivi si fece la sua valente donna chiamare; la quale, essendo bellissima e grande della persona e di ricchi vestimenti ornata, in mezzo di due figlioletti che parevan due agnoli, se ne venne davanti a costoro e piacevolemente gli salutò.

Essi, veggendola, si levarono in piè e con reverenza la ricevettero, e fattala seder tra loro, gran festa fecero de' due belli suoi figlioletti. Ma poi che con loro in piacevoli ragionamenti entrata fu, essendosi alquanto partito messer Torello, essa piacevolmente donde fossero e dove andassero gli domandò; alla quale i gentili uomini così risposero come a messer Torello avevan fatto.

Allora la donna con lieto viso disse: — Adunque, veggio io che il mio feminile avviso sarà utile, e per ciò vi priego che di spezial grazia mi facciate di non rifiutare né avere a vile quel piccoletto dono il quale io vi farò venire; ma considerando che le donne, secondo il lor piccol cuore, piccole cose dànno, più al buono animo di chi dà riguardiate che alla quantità del dono.

E fattesi venire per ciascuno due paia di robe, l'un foderato di drappo e l'altro di vaio, non miga cittadine né da mercatanti ma da signore, e tre giubbe di zendado e pannilini, disse: — Prendete queste: io ho delle robe il mio signore vestito con voi; l'altre cose, considerando che voi siate alle vostre donne lontani, e la lunghezza del cammin fatto e quella di quello che è a fare, e che i mercatanti son netti e dilicati uomini, ancor che elle vaglian poco, vi potranno esser care.

I gentili uomini si maravigliarono ed apertamente conobber messer Torello niuna parte di cortesia voler lasciare a far loro, e dubitarono, veggendo la nobiltà delle robe non mercatantesche, di non essere da messer Torel conosciuti; ma pure alla donna rispose l'un di loro: — Queste son, madonna, grandissime cose e da non dover di leggeri pigliare, se i vostri prieghi a ciò non ci stringessero, alli quali dir di no non si puote.

Questo fatto, essendo già messer Torel ritornato, la donna,

to grandeur, they were nevertheless greatly amazed on this occasion. They thought their entertainment was extraordinary when they considered the knight's rank, knowing as they did that he was a private citizen, not a feudal lord.

After the meal, when the tables were removed, they briefly discoursed on lofty matters. Since it was very hot, all the gentlemen from Pavia followed Torello's advice and went for a nap. He remained behind with his three guests, whom he took to another room. So as not to deny them the sight of any of his treasures, he sent for his worthy wife. She, extremely beautiful, tall and richly dressed, came into their presence with her two little boys, looking like two angels, on either side of her, and greeted them amiably.

When they saw her, they stood up and bowed in greeting. Seating her in their midst, they expressed delight at her two handsome sons. But, after she had begun to converse pleasantly with them, Torello left them for a while, and she amiably asked them where they were from and where they were going. The gentlemen gave her the same answer they had given Torello.

Then, with a delighted expression, the lady said: "So I see that my feminine intuition will be useful! Therefore I beg you, as a special favor, not to refuse or look down on the little gift I'm going to send for. If you reflect that women, who aren't great-hearted, necessarily give only little gifts, you will pay more mind to the giver's good intentions than to the size of the gift."

For each of them she sent for two pairs of robes, one pair lined with silk and the other lined with fur—robes befitting not townspeople or merchants but great lords—as well as three jackets of fine silk and breeches, and she said: "Please accept these. As for the robes, they are just like the ones in which I have dressed my husband. The other garments, seeing that you are far from your wives, that you have already come a long way and still have a long road ahead of you, and that merchants are clean and fastidious men, may be useful to you, even though they're not very valuable."

The gentlemen were amazed and clearly realized that Torello didn't wish to be behindhand in any way in his hospitality. Seeing the high quality of the robes, much too good for merchants, they were afraid Torello had recognized them. Nevertheless, one of them said to their hostess: "Madame, these are splendid things, not to be lightly accepted, were it not that your entreaties have compelled us to do so, because it is impossible to refuse them."

After this, when Torello had returned, the lady wished them

accomandatigli a Dio, da lor si partì, e di simili cose di ciò, quali a loro si convenieno, fece provvedere a' famigliari. Messer Torello con molti prieghi impetrò da loro che tutto quel dì dimorasson con lui; per che, poi che dormito ebbero, vestitesi le robe loro, con messer Torello alquanto cavalcâr per la città, e l'ora della cena venuta, con molti onorevoli compagni magnificamente cenarono.

E quando tempo fu, andatisi a riposare, come il giorno venne, sù si levarono, e trovarono in luogo de' loro ronzini stanchi tre grossi pallafreni e buoni, e similmente nuovi cavalli e forti alli lor famigliari. La qual cosa veggendo il Saladino, rivolto a' suoi compagni disse: — Io giuro a Dio che più compiuto uom né più cortese né più avveduto di costui non fu mai; e se li re cristiani son così fatti re verso di sé chente costui è cavaliere, al soldano di Babilonia non ha luogo l'aspettarne pure un, non che tanti quanti, per addosso andargliene, veggiam che s'apparecchiano!

Ma sappiendo che il rinunziargli non avrebbe luogo, assai cortesemente ringraziàndonelo, montarono a cavallo. Messer Torello con molti compagni gran pezza di via gli accompagnarono fuori della città, e quantunque al Saladino il partirsi da messer Torello gravasse, tanto già innamorato se n'era, pure, strignendolo l'andata, il pregò che indietro se ne tornasse; il quale, quantunque duro gli fosse il partirsi da loro, disse:

— Signori, io il farò poi che vi piace, ma così vi vo' dire: io non so chi voi vi siete, né di saperlo più che vi piaccia addomando, ma chi che voi vi siate, che voi siate mercatanti non lascerete voi per credenza a me questa volta; ed a Dio v'accomando.

Il Saladino, avendo già da tutti i compagni di messer Torello preso commiato, gli rispose dicendo: — Messere, egli potrà ancora avvenire che noi vi farem vedere di nostra mercatantìa, per la quale noi la vostra credenza raffermeremo; ed andatevi con Dio.

Partissi adunque il Saladino ed i compagni, con grandissimo animo, se vita gli durasse e la guerra la quale aspettava nol disfacesse, di fare ancora non minore onore a messer Torello che egli a lui fatto avesse; e molto e di lui e della sua donna e di tutte le sue cose ed atti e fatti ragionò co' compagni, ogni cosa più commendando. Ma poi che tutto il Ponente non senza gran fatica ebbe cercato, entrato in mare, co' suoi compagni se ne tornò in Alessandria, e pienamente informato, si dispose alla difesa.

Messer Torello se ne tornò in Pavia, ed in lungo pensier fu chi questi tre esser potessero, né mai al vero non aggiunse né s'appressò. Venuto il tempo del passaggio e faccendosi

Godspeed and took her leave. Then she had their servants given similar things in accordance with their station. After much pleading, Torello obtained their consent to remain in his home for the rest of the day. After they had slept, they donned their robes, and took a ride through the city with Torello. At suppertime they enjoyed a splendid meal with many honorable companions.

They went to bed at the proper time and arose at daybreak. In place of their tired-out, less-than-pedigreed horses, they found three fine, stout parade horses, as well as new, strong mounts for their servants. Seeing this, Saladin turned to his companions and said: "I swear to God that there has never been a more perfect, courteous, and perceptive man than this one! If the kings of Christendom are as genuinely kingly as this man is knightly, the sultan of Cairo won't be able to withstand even one, let alone the multitude of them that we see preparing to attack him!"

But, knowing it was out of the question to refuse the horses, they thanked him for them most courteously and mounted. Torello, with many companions, escorted them a long way out of town. Even though it grieved Saladin to part with Torello, for he had already taken such a liking to him, nevertheless, deeming it urgent to proceed, he begged him to turn back. Though Torello found it hard to part with them, he said:

"Gentlemen, I'll do so, since it's your wish, but I want to tell you this: I don't know who you are, nor do I seek to know more than you wish to say, but whoever you are, you can't make me believe for the present that you're merchants! And so, Godspeed!"

Saladin, after taking leave of all of Torello's companions, said to him: "Sir, some day the time may come for us to show you our merchandise, and thus assure you we really are merchants! Go with God!"

And so Saladin and his friends left, the sultan with the firm resolve that, if he lived long enough and wasn't killed in the upcoming war, he would some day show Torello no lesser hospitality than the Italian had shown him. He spoke at length to his companions about him, his wife, and all his possessions, actions, and doings, praising everything highly. But after he had investigated the entire Occident quite laboriously, he took ship and returned to Alexandria with his companions. In full possession of the information he had sought, he took defensive measures.

Torello returned to Pavia, where he pondered at length over the identity of his three guests, but never arrived at the truth or even came close. When it was time to join the crusade and great

l'apparecchiamento grande per tutto, messer Torello, nonostanti i prieghi della sua donna e le lagrime, si dispose ad andarvi del tutto; ed avendo ogni appresto fatto ed essendo per cavalcare, disse alla sua donna, la quale egli sommamente amava:

— Donna, come tu vedi, io vado in questo passaggio sì per onor del corpo e sì per salute dell'anima; io ti raccomando le nostre cose ed il nostro onore, e per ciò che io sono dell'andar certo, e del tornare, per mille casi che posson sopravvenire, niuna certezza ho, voglio io che tu mi facci una grazia: che che di me s'avvenga, ove tu non abbi certa novella della mia vita, che tu m'aspetti uno anno ed un mese ed un dì senza rimaritarti, incominciando da questo dì che io mi parto.

La donna, che forte piagneva, rispose: — Messer Torello, io non so come io mi comporterò il dolore nel qual, partendovi, voi mi lasciate; ma dove la mia vita sia più forte di lui ed altro di voi avvenisse, vivete e morite sicuro che io viverò e morrò moglie di messer Torello e della sua memoria.

Alla qual messer Torel disse: — Donna, certissimo sono che, quanto in te sarà, che questo che tu mi prometti avverra; ma tu se' giovane donna e se' bella e se' di gran parentado, e la tua vertù è molta ed è conosciuta per tutto; per la qual cosa io non dubito punto che molti grandi e gentili uomini, se niente di me si suspicherà, non ti domandino a' tuoi fratelli e parenti, dagli stimoli de' quali, quantunque tu vogli, non ti potrai difendere e per forza ti converrà compiacere a' voler loro; e questa è la cagion per la quale io questo termine e non maggior ti domando.

La donna disse: — Io farò ciò che io potrò di quello che detto v'ho; e quando pure altro far mi convenisse, io v'ubbidirò, di questo che m'imponete, certamente. Priego io Iddio che a così fatti termini né voi né me rechi a questi tempi.

Finite le parole, la donna piagnendo abbracciò messer Torello, e tràttosi di dito uno anello, gliele diede dicendo: — Se egli avviene che io muoia prima che io vi riveggia, ricòrdivi di me quando il vedrete.

Ed egli prèsolo, montò a cavallo, e detto ad ogni uomo addio, andò a suo viaggio; e pervenuto a Genova con sua compagnia, montato in galea, andò via, ed in poco tempo pervenne ad Acri e con l'altro esercito de' cristian si congiunse. Nel quale quasi a mano a man cominciò una grandissima infermeria e mortalità, la qual durante, qual che si fosse l'arte o la fortuna del Saladino, quasi tutto il rimaso degli scampati cristiani da lui a man salva fûr presi, e per molte città divisi ed imprigionati; tra' quali presi, messer Torello fu uno, ed in Alessandria menato in prigione.

preparations were being made on all sides, Torello, despite his wife's tears and supplications, definitely decided to go. After preparing everything, on the point of riding away, he said to his wife, whom he adored:

"Lady, as you see, I am departing on this crusade both for my personal honor and for my soul's salvation. I entrust to you our property and our honor. Because I'm sure about going, but, because of a thousand things that may happen, I'm not at all sure about coming back, I want you to do me a favor. No matter what happens to me, if you don't receive reliable word that I'm alive, I want you to wait a year, a month, and a day before remarrying, counting from today, the day of my departure."

His wife, loudly weeping, replied: "Torello, I don't know how I'll stand the grief in which you leave me at your departure. But if my vital forces are strong enough to overcome it, and then something should happen to you, you can live and die assured that I shall live and die as the wife of Torello and of his memory."

Torello replied: "Lady, I am perfectly certain that, so far as it lies in your power, what you promise me will prove to be so. But you're a young woman, beautiful, with powerful relatives, and your great virtue is known everywhere. And so I have no doubt that, if there's the slightest rumor of my death, many great gentlemen will ask your hand of your brothers and kinsmen. Even if you want to, you won't be able to resist their urgings and you'll be forced to comply with their wishes. That's why I ask you for this length of time and not a longer one."

The lady said: "I will do all I can to keep the promise I just made, but if I must do otherwise, I shall certainly obey your commands. I pray to God that He will not hold either you or me to such terms at this time."

After she spoke, the lady embraced Torello in tears. Drawing a ring from her finger, she gave it to him, saying: "If I should die before I see you again, think of me whenever you look at this."

He took it, mounted his horse, bade everyone farewell, and departed on his journey. Reaching Genoa with his men, he embarked on a galley and sailed away. Not long afterward he reached Acre, where he joined forces with the other Christian troops. Almost immediately a terrible, death-dealing plague broke out among them, during which Saladin, whether by his skill or his good fortune, captured almost all the Christian survivors unharmed, imprisoning them in many different cities. Among the captives was Torello, who was brought to a prison in Alexandria.

Dove non essendo conosciuto e temendo esso di farsi conoscere, da necessità costretto, si diede a conciare uccelli, di che egli era grandissimo maestro; e per questo a notizia venne del Saladino, laonde egli di prigione il trasse e ritennelo per suo falconiere.

Messer Torello, che per altro nome che «il cristiano» dal Saladino non era chiamato, il quale egli non riconosceva né il soldan lui, solamente in Pavia l'animo avea e più volte di fuggirsi avea tentato, né gli era venuto fatto; per che esso, venuti certi Genovesi per ambasciadori al Saladino per la ricompera di certi lor cittadini, e dovendosi partire, pensò di scrivere alla donna sua come egli era vivo ed a lei come più tosto potesse tornerebbe, e che ella l'attendesse; e così fece, e caramente pregò un degli ambasciatori, che conoscea, che facesse che quelle alle mani dell'abate di San Pietro in Cieldoro, il quale suo zio era, pervenissero.

Ed in questi termini stando messer Torello, avvenne un giorno che, ragionando con lui il Saladino di suoi uccelli, messer Torello cominciò a sorridere e fece uno atto con la bocca il quale il Saladino, essendo a casa sua a Pavia, aveva molto notato, per lo quale atto al Saladino tornò alla mente messer Torello; e cominciò fiso a riguardarlo e parvegli desso; per che lasciato il primo ragionamento, disse: — Dimmi cristiano: di che paese se' tu di Ponente?

— Signor mio, — disse messer Torello, — io son lombardo, d'una città chiamata Pavia, povero uomo e di bassa condizione.

Come il Saladino udì questo, quasi certo di quel che dubitava, tra sé lieto disse: — Dato m'ha Iddio tempo di mostrare a costui quanto mi fosse a grado la sua cortesia!

E senza altro dire, fattisi i suoi vestimenti in una camera acconciare, vel menò dentro, e disse: — Guarda, cristiano, se tra queste robe n'è alcuna che tu vedessi già mai.

Messer Torello cominciò a guardare e vide quelle che al Saladino aveva la sua donna donate, ma non estimò dover potere essere che desse fossero, ma tuttavia rispose: — Signor mio, niuna ce ne conosco; è ben vero che quelle due somiglian robe di che io già con tre mercatanti che a casa mia capitaron, vestito ne fui.

Allora il Saladino, più non potendo tenersi, teneramente l'abbracciò, dicendo: — Voi siete messer Torel di Strà, ed io son l'un de' tre mercatanti a' quali la donna vostra donò queste robe; ed ora è venuto il tempo di far certa la vostra credenza qual sia la mia mercatanìa, come nel partirmi da voi dissi che potrebbe avvenire.

Messer Torello, questo udendo, cominciò ad esser lietissimo ed a vergognarsi: ad esser lieto d'aver avuto così fatto oste, a vergo-

There, unrecognized and fearing recognition, but needing some means of support, he devoted himself to training hawks, in which he was a past master. He thereby came to the notice of Saladin, who released him from prison and kept him on as his own falconer.

Torello, whom Saladin referred to solely as "the Christian," neither one of them recognizing the other, thought of nothing but Pavia. He had tried several times to escape but had failed. And so, when certain Genoese came as envoys to Saladin to ransom some of their fellow townsmen, and they were about to leave again, he decided to write to his wife saying that he was alive, and would come back to her as soon as he could, and that she should wait for him. He did so, and ardently begged one of the envoys, a man he knew, to see that the letter reached the hands of the abbot of San Pietro in Ciel d'Oro, who was his uncle.

Torello being in this situation, one day, while Saladin was talking to him about his hawks, Torello happened to smile, twisting his mouth in a way that Saladin had frequently observed while his guest in Pavia. This facial expression caused Saladin to remember Torello; he started to look hard at him, and finally recognized him. So, changing the topic of conversation, he said: "Tell me, Christian, what land in the West are you from?"

"My lord," said Torello, "I'm a Lombard from a city called Pavia, a poor man of low status."

When Saladin heard that, his suspicions were all but confirmed, and he said to himself joyfully: "God has furnished me with an occasion to show this man how much I appreciated his courtesy!"

And, saying no more, he ordered his robes to be laid out in a room, led Torello there, and said: "Look, Christian, and tell me whether you've ever seen any of these robes."

Torello began to peruse them, and saw the ones his wife had given Saladin, but he didn't believe it possible that they were the same ones; nevertheless he replied: "My lord, I don't recognize any of them, though it's true that those two resemble robes once worn by me and by three merchants who chanced to visit me."

Then Saladin, no longer able to contain himself, embraced him affectionately, saying: "You are Messer Torello da Strada, and I am one of the three merchants to whom your wife gave these robes. The time has now come to assure you I'm a merchant by exhibiting my merchandise; when I departed, I told you that might happen."

Hearing this, Torello began feeling both happiness and shame: happiness at having had such an eminent guest, and shame because he

gnarsi che poveramente gliele pareva aver ricevuto; a cui il Saladin disse: — Messer Torello, poi che Iddio qui mandato mi v'ha, pensate che non io oramai, ma voi qui siate il signore.

E fattasi la festa insieme grande, di reali vestimenti il fe' vestire, e, nel cospetto menatolo di tutti i suoi maggiori baroni e molte cose in laude del suo valor dette, comandò che da ciascun che la sua grazia avesse cara, così onorato fosse come la sua persona; il che da quindi innanzi ciascun fece, ma molto più che gli altri i due signori li quali compagni erano stati del Saladino in casa sua.

L'altezza della sùbita gloria nella quale messer Torel si vide, alquanto le cose di Lombardia gli trasse della mente, e massimamente per ciò che sperava fermamente le sue lettere dovere essere al zio pervenute.

Era nel campo o vero esercito de' cristiani, il dì che dal Saladin furon presi, morto e sepellito un cavalier provenzale di piccol valore il cui nome era messer Torel di Dignes; per la qual cosa, essendo messer Torel di Strà per la sua nobiltà per l'esercito conosciuto, chiunque udì dire: «Messer Torello è morto», credette di messer Torel di Strà e non di quel di Dignes; ed il caso, che sopravvenne, della presura, non lasciò sgannar gl'ingannati. Per che molti Italici tornarono con questa novella, tra' quali furon de' sì presuntuosi, che ardiron di dire sé averlo veduto morto ed essere stati alla sepoltura; la qual cosa saputa dalla donna e da' parenti di lui fu di grandissima ed inestimabile doglia cagione, non solamente a loro, ma a ciascuno che conosciuto l'avea.

Lungo sarebbe a mostrare qual fosse e quanto il dolore e la tristizia ed il pianto della sua donna; la quale, dopo alquanti mesi che con tribulazion continua doluta s'era, ed a men dolersi avea cominciato, essendo ella da' maggiori uomini di Lombardia domandata, da' fratelli e dagli altri suoi parenti fu cominciata a sollecitar di maritarsi, il che ella molte volte e con grandissimo pianto avendo negato, costretta, alla fine le convenne far quello che vollero i suoi parenti, con questa condizione, che ella dovesse stare senza a marito andarne tanto quanto ella aveva promesso a messer Torello.

Mentre in Pavia eran le cose della donna in questi termini, e già forse otto dì al termine del doverne ella andare a marito eran vicini, avvenne che messer Torello in Alessandria vide un dì uno, il quale veduto avea con gli ambasciador genovesi montar sopra la galea che a Genova ne venìa; per che, fattolsi chiamare, il domandò che viaggio avuto avessero e quando a Genova fosser giunti. Al quale costui disse:

felt he had been inadequate as a host. Saladin said: "Messer Torello, since God has sent you here to me, consider yourself the master here from now on, and not me."

Both rejoiced in their reunion. Saladin had Torello dressed in royal robes, and, leading him into the presence of all his greatest dignitaries, to whom he said many things in praise of his good qualities, he ordered each of them, if they valued his good graces, to honor Torello like himself. From then on, each of them did so, but, above all the rest, the two lords who had been Saladin's companions in his home.

The dizzy heights of sudden glory on which Torello found himself made him forget his concerns in Lombardy to some extent, especially because he had strong hopes his letter had reached his uncle.

On the day they were captured by Saladin, in the field, or rather camp, of the Christians, an undistinguished Provençal knight had been killed and buried; his name was Torello of Digne;[1] and so, because Torello da Strada was known throughout the army for his worth, everyone who heard that Torello was dead thought it was Torello da Strada and not the one from Digne. Then his ensuing capture didn't allow the error to be rectified. And so, many Italians brought that news home, some of whom had so much nerve that they dared to say they had seen him die and were present when he was buried. When this story came to the notice of his wife and kinsmen, it caused great and unspeakable sorrow not only to them, but to all who had known him.

It would take many words to depict the depth and extent of his wife's grief, sadness, and weeping. After several months of mourning in uninterrupted heartache, when she was just beginning to grieve less violently, her hand was sought by the greatest magnates in Lombardy, and her brothers and other relatives began to urge her to remarry. She refused many times, in a flood of tears, but finally, under compulsion, she had to do what her relatives wanted. But she imposed the condition that she would refrain from marrying for the period she had promised to Torello.

While his wife's situation in Pavia was as described, and it was already only a week or so before the day she would have to remarry, in Alexandria Torello happened to meet someone whom he had seen in the entourage of the Genoese envoys when they boarded the galley bound for Genoa. And so, having him summoned, he asked him how

---

[1] A town in the Provençal Alps.

— Signor mio, malvagio viaggio fece la galea, sì come in Creti sentii, là dove io rimasi; per ciò che, essendo ella vicina di Cicilia, si levò una tramontana pericolosa che nelle secche di Barberia la percosse, né ne scampò testa, ed intra gli altri, due miei fratelli vi perirono.

Messer Torello, dando alle parole di costui fede, che eran verissime, e ricordandosi che il termine ivi a pochi dì finiva da lui domandato alla sua donna, ed avvisando niuna cosa di suo stato doversi sapere a Pavia, ebbe per costante la donna dovere essere rimaritata; di che egli in tanto dolor cadde, che, perdutone il mangiare ed a giacer postosi, diliberò di morire.

La qual cosa come il Saladin sentì, che sommamente l'amava, venne da lui; e dopo molti prieghi e grandi fattigli, saputa la cagion del suo dolore e della sua infermità, il biasimò molto che avanti non gliele aveva detto, ed appresso il pregò che si confortasse, affermandogli che, dove questo facesse, egli adopererebbe sì, che egli sarebbe in Pavia al termine dato; e dissegli come. Messer Torello, dando fede alle parole del Saladino, ed avendo molte volte udito dire che ciò era possibile e fatto s'era assai volte, s'incominciò a confortare ed a sollecitare il Saladino che di ciò si diliberasse.

Il Saladino ad un suo nigromante, la cui arte già espermentata aveva, impose che egli vedesse via come messer Torello sopra un letto in una notte fosse portato a Pavia; a cui il nigromante rispose che ciò saria fatto, ma che egli per ben di lui il facesse dormire. Ordinato questo, tornò il Saladino a messer Torello, e trovandol del tutto disposto a voler pure essere in Pavia al termine dato, se esser potesse, e se non potesse, a voler morire, gli disse così:

— Messer Torello, se voi affettuosamente amate la donna vostra e che ella d'altrui non divenga dubitate, sallo Iddio che io in parte alcuna non ve ne so riprendere, per ciò che di quante donne mi parve veder mai, ella è colei li cui costumi, le cui maniere ed il cui abito, lasciamo star la bellezza che è fior caduco, più mi paion da commendare e da aver care. Sarebbemi stato carissimo, poi che la fortuna qui v'aveva mandato, che quel tempo che voi ed io viver dobbiamo, nel governo del regno che io tengo, parimente signori, vivuti fossimo insieme; e se questo pur non mi doveva esser conceduto da Dio, dovendovi questo cader nell'animo, o di morire o di ritrovarvi al termine posto in Pavia, sommamente avrei disiderato d'averlo saputo a tempo che io con quello onore, con quella grandezza, con quella compagnia che la vostra vertù merita v'avessi fatto porre a casa vostra; il che poi che conceduto non m'è, e voi pur disiderate d'esser là di presente, come io posso, nella forma che detto v'ho, ve ne manderò.

their voyage had been and when they had arrived in Genoa. The man replied: "My lord, the galley had an evil voyage, as I heard in Crete, where I left ship; because, when it was near Sicily, a dangerous north wind sprang up that dashed it against the North African shoals. No one escaped, and among the dead were two brothers of mine."

Torello, trusting the man's report, which was perfectly true; recalling that the period he had asked his wife to observe would be up in a few days; and realizing that no news of his situation could have reached Pavia, was certain that his wife would remarry. This caused him such grief that he lost his appetite. He lay down in bed and prepared to die.

When Saladin heard this, he visited him out of his great affection for him. Learning the reason for his grief and sickness after many intense entreaties, he reproached him severely for not informing him sooner. Then he begged him to take heart, assuring him that, if he did so, he, Saladin, would arrange for him to be in Pavia within the deadline. And he told him how. Torello, trusting Saladin's words, since he had often heard this was possible and had occurred any number of times, began to take heart and to urge Saladin to arrange it.

Saladin ordered one of his sorcerers, whose skill he had already witnessed, to find a way for Torello to be carried on a bed to Pavia in one night. The sorcerer replied that it would be done, but that for his own good Torello should be made to sleep. When this was settled upon, Saladin returned to Torello. Finding him fully determined either to be in Pavia in time, if possible, or else to die, if that were not possible, he said:

"Messer Torello, if you are devoted to your wife and are alarmed at her belonging to another man, God knows I can't blame you in the least, because of all the women I've ever seen, she is the one whose habits, manners, and behavior—not to speak of beauty, which is a flower that withers—seem to me most commendable and lovable. Once fortune had sent you this way, it would have been my first choice for us to have lived out the rest of our lives as co-rulers of the realm I possess. And if God was not to grant me that, because you necessarily had to determine either to die or to be back in Pavia on time, I would most sincerely have wished to learn about it so far in advance that I could have arranged your return home with the honor, grandeur, and retinue that your virtue deserves. Since this, too, is not granted to me, and your constant desire is to be there at once, I shall do what I can, and send you home in the manner I described."

Al quale messer Torel disse: — Signor mio, senza le vostre parole, m'hanno gli effetti assai dimostrata della vostra benivolenza, la quale mai da me in sì suppremo grado non fu meritata, e di ciò che voi dite, eziandio non dicendolo, vivo e morrò certissimo; ma poi che così preso ho per partito, io vi priego che quello che mi dite di fare si faccia tosto, per ciò che domane è l'ultimo dì che io debbo essere aspettato.

Il Saladino disse che ciò senza fallo era fornito; ed il seguente dì, attendendo di mandarlo via la vegnente notte, fece il Saladin fare in una gran sala un bellissimo e ricco letto di materassi, tutti, secondo la loro usanza, di velluti e di drappi ad oro, e fecevi por suso una coltre lavorata a certi compassi di perle grossissime e di carissime pietre preziose, la qual fu poi di qua stimata infinito tesoro, e due guanciali quali a così fatto letto si richiedeano; e questo fatto, comandò che a messer Torello, il quale era già forte, fosse messa indosso una roba alla guisa saracinesca, la più ricca e la più bella cosa che mai fosse stata veduta per alcuno, ed in testa alla lor guisa una delle sue lunghissime bende gli fé ravvolgere.

Ed essendo già l'ora tarda, il Saladino con molti de' suoi baroni nella camera là dove messer Torello era, se n'andò, e postoglisi a sedere allato, quasi lagrimando, a dir cominciò: — Messer Torello, l'ora che da voi dividermi dée, s'appressa, e per ciò che io non posso né accompagnarvi né farvi accompagnare, per la qualità del cammino che a fare avete, che nol sostiene, qui in camera da voi mi conviene prender commiato, al qual prendere venuto sono. E per ciò, prima che io a Dio v'accomandi, vi priego per quello amore e per quella amistà la quale è tra noi, che di me vi ricordi, e se possibile è, anzi che i nostri tempi finiscano, che voi, avendo in ordine poste le vostre cose di Lombardia, una volta almeno a vedermi vegnate, acciò che io possa in quella, essendomi d'avervi veduto rallegrato, quel difetto supplire che ora per la vostra fretta mi convien commettere; ed infino che questo avvenga non vi sia grave visitarmi con lettere e di quelle cose che vi piaceranno richiedermi, che più volentier per voi che per alcuno uom che viva le farò certamente.

Messer Torello non poté le lagrime ritenere, e per ciò, da quelle impedito, con poche parole rispose, impossibil cosa esser che mai i suoi benefici ed il suo valore di mente gli uscissero, e che senza fallo quello che egli comandava farebbe, dove tempo gli fosse prestato. Per che il Saladino, teneramente abbracciatolo e baciatolo, con molte lagrime gli disse: — Andate con Dio — e della camera s'uscì, e gli altri baroni appresso tutti da lui s'accommiatarono e col Saladino in quella sala ne vennero, là dove egli aveva fatto il letto acconciare.

Torello replied: "My lord, even if you hadn't spoken, your actions have clearly proved your benevolence to me, which I have never merited in such a supreme degree; and I shall live and die confiding perfectly in the truth of what you say, even if you hadn't said it. But, now that I have made this decision, I beg you to do at once what you say you will do, because tomorrow is the last day on which I am still to be awaited."

Saladin said that it was all arranged without fail. The next day, waiting until nightfall to send him off, Saladin had a beautiful, opulent bed made in a great hall. All the mattresses were of velvet and cloth of gold, as their custom is, and on top he had a coverlet placed which was divided into sections by very large pearls and most costly precious stones (later on, in Italy, it was accounted as an inexhaustible treasure); in addition, there were two pillows in keeping with the richness of the bed. Then he ordered that Torello, who had recovered his strength by this time, should be dressed in a Saracen-style robe, the richest and most beautiful thing anyone has ever seen, and he had one of his very long turbans wrapped around his head in their manner.

The hour now being late, Saladin proceeded with many of his dignitaries to the room where Torello was. Sitting down beside him, and almost in tears, he began to say: "Messer Torello, the hour is approaching that is to separate me from you; and, since I can neither accompany you nor send anyone else along, because of the nature of the journey you must make, which doesn't allow it, here in this room I must take leave of you, and I have come to do so. Therefore, before I commend you to God, I beg you, in the name of the love and friendship that exist between us, to remember me and, if possible, before we both die, to come and see me at least once, after settling your affairs in Lombardy, so that on that occasion, in my joy at seeing you again, I can make up all the shortcomings which your hasty departure now causes. Until that occurs, please don't consider it a burden to 'visit' me through letters, asking me to give you anything you like, because I shall do so more gladly for you than for anyone else alive."

Torello was unable to keep back his tears and so, hindered by them, he made only a brief reply: that he could never forget Saladin's kindness and merit, and would do without fail what he ordered, if enough time was vouchsafed to him. And so Saladin, hugging and kissing him affectionately, said tearfully: "Godspeed!" and left the room. Then all the other dignitaries bade him farewell and joined Saladin in the hall where he had had the bed made.

Ma essendo già tardi ed il nigromante aspettando lo spaccio ed affrettandolo, venne un medico con un beveraggio, e fattogli vedere che per fortificamento di lui gliele dava, gliel fece bere; né stette guari, che addormentato fu. E così dormendo, fu portato per comandamento del Saladino in sul bel letto sopra il quale esso una grande e bella corona pose di gran valore, e sì la segnò, che apertamente fu poi compreso, quella dal Saladino alla donna di messer Torello esser mandata.

Appresso mise in dito a messer Torello uno anello nel quale era legato un carbunculo tanto lucente, che un torchio acceso pareva, il valor del quale appena si poteva stimare; quindi gli fece una spada cignere il cui guernimento non si saria di leggeri apprezzato, ed oltre a questo, un fermaglio gli fe' davanti appiccare, nel quale erano perle mai simili non vedute con altre care pietre assai, e poi da ciascun de' lati di lui due grandissimi bacin d'oro pieni di doble fe' porre; e molte reti di perle ed anella e cinture ed altre cose, le quali lungo sarebbe a raccontare, gli fece metter da torno.

E questo fatto, da capo baciò messer Torello ed al nigromante disse che si spedisse; per che incontanente in presenza del Saladino il letto con tutto messer Torello fu tolto via, ed il Saladino co' suoi baroni di lui ragionando si rimase. Era già nella chiesa di San Pietro in Cieldoro di Pavia, sì come domandato avea, stato posato messer Torello con tutti i sopraddetti gioielli ed ornamenti, ed ancor si dormiva, quando, sonato già il matutino, il sagrestano nella chiesa entrò con un lume in mano, ed occorsogli subitamente di vedere il ricco letto, non solamente si maravigliò, ma avuta grandissima paura, indietro fuggendo si tornò; il quale l'abate ed i monaci veggendo fuggire, si maravigliarono e domandaron della cagione. Il monaco la disse.

— Oh! — disse l'abate — e sì non se' tu oggimai fanciullo né se' in questa chiesa nuovo, che tu così leggermente spaventarti debbi; ora andiam noi: veggiamo chi t'ha fatto baco.

Accesi adunque più lumi, l'abate con tutti i suoi monaci nella chiesa entrati, videro questo letto così maraviglioso e ricco, e sopra quello il cavalier che dormiva; e mentre dubitosi e timidi, senza punto al letto accostarsi, le nobili gioie riguardavano, avvenne che, essendo la vertù del beveraggio consumata, che messer Torel, destatosi, gittò un gran sospiro. Li monaci come questo videro, e l'abate, con loro, spaventati e gridando: — Domine, aiutaci! — tutti fuggirono.

Messer Torello, aperti gli occhi e da torno guardatosi, conobbe manifestamente sé essere là dove al Saladino domandato avea, di

But, now that it was already late, and the sorcerer was awaiting the moment of action and hastening it along, a doctor came with a potion. Informing Torello that he was giving it to him to fortify him, he made him drink it. In a few moments he was asleep. And in that dormant state he was borne by Saladin's orders to the beautiful bed, on which the sultan placed a large, beautiful tiara of great value, marking it in such a way that it was later publicly understood that it had been sent by Saladin for Torello's wife.

Then he placed on Torello's finger a ring in which was set a ruby so bright it resembled a lighted torch; its value could hardly be calculated. Next, he had him girt with a sword whose ornaments couldn't be easily appraised. In addition, he had a clasp attached to his chest containing pearls whose like was never seen, along with many other gems. Then, on either side of him, he ordered them to place a very large golden bowl filled with doubloons. All around him he caused to be placed numerous pearl hairnets, rings, belts, and other objects, too many to list.

After that, he kissed Torello once more and told the sorcerer to hurry. And so, immediately, in the presence of Saladin, the bed, with Torello on it, was whisked away, leaving Saladin and his dignitaries behind talking about him. Torello and all the aforesaid jewels and ornaments had already been set down in the church of San Pietro in Ciel d'Oro in Pavia, in accordance with his request, and Torello was still asleep, when, matins having already been rung, the sacristan of the church entered with a light in his hand. Happening to see the rich bed all of a sudden, he was not merely amazed but also terribly frightened, and he ran back the way he had come. When the abbot and the monks saw him fleeing, they were surprised and asked him the reason. The monk told them the reason.

"Oh," said the abbot, "you're not a child anymore, and you're not new to this church, so why are you so easily frightened? Let's go now and see who turned you into a fraidy-cat."

So, lighting more lamps, the abbot entered the church with all his monks, and they saw that marvelous, rich bed and the knight sleeping on it. While, in their doubt and timidity, they were looking at the remarkable jewels, without getting anywhere near the bed, the power of the potion happened to wear off and Torello awoke, heaving a great sigh. When the monks saw that, and the abbot with them, they were scared and ran away crying: "Lord help us!"

Torello, opening his eyes and looking around, clearly observed that he was where he had asked Saladin to convey him, and he was greatly

che forte fu seco contento; per che, a seder levatosi e partitamente
guardando ciò che da torno avea, quantunque prima avesse la magnificenza del Saladin conosciuta, ora gli parve maggiore, e più
la conobbe. Nonpertanto, senza altramenti mutarsi, sentendo
i monaci fuggire ed avvisatosi il perché, cominciò per nome a
chiamar l'abate ed a pregarlo che egli non dubitasse, per ciò che
egli era Torel suo nepote.

L'abate, udendo questo, divenne più pauroso, come colui che per
morto l'avea dimolti mesi innanzi; ma dopo alquanto, da veri argo-
menti rassicurato, sentendosi pur chiamare, fattosi il segno della santa
croce, andò a lui; al qual messer Torel disse: — O padre mio, di che
dubitate voi? Io son vivo, la Dio mercé, e qui d'oltremar ritornato.

L'abate, con tutto che egli avesse la barba grande ed in abito
arabesco fosse, pur dopo alquanto il raffigurò, e rassicuratosi tutto,
il prese per la mano, e disse: — Figliuol mio, tu sii il ben tornato!

— E seguitò: — Tu non ti déi maravigliare della nostra paura, per
ciò che in questa terra non ha uomo che non creda fermamente che
tu morto sii, tanto che io ti so dire che madonna Adalieta tua
moglie, vinta da' prieghi e dalle minacce de' parenti suoi e contra
suo volere, è rimaritata; e questa mattina ne dée ire al nuovo marito, e le nozze e ciò che a festa bisogno fa, è apparecchiato.

Messer Torello, levatosi d'in sul ricco letto e fatta all'abate ed a'
monaci maravigliosa festa, ognun pregò che di questa sua tornata
con alcun non parlasse infino a tanto che egli non avesse una sua
bisogna fornita. Appresso questo, fatte le ricche gioie porre in
salvo, ciò che avvenuto gli fosse infino a quel punto raccontò all'a-
bate. L'abate, lieto delle sue fortune, con lui insieme rendé grazie
a Dio. Appresso questo, domandò messer Torel l'abate, chi fosse il
nuovo marito della sua donna.

L'abate gliele disse; a cui messer Torel disse: — Avanti che di mia
tornata si sappia, io intendo di veder che contenenza fia quella di
mia mogliere in queste nozze; e per ciò, quantunque usanza non sia
le persone religiose andare a così fatti conviti, io voglio che per
amor di me voi ordiniate che noi v'andiamo.

L'abate rispose che volentieri; e come giorno fu fatto, mandò al
nuovo sposo, dicendo che con un compagno voleva essere alle sue
nozze; a cui il gentile uom rispose che molto gli piacea. Venuta adunque
l'ora del mangiare, messer Torello, in quello abito che era, con l'abate
se n'andò alla casa del novello sposo, con maraviglia guatato da chiunque il vedeva, ma riconosciuto da nullo; e l'abate a tutti diceva, lui essere un saracino mandato dal soldano al re di Francia ambasciadore.

pleased in his mind. And so, sitting up and examining his whereabouts in detail, even though he had realized before how great Saladin's munificence was, now he found it even greater and acknowledged it more fully. Nonetheless, without otherwise moving, when he heard the monks flee and guessed their reason for doing so, he started to call the abbot by name, begging him to have no fear, because he was his nephew Torello.

Hearing this, the abbot became even more frightened, because he had heard many months earlier that he was dead. But after a while, reassured by cogent proofs, and hearing himself constantly called for, he made the sign of the Holy Cross and went up to him. Torello said: "Father, what are you afraid of? I'm alive, thank God, and I'm back here from overseas."

Even though Torello had a big beard and was dressed in Arab clothes, nevertheless the abbot recognized him after a while. Completely reassured, he took him by the hand and said: "My son, welcome home!" And he continued: "You shouldn't be surprised at our fear, because there's not a man in this city who doesn't firmly believe you're dead. So much so, that I can tell you your wife Adalieta, yielding to her relatives' entreaties and threats, is being remarried against her will. And this very morning she is to be united to her new husband; the wedding feast, with all its appurtenances, is prepared."

Torello, rising from the rich bed and greeting the abbot and the monks with extreme joy, begged them all not to talk to anyone about his return before he accomplished a piece of business he had. Then, having the rich gems placed in safe-keeping, he related to the abbot everything that had happened to him down to that moment. The abbot, happy over his good luck, gave thanks to God together with him. Then Torello asked the abbot who was to be his wife's new husband.

The abbot told him, and Torello replied: "Before the news of my return spreads, I intend to see how my wife acts at that wedding. And so, although it's not customary for monks to attend such parties, I want you, for my sake, to arrange for us to go there."

The abbot replied that he'd gladly do so. When day broke, he sent word to the bridegroom that he wanted to attend the wedding with a friend. The gentleman replied that he was most pleased. And so, when mealtime arrived, Torello, wearing the clothes he had come in, went to the bridegroom's house with the abbot; everyone who saw him stared at him in wonder, but no one recognized him, and the abbot told everyone he was a Saracen sent by the sultan as an ambassador to the king of France.

Fu adunque messer Torello messo ad una tavola appunto di rimpetto alla donna sua, la quale egli con grandissimo piacer riguardava; e nel viso gli pareva turbata di queste nozze. Ella similmente alcuna volta guardava lui, non già per riconoscenza alcuna che ella n'avesse, ché la barba grande e lo strano abito e la ferma credenza che aveva che egli fosse morto, gliele toglievano, ma per la novità dell'abito. Ma poi che tempo parve a messer Torello di volerla tentare se di lui si ricordasse, recatosi in mano l'anello che dalla donna nella partita gli era stato donato, si fece chiamare un giovanetto che davanti a lei serviva, e dissegli:

— Di' da mia parte alla nuova sposa che nelle mie contrade s'usa, quando alcun forestier, come io son qui, mangia al convito d'alcuna sposa nuova, come ella è, che, in segno d'aver caro che egli venuto vi sia a mangiare, ella la coppa con la qual bee gli manda piena di vino; con la qual poi che il forestiere ha bevuto quello che gli piace, ricoperchiata la coppa, la sposa bee il rimanente.

Il giovanetto fe' l'ambasciata alla donna, la quale, sì come costumata e savia, credendo costui essere un gran barbassoro, per mostrare d'avere a grado la sua venuta, una gran coppa dorata la qual davanti avea, comandò che lavata fosse ed empiuta di vino e portata al gentile uomo; e così fu fatto.

Messer Torello, avendosi l'anello di lei messo in bocca, sì fece, che bevendo il lasciò cader nella coppa, senza avvedersene alcuno, e poco vino lasciatovi, quella ricoperchiò e mandò alla donna. La quale presala, acciò che l'usanza di lui compiesse, scoperchiata, la si mise a bocca e vide l'anello e senza dire alcuna cosa alquanto il riguardò; e riconosciuto che egli era quello che dato avea nel suo partire a messer Torello, presolo e fiso guardato colui il qual forestier credeva, e già conoscendolo, quasi furiosa fosse, gittata in terra la tavola che davanti aveva, gridò: — Questi è il mio signore, questi veramente è messer Torello!

E corsa alla tavola alla quale esso sedeva, senza avere riguardo a' suoi drappi o a cosa che sopra la tavola fosse, gittatasi oltre quanto poté, l'abbracciò strettamente, né mai dal suo collo fu potuta, per detto o per fatto d'alcun che quivi fosse, levare, infino a tanto che per messer Torello non le fu detto che alquanto sopra sé stesse, per ciò che tempo da abbracciarlo le sarebbe ancora prestato assai.

Allora ella dirizzatasi, essendo già le nozze tutte turbate ed in parte più liete che mai per lo racquisto d'un così fatto cavaliere, pregandone egli, ogni uomo stette cheto; per che messer Torello dal dì della sua partita infino a quel punto ciò che avvenuto gli era

And so, Torello was seated at a table directly opposite his wife's; he observed her with the greatest pleasure. It seemed to him that her face showed distress at that wedding. On her part, she looked at him from time to time, not because she recognized him at all, since his full beard and foreign clothing and her firm belief that he was dead prevented her from so doing, but because of the strangeness of his attire. But when Torello thought the time had come to see whether she remembered him, he took in his hand the ring his wife had given him on his departure, summoned a boy who was waiting at her table, and said:

"Tell the bride from me that where I come from it's the custom, when a foreigner like me dines at the banquet of a bride like her, for her to send him the goblet from which she drinks filled with wine, to show that she is pleased at having him attend. After the foreigner has drunk as much as he wants, he puts the lid back on the goblet, returns it, and the bride drinks whatever is left."

The boy brought the message to the lady, who, being well-bred and wise, and thinking he was a man of lofty station, to show that she appreciated his coming, ordered the large gilt goblet in front of her to be washed, filled with wine, and taken to the gentleman; and this was done.

Torello, having placed her ring in his mouth, dropped it into the goblet while he was drinking, without anyone noticing; when only a little wine was left, he replaced the lid and sent the goblet back to the lady. She took it, in order to comply with his custom, lifted the lid, put the goblet to her lips, and saw the ring; without a word, she looked at it for a moment; recognizing it as the one she had given Torello when he was departing, she took it and stared hard at the man she took for a foreigner. Now recognizing him, she overturned the table in front of her, as if she had gone mad, and shouted: "This is my lord, this is truly Messer Torello!"

She ran over to the table at which he was sitting, with no regard for her clothing or anything on the table, and, leaning as far forward as she could, hugged him tightly; and she couldn't be pulled away from his neck, no matter what anyone there said or did, until Torello told her to contain herself a little, because she would have plenty of time for hugging him later on.

Then she stood up straight. The wedding party was now completely disrupted, but some of the guests were happier than ever to have regained such an excellent knight. At his request, everyone remained calm, and Torello told everyone what had happened to him from the

a tutti narrò, conchiudendo che al gentile uomo, il quale, lui morto credendo, aveva la sua donna per moglie presa, se egli essendo vivo la si ritoglieva, non doveva spiacere. Il nuovo sposo, quantunque alquanto scornato fosse, liberamente e come amico rispose che delle sue cose era nel suo voler quel farne che più gli piacesse.

La donna e l'anella e la corona avute dal nuovo sposo quivi lasciò, e quello che della coppa aveva tratto si mise, e similmente la corona mandatale dal soldano; ed usciti dalla casa dove erano, con tutta la pompa delle nozze infino alla casa di messer Torel se n'andarono, e quivi gli sconsolati amici e parenti e tutti i cittadini, che quasi per un miracolo il riguardavano, con lunga e lieta festa racconsolarono.

Messer Torello, fatta delle sue care gioie parte ed a colui che avute aveva le spese delle nozze ed all'abate ed a molti altri, e per più d'un messo significata la sua felice repatriazione al Saladino, suo amico e suo servidore ritenendosi, più anni con la sua valente donna poi visse, più cortesia usando che mai.

Cotale adunque fu la fine delle noie di messer Torello e di quelle della sua cara donna, ed il guiderdone delle lor liete e preste cortesie. Le quali molti si sforzan di fare, che, benché abbian di che, sì mal farle sanno, che prima le fanno assai più comperar che non vagliono, che fatte l'abbiano; per che, se loro merito non se segue, né essi né altri maravigliarsene dée.

LA PAZIENZA DI GRISELDA [X, 10]

Finita la lunga novella del re, molto a tutti nel sembiante piaciuta, Dionèo ridendo disse: — Il buon uomo, che aspettava la seguente notte di fare abbassare la coda ritta della fantasima, avrebbe dati men di due denari di tutte le lode che voi date a messer Torello. — Ed appresso, sappiendo che a lui solo restava il dire, incominciò:

Mansuete mie donne, per quel che mi paia, questo dì d'oggi è stato dato a re ed a soldani ed a così fatta gente, e per ciò che io troppo da voi non mi scosti, vo' ragionar d'un marchese non una cosa magnifica ma una matta bestialità, come che ben ne gli

day of his departure down to that moment. In conclusion, he stated that his being alive and reclaiming his wife ought not to displease the gentleman who had taken her as a bride in the belief he was dead. The bridegroom, even though this put him in a somewhat ridiculous position, replied generously and amicably that it was up to him to do as he wished with what belonged to him.

The lady left there the rings and the tiara she had been given by the bridegroom, and put on the ring she had taken from the goblet and the tiara sent her by the sultan. Leaving the house they were in, they went to Torello's house, accompanied by all the pomp of the wedding. There, with long, happy rejoicing, they consoled his disconsolate friends and relatives and all the townspeople, who looked on his return almost as a miracle.

Torello, sharing his precious jewels with the man who had borne the cost of the wedding, with the abbot, and with many others, and informing Saladin of his happy homecoming in several messages, assuring him of his friendship and service, lived many more years with his worthy wife, performing more deeds of courtesy than ever before.

And so, this was the end of Torello's misfortunes and those of his dear wife, and the reward for their prompt and willing acts of courtesy. Many people strive to do the same but, even though they have the means, do it so badly that they exact from the recipient more than their generosity is worth before they even bestow it. And so, neither they nor others should be surprised if they receive no merit from it.

PATIENT GRISELDA [X, 10]

When the "King's" long story was finished, and everyone's expression showed how well it had been liked, Dioneo laughed and said: "The poor fool who expected to lower the ghost's erect tail on the following night[1] would have given less than two cents for all the praise you lavish on Torello." Then, knowing that he was the only one left to speak, he began:

My gentle ladies, as far as I can see, today's stories have been devoted to kings, sultans, and people of that sort; and, in order not to diverge too much from your course, I shall speak about a marquess—not, however, recounting a generous deed of his, but an act of mad

---

[1] A reference to story VII, 1, in which a wife makes her husband believe that her lover knocking at their door is a ghost that must be exorcised.

seguisse alla fine; la quale io non consiglio alcun che segua, per ciò
che gran peccato fu che a costui ben n'avvenisse.

Già è gran tempo, fu tra' marchesi di Saluzzo il maggior della
casa un giovane chiamato Gualtieri, il quale, essendo senza moglie
e senza figliuoli, in niuna altra cosa il suo tempo spendeva che in
uccellare ed in cacciare, né di prender moglie né d'aver figliuoli
alcun pensiero avea; di che egli era da reputar molto savio. La qual
cosa a' suoi uomini non piacendo, più volte il pregaron che moglie
prendesse, acciò che egli senza erede né essi senza signor ri-
manessero, offerendosi di trovargliel tale e di sì fatto padre e madre
discesa, che buona speranza se ne potrebbe avere, ed esso con-
tentarsene molto.

A' quali Gualtieri rispose: — Amici miei, voi mi strignete a quello
che io del tutto aveva disposto di non far mai, considerando quanto
grave cosa sia a poter trovar chi co' suoi costumi ben si convenga, e
quanto del contrario sia grande la copia, e come dura vita sia quella
di colui che a donna non bene a sé conveniente s'abbatte. Ed il dire
che voi vi crediate a' costumi de' padri le figliuole conoscere, donde
argomentate di dàrlami tal che mi piacerà, è una sciocchezza, con
ciò sia cosa che io non sappia dove i padri possiate conoscere, né
come i segreti delle madri di quelle; quantunque, pur conoscen-
dogli, sieno spesse volte le figliuole a' padri ed alle madri dissimili.
Ma poi che pure in queste catene vi piace d'annodarmi, ed io voglio
esser contento; ed acciò che io non abbia da dolermi d'altrui che di
me, se mal venisse fatto, io stesso ne voglio essere il trovatore, af-
fermandovi che, cui che io mi tolga, se da voi non fia come donna
onorata, voi proverete con gran vostro danno quanto grave mi sia
l'aver contra mia voglia presa mogliere a' vostri prieghi.

I valenti uomini risposon che eran contenti, sol che esso si recasse a prender moglie. Erano a Gualtieri buona pezza piaciuti i
costumi d'una povera giovanetta che d'una villa vicina a casa sua
era, e parendogli bella assai, estimò che con costei dovesse potere
aver vita assai consolata; e per ciò, senza più avanti cercare, costei
propose di volere sposare, e fattosi il padre chiamare, con lui, che
poverissimo era, si convenne di tôrla per moglie. Fatto questo, fece
Gualtieri tutti i suoi amici della contrada adunare, e disse loro:

— Amici miei, egli v'è piaciuto e piace che io mi disponga a tôr
moglie, ed io mi vi son disposto più per compiacere a voi che per
disidéro che io di moglie avessi. Voi sapete quello che voi mi
prometteste, cioè d'esser contenti e d'onorar come donna
qualunque quella fosse che io togliessi; e per ciò venuto è il tempo

brutality, even though it came out well for him in the end. I don't advise anyone to emulate his cruelty, because it was a great shame that he derived any good from it.

Long ago, among the marquesses of Saluzzo the head of the family was a young man named Gualtieri, who, having no wife or children, spent every bit of his time hawking and hunting with hounds. He had no intention of marrying or having children, for which he should have been considered very wise. This state of affairs displeased his vassals, who often asked him to marry, so that he would not be left without an heir nor they without a lord. They offered to find him such a fine wife, the daughter of such a fine father and mother, that their hopes would be fulfilled and he himself would be very pleased.

Gualtieri replied: "My friends, you are compelling me to do something I had firmly proposed never to do, considering how hard it is to find a woman whose ways are compatible with one's own, how easy it is to find just the opposite, and how difficult life is for a man who hits upon a woman that doesn't suit him. And your saying that you think you can know the daughter by her father's character, and your consequent assertion that you can find me a woman I'll like—that's pure folly, because I don't know how you can even know the father, or her mother's secrets. And yet, even when all that is well known, the daughter is often unlike her father and mother. But since you insist on entangling me in these chains, I, too, want to be satisfied. In order that I won't be able to blame anyone but myself, if things work out badly, I myself want to be her discoverer. And I assure you that, no matter whom I choose, if you don't honor her as your liege lady, you'll learn to your great sorrow how hard I find it to have married against my will to please you."

The worthy men replied that they were satisfied, as long as he actually got married. For some time Gualtieri had admired the character of a penniless young woman living in a village near his home. Finding her quite beautiful as well, he thought he could lead quite a contented life with her. And so, looking no further, he determined to marry her. Summoning her father, who was very poor, he arranged a betrothal with her. Then Gualtieri assembled all his friends in the region and said:

"My friends, it has pleased you, and pleases you now, for me to decide to take a wife, and I have so decided, more to oblige you than to satisfy any desire I had for a wife. You know what you promised me— to be contented with any woman I chose and to honor her as your lady. Therefore the time has come for me to keep my promise to you,

che io sono per servare a voi la promessa e che io voglio che voi a me la serviate. Io ho trovata una giovane secondo il cuor mio, assai presso di qui, la quale io intendo di tôr per moglie e di menàrlami tra qui a pochi dì a casa; e per ciò pensate come la festa delle nozze sia bella e come voi onorevolmente riceverla possiate, acciò che io mi possa della vostra promission chiamar contento, come voi della mia vi potrete chiamare.

I buoni uomini lieti tutti risposero ciò piacer loro e che, fosse chi volesse, essi l'avrebber per donna ed onorerebbonla in tutte cose sì come donna; ed appresso questo, tutti si misero in assetto di far bella e grande e lieta festa, ed il simigliante fece Gualtieri. Egli fece preparar le nozze grandissime e belle, ed invitarvi molti suoi amici e parenti e gran gentili uomini ed altri da torno; ed oltre a questo, fece tagliare e far più robe belle e ricche al dosso d'una giovane la quale della persona gli pareva che la giovanetta la quale aveva proposto di sposare, ed oltre a questo, apparecchiò cinture ed anella ed una ricca e bella corona, e tutto ciò che a novella sposa si richiedea.

E venuto il dì che alle nozze predetto avea, Gualtieri in su la mezza terza montò a cavallo, e ciascuno altro che ad onorarlo era venuto; ed ogni cosa opportuna avendo disposta, disse: — Signori, tempo è d'andare per la novella sposa.

E messosi in via con tutta la compagnia sua, pervennero alla villetta, e giunti a casa del padre della fanciulla, e lei trovata che con acqua tornava dalla fonte in gran fretta, per andar poi con altre femine a veder venire la sposa di Gualtieri; la quale come Gualtier vide, chiamatala per nome, cioè Griselda, domandò dove il padre fosse; al quale ella vergognosamente rispose: — Signor mio, egli è in casa.

Allora Gualtieri, smontato e comandato ad ogni uom che l'aspettasse, solo se n'entrò nella povera casa, dove trovò il padre di lei, che avea nome Giannùcolo, e dissegli: — Io sono venuto a sposar la Griselda, ma prima da lei voglio sapere alcuna cosa in tua presenza.

E domandolla se ella sempre, togliendola egli per moglie, s'ingegnerebbe di compiacergli e di niuna cosa che egli dicesse o facesse non turbarsi, e se ella sarebbe obediente e simili altre cose assai, delle quali ella a tutte rispose del sì. Allora Gualtieri, presala per mano, la menò fuori, ed in presenza di tutta la sua compagnia e d'ogni altra persona la fece spogliare ignuda; e fattisi quegli vestimenti venire che fatti avea fare, prestamente la fece vestire e calzare, e sopra i suoi capelli, così scarmigliati come erano, le fece

just as I want you to keep yours. I have found a young woman after my own heart who lives very near here. I intend to become betrothed to her and to bring her home as my wife in a few days from now. Therefore, arrange a fine wedding banquet and an honorable reception for her, so that I can say I am as pleased with your part of the bargain as you will be with mine."

The good men, overjoyed, all replied that they were satisfied, and that, whoever she might be, they would acknowledge her as their lady and honor her accordingly in every way. Then they all made preparations for a great, beautiful, and happy celebration; and so did Gualtieri. He arranged for a splendid, fine wedding, inviting many friends, relatives, high-ranking gentlemen, and others from the vicinity. In addition, he had a number of beautiful, sumptuous dresses cut and sewn to the measure of a young woman who, he thought, had the same figure as the girl he had decided to marry. Moreover, he prepared belts and rings and a splendid, beautiful tiara, and everything appropriate for a young bride.

When the day he had set for the wedding arrived, about an hour and a half after sunrise Gualtieri mounted his horse, and all those who had come to do him honor mounted theirs. When he had made all necessary arrangements, he said: "Gentlemen, it's time to fetch the bride."

He set out with his entire retinue, they reached the village, and they proceeded to the girl's father's house. They found her returning home hastily with water from the fountain, so she could join the other women who were awaiting the arrival of Gualtieri's bride. When Gualtieri saw her, he called her by her name, which was Griselda, and asked her where her father was. Shyly she replied: "My lord, he is at home."

Then Gualtieri, dismounting and ordering everyone to await him, entered the humble house alone. There he found her father, whose name was Giannucolo, and said to him: "I've come to wed Griselda, but first I want to hear something from her in your presence."

He asked her whether, if he married her, she would always strive to oblige him, never becoming vexed at anything he said or did, and whether she would be obedient, and many other things of the sort; she said yes to every question. Then Gualtieri took her hand and led her outside, where, in the presence of his entire retinue and everyone else, he had her stripped naked. Calling for the garments he had had made, he immediately had her put on a dress and shoes. On her hair, disheveled as it was, he had a tiara placed, and then, while

mettere una corona, ed appresso questo, maravigliandosi ogni uomo di questa cosa, disse: — Signori, costei è colei la quale io intendo che mia moglie sia, dove ella me voglia per marito.

E poi, a lei rivolto, che di se medesima vergognosa e sospesa stava, le disse: — Griselda, vuòimi tu per marito?

A cui ella rispose: — Signor mio, sì.

Ed egli disse: — Ed io voglio te per mia moglie. — Ed in presenza di tutti la sposò; e fattala sopra un pallafren montare, orrevolmente accompagnata a casa la si menò. Quivi furon le nozze belle e grandi e la festa non altramenti che se presa avesse la figliuola del re di Francia.

La giovane sposa parve che co' vestimenti insieme l'animo ed i costumi mutasse. Ella era, come già dicemmo, di persona e di viso bella, e così come bella era, divenne tanto avvenevole, tanto piacevole e tanto costumata, che non figliuola di Giannùcolo e guardiana di pecore pareva stata, ma d'alcun nobile signore, di che ella faceva maravigliare ogni uom che prima conosciuta l'avea; ed oltre a questo, era tanto obediente al marito e tanto servente, che egli si teneva il più appagato uomo del mondo, e similmente verso i sudditi del marito era tanto graziosa e tanto benigna, che niun ve n'era che più che sé non l'amasse e che non l'onorasse di buon grado, tutti per lo suo bene e per lo suo stato e per lo suo esaltamento pregando, dicendo, dove dir soleano Gualtieri aver fatto come poco savio d'averla per moglie presa, che egli era il più savio ed il più avveduto uomo che al mondo fosse, per ciò che niuno altro che egli avrebbe mai potuto conoscere l'alta vertù di costei nascosa sotto i poveri panni e sotto l'abito villesco.

Ed in brieve, non solamente nel suo marchesato ma per tutto, anzi che gran tempo fosse passato, seppe ella sì fare, che ella fece ragionare del suo valore e del suo bene adoperare, ed in contrario rivolgere, se alcuna cosa detta s'era contro al marito per lei quando sposata l'avea. Ella non fu guari con Gualtieri dimorata che ella ingravidò, ed al tempo debito partorì una fanciulla, di che Gualtieri fece gran festa.

Ma poco appresso, entratogli un nuovo pensier nell'animo, cioè di volere con lunga esperienza e con cose intollerabili provare la pazienza di lei, primieramente la punse con parole, mostrandosi turbato e dicendo che i suoi uomini pessimamente si contentavano di lei per la sua bassa condizione, e spezialmente poi che vedevano che ella portava figliuoli, e, della figliuola che nata era tristissimi, altro che mormorar non faceano.

everyone was marveling at his actions, he said: "Gentlemen, this is the woman I have chosen for my wife, if she wants me for her husband."

Then, turning to face her, as she stood there ashamed and hesitant, he said: "Griselda, do you want me for a husband?"

She replied: "Yes, my lord."

And he said: "Then I want you for my wife." And in front of everyone he married her. Mounting her on a palfrey, he brought her home with an honorable escort. There the wedding celebration was as beautiful and splendid, and the merriment as great, as if he had married the daughter of the king of France.

The young bride seemed to have changed her spirit and her ways along with her clothes. As we said before, she was beautiful in face and body. Now, to match her beauty, she became so attractive, charming, and well-bred that she seemed to have been not Giannucolo's shepherdess daughter, but the child of some noble lord. And so she instilled amazement in everyone who had known her earlier. In addition, she was so obedient and obliging to her husband that he considered himself the most contented man in the world. Likewise, she was so gracious and kind to her husband's subjects that there was no one who didn't love her more than himself, or who didn't voluntarily honor her. Everyone prayed for her welfare, health, and prosperity. Whereas they had once said that Gualtieri showed little wisdom in marrying her, now they said he was the wisest and most perceptive man in the world, because he and he alone was able to recognize her lofty virtue when it was hidden beneath her humble clothes and rustic manners.

In short, before much time had passed, she brought it about that, not only in his marquisate but everywhere, she made people talk about her good qualities and fine actions, and made them change their mind if they had said anything against her husband on her account when he married her. She hadn't been living with Gualtieri long when she became pregnant. When her term had come, she gave birth to a girl, and Gualtieri was very happy about it.

But not long afterward, he got a bizarre idea into his head: to test her patience with drawn-out trials involving unbearable conditions. First he wounded her with words, acting angry and saying that his vassals were highly displeased with her because of her low origins, especially now that they saw she was bearing children: they were very unhappy over the daughter who had been born, and they did nothing but grumble.

Le quali parole udendo la donna, senza mutar viso o buon proponimento in alcun atto, disse: — Signor mio, fa' di me quello che tu credi che più tuo onore o consolazion sia, ché io sarò di tutto contenta, sì come colei che conosco che io sono da men di loro e che io non era degna di questo onore al quale tu per tua cortesia mi recasti.

Questa risposta fu molto cara a Gualtieri, conoscendo costei non essere in alcuna superbia levata per onore che egli o altri fatto l'avesse. Poco tempo appresso, avendo con parole generali detto alla moglie che i sudditi non potevan patir quella fanciulla di lei nata, informato un suo famigliare, il mandò a lei, il quale con assai dolente viso le disse: — Madonna, se io non voglio morire, a me convien far quello che il mio signor mi comanda. Egli m'ha comandato che io prenda questa vostra figliuola e che io . . . — E non disse più.

La donna, udendo le parole e veggendo il viso del famigliare, e delle parole dette ricordandosi, comprese che a costui fosse imposto che egli l'uccidesse; per che prestamente, presala della culla e baciatala e benedettala, come che gran noia nel cuor sentisse, senza mutar viso, in braccio la pose al famigliare e dissegli: — Te', fa' compiutamente quello che il tuo e mio signore t'ha imposto; ma non la lasciar per modo che le bestie e gli uccelli la divorino, salvo se egli nol ti comandasse.

Il famigliare presa la fanciulla e fatto a Gualtier sentire ciò che detto aveva la donna, maravigliandosi egli della sua costanza, lui con essa ne mandò a Bologna ad una sua parente, pregandola che, senza mai dire cui figliuola si fosse, diligentemente l'allevasse e costumasse.

Sopravvenne appresso che la donna da capo ingravidò, ed al tempo debito partorì un figliuol maschio, il che carissimo fu a Gualtieri; ma, non bastandogli quello che fatto avea, con maggior puntura trafisse la donna, e con sembiante turbato un dì le disse: — Donna, poscia che tu questo figliuol maschio facesti, per niuna guisa con questi miei viver son potuto, sì duramente si ramaricano che un nepote di Giannùcolo dopo me debba rimaner lor signore; di che io mi dótto, se io non ci vorrò esser cacciato, che non mi ci convenga fare di quello che io altra volta feci, ed alla fine lasciar te e prendere un'altra moglie.

La donna con paziente animo l'ascoltò, né altro rispose se non: — Signor mio, pensa di contentar te e di sodisfare al piacer tuo, e di me non avere pensiero alcuno, per ciò che niuna cosa m'è cara se non quanto io la veggio a te piacere.

When the lady heard those words, she didn't change her expression or her good intentions in any way, but said: "My lord, do with me whatever you think your honor or your pleasure demands, for I will be satisfied with everything, since I know I am beneath their rank and that I was unworthy of the honor to which you raised me through your courtesy."

This reply was most welcome to Gualtieri, who realized that she hadn't been made haughty by any honor he or others had done her. Shortly after that, having told his wife in imprecise terms that his subjects couldn't abide that girl she had given birth to, he gave instructions to a servant and sent him to her. With a very sad expression the servant said: "My lady, if I don't want to die, I must do what my master orders. He has ordered me to take this daughter of yours and to . . ." And he fell silent.

Hearing the servant's words and seeing his face, and remembering what had been said to her earlier, the lady understood he had been ordered to kill the infant. And so she quickly took her out of the cradle, kissed her, and gave her her blessing. Even though she felt great grief in her heart, she kept her face calm, and placed the child in the servant's arms, saying: "Here, do exactly what your master and mine has ordered you to. But don't leave her where the birds and beasts will devour her, unless he has commanded you to."

The servant took the baby girl and reported to Gualtieri what the lady had said. The marquess, marveling at her firmness of mind, sent him with the child to a kinswoman of his in Bologna, asking her to raise and educate the girl, but never to say whose daughter she was.

Afterward, the lady became pregnant again, and in due course gave birth to a baby boy, which was wonderful news to Gualtieri. But, not contented with what he had already done, he inflicted a greater wound on the lady. One day, pretending to be angry, he said to her: "Lady, ever since you produced this boy, I have been totally unable to live with my vassals, because they complain so grievously that a grandson of Giannucolo is to be left as their lord after my death. And so I fear, if I am not to be driven into exile, that I must take the same measures I took before, and that I must at last drop you and marry someone else."

The lady listened to him with a patient spirit, and her only reply was: "My lord, just satisfy yourself and see to your own pleasure. Don't worry at all about me, because I care about nothing but pleasing you in every way."

Dopo non molti dì Gualtieri, in quella medesima maniera che mandato aveva per la figliuola, mandò per lo figliuolo, e similmente dimostrato d'averlo fatto uccidere, a nutricar nel mandò a Bologna, come la fanciulla aveva mandata; della qual cosa la donna né altro viso né altre parole fece che della fanciulla fatto avesse, di che Gualtieri si maravigliava forte, e seco stesso affermava niuna altra femina questo poter fare che ella faceva; e se non fosse che carnalissima de' figliuoli, mentre gli piacea, la vedeva, lei avrebbe creduto ciò fare per più non curarsene, dove come savia lei farlo conobbe.

I sudditi suoi, credendo che egli uccidere avesse fatti i figliuoli, il biasimavan forte e reputavanlo crudele uomo, ed alla donna avevan grandissima compassione; la quale con le donne le quali con lei de' figliuoli così morti si condoleano, mai altro non disse, se non che quel ne piaceva a lei che a colui che generati gli avea.

Ma essendo più anni passati dopo la natività della fanciulla, parendo tempo a Gualtieri di fare l'ultima pruova della sofferenza di costei, con molti de' suoi disse che per niuna guisa più sofferir poteva d'aver per moglie Griselda e che egli conosceva che male e giovenilmente aveva fatto quando l'aveva presa, e per ciò a suo potere voleva procacciar col papa che con lui dispensasse che un'altra donna prender potesse e lasciar Griselda; di che egli da assai buoni uomini fu molto ripreso, a che nulla altro rispose, se non che conveniva che così fosse.

La donna, sentendo queste cose e parendole dovere sperare di ritornare a casa del padre, e forse a guardar le pecore come altra volta aveva fatto, e vedere ad un'altra donna tener colui al quale ella voleva tutto il suo bene, forte in se medesima si dolea; ma pur, come l'altre ingiurie della fortuna aveva sostenute, così con fermo viso si dispose a questa dover sostenere.

Non dopo molto tempo Gualtieri fece venire sue lettere contraffatte da Roma, e fece veduto a' suoi sudditi, il papa per quelle aver seco dispensato di poter tôrre altra moglie e lasciar Griselda; per che, fàttalasi venir dinanzi, in presenza di molti le disse: — Donna, per concession fattami dal papa, io posso altra donna pigliare e lasciar te; e per ciò che i miei passati sono stati gran gentili uomini e signori di queste contrade, dove i tuoi stati son sempre lavoratori, io intendo che tu più mia moglie non sia, ma che tu a casa Giannùcolo te ne torni con la dota che tu mi recasti, ed io poi un'altra, che trovata n'ho convenevole a me, ce ne menerò.

La donna, udendo queste parole, non senza grandissima fatica,

Not many days later, Gualtieri sent for the baby boy in the very same way he had sent for his daughter. In like manner, he pretended he had had him killed, but really sent him to Bologna to be raised, just as he had done with the girl. When this occurred, the lady made no more show of emotion and said no more than she had done in the case of the girl; so that Gualtieri was mightily amazed, declaring to himself that no other woman could do what she was doing. If he weren't perfectly aware that she loved her children intensely, as long as that was his pleasure, he would have thought she was acting that way to rid herself of the trouble they caused; whereas he knew she was acting that way out of a philosophic frame of mind.

His subjects, believing he had killed his children, reproached him greatly and considered him a cruel man, while they felt great pity for his wife. For her part, the only thing she ever said to the women who condoled with her over her children who had died in that way, was that she was satisfied with whatever satisfied the man who had begotten them.

But when several years had passed after the birth of the girl, Gualtieri thought it was time to put Griselda's patience to the final test. He told many of his men that he could absolutely no longer tolerate having Griselda as his wife; that he knew he had acted badly and like a foolish youngster when he had married her; and that therefore he intended to do all he could to obtain a dispensation from the Pope to marry another woman and put Griselda aside. When reproached by many good men for this, his only reply was that it had to be so.

When the lady heard this, and thought she must expect to return to her father's house, perhaps to resume her former life as a shepherdess, and to see another woman in possession of the man she loved wholeheartedly, she was enormously grieved inwardly. And yet, just as she had borne the other affronts of fortune, so now she prepared to undergo this one with an unflinching face.

Not long afterward, Gualtieri caused false papers to be sent from Rome, and gave his subjects to believe that in them the Pope had granted him a dispensation to take another wife and put Griselda aside. And so, summoning her, with many people present, he said to her: "Lady, by a concession granted to me by the Pope, I am able to marry another woman and divorce you. Because my ancestors were eminent noblemen and lords of this territory, whereas your people have always been farmers, my will is that you are no longer to be my wife, but to return to Giannucolo's house with the dowry you brought me, so that I can then marry another woman I find suitable to me."

When the lady heard this, she held back her tears with the greatest

oltre alla natura delle femine, ritenne le lagrime, e rispose: — Signor mio, io conobbi sempre la mia bassa condizione alla vostra nobiltà in alcun modo non convenirsi e quello che io stata son con voi, da Dio e da voi il riconoscea, né mai come donatolmi, mio il feci o tenni, ma sempre l'ebbi come prestàtomi; piàcevi di rivolerlo, ed a me dée piacere e piace di rènderlovi: ecco il vostro anello col quale voi mi sposaste, prendetelo. Comandatemi che io quella dota me ne porti che io ci recai, alla qual cosa fare né a voi pagatore né a me borsa bisognerà né somiere, per ciò che di mente uscito non m'è che ignuda m'aveste; e se voi giudicate onesto che quel corpo nel quale io ho portati figliuoli da voi generati, sia da tutti veduto, io me n'andrò ignuda; ma io vi priego, in premio della mia virginità che io ci recai e non ne la porto, che almeno una sola camicia sopra la dota mia vi piaccia che io portarne possa.

Gualtieri, che maggior voglia di piagnere aveva che d'altro, stando pur col viso duro, disse: — E tu una camicia ne porta.

Quanti dintorno v'erano il pregavano che egli una roba le donasse, ché non fosse veduta colei che sua moglie tredici anni o più era stata di casa sua così poveramente e così vituperosamente uscire, come era uscirne in camicia; ma invano andarono i prieghi, di che la donna in camicia e scalza e senza alcuna cosa in capo, accomandatigli a Dio, gli uscì di casa ed al padre se ne tornò, con lagrime e pianto di tutti coloro che la videro.

Giannùcolo, che creder non avea mai potuto questo esser vero, che Gualtieri la figliuola dovesse tener moglie, ed ognidì questo caso aspettando, guardati l'aveva i panni che spogliati s'avea quella mattina che Gualtieri la sposò; per che recàtigliele ed ella rivestìtiglisi, a' piccoli servigi della paterna casa si diede sì come far soleva, con forte animo sostenendo il fiero assalto della nemica fortuna.

Come Gualtieri questo ebbe fatto, così fece veduto a' suoi che presa aveva una figliuola d'un de' conti da Panago, e faccendo fare l'appresto grande per le nozze, mandò per la Griselda che a lui venisse; alla quale venuta disse: — Io meno questa donna la quale io ho nuovamente tolta, ed intendo in questa prima venuta d'onorarla; e tu sai che io non ho in casa donne che mi sappiano acconciar le camere né fare molte cose che a così fatta festa si richeggiono; e per ciò tu, che meglio che altra persona queste cose di casa sai, metti in ordine quello che da far c'è, e quelle donne fa invitar

difficulty, conquering her feminine nature, and replied: "My lord, I have always known that my low status in no way matched your nobility, and I recognized that the rank I held with you came from God and from you; I never made or considered it my own as an outright gift, but always judged it to be a loan. It now pleases you to take it back; and it ought to please me, as it does, to give it back to you. Here is the ring with which you wedded me, take it. You order me to take away with me the dowry I brought here; to do that, you need no one to disburse it, and I need no purse or pack animal, because I haven't forgotten that you received me naked. If you deem it honorable that the body in which I have carried children of your begetting should be seen by everybody, I shall depart from here naked. But I beg you, as compensation for the virginity which I brought here and cannot take away with me, that you deign to allow me to wear a single shift, over and above my dowry."

Gualtieri, who felt more like crying than anything else, nevertheless kept his features firm, and said: "And you *shall* wear a shift!"

All the people around him begged him to give her a dress, so that the woman who had been his wife for thirteen years or more should not be seen leaving his house so impoverished and in such a state of disgrace, wearing a mere shift. But their entreaties were in vain, so that the lady, dressed in a shift, barefoot, and with no head covering, commended them to God, left his house, and returned to her father, accompanied by the tears and lamenting of all who saw her.

Giannucolo, who had never been able to believe it true that Gualtieri would stay married to his daughter, but expected this turn of events to come any day, had kept the clothes she had removed on the morning when Gualtieri married her. And so he brought them to her and she put them back on; she resumed the lowly chores in her father's house she had done before, bearing up under the fierce assault of hostile fortune with a brave spirit.

After Gualtieri had done that, he gave his people to believe that he had chosen the daughter of one of the Counts of Panico;[2] making great preparations for the wedding, he summoned Griselda into his presence and, when she had come, he said: "I am marrying this lady to whom I was recently betrothed, and I intend to honor her upon her arrival here. You know there are no women in my house who can arrange the rooms or do the many things required for such a celebration. So I want you, because you are more familiar with these domestic details than anyone else, to make all the necessary arrangements

[2]A fief in the vicinity of Bologna.

che ti pare e ricèvile come se donna di qui fossi; poi, fatte le nozze, te ne potrai a casa tua tornare.

Come che queste parole fossero tutte coltella al cuor di Griselda, come a colei che non aveva così potuto por giù l'amore che ella gli portava, come fatto aveva la buona fortuna, rispose: — Signor mio, io son presta ed apparecchiata.

Ed entratasene co' suoi pannicelli romagnuoli e grossi in quella casa della qual poco avanti era uscita in camicia, cominciò a spazzar le camere ed ordinarle, ed a far porre capoletti e pancali per le sale, a fare apprestar la cucina, e ad ogni cosa, come se una piccola fanticella della casa fosse, porre le mani; né mai ristette, che ebbe tutto acconcio ed ordinato quanto si conveniva.

Ed appresso questo, fatto da parte di Gualtieri invitar tutte le donne della contrada, cominciò ad attender la festa; e venuto il giorno delle nozze, come che i panni avesse poveri indosso, con animo e costume donnesco tutte le donne che a quelle vennero, e con lieto viso, ricevette. Gualtieri, il quale diligentemente aveva i figliuoli fatti allevare in Bologna alla sua parente che maritata era in casa de' conti da Panago, essendo già la fanciulla, d'età di dodici anni, la più bella cosa che mai si vedesse (ed il fanciullo era di sei) aveva mandato a Bologna al parente suo pregando che gli piacesse di dovere con questa sua figliuola e col figliuolo venire a Saluzzo ed ordinare di menar bella ed onorevole compagnia con seco, e di dire a tutti che costei per sua mogliere gli menasse, senza manifestare alcuna cosa ad alcuno che ella si fosse altramenti.

Il gentile uomo, fatto secondo che il marchese il pregava, entrato in cammino, dopo alquanti dì, con la fanciulla e col fratello e con nobile compagnia, in su l'ora del desinare, giunse a Saluzzo, dove tutti i paesani e molti altri vicini da torno trovò, che attendevan questa novella sposa di Gualtieri. La quale dalle donne ricevuta e nella sala dove erano messe le tavole venuta, Griselda, così come era, le si fece lietamente incontro, dicendo: — Ben venga la mia donna!

Le donne, che molto avevano, ma invano, pregato Gualtieri che o facesse che la Griselda si stesse in una camera o che egli alcuna delle robe che sue erano state le prestasse, acciò che così non andasse davanti a' suoi forestieri, furon messe a tavola e cominciate a servire. La fanciulla era guardata da ogni uomo, e ciascun diceva che Gualtieri aveva fatto buon cambio; ma intra gli altri Griselda la lodava molto, e lei ed il suo fratellino.

Gualtieri, al qual pareva pienamente aver veduto quantunque di-

and to invite the ladies you think should attend and welcome them as if you were mistress here. Then, after the wedding, you can go home again."

Though all these words were knives in Griselda's heart, because she had been unable to put aside her love for him as she had put aside her good fortune, she replied: "My lord, I am ready and prepared."

And, in her rough homespun clothes, she entered the house she had shortly before left in a shift; she began to sweep out the bedrooms and tidy them, to have wall cloths and bench coverings placed in the assembly rooms, to prepare the kitchen, and to put her hand to everything, as if she were a lowly chambermaid of the household. She didn't rest until she had cleaned and arranged everything properly.

After that, she invited all the local ladies in Gualtieri's name, and began to await the celebration. When the wedding day arrived, although she was wearing those humble clothes, she welcomed all the lady guests in a lordly spirit and fashion, and with a smile on her face. Gualtieri had taken pains to have his children raised in Bologna by his kinswoman who had married into the house of the Counts of Panico. The girl, now twelve, was the most beautiful creature ever seen, and the boy was six. Now he had sent word to his kinsman in Bologna, asking him to be so good as to come to Saluzzo with his daughter and son, arranging to bring along a fine, honorable retinue; he was to tell everyone he was bringing her to be Gualtieri's wife, and not to let anyone know who she really was.

This gentleman, complying with the marquess's wishes, set out, and arrived in Saluzzo at the dinner hour a few days later, along with the girl, her brother, and a noble escort. There he found all the townspeople, as well as many other people from the vicinity, waiting to greet this new bride of Gualtieri's. When she had been welcomed by the ladies and had come into the hall where the tables were set, Griselda, dressed as she was, came forward cheerfully to greet her, saying: "Welcome to my mistress!"

The ladies, who had long implored Gualtieri in vain either to keep Griselda out of sight in a chamber, or else to lend her one of her former dresses so she might not have to greet her guests looking like that, were now seated at their tables, where they began to be served. Everyone looked at the girl, saying that Gualtieri had made a good exchange. But along with the others Griselda praised her highly, and her little brother as well.

Gualtieri, to whom it seemed that now he had fully seen all he

siderava della pazienza della sua donna, veggendo che di niente la
novità delle cose la cambiava, ed essendo certo ciò per mente-
cattaggine non avvenire, per ciò che savia molto la conoscea, gli
parve tempo di doverla trarre dell'amaritudine, la quale stimava
che ella sotto il forte viso nascosa tenesse; per che, fàttalasi venire,
in presenza d'ogni uomo sorridendo le disse: — Che ti par della
nostra sposa?

— Signor mio, — rispose Griselda, — a me ne par molto bene;
e se così è savia come ella è bella, che il credo, io non dubito punto
che voi non dobbiate con lei vivere il più consolato signor del
mondo; ma quanto posso vi priego che quelle punture, le quali al-
l'altra che vostra fu già, déste, non diate a questa, ché appena che
io creda che ella le potesse sostenere, sì perché più giovane è, e sì
ancora perché in dilicatezze è allevata, ove colei in continue fatiche
da piccolina era stata.

Gualtieri, veggendo che ella fermamente credeva, costei dovere
esser sua moglie, né per ciò in alcuna cosa men che ben parlava, la
si fece sedere allato e disse: — Griselda, tempo è ormai che tu
senta frutto della tua lunga pazienza e che coloro, li quali me hanno
reputato crudele ed iniquo e bestiale, conoscano che, ciò che io
faceva, ad antiveduto fine operava, volendoti insegnar d'essere
moglie ed a loro di saperla tenere, ed a me partorire perpetua quie-
te mentre teco a vivere avessi; il che, quando venni a prender
moglie, gran paura ebbi che non m'intervenisse; e per ciò, per
pruova pigliare, in quanti modi tu sai ti punsi e trafissi. E però che
io mai non mi sono accorto che in parola né in fatto dal mio piacere
partita ti sii, parendo a me aver di te quella consolazione che io
disideravo, intendo di rendere a te ad una ora ciò che io tra molte
ti tolsi e con somma dolcezza le punture ristorare che io ti diedi; e
per ciò con lieto animo prendi questa che tu mia sposa credi, ed il
suo fratello, per tuoi e miei figli; essi sono quegli li quali tu e molti
altri lungamente stimato avete che io crudelmente uccider facessi,
ed io sono il tuo marito, il quale sopra ogni altra cosa t'amo, credendomi poter dar vanto che niuno altro sia che, sì come io, si
possa di sua moglier contentare.

E così detto, l'abbracciò e baciò, e con lei insieme, la qual
d'allegrezza piagnea, levatosi, n'andarono là dove la figliuola,
tutta stupefatta queste cose ascoltando, sedea; ed abbracciatala
teneramente, ed il fratello altresì, lei e molti altri che quivi
erano sgannarono. Le donne lietissime, levate dalle tavole, con
Griselda n'andarono in camera e con migliore augurio trattile i

wanted to concerning his wife's patience, saw that her character was unaltered by any strange occurrence, and he was sure that this was not because she was foolish, since he knew how intelligent she was. He deemed it was time to release her from the bitter sorrow he thought she must be feeling, hiding it beneath her brave exterior. And so, sending for her, in the presence of all, he asked her with a smile: "What do you think of our bride?"

"My lord," Griselda replied, "I think she's very nice. And if she is as clever as she is beautiful, which I believe is the case, I have no doubt whatsoever that you will be the most contented man in the world, living with her. But I beg you with all my might to spare her the wounds you inflicted on that other wife you once had, since I can scarcely believe she would be able to bear them, both because she's younger and because she was raised in luxury, whereas that other woman had been engaged in constant toil since early childhood."

Gualtieri, seeing that she firmly believed the girl was to be his wife, and yet had only the kindest words for her, had her sit down next to him, and said: "Griselda, it's now time for you to be rewarded for your long patience, and for those who deemed me cruel, unjust, and brutal to know that I acted as I did with a planned purpose in mind. I wanted to teach you how to be a wife and teach them how to keep a wife, and I wanted to obtain lasting peace of mind all the days I was to live with you. When it came time for me to marry, I greatly feared that that wouldn't be my lot; and so, to test you, I wounded and saddened you in all the ways you already know. And because I have never perceived that you departed from my wishes in word or deed, and I believe I have been as contented with you as I desired to be, it is now my will to restore to you in one hour what I took from you over many hours, and through enormous pleasure to heal the wounds I gave you. Therefore, with a happy heart, greet this girl you believe to be my bride, and her brother, as your children and mine. They are the ones you and many others have long thought I cruelly had killed, and I am your husband, who loves you above all else, believing I can boast that no other man can be so satisfied with his wife."

Saying this, he hugged and kissed her, and, rising with her, while she was weeping with joy, went over to where their daughter was sitting dumbfounded at hearing all this. He hugged her and her brother affectionately, revealing the truth to her and many others present. The ladies, overjoyed, left their tables and entered a chamber with Griselda. There, with a better portent of good fortune [than on her

suoi pannicelli, d'una nobile roba delle sue la rivestirono, e come donna, la quale ella eziandio negli stracci pareva, nella sala la rimenarono.

E quivi fattasi co' figliuoli maravigliosa festa, essendo ogni uomo lietissimo di questa cosa, il sollazzo ed il festeggiar multiplicarono ed in più giorni tirarono; e savissimo reputaron Gualtieri, come che troppo reputassero agre ed intollerabili l'esperienze prese della sua donna, e sopra tutti savissima tenner Griselda. Il conte da Panago si tornò dopo alquanti dì a Bologna, e Gualtieri, tolto Giannùcolo dal suo lavorìo, come suocero il pose in istato che egli onoratamente e con gran consolazione visse e finì la sua vecchiezza. Ed egli appresso, maritata altamente la sua figliuola, con Griselda, onorandola sempre quanto più si potea, lungamente e consolato visse.

Che si potrà dir qui, se non che anche nelle povere case piovono dal cielo de' divini spiriti, come, nelle reali, di quegli che sarien più degni di guardar porci che d'avere sopra uomini signoria? Chi avrebbe altri che Griselda potuto col viso non solamente asciutto ma lieto, sofferir le rigide e mai più non udite pruove da Gualtier fatte? Al quale non sarebbe forse stato male investito d'essersi abbattuto ad una che, quando fuor di casa l'avesse in camicia cacciata, s'avesse sì ad uno altro fatto scuotere il pilliccione, che riuscito ne fosse una bella roba.

wedding day], they took off her humble clothes and dressed her in one of her noble gowns. Then they led her back into the great hall as a noble lady, which she had looked like even when dressed in rags.

There she enjoyed a wonderfully happy reunion with her children. Everyone was overjoyed at these events, and they increased their pleasure and celebration, prolonging it for several days. They considered Gualtieri very wise, even though they deemed the trials to which he had subjected his wife too harsh and unbearable. They considered Griselda wisest of all. A few days later, the Count of Panico returned to Bologna. Gualtieri, relieving Giannucolo of his labors, acknowledged him as his father-in-law and placed him in a position where he could live in honor and great contentment; and so the old man lived till the end of his days. Then, after providing his daughter with a husband of high rank, Gualtieri lived long and contentedly with Griselda, always honoring her as much as he could.

What can I say here, except that angelic natures may be vouchsafed by heaven even to humble homes, just as royal homes may shelter people more fitted to herd swine than to govern men? Who but Griselda could have suffered the harsh, unheard-of trials imposed by Gualtieri with a face not only unwashed by tears but even cheerful? Perhaps it wouldn't have been a bad thing if Gualtieri had stumbled upon a woman who, when driven from home in a shift, had showed some other man such a good time in bed[3] that she would have gotten a nice dress out of it!

---

[3]Literally, "had had some other man shake her fur-lined robe." A multiple word play: the word *pelliccione* (also slang for the female pudenda) adds a third garment to the shift and the dress already mentioned in the sentence.

A CATALOG OF SELECTED DOVER
BOOKS IN ALL FIELDS OF INTEREST

ABC BOOK OF EARLY AMERICANA, Eric Sloane. Artist and historian Eric Sloane presents a wondrous A-to-Z collection of American innovations, including hex signs, ear trumpets, popcorn, and rocking chairs. Illustrated, hand-lettered pages feature brief captions explaining objects' origins and uses. 64pp. 0-486-49808-5

ADVENTURES OF HUCKLEBERRY FINN, Mark Twain. Join Huck and Jim as their boyhood adventures along the Mississippi River lead them into a world of excitement, danger, and self-discovery. Humorous narrative, lyrical descriptions of the Mississippi valley, and memorable characters. 224pp. 0-486-28061-6

ALICE STARMORE'S BOOK OF FAIR ISLE KNITTING, Alice Starmore. A noted designer from the region of Scotland's Fair Isle explores the history and techniques of this distinctive, stranded-color knitting style and provides copious illustrated instructions for 14 original knitwear designs. 208pp. 0-486-47218-3

ALICE'S ADVENTURES IN WONDERLAND, Lewis Carroll. Beloved classic about a little girl lost in a topsy-turvy land and her encounters with the White Rabbit, March Hare, Mad Hatter, Cheshire Cat, and other delightfully improbable characters. 42 illustrations by Sir John Tenniel. A selection of the Common Core State Standards Initiative. 96pp. 0-486-27543-4

THE ARTHUR RACKHAM TREASURY: 86 Full-Color Illustrations, Arthur Rackham. Selected and Edited by Jeff A. Menges. A stunning treasury of 86 full-page plates span the famed English artist's career, from *Rip Van Winkle* (1905) to masterworks such as *Undine, A Midsummer Night's Dream,* and *Wind in the Willows* (1939). 96pp.
0-486-44685-9

THE AWAKENING, Kate Chopin. First published in 1899, this controversial novel of a New Orleans wife's search for love outside a stifling marriage shocked readers. Today, it remains a first-rate narrative with superb characterization. New introductory note. 128pp. 0-486-27786-0

THE CALL OF THE WILD, Jack London. A classic novel of adventure, drawn from London's own experiences as a Klondike adventurer, relating the story of a heroic dog caught in the brutal life of the Alaska Gold Rush. Note. 64pp. 0-486-26472-6

THE CARTOON HISTORY OF TIME, Kate Charlesworth and John Gribbin. Cartoon characters explain cosmology, quantum physics, and other concepts covered by Stephen Hawking's *A Brief History of Time.* Humorous graphic novel–style treatment, perfect for young readers and curious folk of all ages. 64pp. 0-486-49097-1

A CHRISTMAS CAROL, Charles Dickens. This engrossing tale relates Ebenezer Scrooge's ghostly journeys through Christmases past, present, and future and his ultimate transformation from a harsh and grasping old miser to a charitable and compassionate human being. 80pp. 0-486-26865-9

CRIME AND PUNISHMENT, Fyodor Dostoyevsky. Translated by Constance Garnett. Supreme masterpiece tells the story of Raskolnikov, a student tormented by his own thoughts after he murders an old woman. Overwhelmed by guilt and terror, he confesses and goes to prison. A selection of the Common Core State Standards Initiative. 448pp. 0-486-41587-2

DOOMED SHIPS: Great Ocean Liner Disasters, William H. Miller, Jr. Nearly 200 photographs, many from private collections, highlight tales of some of the vessels whose pleasure cruises ended in catastrophe: the *Morro Castle, Normandie, Andrea Doria, Europa,* and many others. 128pp. 0-486-45366-9

DUBLINERS, James Joyce. A fine and accessible introduction to the work of one of the 20th century's most influential writers, this collection features 15 tales, including a masterpiece of the short-story genre, "The Dead." 160pp. 0-486-26870-5

ETHAN FROME, Edith Wharton. Classic story of wasted lives, set against a bleak New England background. Superbly delineated characters in a hauntingly grim tale of thwarted love. Considered by many to be Wharton's masterpiece. 96pp. 0-486-26690-7

FLATLAND: A Romance of Many Dimensions, Edwin A. Abbott. Classic of science (and mathematical) fiction — charmingly illustrated by the author — describes the adventures of A. Square, a resident of Flatland, in Spaceland (three dimensions), Lineland (one dimension), and Pointland (no dimensions). 96pp. 0-486-27263-X

FRANKENSTEIN, Mary Shelley. The story of Victor Frankenstein's monstrous creation and the havoc it caused has enthralled generations of readers and inspired countless writers of horror and suspense. With the author's own 1831 introduction. 176pp. 0-486-28211-2

THE GARGOYLE BOOK: 572 Examples from Gothic Architecture, Lester Burbank Bridaham. Dispelling the conventional wisdom that French Gothic architectural flourishes were born of despair or gloom, Bridaham reveals the whimsical nature of these creations and the ingenious artisans who made them. 572 illustrations. 224pp. 0-486-44754-5

HEART OF DARKNESS, Joseph Conrad. Dark allegory of a journey up the Congo River and the narrator's encounter with the mysterious Mr. Kurtz. Masterly blend of adventure, character study, psychological penetration. For many, Conrad's finest, most enigmatic story. 80pp. 0-486-26464-5

THE HOUND OF THE BASKERVILLES, Sir Arthur Conan Doyle. A deadly curse in the form of a legendary ferocious beast continues to claim its victims from the Baskerville family until Holmes and Watson intervene. Often called the best detective story ever written. 128pp. 0-486-28214-7

HOW TO DRAW NEARLY EVERYTHING, Victor Perard. Beginners of all ages can learn to draw figures, faces, landscapes, trees, flowers, and animals of all kinds. Well-illustrated guide offers suggestions for pencil, pen, and brush techniques plus composition, shading, and perspective. 160pp. 0-486-49848-4

JANE EYRE, Charlotte Brontë. Written in 1847, *Jane Eyre* tells the tale of an orphan girl's progress from the custody of cruel relatives to an oppressive boarding school and its culmination in a troubled career as a governess. A selection of the Common Core State Standards Initiative. 448pp. 0-486-42449-9

JUST WHAT THE DOCTOR DISORDERED: Early Writings and Cartoons of Dr. Seuss, Dr. Seuss. Edited and with an Introduction by Rick Marschall. The Doctor's visual hilarity, nonsense language, and offbeat sense of humor illuminate this compilation of items from his early career, created for periodicals such as *Judge, Life, College Humor,* and *Liberty.* 144pp. 0-486-49846-8

THE LADY OR THE TIGER?: and Other Logic Puzzles, Raymond M. Smullyan. Created by a renowned puzzle master, these whimsically themed challenges involve paradoxes about probability, time, and change; metapuzzles; and self-referentiality. Nineteen chapters advance in difficulty from relatively simple to highly complex. 1982 edition. 240pp. 0-486-47027-X

LINE: An Art Study, Edmund J. Sullivan. Written by a noted artist and teacher, this well-illustrated guide introduces the basics of line drawing. Topics include third and fourth dimensions, formal perspective, shade and shadow, figure drawing, and other essentials. 208pp. 0-486-79484-9

MANHATTAN IN MAPS 1527-2014, Paul E. Cohen and Robert T. Augustyn. This handsome volume features 65 full-color maps charting Manhattan's development from the first Dutch settlement to the present. Each map is placed in context by an accompanying essay. 176pp. 0-486-77991-2

THE METAMORPHOSIS AND OTHER STORIES, Franz Kafka. Excellent new English translations of title story (considered by many critics Kafka's most perfect work), plus "The Judgment," "In the Penal Colony," "A Country Doctor," and "A Report to an Academy." A selection of the Common Core State Standards Initiative. 96pp. 0-486-29030-1

THE ODYSSEY, Homer. Excellent prose translation of ancient epic recounts adventures of the homeward-bound Odysseus. Fantastic cast of gods, giants, cannibals, sirens, other supernatural creatures — true classic of Western literature. A selection of the Common Core State Standards Initiative. 256pp. 0-486-40654-7

THE PICTURE OF DORIAN GRAY, Oscar Wilde. Celebrated novel involves a handsome young Londoner who sinks into a life of depravity. His body retains perfect youth and vigor while his recent portrait reflects the ravages of his crime and sensuality. 176pp. 0-486-27807-7

PRIDE AND PREJUDICE, Jane Austen. One of the most universally loved and admired English novels, an effervescent tale of rural romance transformed by Jane Austen's art into a witty, shrewdly observed satire of English country life. A selection of the Common Core State Standards Initiative. 272pp. 0-486-28473-5

RELATIVITY SIMPLY EXPLAINED, Martin Gardner. One of the subject's clearest, most entertaining introductions offers lucid explanations of special and general theories of relativity, gravity, and spacetime, models of the universe, and more. 100 illustrations. 224pp. 0-486-29315-7

THE SCARLET LETTER, Nathaniel Hawthorne. With stark power and emotional depth, Hawthorne's masterpiece explores sin, guilt, and redemption in a story of adultery in the early days of the Massachusetts Colony. A selection of the Common Core State Standards Initiative. 192pp. 0-486-28048-9

SKETCHING OUTDOORS, Leonard Richmond. This guide offers beginners step-by-step demonstrations of how to depict clouds, trees, buildings, and other outdoor sights. Explanations of a variety of techniques include shading and constructional drawing. 48pp. 0-486-46922-0

TREASURE ISLAND, Robert Louis Stevenson. Classic adventure story of a perilous sea journey, a mutiny led by the infamous Long John Silver, and a lethal scramble for buried treasure — seen through the eyes of cabin boy Jim Hawkins. 160pp. 0-486-27559-0

WORLD WAR II: THE ENCYCLOPEDIA OF THE WAR YEARS, 1941-1945, Norman Polmar and Thomas B. Allen. Authoritative and comprehensive, this reference surveys World War II from an American perspective. Over 2,400 entries cover battles, weapons, and participants as well as aspects of politics, culture, and everyday life. 85 illustrations. 960pp. 0-486-47962-5

WUTHERING HEIGHTS, Emily Brontë. Somber tale of consuming passions and vengeance — played out amid the lonely English moors — recounts the turbulent and tempestuous love story of Cathy and Heathcliff. Poignant and compelling. 256pp. 0-486-29256-8

Browse over 10,000 books at www.doverpublications.com